A Family Matter

James Roosevelt
with Sam Toperoff

Simon and Schuster
New York

Copyright © 1980 by James Roosevelt and Sam Toperoff
All rights reserved
including the right of reproduction
in whole or in part in any form
Published by Simon and Schuster
A Division of Gulf & Western Corporation
Simon & Schuster Building
Rockefeller Center
1230 Avenue of the Americas
New York, New York 10020
SIMON AND SCHUSTER and colophon are trademarks of Simon & Schuster
Designed by Carole Stephens
Manufactured in the United States of America
Printed and bound by Fairfield Graphics, Inc.
1 2 3 4 5 6 7 8 9 10
Library of Congress Cataloging in Publication Data

Roosevelt, James, 1907–
    A family matter.

    1. Roosevelt, Franklin Delano, Pres. U.S., 1882–1945
—Fiction. I. Toperoff, Sam, joint author. II. Title.
PZ4.R7794Fam   [PS3568.0638]   813'.54   80–11759

ISBN 0–671–24621–6

Wil.

Part One

"Sailor, Home from the Sea"

Chapter

1

THE PRESIDENT's black Packard touring car came to a halt near the corner where it was supposed to turn into the Soviet embassy grounds. The delay caused Mike Reilly, the smiling Irishman in charge of FDR's security, to move up against the President and shout to the Marine sergeant who was driving, "Hit the horn a few times, Sarge. See if we can move this crowd back a little."

The driver tapped the horn in staccato bursts, but the milling Iranians who had closed off the narrow street now came even closer to the car. The Russian military motorcyclists who had been leading the way into the new quarter of Teheran from the Amerabad airfield were also unable to open a path.

Three local policemen were barely keeping some of the more aggressive Iranians from touching the car, but Mike Reilly was clearly worried; it was potentially as dangerous a situation as he had ever been in with the President. *A bomb thrower would have easy pickin's,* he thought. So Mike

Reilly said, " 'Scuse me, sir," pulled a Colt .45 automatic pistol from under his suit jacket, and circled it high in the air. At the same time he seemed to enlarge his already ample body while throwing his arm around the President, hooking his forearm on FDR's shoulder, and spreading his huge left hand over Franklin Roosevelt's heart.

Ordinarily, the situation and Reilly's response would have brought a Roosevelt wisecrack, but now, in November 1943, FDR remained silent. His anticipation of the Big Three conference, of his first, long-delayed meeting with Joseph Stalin, had been dulled by his impressions of Teheran itself. The expressions on the sun-darkened faces he had seen as his car moved through the outskirts of the city, expressions of weariness, hunger and despair, had depressed him. In the people's eyes he saw a general and unrelieved hopelessness. Abject poverty was the invariable backdrop. The only smile he saw was on a toothless, turbaned beggar, and it was the wild grin of a madman.

Never before had he seen so much concentrated misery and misfortune. Scores of amputees and lunatics, torn and filthy clothes the norm; garbage strewn everywhere; and scrawny dogs edging slyly against the walls of passageways, their eyes with that same hollow, desperate expression. In darkened doorways FDR saw shadowy suggestions of humanity: a hand moving quickly to cover a face, a head turning back over a shoulder and looking away as suddenly. Indeed, FDR's depression had deepened during the ten-minute ride through the squalid old section of the city. What in the world, Franklin Roosevelt wondered, had brought him to this hopeless place?

By the time the limousine had entered the new quarter of the city—the European pride of the King, Reza Shah Pahlevi—the American President's mood had begun to approach despondency even though the people in the pressing crowds now were cleaner, better dressed, animated. Some even shouted recognizable approximations of his name, and a comic chant developed: "Rooz-vel, Rooz-vel, Rooz-vel." That's when the forward progress stopped, and Mike Reilly, having known for weeks that the Iranian capital was rife with enemy agents and assassins, decided to force the issue. "Lean on that horn and stay on it," he now ordered the driver.

For the next half minute the horn wailed continually in pulsing cycles until Russian soldiers running from the embassy with machine guns strapped around their necks opened a path to the stranded Packard. Only after the iron gates were behind them did Reilly undrape himself from the President, explaining as he did so, "The Secret Service and Army security had word of some desperadoes in the neighborhood, Mr. President. Don't want you to think I overreacted." He blew some imaginary smoke away from the barrel of his gun before putting it back under his jacket, executing an exaggerated sign of the cross and looking heavenward as he did.

FDR smiled, but it was a distracted, preoccupied gesture. A moment later, when he said, "I'm surprised at you, Reilly —they can't kill us," his heart still wasn't in it.

Mike Reilly touched the tip of his nose in a familiar gesture of sudden seriousness. "Anybody can kill anybody in this world, Mr. President."

Roosevelt laughed his deep, genuine laugh. "Always the optimist, aren't you, Reilly?"

Against the dull grays and ochers of the low buildings in the Soviet compound, two things of incredible brightness stood out. The first was a peacock in full show of plumage strutting off the gravel path and into the parched garden. The second, even more colorful, was the extraordinary row of ribbons and medals on the chest of the Russian general who awaited him on the steps of the legation. Fortunately, Charles "Chip" Bohlen, the young State Department interpreter, was already there to help the President over the rough spots. When the car stopped, Reilly jumped out and began to remove the wheelchair from the trunk of the Packard. "Later, Mike," the President ordered. "Just give me a hand getting out."

With Reilly supplying more than enough support, FDR moved slowly toward the chest full of glistening Soviet victories, which began to step quickly forward to meet him. "Mr. President," Charles Bohlen announced, "General Voroshilov, Commissar of War of the Soviet People's Republic." The General, his ruddy face a mixture of pomp and respect, snapped rigidly to attention and cut a precise salute. FDR smiled and returned the salute in a far less military manner. Bohlen translated the President's words: "The people of the entire world are grateful, General Voroshilov, for the valiant stand of the Russian army and the wisdom of its leader and its generals in reversing the tide of the war." Voroshilov beamed.

During the brief silence that followed the message, there came from the formal garden a mournful sound unlike any FDR had ever heard. *Laaay-ooon*. And again, *Laaay-ooon*. Part moan, part cry, part judgment. It seemed to capture in sound the plaintive look Roosevelt had seen in eyes throughout the old city.

All the men standing at the steps of the embassy turned toward the sound. Bohlen translated the General's explanation: "There are many peacocks on the grounds. This is their mating call."

His regular midafternoon nap, given his physical weariness, should have come easily, but for reasons Franklin Roosevelt could not determine, he was unable to fall asleep. The difficult flight in his plane, the *Sacred Cow*, on the last leg of this monumental journey, had, even after a day of recuperation in Cairo, left him weak and slightly sick to his stomach. He tossed continually, his body seemingly buzzing with an awareness of its weariness. Perhaps he should have had his leg braces removed. His active mind began to wander, and he was unable, or maybe unwilling, to bring it back to the political matters at hand. The peacocks' cries came at irregular intervals; he found himself trying to anticipate them, an exotic alternative to counting sheep.

Then a soft knock on the bedroom door told him of the impending visit, the significant first meeting, with Joseph Vissarionovich Stalin. He said, "Yes, yes." Two scowling, stocky men entered; they wore the starched white jackets of waiters; in this case, however, the uniforms barely concealed large shoulder holsters. Reilly and Bohlen were a step behind, and Reilly said, "Sir, I've just had a talk with Colonel Vertinski, their man in charge of security. Everyone in the compound has been cleared. All the servants are NKVD." He smiled broadly and his eyes singled out the white coats.

FDR nodded.

Bohlen said, his voice sounding very dry, "Marshal Stalin is on the grounds now. He wishes to visit briefly, if it is all right with you, Mr. President."

"Certainly. I'll need a minute."

Bohlen spoke in Russian to the waiters and they disappeared.

"Reilly," FDR said, "I'd like to be standing over there." He had looked around the room and pointed to a tall, ornate chair with a tapestry design of a large, colorful bird on the backrest. "I'll use it for support." It was important to FDR, as both symbol and tactic, that he be standing during his first meeting with Stalin. He assumed that any sign of weakness was certain to be exploited. In fact, he had left his leg braces on in anticipation of the meeting that was about to occur. Mike Reilly moved the President into place.

When Stalin finally entered, neither his manner nor his weak handshake was at all what Roosevelt had expected. He spoke softly, almost apologetically, swallowing so many of his words that Bohlen was translating gesture as often as language.

Other things were unexpected as well: Stalin proved to be

surprisingly short and wore a gray uniform buttoned to the collar and utterly without adornment. He did not maintain eye contact with Roosevelt but tended to look at the American's chest most of the time while stealing only occasional glances at his face. No, this historic meeting was not at all what FDR had anticipated.

It was not until FDR mentioned Stalingrad that the Marshal showed signs of being the force Roosevelt had anticipated. Stalin stepped forward, his small brown eyes now wide open, his pockmarked face turned directly up to his guest's. "Ah, yes, the turning of the tide at Stalingrad. That stand by the Russian people, alone—that has pulled out all the eggs, has it not?" And Bohlen quickly added that the Marshal's last expression had a Russian meaning akin to our "saving your skin."

"That," FDR said without breaking eye contact or blinking, "is precisely why I have come halfway around the world, to discuss our new military options."

But rather than discussing options, Stalin said defensively, "If it is very far for you to come to meet me, it is because the war in my country is in a delicate state. I cannot permit myself the luxury of being too far away from it. There are military decisions to be made quickly, very quickly. There is no room for error. You and Churchill do not know what it is like to have the enemy on your land, so you cannot understand." There was a distrustful, accusatory note in the voice now.

Of a number of possible responses, the ones FDR came closest to uttering were "I needn't remind you, Marshal Stalin, that we are fighting the Japanese all over the Pacific," and "The English capital is being bombed daily." He decided to say nothing whatsoever.

The silence weighed heavily, and Bohlen cleared his throat. Stalin moved the palm of his hand over his hair, which had been recently clipped and combed straight back off his brow. He slipped back into a posture of diffidence and said, "If you have any needs, no matter what they may be, our entire staff is at your disposal. It will be well to get to our business, will it not?"

FDR answered, "Very well indeed."

After the other men had left the room, Mike Reilly helped the President back on the bed and removed the heavy leather and steel leg braces. Then FDR, alone again, began to experience an unsettling uneasiness. Uncertainty and intimations of discord had been planted, he didn't know precisely how, but his unerring instinct for anticipating trouble had certainly been activated by Stalin's visit.

Lying quietly in the gaudy, unfriendly room, he said to the hostile gold chandelier, "Why in the world would I have thought it could go smoothly?"

It was not sleep that came, not even a half-conscious doze, but merely the slow receding of his political fears and concerns, an easing of his vague worries about the conference. At least, however, the body, weakened from an exhausting trip, was finally at rest. But in his mind's vision he continued to see the hollow, hungry expression in the eyes of the world's hopeless. He was uncertain if he heard the wail from the garden or if he only imagined it. *Laaay-ooon.*

FDR had been the last of the principles to arrive at the table of the drafty, overdecorated conference room. There had been nods and smiles and handshakes all around. Then, to his embarrassment, it had demanded a greater effort than usual for FDR to collapse the arm of his wheelchair and slide into his high-backed, carved mahogany seat, but the smile never left his face as he struggled. It was understood that the President wished no help, and the men seated around the table had attempted to continue conversing in normal tones while FDR maneuvered, but a restrained hush had settled over the room when finally he had managed to place himself.

The meeting had begun simply enough, with Stalin delivering a short, emphatic statement that had been translated as: "It is good that we are together at last. So let us get down to the business."

Winston Churchill had been clipping the tip of an enormously long cigar. He stopped abruptly, raised his hand, and cleared his throat. "Perhaps it is superstition on my part," he explained while smacking his lips as he lighted the cigar, "but I'd rather not antagonize the gods." Then he made a short speech about how the hopes and expectations of the entire world were focused on this historic meeting at Teheran. FDR watched Stalin's expressionless translator whispering into the Marshal's right ear. When Churchill finally said, "In this year of our Lord 1943, let us pray that He looks kindly upon our efforts."

Stalin smiled broadly and his small eyes twinkled. He said something that was translated as, "Now with God on our side, let us get down to the business." Voroshilov guffawed, and there was a variety of smiles all around the table. FDR had nodded and sipped from a glass of minted tea. He began to think that his earlier misgivings about the conference were all wrong.

Stalin, looking inexpressive in a tight mustard-colored Soviet Army uniform with red and gold epaulets, then reported on the recent turn of military events on the entire 2,000-kilometer-long Russian front. "Yes, the tide has been turned. Finally. Our strategies and sacrifices have proved correct and successful. For the moment, at least. We have taken the initiative. There is no absolute guarantee that we shall hold it." He stopped suddenly. General Voroshilov, sitting to Stalin's left, then gave a lengthy and detailed military report that FDR only appeared to be listening to. Notes were being made around the table. Generals George C. Marshall for the Army and Henry "Hap" Arnold for the Air Force then presented briefly and in broad outline the American military position. Owl-eyed Sir Charles Portal did the same for the British. FDR scribbled some of the numbers and phrases he heard on a pad on the table before him, trying hard to look attentive. He noticed Stalin's gaze darting around the table as the Soviet Marshal filled the bowl of his pipe from a canister he produced miraculously from beneath his chair. FDR noticed also Churchill's eyes following the filigreed molding high on the windowless walls around the room while the reports were being delivered in monotone. The meeting had proceeded in a straightforward, business-like manner.

The anger surfaced suddenly, without apparent provocation. When Lord Portal had finished his report, Stalin looked directly at Roosevelt and spoke; Charles Bohlen, at the President's side, translated: "Forty-two thousand tons of steel wire—7,500 tons delivered. Three thousand tools promised —820 shipped. Stainless steel, 120 tons—22 delivered." Then the Russian leader turned toward Churchill and said, "Two English divisions pledged for the Caucases—do you have any idea how brutal is the fighting in the Caucases?—none have ever yet arrived. Should we still wait for them to come?" He was smiling narrowly.

FDR leaned far back from the round oak table, as though to dissociate himself from the mood that now prevailed. The tips of Churchill's ears were already turning a deep red when he responded. The indignation in his voice came out as impeccably controlled diction. He dabbed at his lips with a folded handkerchief. "The Marshal certainly knows the difference between a wish and a pledge. It was our deepest hope to have been able to send aid in the form of manpower. Herr Hitler, alas, has been uncooperative. He has forced His Majesty's Government to alter that plan. Never, and I repeat, never, had His Majesty's Government made such a pledge. A hope, a wish, sir, is something one would like to be able to do. A pledge, sir, is quite another matter and is always honored by an English government." Churchill seemed mildly distracted by the Russian interpreter's whispers. So he waited until the small, studious man had caught up.

Stalin, however, believing that the Prime Minister had finished, broke into a broad smile and flickered at his mustache with a broad thumb. He said, "Not so sensitive, gentlemen, not so sensitive. There are no grudges here. It is for the record that I speak. These pledges are, as you say, water under the bridge."

Roosevelt and Churchill looked at each other. FDR raised his brow and shrugged slightly.

"We will, gentlemen, have very much time to examine formal positions. This does not interest me at the present moment," Stalin said in translation. "Would it not be better to . . . to . . . to . . ." Bohlen reiterated the final word of Stalin's statement while the Marshal paused. ". . . to put down our hair for some moments. There is tea, coffee, liquors." Bohlen was groping, aware of communicating too literally, poorly. "Informal."

He whispered Stalin's general meaning to the President, "We three should talk a while informally now, not so much for the record and posterity."

After hushed arrangements among each of the delegations, the room began to empty; ribboned, uniformed men leaving first, the diplomats departing after shuffling papers around. All of them men used to having other people adjust to their desires.

A waiter brought in a tray filled with bottles and glasses. Churchill nodded when the white-jacketed man touched the cap of the Scotch and smiled as the amber rose in his glass. FDR accepted a good deal less of the gin. Stalin chose the vodka and had the bottle left on the table, an idea Churchill adopted for the Scotch before the waiter left.

Six men remained in the room: the Big Three and their auxiliary tongues. Now their conversation ranged and rambled. They spoke easily about the war and the world, like men who might have been able to walk around it at will in a dozen or so strides. Each subject—Turkish neutrality, Chiang Kai-shek and China, provisional governments in Eastern

Europe, the African campaign, the war in the Pacific, reforms and population control in India—each received a capsuled opinion from each man. Even though FDR was tired and displaced and his stomach still upset, he enjoyed the give-and-take of this session, recognizing it for exactly what it was—preliminary but deadly serious international sparring.

Stalin's voice lowered perceptibly when he introduced, without benefit of transition, the subject of a second front, of a British-American amphibious landing in northern France. The idea had been the subject of serious discussion for two years; it even had a code name—OVERLORD. Before the Nazi armies had been stopped at Leningrad and Stalingrad, the second front in the West had been seen by Stalin as a matter of life and death, but it had not come. Now, as he spoke, he made geometric designs on the table with a stubby forefinger. His blemished face glistened with perspiration.

Bohlen had become more accustomed to the Marshal's speech rhythms; the translation had fluidity now: "Always new delays, always new excuses. Someone who was cynical might believe you did not truly wish to relieve the pressure the Germans have placed upon the Russian people. We have waited and waited—still we wait—no second front have we gotten." He looked directly at Churchill.

FDR reached for the pack of Camels on the table even though he did not particularly need a cigarette.

Churchill, his voice now openly angry at the accusation, talked about the delays with OVERLORD. "Landing craft. Do you not see, it all comes down to that. We simply do not yet have the numbers of craft we need to place the many thousands of men that will be required on the mainland. It is, of course, one thing to draw arrows on maps; it is quite another to deposit armies of men across the channel. You remember, I hope, that the landing I supported—a southern front in the Adriatic—was a far less grandiose strategy. I see no reason, therefore, why we should not reconsider an Adriatic front."

Stalin, the smile a frozen grimace, continued to trace designs on the wood. "It is well known, Mr. Prime Minister," he said when Churchill had finished, "it is well known that the Adriatic would suit your political inclinations, but the Red Army will be in the Balkans in a matter of months, thank you. If indeed you wish to crush the enemy quickly, a front in the West, a huge pincers, is what is and has been needed."

Churchill sputtered, "Are you implying . . . ?" But he wisely did not finish his thought.

Joseph Stalin said calmly, "It is well known that you find Nazism repugnant; you have to prove nothing on that score. But it is also well known that you lose no love for our communism either. This war, you must certainly tell yourself, will not last forever. Perhaps . . ." It was the Marshal's turn to catch himself and hold his words back.

Winston Churchill leapt to his feet and bent far over the table toward Stalin. FDR leaned even farther back. Stalin took a penknife from his breast pocket and began scraping under his fingernails. The gesture caused Churchill to slap the table with an open palm. Glasses and bottles and ashtrays shook. The Prime Minister's face was a dark lavender; spittle flew from his lips when he spoke. "I can begin to see, sir, that there is no point in a charade of amity here. Either we are allies or we are not. If every difference of opinion—and there must always be some—is to be riddled with accusation and recrimination, then, well then, let us call ourselves temporary associates and be done with it. When the war is over, we can disband. But I was under the impression"—here he looked over at FDR—"I was under the impression, I say, that we were assembled here to discuss, quite openly and free from constraint, all matters. It so happens that His Majesty's Government is not committed to the OVERLORD approach. It believes an attack in Europe up from the south to be preferable strategically. There are some very difficult decisions to be made during these days. I, for one, am here to try to make them, not to be attacked or insulted for my positions. If we set about to make them, fine. If there are differences, so be it. But His Majesty's Government will not sit here and tolerate accusation and innuendo." Winston Churchill made a growling noise as he sat back down.

Stalin's eyes narrowed as he regarded his fingernails. He said slowly and in modulated tones, "Drama is not wanted here. There is much of that already on the battlefields, where men die. I, too, can be dramatic, angry and indignant with good reason. My people have paid very dearly for our recent victories. We have waited for aid. It has not come. We ask questions. We are not stupid." Again, he appeared to have more to say but chose silence.

For Franklin Delano Roosevelt the meeting had a frighteningly surreal quality. Here was basic disagreement, distrust, personal anger and antagonism. Emotions had charged the air around the table; yet the words came in disembodied whispers from the interpreters.

One thing was suddenly clear to him. He had, of course, suspected that only Hitler had given these two men the opportunity to share anything; he was the demon both could focus upon. But the President hadn't expected their essential differences to have surfaced quite so blatantly. What in the world would happen after the devil had been defeated? If the alliance held together long enough for the devil to be defeated! What sort of world would be shaped by this elemental division? The thought alarmed him.

He envisioned a time when these men and their countries would be at one another's throats. So he had no other choice —he must be the peacemaker. Certainly for this evening, at least, and probably for the duration of the conference.

FDR cleared his throat, and his face reflected utter earnestness. "Gentlemen," he said, his voice unusually rich even to his own ears, "if there is anything I did not reckon on or particularly need, it was to travel to the end of the earth to have a misunderstanding. I can assure you I could have gotten into as good a scrap as this without having left Washington—with Eleanor."

His complex mind, however, had already understood that "peacemaker" would certainly not be sufficient for him in the long run. There would have to be something more.

In his bedroom that night Franklin Delano Roosevelt could not sleep. The vague outline of a plan had already begun to take shape in his mind. A plan complex and daring. The last sound he remembered hearing was a mournful *Laaay-ooon.*

Chapter

2

BEFORE HIS trip to Teheran, Franklin Delano Roosevelt had thought of all the great cities of the Middle East as being clumped together someplace "over there." Now he knew better as he lay fully clothed and unable to sleep on the hand-carved bed of the United States embassy on the Avenue of Mehemet Ali in Cairo. The six-hour nonstop flight from Teheran back to Cairo had been a rough one, especially for someone easily prone to sickness in the air. Dizziness and nausea were part of the price he paid for his ignorance of geography.

The darkened bedroom he found himself in was reserved for American dignitaries whose missions had brought them to Cairo. Vice President Henry A. Wallace had used it two years earlier when he negotiated with King Farouk a trade of U.S. wheat and machinery for free access to the Suez Canal. The room had been empty since then until FDR's arrival in early afternoon. A damp mustiness was lingering testimony of disuse.

FDR's head and shoulders propped on a firm beaded pillow afforded him a rare perspective of his body. That numbed body, in a tan pullover and gray flannel slacks, tapered off below like an inverted steeple, the point of which was formed by toes of angular black shoes. He stared hard at those perfect, Presidential shoes, impeccably polished and without any trace of the creases of use across the instep. Their perfection offended him, but he could not break off his gaze. At least when he had had his braces on, he could will some sort of humanly recognizable movement from those legs. Without them he was as helpless as a rag doll.

Across the darkening room a large photograph of the President, the official one in which he pondered thoughtfully with his head cocked ever so slightly to the left, hung below the crossed flags of the United States and Egypt. He could dimly make out the portrait and remembered how buoyant he had felt the afternoon it was taken. While the photographer was setting up in the cabinet room, word had come that John L. Lewis, the tough, intransigent leader of the coal miners' union, had called off a threatened strike. FDR had faced down the old curmudgeon in the most important of their skirmishes. That explained the particularly satisfied look in and around the eyes of the portrait of the thoughtful President. The impression conveyed was unmistakable: Yes, he was confident that everyone would get a fair deal. No, there wasn't the slightest hint of doubt concerning the general state of well-being that knowing face intended to secure. The military reversals of the last two years were too recent to be reflected in the portrait. Good thing, he thought.

He wished he could sleep, even lightly for a few minutes, in the way he sometimes did in the White House at noontime when he could hear the sounds around him—an airplane overhead, a muffled telephone ringing, Fala's gruff bark—but was at the same time being recharged in some deeper, unconscious way. There would be little time to regain lost energies on this trip; it had been sapped even before the last two private sessions at Teheran. He had been running on memory and will power and redirected anger for the last five days. The smile that had become a fixture now began to slip away, making room for a hollow weariness in the cheeks and the dark-rimmed eyes. There was, he realized, that vial of sleeping pills Dr. McIntire had brought along, but that thought, too, melted into indistinctness.

Tiring of gazing at his useless shoes and thinking about not sleeping, Franklin Roosevelt traced the arabesque mosaic on the ceiling and said softly to himself, "A real touch of home." He told himself that sleep was unnecessary, that rest would be sufficient. Ordinarily he didn't lie to himself about himself and his needs. The ceiling tiles were triangular; they blended into large squares that, in turn, formed a grander hexagon with shadowy triangles in the corners. By changing focus and point of view slightly, he found that he could exchange straight-line, geometric forms at will; building and breaking down, adding and subtracting, reshaping the ceiling world. It was tempting for him to make analogies with life, politics, art, future events, but he willed this not to happen this evening and almost smiled at his refusal to take this very attractive step.

From the parapet of the Bulak mosque near the royal palace, the muezzin began to call the faithful to evening prayer. His clear call entered hovel and palace, drifting as clearly into the shuttered room that held the bone-weary American President. FDR listened as the nasal sounds shaped themselves into curious, curling figures, the tones of which always slid toward the unexpected from the incomplete. There was a sultry suspense to the chant which, like the ceiling, trapped his interest, his intellect, like an unfinished riddle that commanded serious attention. It never moved in precisely the direction it promised to go; surprise was the meaning of its form. Such involutions were generally to his taste; now they perfectly captured and held his fatigued uncertainty. Yet he realized that for some who heard the call daily, it had already become mere background noise and allowed them to set their clocks or perhaps even to walk reflexively toward the mosque. That a human voice ranged over a great city each day was a pleasing thought, but it reminded him that he had not yet seen the pyramids or the baths at Luxor, a sudden and deeply unpleasant realization.

He didn't want to see Churchill again tonight and review informally the events of their meetings with Stalin at Teheran. He wanted to be at Warm Springs, floating, napping, swimming again. Becoming stronger and stronger still. Feeling movement in his legs against the water. Becoming so strong that . . .

But it was impossible to cancel this evening with Churchill. Any sign of weakness, especially after the successful effort he had made at Teheran, would be an error, a wedge that would soon be a breach and a well-traveled path soon after that. Appearances meant everything. He begrudged Stalin and Churchill their energies, their robustness. For them negotiations were an all-night, every-night, continuous poker game in which the ability to stay to the bitter end was the most important thing. The storytelling, the drinking into the early hours—this was how issues were being decided, this was when each was measuring each, probing and retreating, noting strengths and weaknesses and dead spots for possible use later.

Now he recalled what Harry Hopkins, his old friend and advisor, had said of Churchill: "The man has everything— everything except vision." FDR smiled at the thought. In intellect and tactic Roosevelt believed himself to be more than a match for either of them, but whereas they seemed to grow stronger as the vodka and Scotch and brandy flowed and the smoke curled and filled the space below the ceiling, he weakened. How noticeably, he couldn't be sure. They didn't miss very much though. But he did not quit: the quitter in this three-handed game was the loser even if he held most of the chips. Resolve, after all, was the trump card. The combination of will power and the high stakes had carried him through Teheran—barely.

He realized then, quite unexpectedly, that he actually preferred dealing with Stalin; with him the attack was usually frontal, emotion the chief weapon in the arsenal, especially where the Germans were concerned. With Stalin some things were negotiable, others were not. He could be flattered a bit, was a transparent liar, and lacked even a trace of true subtlety. Still, like Roosevelt in December of 1943, he was beginning to argue from a position of strength; Leningrad and Stalingrad had changed everything. FDR and Churchill knew his position would grow proportionally stronger and bolder as the Russian counteroffensive gained momentum. OVERLORD had ceased being a lever for the Western Allies; now a landing on the continent was very much in their mutual self-interest.

Dealing with Churchill was another matter entirely. Granted, his bargaining position was becoming more dependent and sometimes untenable; he nevertheless played his hand always looking to force a misplay or take advantage of an error. *"Playing fields of Eton,"* FDR thought cynically. He negotiated always by indirection, qualifying much of what he said, trying for an edge continually, and often getting it. At Teheran it had begun to bother FDR a great deal.

Stalin was Churchill's chief adversary, but Roosevelt was the Prime Minister's most effective way of putting pressure on that adversary, so it was with Churchill that Roosevelt felt the greatest discomfort, with the disarming social manner, with the caricature face and voice that he most felt the need to be on guard. And he had come to resent the sapping of his energy in this way. FDR had worked himself into such a state that he now even blamed Churchill for his inability to rest.

This evening would be no different; probably it would be worse, especially if the President indicated any hint of weakened health or resolve, or made the tempting mistake at this point of spelling out very clearly and precisely what had been upsetting him in Churchill's manner and behavior. There was a fleeting, wistful moment when he missed his overt struggles of will with John L. Lewis. "Well," he whispered, "I guess that's why God saw fit to create Winston Leonard Spencer Churchill."

But FDR had already made himself extremely angry, so he expelled a breath that was more of a snort and ground his molars. Then he considered his body again, the rag doll legs tapering to those distastefully perfect shoes, and wanted to transform his anger into an impetuous, violent kick in the air. He pushed downward on the firm mattress with his hands, and the small of his back was lifted slightly in the air, but the "kick" message ended in deadened nerves and tissues. "Damn it," he shouted, but his shout wasn't given full voice. Always, he realized, there was that damnable sense of controlled emotion.

The muezzin had finished his call and had gone inside the mosque to wash face and hands and feet three times as called for by Moslem ritual. In his mind's eye FDR saw once again the human poverty and despair in the old quarter of Teheran. The face of Franklin Delano Roosevelt, thirty-second President of the United States, smiled confidently from the far wall. The glow of this second floor room in the U.S. embassy had yielded to the blue of Levantine evening.

Immediately upon being wheeled to the opened doorway of the conference room and seeing Churchill in an unguarded moment slumped in the large leather chair that had been placed by the garden window, FDR realized what he had overlooked. The unexpected and unforeseeable were always part of the equation of power and negotiation. Random elements, perhaps, and never to be counted on, but integral nevertheless. Churchill's momentary weakness was suddenly transformed into FDR's momentary strength.

Wishing to savor and seize this privileged moment, FDR silently waved off the young embassy official and Mike Reilly, who had directed his wheelchair toward the opened doors. The room, unlike the impromptu bedroom upstairs that had been prepared for the President, was completely American. Large paintings representing the various sections of America covered the walls; on the tables were American newspapers and magazines—*Life* and *Look* and *The National Geographic*. FDR smiled wickedly and whispered, "My territory this time, Winston."

Then, after a deep breath, he rolled himself briskly forward, ready to take the initiative by taking the Prime Minister by surprise, but the rug impeded his progress a little. It was, of course, an oriental but not the predictable Kirman or Tabriz. The border he had trouble mounting was of rough camel hair in a richly toned geometric design. The center, however, was far more delicately done in a mixture of pale and deeper blues. FDR smiled as he recognized the circular seal of the President woven into it. He planted his right wheel directly on the word "PLURIBUS." He said forcefully, and perhaps a bit too cheerily, "Winston, old man, sorry to keep you waiting. Been on the line to Washington all afternoon. This war will end eventually, but politics just go on forever."

He had caught Churchill in . . . what? Thoughtfulness? Weariness? Sorrow? Perhaps all three and more. Winston Churchill's pink cheeks had a waxy luster, but a distinct pallor was visible beneath. He cocked a glazed eye upward, cleared his throat, and ran a pudgy finger back and forth under his nose. "Ah, quite so, quite so. It may be they only keep us because they don't want to make a change during the war. As soon as it ends, wouldn't be a' tall surprised if they do us in. Not a bad idea, really. Been a bit under the weather m'self. They tell me it's a slight cold. 'Tisn't. Overwork. Run down, lowered resistance. These conferences are killing. Don't know how in the world you do it, Franklin.

Must be a good deal harder on you, after all, what with pulling around . . ." Churchill made a vague hand gesture that encompassed Roosevelt's lower body. "Good job Uncle Joe doesn't get a sense we're a pair of supernumeraries. He'd go right for the jugular then, wouldn't he? That, without a doubt."

We aren't a pair of anythings, Roosevelt thought, petulant over having his psychological advantage undercut, resentful anew because Churchill had the luxury of complaining about poor health while he could not.

Churchill peered over spectacles he wasn't wearing at the time and said, "Listen, I've had the temerity to ask your people here to lay by some good Irish for us. Purely medicinal, of course."

"None for me, Winston. It makes me glow with a false flame, and I can't afford to lose any more body heat. But if you're sure it is prescription stuff, help yourself." And he swept his head magnanimously toward the sideboard.

Churchill reached into the pocket of the beribboned military jacket he had worn to most of the plenary sessions at Teheran—"Wouldn't want our Uncle Joe thinking he's the only military genius at the table"—pulled out a handkerchief, and blew very hard into it twice. "Supernumeraries," he repeated.

The President was vexed. Churchill had not only felt confident enough to drop his guard and let his physical frailty show, he was using that frailty to form a bond of weakness—a "we're-in-the-same-boat-against-this-devil" strategy that Roosevelt absolutely detested. FDR, in this as in all things, was steering his own course, having selected his own objectives, and was moving toward them in his own way and at his own speed. "Pulling all this metal around," he said making the same hand gesture toward Churchill's legs, "may be a virtue in negotiations. Steels the will, you might say, if you can abide so lousy a pun."

Churchill wheezed and waddled over to the early American cherrywood cabinet on the edge of which bottles, glasses and an ice bucket had been laid out. "You realize, of course, Franklin, that we must eventually talk some rather unpleasant politics with our lately successful Uncle. War strategy against a collapsing Hitler is fine stuff—Joe seems amenable enough there now that things appear to have begun to turn in his favor—but the politics of carving up the spoils of war, that will be another matter entirely." A clink of ice punctuated the assessment. FDR, with the privilege of inspecting Winston Churchill from the rear, saw in a crumpled British Army uniform a flat-rumped, paunchy body that was losing the battle to the earth's gravity. The fringe of hair in back of his head was feathery and disheveled. A comic English character actor playing a solicitor in a film of a Dickens novel.

What could not be readily seen, what Winston Churchill had taken pains to conceal over the course of a lifetime, was the intelligence, the brilliance, the tenacity in struggle, the subtlety in negotiation, the complete understanding and evaluation of power and its use—and the decades of training in all these political arts and crafts.

"As I made quite clear to him at Teheran, I do not believe," he was saying while he poured his golden Irish whiskey slowly over the ice, "that an all-out frontal assault against the French coast is our best strategy. No, no, most assuredly a faulty and terribly costly approach." He paused, waiting for FDR to respond. When it became clear that the President had no such intention, he continued pouring and speaking. "But I was overruled. Quite fair and square. And not being one to ever let down the side, I can assure you I will indeed throw myself into the fray as though I'd initiated the plan myself." He had poured himself three thick fingers and returned to his armchair. "That, of course, shouldn't rule out my campaigning for some modified version of my original proposal. In addition, of course, to OVERLORD."

There, thought Roosevelt, *there is the absolute essence of this man.* Reluctantly, and ruled more by politeness than genuine interest, FDR allowed himself to become engaged. "You know, Winston, Joe Louis, the boxer, has something to teach us about strategy. He has devastation, pure thunder, in that right fist of his—he knows it and his opponent knows it also. Over the course of a bout, both of them know it is bound to explode, but the opponent doesn't know when or where. So Louis waits patiently, coming forward, forward, always forward. No great deception until—*BOOM!*" Roosevelt's sudden outburst startled Churchill, and the President laughed at the effect he had intended to produce. "In a short while, if our war production continues at its present rate, we will have Louis' thunder in our right hand, and we'll step forward and throw it right at their chin—the French coast. Nothing too tricky, mind you, no military adventurism. Just a direct knockout blow. Then we'll turn around and take care of the other guy the same way." FDR had been unable to resist that taunt of "adventurism"; it had been Chief of Staff George Marshall's principal complaint against Churchill and the mentality of the British generals. "Those kinds of theatrics will bring us another Gallipoli" was how Marshall had twanged it at Teheran.

"Winston, your plan to land in force in the Balkans was fully discussed and weighed against alternatives. It simply did not make as much sense militarily as a genuine second front in the West, in France. I hope you realize that there certainly wasn't anything personal in it."

"P'rhaps, p'rhaps. But the soft underbelly, Franklin. That's the ticket. Four years now we've fought the bastards, and believe me I know the Hun. Soft underbelly. Drive up from the south, hook into the Ruskies in Poland. . . ." Here he made the same hand motion he had employed to encompass Roosevelt's dormant legs. "You'll forgive me, I hope, if I prefer to believe that my idea was dismissed on purely political grounds, your wonderful Joe Louis analogy notwithstanding. Stalin simply doesn't want us interfering with what will become his sphere of influence after the war. He can smell and taste that territory already."

"Forgive *me* if I prefer to believe it was dismissed on purely military grounds by me and my people."

"But, Franklin, surely you realize that there are hundreds of thousands, nay, millions of good people in Eastern Europe who ought not to be thrown away, who ought not to have to live their lives under the Russians. My God, can you contemplate a more depressing fate than for people who have survived the Germans having to live under the Russians?"

"And so?"

"I'd like your permission to deal with Uncle Joe on this Balkans matter. I think he'll allow a British expedition in Greece, perhaps Yugoslavia, Rumania . . . whatever, to take the pressure off his troops down there. Certainly we'll not have to throw *all* our forces into a French attack. Even your Joe Louis holds something back, doesn't he? I think Stalin might be amenable to a trade-off in the Balkans."

"Specifically, Winston. What are you saying specifically?"

Churchill emptied the whiskey glass with his second draught. He raised the glass to the light and said, "If for no reason other than this, all the sacrifices we have made in Ireland have been well worth it. May I?" With grunting effort he pushed himself out of his chair and waddled again to the bottle. "Specifically, to let me deal directly with Uncle Joe on the Balkans," he repeated. "We all but lost Poland at the table last week, and I'd like to see if I can finesse a few of the smaller pieces away from the old devil. I'd like to be able to say you approve. Of course I'll clear every matter with you personally in advance." Again the clinking of ice cubes was punctuation.

The proposal struck FDR as having the immediate benefit to him of occupying Churchill with an activity that struck the President as something relatively unimportant in the larger scheme. He was inclined to agree. Agreement also seemed the best way of abbreviating the meeting. "Seems fine with me. Just be sure to keep me informed. I'd surely hate to have Uncle Joe ever thinking we're plotting something behind his back. Wouldn't you?" It was FDR's not so subtle way of telling the Prime Minister that he, himself, wouldn't want to be gulled.

At that moment Churchill's body seemed to have become more energetic, the pull of gravity temporarily overcome. He spun around, his eyes shining brightly, the bulldog face animated. He held his drink high as though in a toast. His eyebrows rose cunningly as he said, "Of course, if we get that bomb of ours—fusion, fission or whatever the hell they're calling it now—it would certainly make things with our contrary Uncle a good deal easier, n'est-ce-pas?"

FDR sat expressionless, more exhausted than restrained. He'd been slightly offended by the "ours" as the word that described "bomb." But the truth was that he had all but forgotten the Manhattan Atom Bomb Project, probably because he had just about given up on it as a means for winning the war at one crack. The ultimate Joe Louis punch.

At this moment, however, like Churchill's, his mind was once again excited by its possibilities—political now as well as military. The vague plan that had begun to take shape during that restless night in Teheran took on a bit more definition. He knew that the words "MANHATTAN PROJECT" were going to be an important part of it in some way. FDR swiveled his wheelchair a few degrees, and it now cut across the olive branch on the Great Seal of the United States.

Chapter

3

FOR FRANKLIN Roosevelt, sailing had always had a very special significance. James, his father, had so doted on the miraculous child of his old age that every wish of the boy was immediately gratified, so when Franklin was fourteen, he was given his own twenty-one-foot sailboat and the freedom to roam the Hudson River from Newburgh down to Spuyten Duyvil. His skill as a sailor and navigator came quickly. For the more challenging conditions around Campobello Island, the family's summer retreat off the coast of New Brunswick, Canada, Franklin had his father's yacht, the *Half Moon*, and lessons from Frank Calder, a local fisherman and the island's best sailor. In precise memory now he pictured himself at the tiller of the *Moon* as it sped past the East Quoddy lighthouse during the yearly race around the island. He recalled his crew also: Uncle Fred Delano; Louis Howe, the misshapen little man whose political advice Franklin would follow all the way to the White House; and his teenaged son, Jimmy. Franklin had molded them into a passable crew—barely passable and never good enough to win. Days then had the smell and savor of sea salt and spray.

When he was twenty-one Franklin Roosevelt was the second-best sailor on Campobello, and no one loved the challenge of the sudden fogs and wind changes, the extremity of the tides rolling down from the Bay of Fundy, more than he did. He had gotten so good, in fact, he could loop Deer Island, touch into Blacks Harbour for lunch, and circle back to Campobello in time to catch the long, blazing summer sunset. When he first sailed from Campobello into Dark Harbor, Maine, where his cousin Eleanor had been visiting her aunt in the summer of 1903, he knew exactly how much it would impress her. Now he remembered once again steering the *Half Moon* past the shoals of Dark Harbor, around the bobbing red buoy, and right up the channel toward the town dock. And there she was, fair hair blowing, white dress billowing in the midafternoon sun. Cousin Eleanor. Memory carried him again in its deceptive currents.

Even his first step in national politics had been related to the sea. Woodrow Wilson, the President-elect in 1913, had settled the problem of New York patronage with his selection of young, State Senator Roosevelt, but in precisely what capacity was a slight problem. When Franklin screwed up his courage and said, "Mr. President, all my life I have loved the sea and ships, and have been a student of naval history for as long as I can remember," the matter was settled. FDR recalled the thrill of being appointed assistant secretary of the Navy at thirty-one. Those years, it seemed to him now, had poured away too quickly.

As President he still enjoyed the idea of going to sea. Not only was it an escape from what the land had come to represent after eleven years as President—constraint, endless pressures and constant demands—it was a consolation. His spirit was revived by the timeless rocking, the cold mists and the harsh winds of an ocean crossing. Only messages of the utmost urgency were ever sent along, matters that could be resolved by a direct "yes" or "no." It was supposed to be a time for renewing his strength and replenishing the energies the affairs of the land had stolen, but neither was happening on this particular crossing.

FDR had exhausted himself flying, no doubt about that, hopping all over the Near East, from Oran to Cairo to Teheran, back to Cairo to Tunis, Malta and, finally, Sicily. Nothing in the world wearied and taxed the President quite so much as flying; nothing, not even going head to head with Uncle Joe or bickering with Churchill. But this trip had been especially difficult. And the sea was simply not working its magic. The problem, he believed as he poured some gin into a weighted goblet from the cut-glass flagon in the captain's cabin, was with the ship itself. The U.S.S. *Iowa*, largest battlewagon in the fleet, was so massive and stable that it transformed the undulating, unpredictable sea he loved and needed into a flat extension of the air and land worlds that had stolen his energies.

At least on the cross-Atlantic trip eastward in November there had been the excitement of the topedo that was accidentally fired by a destroyer in the escort. The *Iowa* had swerved and listed so sharply that the President had almost been thrown out of his bed; his wheelchair took on a life of its own as it ran crazily around the cabin. Then the *Iowa*'s five-inch guns set up an immediate deafening salvo. FDR insisted on being wheeled out and lifted up to the bridge for the display. Of course, it was too dark to see very much, but the experience had been bracing indeed. This western crossing, unfortunately, was utterly without incident. If he weren't quite so weary, Franklin Roosevelt would have managed, somehow, to create a bit of interesting mischief.

Earlier in the afternoon he had taken a turn around the first superstructure deck, almost nine hundred feet long, on a sea so calm the only feeling of motion he had came from the engine vibrations. That and the spinning rubber of his wheels against the calluses on the flat of his hands.

FDR's exhaustion seemed to border on fatigue, but he had been at this point before, perhaps too many times before. During the final weeks of the Presidential campaign against Wendell Willkie, he had required very close attention; never, however, had he felt such emptiness, loneliness. Never before had three days at sea failed to recharge his energies or revive his spirits. He had isolated himself because his malady, his weariness, seemed to be of the soul. Franklin Roosevelt saw the reflection of his head and shoulders in a round gold-framed mirror across the room; he placed his fingers on his scalp and combed the thinned hair on top into a more presentable, fuller cover.

His cigarettes, a half-empty package of Camels, were on a table on the far side of the large bed, but he was too tired to make the effort at retrieving them. He smiled bitterly at the irony of his dilemma: the simple desire for privacy *and* a cigarette was for him a luxury, a matter of choice. Then the thought that things would begin to get better, that there would be ease and family and friends and restful days at Warm Springs, Georgia, began to encourage him.

He slid the dispatches, two sheets of rough paper—one pink, the other pale blue—fully out from under an unopened copy of William Shirer's *Berlin Diary*. He had started the book twice and each evening found himself unable to concentrate enough to finish the second page. Placing the first dispatch above the other, he read them once again:

SECRET

URGENT

[NAVY CODE]

MOSCOW 10 DECEMBER 1943

MOST SECRET FOR THE PRESIDENT ONLY FROM HARRIMAN.

MESSAGE HAS BEEN GIVEN ME FROM PERSON HIGHEST IN

AUTHORITY HERE. MESSAGE SEEMS TO CONTRADICT TEHERAN

PROMISE TO HELP DEFEAT . . .

[REMAINDER FOLLOWS IN ARMY CODE]

MOSCOW 10 DECEMBER 1943

UNNUMBERED. MOST SECRET FOR THE PRESIDENT ONLY FROM
HARRIMAN.

. . . THE ENEMY IN THE FAR EAST AFTER DEFEAT OF GERMANS.
IN ADDITION WILL NOT ACCEPT POLISH GOVERNMENT IN EXILE IN
LONDON.

[THIS ENDS MESSAGE IN ARMY CODE] PLEASE FLASH
ACKNOWLEDGMENT AT ASSIGNED TIME AND PLACE.

More than ever, the cabin, spacious as it was, bored him
terribly. FDR's restless frustration had become barely con-
trollable. The three portholes high on the bulkheads presented him with dots of an invariable blue sky. Shifting his
weight on the swivel chair next to the bed, he pulled off the
striped Groton school tie he had loosened a few minutes
earlier. Then he again eyed the distant pack of cigarettes.

Franklin Roosevelt had chosen not to recognize the true
source of his weariness; he had, in fact, willed himself to
blame only the taxing days and weeks of extreme physical
and psychological effort. Intense political maneuvering. Just
as he had willed himself to function as well as he had under
extreme pressure. *Let's face it,* he now allowed himself to
admit, *I'm sixty.* He had once sat on the knee of President
Chester A. Arthur. He unconsciously spread and patted his
thinning hair once again. *Sixty-two!*

The President sat quietly, his hands curled limply in his
lap. He sighed uncharacteristically. *Wasted,* he thought.
*The effort so far all but wasted. Still another enormous effort
ahead.* OVERLORD. *A massed assault on France. Stalin had
forced the issue. But what was the point in the long run?* He
shrugged helplessly and sighed again even more unacharac-
teristically. *Nothing's ever certain, least of all the peace after
the war is won—IF the war is won. Wilson learned that the*

hard way. Here he looked across into the distant mirror. *Tens of thousands will die in the assault—that's the only thing that's certain.*

He removed his pince-nez and glowered at the crutches propped against the foot of the bed. With thumb and forefinger he squeezed the bridge of his nose. The tightening of his stomach, chest and back muscles as he pulled the weighty body off the chair forced a sound—a slight groan, actually—from between his lips. Edging around the bed, supporting himself only by the strength in his arms and balanced by broad palms and outstretched fingers on the solf mattress, FDR moved like a marionette operated by an amateur. Slowly toward the cigarettes and even more slowly back again to the swivel chair—a small but important victory over inertia, coming at a crucial time, given his prevailing thought and mood. He was perspiring profusely when he lit his first cigarette of the day and held the smoke in his throat and lungs for a long while.

He thought about Churchill's smug elation over the possibility of controlling the war and the peace with an atomic weapon, and he realized the truth was that he had really never fully believed such a weapon could win the war all at once with a single blow. Then he distinctly remembered that morning in October four years earlier when Alexander Sachs, his old friend but then acting as a spokesman for Albert Einstein and expatriate physicists Enrico Fermi and Leo Szilard, sat imperially across from his desk, waving a forefinger and saying, "Mr. President, you know, of course, as a student of naval history that Napoleon once rejected Robert Fulton's idea of developing steamships for wartime use." Could an informed American President possibly make the same sort of tactical error again? Of course not. So it was primarily to protect himself against the judgment of history that FDR had taken on the Manhattan Project and the multimillion dollar cost. That and Professor Einstein's signature at the bottom of the urgent letter Sachs had brought him.

It was true that in the spring of forty-two FDR had allowed himself the luxury of hoping for a few short weeks that the mysterious superbomb could be a reality before very long and would soon thereafter alter the course and duration of the war. When Churchill had met with him at Hyde Park in June of that year, Winston's enthusiasm for the Tube Alloys Project, as the British had coded the research project then, had rubbed off on FDR, but only for a week or so; he never had perceived it as anything more than a hope, and hopes were things, finally, to be admired only from a considerable distance.

The cigarette smoke drifted upward and toward the nearest, slightly open porthole. FDR brushed the back of his hand over his face and prolonged the rhythmic scratching of his knuckles on two days' white stubble. The sun had gone behind a long cloud, and the *Iowa* altered course ten degrees south-southwest with only the barest hint of deflection. The captain's cabin darkened.

Bodies. Bodies were going to win this war. Not a superbomb. That's the reality of it. Hundreds of thousands of bodies and the military minds of men like Marshall and King and Eisenhower. There are no shortcuts. That much is certain if anything is. FDR smacked the table loudly with his large, strong hand. "Damn it," he growled. *Stalin, Churchill already jockeying for postwar position and I, like a fool, completely engaged with the war. He fingered the blue dispatch. Got to pay more attention. Do something soon. But I mustn't make Wilson's mistake; I'll not be the naive idealist chewed up and spit out by the sharks.* "Bet your bottom dollar on that," he told the mirror.

Without his being fully aware of it, the competitive juices had begun to flow again. The mind, as politically complex and well trained as any shaped in this century, had begun to throw off its torpor, challenged by the discovery of a contingency that had not been well enough prepared for. There would be a weapon eventually, that much was certain; Churchill, in fact, knew of its development and was counting on it to enforce his own *Pax Britannica*; that, after all, had been the main point of that casual evening at the embassy in Cairo three nights earlier.

FDR's thought pattern was rarely linear. It didn't move through a series of logically related steps; rather, his mind ran in many directions at once, leaping, skipping, pirouetting through, over and around possibilities. Always he knew the results he wanted, and the mind usually fashioned a journey toward that end which few others could have shaped or even fathomed. Characteristic of the final process was that the plan generally had an infinite variety of options when it was finally instituted, deceptions if secretive, and protective covers and very logical explanations should it fail. When it was completely formulated—that process took a few weeks usually—it appeared to be a beautifully tooled and remarkably complicated piece of delicate machinery. Friends termed the mind "brilliant"; enemies called it "devious." It was both.

There were certainly other ways to control the peace besides bombing the world into submission, or continually threatening to do so. Another world organization, *à la* Wilson, wasn't going to be sufficient, even though it might be helpful. He gazed again at the message on the table in front of him: it was, he knew, merely a harbinger of the disagreements, the incompatibilities, that would erupt everywhere when the war ended.

Not a place on this earth that will not become a bone of contention, that will not be fought over as a spoil of war. So it really falls to me. Always suspected it would, and maybe that's as it should be. Just as well. Just hope it's not too late to get going on something. This wasn't the first time he had had such a conversation with himself. It was, however, the first time, the very moment, in fact, when he decided to begin to take the shaping of the postwar world completely into his own hands.

He spoke aloud to himself in the darkening room: "What the hell made Sachs, or even Einstein, think we could control the bomb any more than Napoleon could have controlled the steamboat? There never has been a weapon that hasn't eventually got out to the world for its destruction and misfortune. How long do you think it would be before Uncle Joe had to have one of his very own?"

FDR couldn't imagine Joseph Stalin not having something he really wanted for very long, not being able to get it one way or another. *The bomb would give us a time advantage, though. For how long, I wonder—that's the real question. Of course that advantage would be at the cost of a real peace, would certainly set up a military competition that could . . .* He closed his eyes and allowed the implications to blend into the gloom of his cabin.

He was slightly angry now and more mentally alert than he had been for days. The uranium bomb was undoubtedly the single most important political instrument he had available to him, and he had underestimated its true value and long-term importance—probably because most of the people around him who were privy to the secret had overestimated its tactical, short-term value. His anger was self-directed; he had allowed the matter to rest in the hands of others, to become the province of people he realized now he did not even know particularly well.

Two things were already certain in his mind: first, he must take control of the MANHATTAN PROJECT, and second, it must be done secretly so as to give him the greatest freedom to maneuver. It was a delicate task that required someone he could trust absolutely and who would not tip his hand. Franklin Roosevelt preferred to think of the role he had just created as a "confidant," when, in fact, "agent" was far more accurate. He probably knew whom he wanted for the task well before his instincts had led him to this point.

He won't like it a damned bit. FDR smiled. *Too caught up in the romance of a war fought crawling on his belly in the moonlight*. The President turned Harriman's pink message over and printed boldly:

SECRET

URGENT

[NAVY CODE]

11 DECEMBER 1943

MOST SECRET FOR GEN. GEORGE MARSHALL HEAD JOINT CHIEFS.

PLEASE HAVE FOLLOWING TRANSFER ORDERS CUT AND AUTHORIZED BY YOU IMMEDIATELY . . .

Here he stopped for a moment, long enough to realize that he was still very tired but no longer weary of heart. His spirits had revived; he was active again, thinking, planning —indeed, scheming. The final thought brought a thin smile to his haggard face. *Hell, call it "plotting" and be done with it.* His smile widened.

When he picked up his pencil and finished his message to Marshall, he was almost beaming his reelection smile. He always enjoyed writing the title "COMMANDER IN CHIEF" boldly after his name. As he leaned far over to reach the buzzer alongside the bed, FDR said, his voice capturing his smile, "But he's going to be mad as a hornet's nest when he gets this little invitation."

Chapter

4

TWICE THE twin-engined Curtiss Commando had circled, tipped a wavering wing toward the sun, and come in low over the headquarters quonset. The second time its wheels had touched the volcanic soil of Makin island, kicking up a whirlwind of dust and stones before jumping back into the air for still another approach.

This was the first transport plane that had attempted to land since a larger force of dogfaces had moved in and mopped up the work the Marines had done. A few Hellcats and P-40s had been in and out, but since supplies had started coming in by LST, Colonel Carlson, the Marine commander, had not considered clearing the airstrip a priority job for his tired Raiders.

The Colonel was among the small knot of stiff-backed Marine officers standing in front of the quonset looking skyward. His expression was a mixture of curiosity and disgust; he muttered curses as the plane arced again and began its third approach. "Don't know what in the world could be so damned urgent. I sure to hell hope it's worth it, Roosevelt," he said, increasing his volume to a shout as the plane roared in.

The landing was a series of bumps, bounces and skids that culminated in a dusty slide ending a few feet from the heavy bush. Now the expression of the day was incredulity—raised eyebrows, pursed lips. A lieutenant whistled shrilly, and the island's only truck kicked down the field to help pull the plane back so it could be turned around.

Led by Colonel Carlson and Major Roosevelt, the other men, all junior officers in immaculate fatigue uniforms, began the walk toward the plane. Their movement was as relaxed as their training and rank would permit, a military saunter rather than a march. "You're certain you want to do this, Roosevelt? That plane looks a lot more dangerous than chasing Japs off the rest of these islands," Carlson said, indicating the plane's precarious position with a cock of his head.

Major James Roosevelt smiled weakly. Irony was not Carlson's forte, and his bantering was worse. James opted for the most direct response: "Orders, Colonel. I'd rather stay here and finish the job." Understatement was not wasted on these men; they had shared so many elemental things that unnecessary words could seem an insult.

It was happening to him again. It had happened as long as he could remember—at Groton, at Harvard, in Washington, even here on Makin with the Marines. Always proving himself and always the same no-win situation, and always, of course, the shadow of his father or mother casting everything in doubt or uncertainty. He wanted to tell Carlson he'd be back in a week or two at most. This was, after all, the gravy time. The outfit had fought like hell and paid a price, but now there was time for licking wounds, for resting lazily like sated tigers, for tasting the rare sweetness of their mortality. All before having to do it all over again on some other island—that was how the war was going to be fought in the

Pacific. Now, suddenly, he would not be doing it all over again. He knew it. They knew it. He realized that his recall orders could have come *before* the raid on Makin. He'd been allowed at least that, and now the experience was irrevocable.

Colonel Carlson spared him the embarrassment of many final words. "Roosevelt. You don't have to tell me you don't want to leave. Every man in this outfit knows that. Whatever the reason they're pulling you out, it's got to be dumb as hell. Good thing you have some pull and can find your way back here before too long. My problem is how in the world I'm going to find another able executive officer." Carlson offered his hand.

As they shook, James said, "Two weeks at the outside, sir."

The plane was vibrating heavily as a door above the wing was thrown open. A leather-jacketed Army corporal motioned him, with exaggerated, impatient gestures, to climb aboard. He stretched down a hand for Major Roosevelt, who vaulted up as the plane began to roll. There was time for only one final wave from the doorway before the plane jerked forward in earnest. Every bump and rut was transmitted directly to the new passenger, who had fallen into the first seat he saw. With what sounded like its final reserve of power, the Curtiss Commando edged off the ground and over—just barely over—the quonset and into a steep incline and banking maneuver toward the east, the direction he dreaded most.

James Roosevelt blew his nose into a wrinkled handkerchief, and when he put it away, he remembered the orders folded in his breast pocket. He pulled them out and smoothed them on his lap. His lips moved slightly as he read. All was, of course, in order:

4th Endorsement

FROM: Gen. G. C. Marshall, Head Jt. Chiefs
TO: Maj. James Roosevelt, U.S. Marine Corps

1. You will stand relieved temporarily from present duties and will proceed by air to Marine Corps Base, SD Cal and thereafter report to Alex. Va. Marine Repl. Depot no later than 17 December 1943.

2. This transfer should be effected through channels in a normal and unexceptional manner.

3. The travel herein enjoined is necessary in the public interest.

His eyes carried up the page and fastened again on the word "temporarily." He reread the orders. Marshall might have issued them, but James clearly perceived his father's hand. He hoped there was at least some purpose to them, not merely a sudden swell of parental concern over his safety in combat.

The last time he had seen his mother and father together was nine months earlier, on the ninth of March, actually. He remembered the date exactly because it was that of one of FDR's regular monthly press conferences and James had attended. There had been some strong needling by May Craig, the reporter for the Portland *Press Herald*, who had managed to upset the President on the subject of Lend-Lease. It was James's final leave before combat, and he had flown back East from California for a few days at his mother's urging. But the family was so far-flung and occupied, it wasn't until his last evening that he could spend even a few moments alone with his parents. His time with Romelle, his wife, had been particularly strained. The war in the Pacific was, in a sense, an escape from the pressures and responsibilities of the life that had been chosen for him and over which he had very little control.

Over tea with his parents in the Green Room, the unspoken tensions grew rather strong. Eleanor stirred and tinkled her spoon in her cup. "I don't see," she said finally without preamble, "why you have to take such risks, Jimmy. There are a great many reasonable and significant ways to

46

participate in this war without taking such chances. Elliott is quite bad enough, but you, you've always been so much more . . . " She didn't finish her sentence; she merely shrugged and brushed a wisp of hair from her forehead. Then there was a long silence, and James was reminded that there had been many such in this family. His eyes fastened on the quivering blue feather atop his mother's hat.

FDR said, finally and emphatically, "Never, James. I want you to know that I would never ask for special treatment for you, or any of the boys. And that's a promise. Why, I wouldn't dream of putting myself on that kind of spot politically." As had many such silences in this family, it ended with the father's making a joke. The son and father forced laughs. Eleanor put the spoon in the saucer and lifted the green china teacup, the legacy of Lincoln's Presidency, to her lips.

For Major James Roosevelt, child of privilege with eyesight not strictly up to Marine Corps standards, the simple notion of "home" was a very complicated matter. Where was it, really? The family house in Hyde Park? The apartment in Washington he shared less and less with Romelle? Or was it the White House and the whole knot of ambiguous feelings that place and his parents gave him?

The December 17 target date for his arrival, which had seemed reasonable the previous week, had not been easy to make even with a Top Priority clearance. There had been a long delay in San Diego, doubling back and postmidnight transfers to freezing cargo planes at Phoenix and Waco and Akron and Greensboro as he zigzagged his way eastward. He finally arrived at the Alexandria, Virginia, Marine Replacement Depot shortly after midnight of the seventeenth.

Turning his orders over to the unsmiling clerk in the headquarters orderly room, he was handed a note. "Call me soon as you arrive. Import. Hassett. WA 5-1010."

Of all the people he might have expected to contact him on arrival, Bill Hassett, his father's aide and secretary, was one of the most likely. Although General Marshall's name was on the orders, James had never doubted for a single moment that his father was really behind the whole thing. So the note from Hassett made perfect sense.

The phone rang half a dozen times, and the receiver was juggled and dropped before a tired, cracking voice said, "Hassett here."

"Bill, sorry, I just got in. Your note said 'important.' "

"Jimmeeee. Swell to hear your voice. Darned swell." The 'darned swell' was Hassett in a nutshell. "We've been hearing some awfully good things about you out there, son."

There was a pause that demanded filling, and James considered "Don't believe everything you hear, Bill," but he opted for a simple "Thanks. What's up?"

"Well, Jimmy, there's been a delay. The President's been called away. All very hush-hush. Latest has it he'll be back day after tomorrow. But he called this morning and said he wants to see you the very first thing he gets home. I'd figure maybe Sunday morning."

"How's he doing? Did the trip take too much out of him?"

"Trip?"

"Teheran."

"Oh. Then you've seen the communiqué in the papers. Well, he's handling it about as well as can be expected." James didn't like the way that sounded, but before he could follow up, Hassett said, "You planning to move back in, Jim?"

"Back in where?"

"Why, the White House."

"No. I've got orders for this company. In fact, I had the distinct impression this was going to be T.D.Y."

Hassett was confused. "T.D.Y.?"

"Temporary duty."

"Oh—"

"Bill. Do you know something I don't and that maybe I ought to?"

"Absolutely not, Major. Absolutely not. I only thought that since—"

"Well, I did actually plan to come by and see Mother tomorrow afternoon."

"You'd be disappointed, Major. Come to think of it, you're the only living Roosevelt who's anywhere near Washington. And will be until the Chief comes back on Sunday."

"Hurry up and wait, eh? Well, I guess I'll just sit tight here for a while. Nothing for the press, okay, Bill? In fact, let's keep this whole thing very quiet."

"Naturally, Major. Your father made that very clear when he forwarded your orders."

There was not the slightest hint of curiosity in James's voice when he said, "Was Mother with him?"

"No, he was flying solo in Teheran."

James said, "I'd like to have some time to catch up on my reading, Bill. So, as I've said, let's keep this on the Q.T., okay?"

"Far as I'm concerned, Jimmy, you're still in the Pacific."

"Let's not overdo it, Bill."

When he hung up, James Roosevelt was vaguely upset but more curious. Washington certainly was, he realized, a very difficult place.

Certainly he did not expect the changes he saw in the White House after his only nine months away. Soldiers now guarded the entire perimeter, and heavy chains barred all the gates. Antiaircraft guns were visible on the roof and barely concealed behind false terraces on the lawns. No more tourists passing through the first-floor rooms; all employees and visitors had to be issued passes; most were searched. James, wearing his short-waisted campaign jacket, looked around for other changes as he was escorted to the entrance of the East Wing by a Secret Service man who remembered him. There he was turned over to an attractive red-haired WAC captain at an admissions desk, a cheerfully efficient young woman who welcomed him and spoke pleasantly about the unseasonable weather as he signed the register in two places. In almost any other situation, at almost any other time, James would have engaged her in conversation. His return to the White House, however, had disoriented and vaguely depressed him.

On this clear winter day, the morning sun was streaming through the triple windows of the President's second-floor oval study. Shortly there would be a resolution. James looked around while he waited for his father. In this room he had been administrative assistant, advisor, confidant, confessor, secretary, sounding board, devil's advocate and sometimes even son to Franklin Delano Roosevelt.

He rested, anxious yet semireclined, with one leg up on the soft leather couch. He was partially at ease in this room, a decade of use having submerged its history to matter-of-factness. He hadn't even noticed how cluttered it had become with ship models and mementos. With his finger he absently swiveled the tiller of the *Half Moon*, the family boat on which he and his father and the other boys had cruised and island-hopped up at Campobello, at least until his father had been stricken with polio.

It was a few minutes after ten. Suddenly the door from the bedroom opened and Arthur Prettyman, the President's valet, poked his head in. He smiled broadly, shifted his weight from one foot to the other, and said, "Mo'nin', Mr. Jimmy. It sure be good to see you standin' here nice an' tall."

James recalled Arthur's regular greeting, breathed deeply, walked over, and shook hands.

From the adjoining bedroom the President's voice boomed. "Damn it all, Arthur, don't block my way. I want to see him." The valet backed out of the doorway and wheeled the President into the room. Franklin Roosevelt, apparently near full strength and vigor again, sat tall in his chair, smiled even more broadly than his valet, and held his arms out, palms upward, far in front of him. "My God, Jimmy, look at you. You're a bloody enlistment poster. For the first time I understand what they mean when they say, 'There's no such thing as an ex-Marine.' It looks as though they've marked you for life. And for the better. You look marvelous." The two men looked at each other for a few silent beats before James stepped forward, bent at the waist, and embraced his father's shoulders tightly. When James stepped back, Arthur Prettyman was gone.

"Really, Jimmy," the father said, "you've never looked so well. Shame Ma isn't here to see you." The mention of his mother revived some of the son's old confusion. It didn't rest long, however, because FDR said, "Believe me, Jimmy, if there had been anyone else I could have trusted with this matter, I never would have . . . " FDR had begun the explanation, but he let the specifics expire with a vague hand gesture. At that moment the son began to notice a change in his father's body. It began to deflate. The long arms dropped. The smile took on the fixed quality of a painting. The collar and lapels of his green morning robe appeared to rise on his neck and shoulders. James had the sudden sense of the sheer physical effort that had gone into the welcome now that it was being so quickly dissipated.

"It must have been a very rough trip," James said matter-of-factly.

FDR cocked a brow.

"It usually takes you almost a week to get your land legs back after so much flying and ocean sailing. Unless, of course, you're posing for a photographer; then you look healthier than a circus strong man, no matter where you've been or what you've been doing."

FDR smiled and nodded a sad agreement. "Actually, it would have taken a circus rubber man to adjust to those two—Stalin, Churchill. And let me tell you, Jimmy, no sooner had I arrived in Teheran when I began to decide to have your transfer orders cut. Believe me, I held off as long as I could. I can assure you, though, it was not done without weighing a great many factors. But more of that by and by. Notice anything different?" And FDR wheeled himself in a tight circle, looking over his shoulder when his back was turned toward his eldest son. The object of this coy turn was a khaki pouch attached to the rear of the wheelchair.

"What the devil is it, Pa?" James asked.

"Gas mask," answered the father proudly. "Silly thing, but they tell me I'm a likely target for attack. Only trouble is, it falls off every time I spring around too fast."

"I noticed that the entire place has become a little like an armed camp."

"I know, Jimmy, and it's depressing, but they assure me it's all necessary. You've simply got to go along with some of these things. I told the cabinet meeting the other day that if Hitler got us all with a bomb except for Frances Perkins, we'd have a woman President. I said I didn't believe even that madman would take such a chance." James smiled weakly but didn't say anything; he knew his father well enough to appreciate the importance to him of scenario and orchestration. So he decided to let things unfold; he really had no alternative.

The President rolled his chair over to his cluttered desk, lifted off the day's appointments sheet—a light Sunday schedule, mostly names at fifteen-minute intervals with the word "hello" typed next to each—and handed it to James. That meant it had just been canceled. James, remembering his days as his father's administrative assistant, looked down at the neatly typed page and walked toward the door of the outer office. He opened the door and without a word handed the sheet to Bill Hassett, who winced. It meant a dozen cancellation phone calls.

FDR had taken the dispatches from the War Department pouch on his desk but was having trouble with the seal of the first envelope. He handed it to James and put his hands limply forward: the gesture said, "How about a little help; I just can't manage it this morning."

While the President read the dispatch, Jimmy experienced a sudden and dizzying sense of displacement. It was, however, arrested by the firmness of his father's voice, once again becoming sure and hearty: "A Tartar. The man's an absolute Tartar, Jimmy. Take a look at this." Suddenly FDR was smiling, the large head thrown back, pinching at the bridge of his nose. As James took the note from his father, he felt the muscles in his neck and upper back tighten.

He glanced first at the name on the bottom. *Joseph Stalin.* Because his father kept repeating the phrases "a Tartar" and "the temerity of a burglar," James could not fully concentrate on the text. There were some formalities early: "The great pleasure to have met with you at last . . . prefer to deal with friends face to face . . . we are, after all, human beings, not machines who write dispatches—"

"Down there," the President said impatiently, "down there," tapping the middle of the third paragraph. The line read: ". . . to tell our mutual friend Churchill that the government in Poland will most assuredly be the one that remained behind, suffered, and fought the enemy at great personal risk, not the exiled lawyers and diplomats who live in the lap of luxury in London."

"And no more than a week or so after we'd all agreed that the Polish question would remain open until we had established a clear military advantage," the President said, shaking his head. "The man's a Tartar."

James did not quite know what to make of his father's reaction. There was annoyance, certainly; but overlaid were an exasperated respect and just the barest suggestion of admiration. James said, "Is it really important, Pa?"

FDR didn't answer, hadn't, in fact, even heard his son's question. And just as well. "Trouble is," he said as much to himself as to his son, "trouble is that these conferences are always out of sync. We are always reacting, trying to catch up with things well after the fact. So we meet in Persia to coordinate our military strategies when actually we should begin anticipating these"—he tapped the dispatch with the back of his hand—"these political problems."

James opted for his "sounding board" tone. "Maybe Uncle Joe's politics take care of themselves every day his army moves westward. *De facto* politics. That's what this dispatch seems to be saying, if I read it right."

"That's it precisely, Jimmy. Precisely. The Tartar's clever. Farther through Poland every day. Then Hungary, Czechoslovakia. Austria and Germany itself. Saying whatever we want to hear; doing whatever he damned well pleases. That's what Teheran was all about for me, let me tell you. That's why I want to have our front in France by late spring and begin to squeeze the Germans till there's nothing left. Have to; can't let him have things all his own way. My God, we all knew that before we ever got to the table. But now he's starting to send out new signals. New and powerful signals." Here FDR's voice changed, as though he were mimicking the deep-throated Russian. "Our terms have changed, *tovarich*. We no longer run, scorch the earth and hide. No longer do we sacrifice to buy time. Now we are on the move. Now we have time. We will be moving even faster tomorrow and the day after that. Maybe the end of the war will not even stop us."

"Wouldn't be a bad idea, Pa, if we could get him involved and moving eastward against the Japs. That one's not going to be so easy, believe me."

The phone buzzed. James walked over to the desk and picked it up. The call had been cleared through Hassett, so it must have been priority. "It's Hopkins's secretary," James said to his father.

"No, not right now," the President said, "I want to finish with this first."

James flushed. Never had he known FDR to hold off

Harry Hopkins. In fact, it was surprising that Hopkins wasn't in the room. His absence gave the President's orchestration an air of authenticity. It seemed reasonable that whatever was involved in bringing James to Washington was fairly genuine—not merely a matter of protecting his eldest son from the risks of yet another amphibious landing in the Pacific.

FDR was never happier than when he was hatching something, even a surprise party for his grandchildren, and the obvious realization now by his son gave the father a vigor that hadn't been there five minutes earlier. Now a glint was in the eye, the voice resonated. "You read that newspaper every day?" His father directed his chin to a *New York Times* that James had been leafing through earlier.

"Delivery is a bit slow in the Pacific, Pa."

Unhearing, the President said quickly, "Do you recall reading about a speech the Pope delivered before the Pontifical Academy of Science in the spring? You might have still been in the States. The *Times* was the only paper that carried it."

Major Roosevelt shrugged.

"Good thing no one ever takes the Holy Father very seriously. Anyway, in his speech he warned against the destructive use of atomic energy. I wonder where the hell he gets his intelligence." At this moment FDR placed his hand heavily atop his son's; there was ritual to the act, as though a pact were about to be made. "There's nothing definite yet, Jimmy. It's all the merest conjecture at this point. Nevertheless, nothing must leave this room." He squeezed his son's fingers. There was surprising strength in the grip now.

James responded with a glance, with a weary earnestness that reaffirmed the bond too often strained during their times apart—and often during their hours together.

When FDR continued, the original disclaimers were all repeated as though he were breaking a story to a reporter, with the phrase "purest supposition" added a few times just for good measure. James had concluded that his father's mind had all but settled on something unusual and daring. "I've been informed that the MANHATTAN PROJECT will bear fruit fairly soon. In about a year, maybe less. It's been a hell of a long time in coming." His eyes flashed and looked away abruptly during the dramatic pause he had manufactured.

"Jimmy. We will have the most powerful weapon in the history of mankind. This is our best estimate, latest word from Chicago. It could be so powerful that the real problem won't be in how to use it but how not to have to use it. You follow?"

The Major nodded partially even though the question was rhetorical.

"And we're going to have to decide fairly soon what the hell to do with it. Consider the options. If we drop a bomb, it could conceivably end the war; in fact, I've been told we might even end the war with just a demonstration of its power. But this is nothing new to you, James." It was indeed new, and they both knew it. "I've lived with the realization of having to make that decision for a good many months now, but I want to tell you that Teheran has turned my head around, turned it quite a bit, m'boy."

The "m'boy" bothered James, but he only said, "In what way?"

"The Tartar has changed my view of everything. Now he stands over his tactical maps and nudges a division forward here, a tank brigade there. The Germans had things their own way for two years; now it's Uncle Joe's turn, and he's sure to repay them in kind—and with plenty of interest. He's so preoccupied with territory and revenge now that he's not even thinking in terms of a superweapon."

"All the more reason to beat him to it, Pa. Put us completely in the driver's seat when the war is over."

"Ah, there's the elemental rub. Would it, Jimmy? Would it really?" Here the phone buzzed again. Hopkins calling back.

James began to rise; his father touched his knee and he sank back. The phone buzzed once more and was silent. "If we ever do have such a wapon, the Tartar will not rest until he has a comparable one. Only a matter of time, Jimmy, I can assure you. By then we could have an atomic competition that would make your head spin. The man would never give up. Never. And with his espionage network . . ."

"But we've got to go ahead with our project. If we sit back and let anyone get it before we do—"

"Of course, of course." The slightest note of exasperation crept into the President's voice. "That's exactly the point. There's going to be a superbomb one way or another—that much we now know. And either way, there's going to be a terrible competition, maybe even a headlong race toward destruction." The President pursed his lips and raised one eyebrow as he noted the last phrase; there would certainly be use for it in a speech somewhere further down the line.

It was clear to James now that—all qualifications aside— his father had a rather definite and complicated strategy already in mind. Perhaps no specific plan quite yet, but certainly a strategy. There had been other, earlier such revelatory moments with this man, never more of an impressive stranger to his son than when he was reshaping the American economic or judicial systems or, as in this case, assaying the future of life on the planet. There was always, as now, more behind the blue eyes than was ever translated into words.

FDR delivered his conclusion, dropped a pencil emphatically into his lap, and with a defiant jut of jaw said, "Stalemate. That's what we want. It's the only possible 'victory.' And the only way to achieve it is if each side has exactly the same superweapon as the other. That would rule out atomic blackmail."

Franklin Roosevelt had delivered the most astounding sentence of his astounding life, and like a great actor, he had underplayed it, almost, in fact, had thrown the line away.

James realized that he was expected to respond at this point, but nothing came. The suddenness of the suggestion, its vague implications, confused him.

"Your slack jaw, Major Roosevelt, is probably the mildest reaction we'd get on this if word ever got out what it was we were concocting here today. It's all just speculation now of course." The broadest of Roosevelt grins broke out. "Yet, with a few simple strokes, we do have the chance for parity and stability, for working out a peace that has a chance to endure. After all, what is really involved here is the giving up of a brief time advantage in order to establish an atomic stalemate without risking the endless rounds of weapons competition, any of which could prove fatal to both sides." FDR hoped for some responsive words this time, but James had just begun to play with the stunning ramifications. "It's just the enormity of the premise that would confuse lesser souls, congressmen and generals," FDR said with a curl on his lips.

"Not to mention cabinet members, newspapermen, the American public," James added as a partial list.

"Ah, but, Jimmy, once you get beyond the premise, it's amazing how nicely things begin to fall into place. Not at all unlike Keynes's idea about spending money you don't have. Don't you see, if the Tartar has the same power we have, there'll be no need for him to behave like a Tartar with it, at least not quite as often as he does now."

"Unless," James added, "he wants the whole world to play with, not just Poland."

"But we'll still be there to tell him that's not allowed. And we'll have our bombs to back us up. Well, what do you think?"

Unwillingly, James found himself already pulled into his father's orbit. He said, "I'm not quite certain yet, Pa, exactly who the real Tartar is in this matter."

FDR's laugh burst to the ceiling. He was operating near full strength again. "But," he said softly, "the timing's cru-

cial. There's no telling if we'll actually have an atomic anything next time I meet with him. But the next time we do
meet, it'll be to divide up the spoils of war, most likely, and
that's when the real problems are going to be on the table. It
would be very nice to have a little something in my pocket if
I had to use it."

"You know, Pa, to hit me with something like this right
out of the blue is a bit much. But there *is* something—or
rather, someone—that you seem to be overlooking in all this.
Churchill. There's the agreement you made with him in
Quebec to share all atomic secrets with the British. He'd
never stand for any of this, and you know it. So how in the
world do you intend to handle him?"

"Well, we could probably think of something really devious, couldn't we? Or, we could handle him the same way
you just *handled* Hopkins. As for the agreement at Quebec,
we'd share our secrets with him—eventually." FDR took a
deep breath and spoke in a voice much more his own. "I
realized something important about Churchill this time
around too, Jimmy. I don't know how I missed it before.
Really. Did you know that when he was a young man he
participated in a cavalry charge in South Africa, the last one
in history, to the best of my knowledge. Think of it, a line
of horsemen advancing on command into the teeth of
their guns." James didn't see the point but said nothing.
"And do you know that he carries a loaded pearl-handled
revolver in his belt at all times? I saw it at Teheran." James
still did not comprehend. "The point is that for him the
world is still South Africa and the Tartar will have to be
whipped into line. He wants to make the bear dance an
English air when this war is over. We could find ourselves in
another war before the smoke from this one clears."

"But he's been in on this from the beginning. He's going to
have to know what happens to it—how it's to be used."

The President nodded in the way he always did when he
disagreed, firmly, with his large head making abrupt arcs

forward and downward. "I need you, Jimmy. Our thing will be strictly a family matter." His voice became overtly and sweetly conspiratorial. Then, after another dramatic pause and a final, vigorous tug on the right wheel of his chair, Franklin Delano Roosevelt swung a ninety-degree turn and rolled toward the door. His gas mask shook but did not slip off.

James had seen that movement too many times before. It meant, "That's it; there won't be anything of substance until I'm ready to discuss it further." But James wasn't a mere petitioner or a politician with something to trade; he was someone who didn't even want to be there, someone who had been summoned from half a world away. He was this man's eldest son. In anger he said, "Would you please tell me what all this mumbo jumbo means in terms of separation from my outfit?"

"We'll have plenty of time to talk about that later." FDR was almost to the door.

"I beg your pardon, sir." His father stopped. "You have taken me away from the most important duty of my life. You've spoken in generalities about world conditions I could have read about in the newspaper. And you won't even do me the courtesy of telling me what specifically, if there *is* anything specific, you have in mind for me, what I will be doing or how long it will last. And I think, sir—"

His father said, over his shoulder, "There is nothing definite at this time, James. Just think about what I've told you. We'll talk about it again fairly soon. Might even be a good idea if you made up a code name for it—that's what's done these days. Something really arch that smacks of treachery and deceit."

James heard himself say hotly, "You realize, of course, that no one, not even the President of the United States, for whatever reason, has the right to peddle our national secrets."

The President of the United States rolled around smoothly

—at least James felt that he had forced some response—and, smiling very broadly, said, "Why, that's all just conjecture, Major, the purest fanciful conjecture on your part. If one is responsible for charting the future course of a powerful nation, such as ours, in this world, then one must think of a whole range of possible strategies before acting. Shame. I thought you had learned that much in this family. The objection you raise, however, is merely a problem of semantics. Easily solved. You see, I don't think *we* have to *peddle* anything. No, no, no, not at all. We might simply let the Tartar *steal* what we want him to have. Or at least make it look that way. After all, he's such an unscrupulous man. Now let's go to breakfast; I could eat half of Dutchess County."

Arthur Prettyman appeared in the doorway and stepped behind the President's chair.

James took off his glasses and pinched the bridge of his nose hard between a suntanned thumb and forefinger, not even realizing that it was an inherited gesture. The enormity of what he had just heard, or thought he'd heard, bewildered him.

"You know," his father was saying, "your mother's expected back by midweek. She'll be very happy to see you all in one piece."

Chapter

5

As MAJOR Roosevelt, sufficiently battened down in a borrowed overseas coat and gloves, made his way along the windy path from Pennsylvania Avenue to the East Wing entrance of the White House, his chief concern was keeping his hat on. He found himself mildly curious also about whether or not that redheaded WAC captain would be on duty when he stepped inside. No one was seated behind the table; James was momentarily disappointed. From behind him a cheerful voice said, "Good morning, Major Roosevelt," and he was as quickly pleased and reassured. "If you'd like," she added cheerfully, "you might want to hang your coat here and pick it up as you leave. It's part of the service." He accepted the invitation, placed his cap in an overcoat pocket, and hung his coat on the temporary rack.

She was tall, fair-skinned and lightly freckled. Superb smile. An inner voice unexpectedly warned him: "Good God, Jimmy, be reasonable. Not another woman." He felt the smile on his lips begin to fade.

She sat and turned the register for him to sign while she fingered a pile of yellow memos. "There's something here for you that came through earlier this morning, Major."

Leaning over the table, James could not resist taking a deep breath and smelling a sweetness, a fruity aroma coming from her hair, which had been pulled tightly back off her face and caught in a neat bun at her neck. He closed his eyes and weakened for a moment. He hadn't been this close to any woman for almost nine months; before he spoke, he willed his voice not to betray him. "Since it appears that I'll be seeing you fairly often, Captain, shouldn't I really know your name?" He smiled a bit too confidently, he thought.

She touched the name tag on her pocket. It read: "FIELD-ING."

"I mean the first name," James said.

She looked both ways before she whispered, "It's May." She said nothing else and handed James the memo she had been looking for. Her response, although brief, was not curt or coy, merely straightforward. Indeed, James had the distinct impression that in another time and place she would have been someone worth listening to and knowing a little better. The idea of asking her to lunch flitted through his mind, but he was now already focusing on the memo. It was printed boldly in dark, thick pencil lines with the date and time of receipt stamped at a slight angle near the top:

WHITE HOUSE
27 DECEMBER 1943
08:28
    YOUR MOTHER WOULD LIKE TO SEE YOU IN HER OFFICE.   THIS
MORNING.   YOUR CONVENIENCE. WELCOME BACK.

                                                  TOMMY

James was at first puzzled by the signature. "Tommy," he then remembered, was Malvina Thompson, his mother's secretary, and more, her shield, faithful right arm, blocking back and supplementary memory. He was at the elevator behind the main hallway cloakroom when he realized that he didn't remember leaving the Captain's presence, couldn't even recall if he'd said goodbye. He hadn't. At precisely the moment he decided to walk back to her table and apologize, the elevator door rolled open and a crew-cut Marine asked, "Floor, sir?"

James had been "home" for more than a week, suffered through a lonely Christmas, and found his sense of displacement totally undiminished. He had great trouble sleeping and concentrating on anything; the more familiar the places and people, the more strange. In addition, his body did not even seem quite his own; he usually felt a slight buzzing sensation, as though a very mild electric charge ran through him. The young Marine repeated the question and then asked to see the Major's pass.

Major Roosevelt blinked and looked again at the note. The phrase "her office" was far from clear. It could mean her sitting room upstairs on the second floor of the White House proper that had become the center of her administrative affairs in Washington. From another large room in the West Wing, where a host of secretaries worked on her mail, she was known to conduct business for days at a stretch. While in a downstairs East Wing office near the pool, five staff members labored continually on her press relations and for organizations to which she had lent her name and support. In fact, her "office" was wherever she happened to be sitting at the time. He showed the memo and said, "Second floor, please."

"I'm afraid you'll need special clearance for that, sir."

"I'm Mrs. Roosevelt's son, Corporal."

The young Marine cleared his throat and said, "I guess it'll be okay then."

James admired what his mother had made of her life, admired how by sheer will and intelligence—particularly by will—she had refused to accept the options offered her, how she chose and shaped new ones. A very impressive woman. *Mother* was, however, a very different matter. As long as James kept the two things separate and managed a certain distance, theirs was an acceptable relationship. *Perhaps,* James thought as he stepped off the elevator and turned left into the narrow beige hallway on the second floor, *perhaps this is the best of all possible situations with such a mother.* He hadn't remembered the clutter of bookcases and lopsided photographs and prints in the hallway as he passed the soldier who guarded them. Then he was struck by the incredible and sudden realization that thirty-six years earlier he had actually issued forth from Eleanor Roosevelt. A child of her womb. *Mother* meant that he was indeed flesh of her flesh.

He stood stock-still on the thick green carpet before her sitting room. He was smiling in a distracted way. Then a poignancy inherent in the confusion of his thoughts and feelings entered; the smile faded slowly but not completely; his eyes narrowed and he tilted his head. She clearly belonged to the world while he had been struggling like the devil just to belong to himself. He pulled a long breath, smiled a resignation, and turned the polished bronze knob.

The room had been a pink and gold sitting room with lots of brocade and a Louis Quatorze feel to it when he had first visited it, the vestige of Mrs. Harding's attempt to lighten the first Mrs. Roosevelt's morbid sense of decor. Now James stepped into a room completely transformed, no longer a sitting room at all but a legitimate office in which tans and grays and polished wood immediately proclaimed a serious commitment to work, a room in which subdued mechanical sounds—hums and clacks and buzzes—and the hushed activity of women at desks and before filing cabinets made a visitor feel like an intruder. The son stood in the doorway for a few seconds before realizing that he was entitled to enter unannounced.

James heard his mother's voice through the half-opened

inner door before he saw her, the same strained coloratura that had become the friendly butt of comedians and mimics. Her back was toward him; her loose, flowered dress draped her stooped, elongated body. She shifted her weight slightly from leg to leg as she spoke in short, authoritative phrases. Through the window before her the Washington Monument, the reflecting pool and the Lincoln Memorial lay cloaked in a bleak winter mist. She saw her eldest son's reflection in the same glass, covered the telephone with her palm, turned and said, "Jimmy. You surprised me. These foolish details." She seemed at once terribly efficient and terribly vulnerable. James stepped around the desk, took her free hand, and brought it to his cheek as she said into the phone, "No motorcade under any circumstances. None. Two plain, unmarked vehicles at the airport—right at the foot of the ramp, mind—and a direct drive to the arena. Nothing more. Understood?" The back of her hand, James realized, had become spotted with the marks of age. He could not remember how long it had been since he'd held it like this. He was close enough to her face to see a leathery cross-hatching of creases; he could see the blond down he remembered on the sides of her forehead, her cheeks, her upper lip. He examined her closely until she was finished and had left word not to be disturbed.

Then they embraced. The smell of lilac water was still about her. He felt how fragile she actually was beneath that imposing presence; she was pleased to be touched by the strength of his youth. Nothing was said for a long while. At precisely the same moment, mother and son stepped back and sat down.

"You are to know right off, Jimmy, that it wasn't at my instigation that your father decided to terminate your career as a daredevil Marine. Although I must say, it wasn't at all a bad idea." She was not looking at him but at her hands smoothing her dress in her lap. Her voice suddenly throbbed with grateful welcome: "I'm *so* glad you're back safely."

"Thanks, Ma, but being retired prematurely from the war has not been the easiest thing in the world for me. If, in fact, I am retired."

"Still, I wanted you to know that your transfer was none of my doing." She looked away and continued to smooth her dress, now the sleeves and cuffs. "I've spoken with Romelle."

"That's more than you can say for me." He didn't like himself when sarcasm leapt out uncontrolled. But he didn't much welcome being lectured on his marriage by his mother either.

Now she looked directly at him, her face severe under her parted and taut hair. Her gray eyes, however, were the counterforce, alert, sensitive and even a little frightened. When she spoke next, all her features softened suddenly; her voice lost its certainty. "She's afraid to approach you. Afraid of a rebuff, so she asked me . . ." She was almost whispering when she broke off. "If you don't see her at all after they find out you're home, the publicity will be ferocious."

"Ma, *they* know I'm home, in the first place. In the second place, Romelle and I were in fact separated before I left for California. And in the third place, when have you ever been that concerned with bad publicity?"

"Oh, you're right, of course; it's not the publicity. It's Romelle herself. I've really come to like her. I told her I'd say something to you. She seemed desperate. She's a very good person, Jimmy."

"We're all good persons, Ma. That's precisely the problem."

"Of course. But that's not what I'm trying to tell you. And it's not my intention to meddle in your business. I know I don't quite have the credentials of a marriage counselor; I don't even have the right to advise. I know that it may be better sometimes, after all, to break a marriage cleanly than to carry it on as a matter of form, especially when there are no children. I know that. A second marriage, however, so soon after the first . . ." Eleanor Roosevelt looked above and beyond her son. "Your father and I have been far from perfect parents. There's no need to go into that."

Neither mother nor son was in any way prepared for what occurred then. Neither was aware that eyes had begun welling with tears or that emotion would make it difficult for them to speak. When James struggled for self-control, he maintained it barely, mostly through the consciousness of having to breathe regularly. His greatest fear was of breaking down and crying like a child: the bursting forth of an accusatory phrase and the gasping for breath until all was reduced to unclear words and sucking noises and the humiliation then of having lost control. Such things had never been permissible for Roosevelts.

But it came quite suddenly and quite out of the blue. He didn't speak in sentences but in carefully controlled fragments about the double pneumonia incident of almost twenty years earlier. "Coming home. All the way from Boston. Sick as a dog. Turned away. Didn't even take—take time for me from your party." By increments the history was recounted and tallied.

She remembered, vaguely at first, then more precisely. James had been sent home from school; ill with flu, he had burst in on a dinner party at the Governor's mansion. The butler didn't even know who he was and kept him waiting at the door. Then she'd sent him off to bed. It became pneumonia. And he'd begun to lose his hair shortly after.

James had started to approach sentences and make logical connections. "Do you have any idea, Mother, the humiliation of going bald when you're still in college?" He tapped the side of his head with the tips of two fingers. "How it is to feel that so many things could have been very different if you hadn't been so terribly neglected? Look at all the children. Not a one of us who hasn't been marked in some way or other. Not a one of us who's a whole, really solid human being. It's no wonder we can't make our marriages work."

There was, of course, a great deal more to be said, but James had compressed everything and spent himself quickly, so he merely repeated his final sentence slowly.

His mother had fastened on the word "neglected." Privately she took a good measure of responsibility for her children's ragged lives. To label her maternal offense as clearly and specifically as James had was something new and rather stunning. And, she knew, true.

No defense was possible, none was attempted. She began to blink and purse her lips rhythmically. "Your father and I might have divorced at one time. I suspect you know the story. But we did not. We arranged, for want of a better word, to stay together and maintain a family, such as it has been. No, not for the children's sakes. If that had been the case, we'd have *all* been unremitting failures. We did it for our own sakes and for the sake of appearances. That you've only been as 'neglected' as you have is a miracle of sorts. In the world, most people are far more neglected than you've been. But I must ask you something, Jimmy, I might not have the right to ask."

James had begun to feel shame; it came in the form of warmth on the back of his neck and his ears. He nodded.

"Jimmy, do you hold the same resentment against your father as you do for me?"

He was shaking his head even as he tried to consider the implications of his response; the moment, however, commanded honesty. "No, Ma, I don't think I do, at least not in the same way. I can't say why exactly, but I don't. I guess I expected more from you for some reason."

She nodded, smoothed her dress again, blinked and pursed. "At any rate, Romelle wanted me to say something and I have. She really does strike me as a very decent person, James."

He said, "I'd rather not see her for a while. I'll be staying at the base over in Alexandria. Lying low."

Eleanor fondled a jeweled pin shaped like a mushroom that was clasped at her bosom. "Come," she said with a shrug of resignation, "let's walk out together."

"Certainly, Ma," he said with a smile, and they hooked arms and walked through the buzzing and clacking of one of Eleanor Roosevelt's many offices. They touched cheeks lightly when they reached the hallway.

James thought again of the WAC captain on duty downstairs and felt glad he'd get to see her again today. A fleeting thought but a satisfying one. He had almost reached the elevator when a voice from behind called, "Major Roosevelt. Yoh, Jim."

The few hurried steps that brought Steve Early, FDR's press secretary, alongside James also caused the older man to puff and wheeze. "Heard you were back," he said with the charming Virginia drawl that worked on some of the White House reporters some of the time. While shaking James's hand, he added, "The boys in the pressroom who are in the know tell some pretty hairy stories about you out in the Pacific, young man."

"Don't believe everything you read in the papers, Steve. Pure exaggeration by some very unstable elements, I can assure you."

"Well, I think we might want to let some of it get to the public now, exaggeration or not. Might have to in light of what Hearst's starting to pull."

James's lips rounded the name: "Hearst?"

"Your daddy's mad as hell about it, let me tell you. C'mon, I've got it downstairs, my office. You'd better see for yourself. We'll have to decide what we want to do about it pretty quick." Early's normally rosy face had turned purple. "This way; the steps are faster."

As they descended and walked through the maze of broken hallways in the East Wing, Early spoke continuously about how busy he'd been and how he didn't need this new problem. His increased puffing and wheezing as he bobbed alongside James seemed to be offered up as proof of his professional exertions. James's thoughts were only on what he was walking into.

"Hey," Steve Early said, stopping at the north foyer entrance, "just had a brainstorm. We don't have any recent photos of you. How'd you like to sit for a couple today. You've got a great tan, and the uniform could really look snazzy. Yep, it's just the sort of thing to send out to the Sunday rotogravures. Take Hearst on where it matters." Steve Early was almost plum-colored with excitement.

"Let's see what it is you want to show me, Steve. Then we'll decide what we want to do about it." Major Roosevelt admired his own control. He discovered that he was grateful to be out of his mother's office; apparently he could handle just about anything that wasn't "family."

Early led the way through the pressroom, where a few reporters sprawled lazily and the Teletype machines clattered. None of the people in the room recognized FDR's son, even though they looked at him as he entered. They saw just another military big shot on a guided tour of the White House.

Inside his private office, Steve Early took a tabloid from his desk and offered it to James. He withdrew it suddenly. "Remember, son, don't hold the messenger responsible for the message." Then he handed it over. "Last night's New York *Daily Mirror*. The editorial's the thing. Same in every single one of his papers today from coast to coast. His radio stations, too, most likely."

James had opened the paper on Early's desk and, resting his weight on the heels of his hands, leaned over and began reading the two-column editorial.

This newspaper has and will continually speak out against injustice. Never louder and clearer than when the rich and the powerful take advantage of their positions and refuse to pull their fair share of this great country's load. In typical, and perhaps a bit naive, Yankee fashion, we have always associated privilege with the decadent, class-conscious societies of Europe, not the 'one-man-is-as-good-as-anybody' ideal we are fighting and dying for today.

Whenever we see an abuse of privilege, we will speak out. Whenever preferential treatment is obtained for the very people who give loudest lip service to American ideals, we become disgusted with their transparent hypocrisy. Whenever, because of this blatant double standard, some men will be killed in battle while others live safe and comfortable in the lap of luxury, we believe every American ought to know it and give proper vent to his anger.

We are talking not about something abstract here. No indeed. We are talking about that great equalitarian American family, recently memorable for their reluctance in having their sons carry out the policies of the father, in having them all but pressed kicking and screaming into military service. (We won't even mention their bad taste in having house pets transferred on military aircraft during wartime at taxpayers' expense.)

Yes indeed, ladies and gentlemen, the democratic Roosevelts are at it again.

The President's eldest son, Marine Corps Major James Roosevelt—a man whose rank certainly appears to outstrip his military accomplishments by a far piece—has been swiftly and silently recalled to Washington. The transfer was for him alone and comes just before his outfit was slated to engage the enemy.

Now we don't know what fumbling explanations, if any, will be given from on high in those dulcet tones, but this sure sounds like a simple case of privilege to us!

What's the matter, Mr. President, were things getting a little too hot for sonny out in the Pacific? Or do you plan to rotate all of our sons in this manner eventually? Perhaps it was just sheer chance your own son's name happened to be drawn first!

The words were like a slap in the face to a sleepwalker. But with the slap something combative had been activated, and with it came a rush of anger that carried energy and direction.

Major Roosevelt reread the editorial, unaware that Steve Early was observing him carefully. Certain distinct Hearst touches leapt out on second reading. The innocence of "typical . . . Yankee fashion," the downright meanness of "we won't even mention" followed by the specific mention, and the taunt in "What's the matter, Mr. President . . . ?" James knew that they would all find their mark in his father's feelings.

It was Hearst at work himself, not an editorial man—that much was certain. The attack was too personal, too vicious in a very distinctive way. The tone might be slightly elevated in spots, but this was the same pen that had referred to FDR as "Stalin Delano Roosevelt." Yes indeed, this was certain to find its true target by getting to the father through the son.

"Well," Steve Early said anxiously, "can I arrange for that photo of the hero home from the wars now?"

"I think not, Steve. Sorry. We've got other fish to fry right now." He picked up the telephone. "How do I get my father's office?"

"9-9."

James dialed and waited. The telephone voice was Louise Hackmeister's, the main switchboard operator. "Hello, Hacky, this is Major Roosevelt. I'm calling from Steve Early's office downstairs. Can you put me through to the President, please?"

"He's in a cabinet meeting now, Major. Left explicit instructions not to be disturbed. Grace is taking all his calls today. Shall I put you through to her?"

James had forgotten how rarely things in the White House ran on an express routing. In this respect, at least, it was like the Corps. "Please," he said.

Two clicks and buzzes. "Miss Tully."

"Hello, Grace. This is Major Roosevelt. When will I be able to get through to the President on an important matter?"

"Well, they've just ordered hot trays to be sent in. That usually means an all-day session. If you'd like to have a note sent in on his tray . . . ?"

"No, no, I think not."

"Well, if you could call back at, say, three o'clock, I may have some information for you then."

"I'll call back then. And thank you, Grace."

"You're welcome and . . ."

"Yes."

"Welcome home, Jimmy."

Something in her voice communicated a sense of certainty, of finality. He extracted from it the understanding that there was nothing temporary in his reassignment. He pursed his lips before placing the receiver on the cradle.

Steve Early reached up, clapped the tall Marine across the shoulders, and said, "C'mon. I'm springing for lunch. National Press Club. We might as well get right out front and show 'em what the Roosevelts are made of."

"Might as well," James said dreamily.

By the time the two men had walked to the East Wing entrance, where the Major would reclaim his coat and once again see the young woman whose face had begun to be a part of his memory, Steve Early had almost recovered his innocent pink complexion. At the desk, James bent over to countersign the register, but the face that looked up into his was broader than it was long, the skin was a brown berry color, and the eyes were almond-shaped. She wasn't there. James's sense of loss was greater than he would have expected.

Chapter

6

THE DULL pain was not restricted to his temple, so it could not technically be considered a headache. The ache permeated the entire left side of his face—ear, cheek, upper jaw. "Neuralgia," he had told Dr. McIntire authoritatively during his pre-Teheran physical examination in November. "Runs in my mother's side of the family, brought on by dry heat indoors. Really only is a problem in the winter. It's only bothered me then. Always has."

The tingling numbness on the side of his face now made him feel that his smile was frozen on slightly lopsided, but none of the people in the room appeared to take notice. What bothered him more than the physical discomfort, as he sat behind his desk in the oval study, was that he was required to become again master of ceremonies of a ritual event he had allowed to become much too infrequent these days—Friday evening "happy hour" at the White House.

Would a Presidential historian, he wondered, ever be clever enough to trace the course of his Presidency in terms of his changing martinis. Back in thirty-three he mixed them just about half and half; the second-term ratio slid from about three to five parts gin to every one of vermouth. The drinks he mixed before December 7, 1941, before his "date that will live in infamy," was 8 to 1 or slightly higher. Now there was some question if any vermouth at all ever found its way into his glass, but he still called them martinis.

Fala was being buffeted on FDR's lap as the President circled the chilled cocktail shaker in the air like a magician making a pass. "Please note, ladies and gentlemen," he announced to the collected cabinet members, aides and staff, "the accepted technique for approaching the proper temperature and aerating your basic clear liquid. And now, Arthur, the vermouth, please." Said to Arthur Prettyman like a prestidigitator to his assistant.

The valet was up to the performance expected of him. He lifted the sleeve of his white jacket and plucked the small bottle from among the dozen or so on the bar cart with the style of an accomplished second banana.

The President said, "The cap, please." And the valet spun the top so strongly that it appeared to leap into the air before he caught it. Then FDR put out a finger dramatically; Arthur placed the green vermouth bottle beneath and elevated it until the Presidential fingertip was moistened. The magician nodded, and the bottle was lowered and removed. A single drop of vermouth glistened and was then flicked into the mixer. "The perfect balance, a secret discovered only after many years of difficult experimentation," FDR said as he whirled the liquid with a cocktail spoon. Everyone was smiling. He poured the elixir into a glass that held two olives, raised it to his eyes and nose and lips and announced, "The acid test, ladies and gentlemen."

"Literally or figuratively speaking, Mr. President?" quipped Henry Morgenthau, secretary of the Treasury.

FDR pretended he did not hear the comment. He sipped. Then, pursing his lips for some dramatic seconds, he said,

"It'll do, Henry. It'll do. But you were a trifle too strong with the vermouth, Arthur."

The valet managed to look properly forlorn.

"In case there are those of you a bit fearful of a Roosevelt martini, Arthur here can produce just about any other poison you'd like to inflict upon yourselves." Then there was some milling about and quiet conversation in the room, a general release of tensions, and the beginning of a slight winding down before things would begin to be rewound for the following week.

Bernie Baruch was pointing toward the still fogbound Potomac and telling Judge Sam Rosenman and Bill Hassett in which direction he believed South Carolina to be. Grace Tully and Missy LeHand sat across from each other at a small table trying to decide how they would handle Senator George when he came storming in on Monday morning, annoyed by the President's arm-twisting of members of his Foreign Relations Committee.

Secretary of War Stimson; Jesse Jones, the commerce secretary; and Frank Knox, the secretary of the Navy, were clustered in a corner, having stayed on after the cabinet meeting to hack out a revised, and supposedly more efficient, Lend-Lease policy. They had looked on politely as the President performed the martini ritual. Now the room began to throb and buzz with conversation; there was muffled laughter and the soft clink of ice cubes in glasses.

FDR sipped his second martini and surveyed the room. He liked what he saw. An ember popped and leapt against the screen of the fireplace. It caught his eye. The original of Dorothy McKay's already famous *Esquire* cartoon had recently been hung over the mantle. FDR looked at it once again: the kid brother had written "ROOSEVELT" in chalk on the pavement, and the caption below, attributed to an apoplectic older sister, read: "Wilfred wrote a bad word." Franklin Roosevelt chuckled, utterly content with the sentiment.

Then he felt obliged, as benevolent lord and patriarch, to offer some more entertainment. He selected Archibald Mac-Leish, resident poet and Librarian of Congress, as his friendly foil. "Were you all aware," he announced, and the buzzing stopped. "Were you all aware that Archie here has asked to be turned loose from his books and manuscripts? Says he wants to participate more actively in the war effort. So"—here the pause for timing he had long since perfected. —"we've struck this little bargain. He's going to become the President for a while and I, I am going over and straighten out his card catalog." MacLeish turned crimson amid the laughter.

At that moment Fala yelped and jumped off the President's lap. He ran to the half-opened door of Hassett's office, where James, backed by Steve Early, had just entered. Fala rested his front paws on James's knees, arched his back and wagged his tail vigorously. While the son scratched the scottie under the chin, his father boomed, "Behold, the sailor, home from the seas, the hero home from the wars."

James could not hide his astonishment when the people in the room rose and softly began to applaud. James let his chin rest on his chest. His father said, "And a reluctant hero at that. How do you like your martinis, Jimmy? A bit on the dry side, I hope."

Then, drink in hand, there was time for James to circulate, to kiss cheeks and shake hands, to renew Washington acquaintances. He was conscious of being severely displaced: half a world away Carlson and the Raiders had begun preparing for another assault.

The end of the slightly abbreviated "happy hour" came when FDR announced, "There's probably no way to keep this from Hearst, folks, but the real reason Jimmy's back is that he captured some Jap letters and noticed that I didn't have the stamps in my collection. We couldn't trust anyone for the transfer." He cocked his head slightly, and looked deeply into his son's eyes. The words and that gesture were sufficient to convey the idea: in a matter of minutes the room had begun to empty.

As the door to the main hallway closed softly, the President said to Steve Early, who had been asked to remain for a minute, "Well, how are we going to handle this Hearst thing?"

"I'd say, Mr. President, that we blitz him. We've pussy-footed long enough, but now we've got some room to maneuver. My God, he's made an attack on the Office of the President in wartime. Attacked the Commander in Chief. We could go after him for treason. And we really should also play up Jimmy's—I mean the Major's—true war record."

James said flatly, "You realize, of course, that there's another alternative. I could just be quietly transferred back to the Raiders. Then he'd have no basis even for rumor, would he?"

The President appeared not to have heard what his son had just said. He looked at the ceiling and wondered aloud, "You know, Hearst was expelled from Harvard for something especially rotten. I'd heard a number of versions, the mildest of which was cheating at cards. I always thought it might have been important to find out the truth, but I never did take the time. I wish I had, though; maybe then I'd understand the malignancy better. The man amazes me; has he absolutely no sense of . . . ?" FDR had taken off his spectacles and begun to rub his eyes. If he actually finished his sentence, neither of them heard it.

"There is a time factor here, Mr. President," Early explained. "You've got a press conference scheduled for Monday morning, and they're going to jump all over you on this thing. Expecting you to fight back. At the very least, sir, we'll need a statement of some sort by then."

"Jimmy and I will hack something out right now, Steve. Stand by downstairs and you'll have your statement for release tonight."

James felt like the defendant in a rigged trial. He knew

that his father had orchestrated something, so he remained silent after Steve Early left.

FDR indicated that he wanted some assistance in transferring himself back into the wheelchair. James leaned down and lifted the torso under the arms and was struck by the dead weight of the lower body. FDR rolled himself slowly toward the window and looked out over the darkened mall. His voice became thinner, yet a bit more his own: "Do you know what they really think of me, Jimmy? No, not the haters. Not the Hearsts, the McCormicks, the Pattersons; they don't matter, not really. They're just a political annoyance and can even be useful if you know how to manipulate their more rabid impulses. The other ones concern me, Jimmy. The respectable ones: the historians, the Presidential scholars, the ones who judge and make reputations. Perhaps they shouldn't matter, and I'd never admit this to anyone else, but they do. D'you know what they think?"

The question was obviously rhetorical; still, FDR paused. His son looked over his shoulder into the darkness.

"They'll have to grant me certain things. Cleverness. Intelligence. Fairly effective as a leader in wartime. Occasional moments of inspiration, maybe even of brilliance. Ambitious —but that cuts both ways, especially if I attempt to become a four-term President."

"Doesn't sound so bad to me, Pa. On balance."

"Trouble is, that except for some specifics, it's pretty much the appraisal they make of Woodrow Wilson. I'd like them to know about the daring, of the will to leave something positive after all this rubble's been cleared away." Then there was a transition—or lack of transition—that confused James. FDR said, "Have you come up with that code word yet?" His son looked puzzled; the father disappointed. "The Tartar, Jimmy. What we spoke about last time."

"No, not really, Pa. Too much has been going on in my mind and around here to get a handle on something like that."

"Well, I have. Let's call it "FAMILY MATTER." That's what it is, after all, and that's what I want it to stay between us." After another long pause, the explanation began to come. "You know this Hearst thing is good luck in a way, don't you think? We're in a perfect position now, Jimmy. He's made you seem absolutely insignificant around here." FDR glanced back and upward; his son was looking straight ahead.

Intuitively, James knew; there was that purr in the voice. "It was you, wasn't it, Pa? You who let the word slip out to Hearst that I was coming back." Now the son looked down and made eye contact. A smile played around the old man's darkened eyes.

James's stomach churned, a mixture of anger and hurt pride. "Why'd you do it, Pa?"

"Because it was absolutely necessary, Jimmy, that's why." The President's body quivered. His voice became slightly nasal with anger. "You think I would have put you through this? Fed you up on a platter to Hearst? Allowed your reputation to be besmirched? All that just to . . ." His rush of emotion cut off his words.

"You mean you knew Hearst would go after me like that?"

"Not quite so vehemently, but it was part of the plan, Jimmy. Unfortunately, a necessary part of the plan. It's the way I'd have handled it with anyone I'd have selected for this A-bomb project. It's what had to be done to protect you—to protect us—for what you're going to have to do on FAMILY MATTER. Pour those last few drops into my glass, will you?"

There was a silence, during which some of the floorboards in the old house groaned as a sudden, stiff wind struck it. James Roosevelt tipped the clear liquid over a wrinkled olive. "Suppose," he said irritably, "you tell me, then; what statement have *we* concocted for the press conference?"

"*We* are not waiting till Monday. Stimson and Baruch will issue a terse joint statement tomorrow saying that because of increased war production and a general military buildup on all fronts, a new office will be set up immediately headed by a military man who will act as a liaison between industry, the government and the military. This person must be someone who knows all three sectors well, who is above influence of any sort, a troubleshooter who could sniff out problems and be tough enough to break logjams. Someone who could cut through red tape and carry the weight of the President at all times. Major James Roosevelt is such a person. He will be our country's new Co-Ordinator of Military Manpower and Materiel. Or some such thing as that."

"Of course. 'Or some such thing,'" James muttered. "Pa, it's so transparent. It's pure nepotism. It makes his first story look even more believable. He'll murder us."

"Precisely, m'boy."

There was that "m'boy" again, James thought.

"It's better for our purposes if Hearst stays on your back for a while. Better if he really gets people thinking I've pulled you back and invented this post in order to save your skin. That's precisely the idea that will give you the mobility we'll need for FAMILY MATTER. You'll have to live with the humiliation, I'm afraid. But all the while you're being 'protected' by your old man, you'll also be able to move around our MANHATTAN PROJECT without being taken very seriously. And that's the whole point." He actually expected his son to brighten suddenly and begin enjoying their new adventure. James didn't. FDR sipped his cocktail glass empty and said, "Oh, buck up, Jimmy. What's a bruised reputation or two among the world's saviors? When this whole thing is over, we can write a book about it and set the record straight."

"Somehow it's not very funny to me quite yet."

FDR's expression said that he knew the price his son would have to pay was going to be high. Working for a year or two with people who didn't respect you, who thought you were probably a coward, could be a ring of hell. Nevertheless, this was the tactic he had decided on. "Jimmy, this may sound cruel, but self-pity has no place whatsoever in this matter. Nor am I *asking* you to begin immediately in your new position—or should I say, positions—I'm *ordering* you, Major, as your Commander in Chief."

"That, at least, is clear and direct, sir."

The President took his empty glass, held it high before him, and moved it toward James. The action was meant as apology and pledge. The son reached forward with a glass he picked off the desk, but there was no contact; he had to lean down farther to produce a satisfying "clink."

"By the way," FDR said, "I've got an office picked out for you in the East Wing. Small, but it should do. Go about the job of picking a staff immediately. A few people with top clearance who you think you can trust. Set it up quickly, and make it look legitimate. I'm going to want you free to look into the bomb project fairly soon."

The most significant difference between father and son had always been the way they handled their feelings. Father had long ago learned to mask emotion, to diffuse and trans-fer it into humor or to delay its effects. In the son emotion took root and lingered, left a residue even after it was trans-ferred, as it was beginning to be now, into a sense of duty. His stomach still churned; to the original mixture had been added the certain loss of his reconstructed life in the Pacific as well as a vague, and contradictory, sense of anticipation. The confusion of feelings left him slightly numbed, but it revealed itself in a soft, breathless laugh.

FDR raised his eyebrows. James remained silent. "Leave the statement to me," the President said finally. "You'll read it in the newspapers tomorrow. Just make yourself scarce when you aren't in the office, and for heaven's sake, don't grant any interviews. Anything more than 'no comment' will be considered grounds for a court-martial, Major."

James touched his father's shoulder lightly. He said, "Roger."

"As you leave, send Arthur in to me. It's been a hell of a day."

"Sure, Pa. Ought to tell you, though, that there is a solution to the problem you mentioned, about your reputation for posterity."

"Oh, and what's that?"

"Just go out and adopt all those historians; then put them to work for you as your sons. You'll never have to worry about not being considered sufficiently daring or willful."

FDR smiled and nodded. "Perhaps, perhaps."

The Major then moved around his father's wheelchair and fronted the President directly in the gloom. "Pa, you know I'm with you all the way in this. I only ask one thing. Since we are both on the same side, how about no more surprises, okay?"

"No more surprises," the President agreed, looking up into identical blue eyes about half as old as his own.

The next surprise, a pleasant one, was less than an hour in coming. James was unlocking the door of his cubicle in the Officers' Quarters at the Replacement Depot when the intercom at the end of the barracks hallway crackled, "Major Roosevelt, telephone call, please. Holding in orderly room. Major Roosevelt, please."

The voice at the other end did not at first identify itself, so James had to say, "Is that you, Steve?"

"Yes it is. Look, Jim, I just got a copy of that statement the War Department is going to put out with the Production Planning Board tomorrow. Congratulations."

"On what?"

"The appointment, of course. I know you'll do a terrific job."

Of his options, "thanks" was the easiest, so James said it.

"Now listen, Major, if I'm off base on this, stop me immediately. I'll understand. But it seems to me that if you're going to have that office in operation within the week, you're going to have to corral some pretty good people in a hurry." He paused as though testing the waters, and James thought momentarily that Early was applying for a job. "Am I out of line, Major?"

"Go on, Steve."

"Well, there's a gal works in the White House. Captain in the WACs. General Fielding's daughter." James paused in the middle of a breath. "Maybe you've seen her. She's sometimes on East Wing security?"

"Very short, fat, dark-haired?" James volunteered, beaming.

"No, not at all. Above average height and a redhead. Very nice-looking girl. You wouldn't forget her, Jim. Anyway, she's terrifically bright, very efficient, discreet—"

"Discreet?"

"Sure. That'll be a sensitive office, Major, and Captain Fielding has top clearance and some OSS training."

"But what's your interest in this, Steve?"

"Friend of the family. Want to see you get top people, nothing more."

James found himself confused by his unexpected elation: the situation didn't quite seem to warrant it. He said, "Sounds awfully good to me, Steve. Why don't you have the War Department set up an immediate transfer."

Roosevelt had become agreeable so abruptly that Early became suddenly defensive. "Listen," he said, "maybe you ought to interview her or screen a few other candidates—"

"Why? She sounds perfect. Go ahead with the transfer."

Steve Early sounded confused when he said, "Sure. Will do. Good night, Major."

James allowed himself the first smile of satisfaction of a long and eventful day. The orderly, an apple-cheeked, crew-cut kid, smiled at the smile he saw and said, "Good news, Major?"

"Let's hope so, Corporal, let's hope so."

Chapter
7

THE BOGUS Office of Military Manpower and Materiel was, in fact, a former custodial supply room on the second floor of the East Wing about twelve feet square now divided into two tiny cubicles by a frosted-glass partition. The inner office of the Co-Ordinator had a large window with a view of the south lawn; the outer office had three desks and four empty filing cabinets where two of each would have fit snugly. The inner office was overheated by a rattling radiator; the outer had no heat at all.

A sign painter had just put the final golden strokes on the glass panel of the door when James arrived, wearing an open raincoat over dress blues. The artist stepped back to admire his work; so satisfied was he that James didn't then have the heart to correct the "a" he had substituted for the final "e" in "Materiel."

"It ain't much in the war effort," the old man explained, "but at least it's done good."

"That's the important thing," mumbled James, more pleased than ever with his self-control. It would make a good story, but he realized he didn't have anyone to tell it to.

The pecking typewriter within reminded him that May Fielding, perhaps the sole consolation of his return to Washington, was as permanent as anything else in his new life. He smiled at the thought of her. And his smile broadened when he saw her, typing rhythmically, head tilted slightly, a wisp of hair falling over her forehead. Her khaki jacket was draped over the back of her chair, and her cuffs were neatly folded back twice. James watched unseen for a moment and observed the bright, open face that pleased him so much. She apparently arrived at an illegible passage in her notebook because she slowed down perceptibly and her tongue pushed out her cheek. When she struck a wrong key, she huffed and said, "Damn."

"Morning, Captain."

"Oh. Major Roosevelt. I didn't see you there. Good morning." She attempted to blow the hair out of her eyes. "There have been some calls. The messages are on your desk. And, oh yes," she added, "Personnel is sending up some people. When would you like to interview them, sir?"

Her smile, broad and straightforward, he imagined now as ironic and enigmatic. "I'm going to leave that to you, Captain. After all, you'll be in charge of running the office, so you might as well satisfy yourself." James flipped his hat on the bentwood rack behind the door. These last moments had driven home for him the difference between the theory and the practice of being a fake; well bred and connected, highly placed and protected—but a fake nonetheless. He didn't like the role.

James sensed that May Fielding was watching him as he sidestepped the blockade of desks and chairs in the cubicle. The messages included calls from Henderson at OPA, Frances Perkins at the Labor Department, and Steve Early. Each military, production and support agency was now required to send a duplicate of every letter, order and memo to James's new office. There would be endless filing and requests for clarifications of previous memos, nothing more than the shuffling of papers, busy work. A blizzard of paper, in the form of copies of files from all over official Washington, would begin to arrive any day now. James wondered how long May Fielding, sharp as she was, could be fooled by its irrelevance.

For his part, Major Roosevelt was to read all Top Secret material before it was filed in a special cabinet; sometimes he'd have to respond. He would compose a letter or two each morning to the head of some governmental bureau or other and to corporation presidents and chairmen. In this correspondence he'd make some laudatory statements thanking so-and-so for efforts promised or already made, raise some questions about the future that required a response, and urge them all on to even greater efforts in the future.

He realized he had been drawing a string of stars across the top of a legal pad. He threw down his pencil and buzzed the outer office.

"Yes, Major."

"Captain Fielding, keep your lunch hour open. We're going to have our first staff meeting. Reserve an inconspicuous table at the Statler."

"I'm not sure there is such a thing these days, Major. Haven't you heard there's a war on?"

"In that case, Captain Fielding, consider it an assault on the Statler."

Captain and Major were merely two officers at a corner table among dozens of others accepting the privileges a grateful nation at war offered them. The room was filled with Washington types, and the combined hushed conversations produced a dull roar only slightly distinguishable from that of a war plant cafeteria.

"I hope you don't mind being seen in public with someone who happens to be married," James said to break the ice. The artificiality of the situation pressed on him suddenly. The weight of beginning a friendship seemed enormous.

Her blue eyes narrowed. "Precisely how does someone *happen* to be married? And by the same token, how do you feel having a married woman running your office for you, Major?" As his face registered first amusement and then puzzlement, May Fielding laughed and finally explained: "Couldn't resist, Major. Actually, I'm not very married."

"Divorced? I've been down that road myself."

"Nooo, not exactly. I've been annulled. Canceled. Voided. And invalidated. You pick it. My father's adjutant. It looked awfully good on paper, but we all know now that life isn't lived on paper."

"How's your father taking it?"

"How's yours?"

"Touché." And James raised a dry martini in her honor. She acknowledged the gesture by tipping her water tumbler. The ease of being with this woman surprised him, made him, in fact, a bit suspicious. Her openness was not easy for him to get used to. She admitted, for example, that her father, General Fielding, had become a vigorous FDR opponent over the issue of a third term but that he also felt Hearst's attacks on Jimmy to be totally unfair. "My father knew, you see, the truth about your service in the Pacific. I love and respect him a lot, Major. It's just that his politics are his and mine are mine." She traced a fold in the tablecloth with a trimmed fingernail as she spoke softly but with confidence.

Most of all, James was happy to hear that she knew he wasn't a coward. He felt the remaining tightness in his chest leave. "Was it he who gave you all those great freckles? Because if it was, I'd be more than willing to overlook his political ignorance."

She laughed. "No, that's my mom. And she didn't even want your father for a first term."

"Well, I'm so hungry that, 'Meatless Tuesday' or not, I'm going to order a steak."

"Now, now, don't get reckless, Major. You wouldn't want Mr. Hearst getting hold of that information, especially when even the walls have ears." She had whispered, and her eyes led his attention to a poster above them that showed a drunken American sailor babbling at a bar. Below, the words: "THE SLIP OF A LIP CAN SINK A SHIP!" Jimmy Roosevelt and May Fielding laughed together, her laugh deeper and warmer than his.

Then they began recounting random incidents of their lives. Most of the stories were humorous: failed exams, missed appointments, embarrassing blind dates, social disasters—the sand and stones and mortar of which the foundation of a friendship can be built. It was uncomplicated, it was pleasant.

They laughed about Steve Early's phone call on her behalf. How James had teased Early with "short" and "fat" and "dark-haired" when he really knew better. And how Early almost fell over himself when James accepted her without a single question or stipulation. They were each smiling and forking a salad when Captain Fielding, again with her expressive eyes, caught his attention and directed it to the maître d', who stood elegantly at James's elbow. "Excuse me please. Major Roosevelt?"

James nodded.

"There is a telephone call for you. You may take it at the front desk, sir."

James folded his napkin and threw it down on the table.

May said quietly, "It is Washington, D.C., Major. And the year is 1944."

"And there's a war on," he muttered. "I'll be right back."

As he walked toward the main desk and the telephone, James recognized a phenomenon almost as old as he was: the curiosity evoked by the Roosevelt name. People had already taken positions from which to steal glances at this particular Roosevelt. Which one was it? They couldn't be sure, but they had heard it was a genuine Roosevelt. He had almost forgotten their looks of expectancy, then the mild disappointment and the search of the face for resemblances. The desk clerk was all smiles and smooth gestures as he turned the phone over to the Major. It was Louise Hackmeister: "You are not an easy man to track down, Major."

"That's purely a matter of point of view, Hacky. What's up?" As he spoke, he looked in the eyes of a gaper or two. That was usually sufficient in getting them to look away.

"Bill Hassett wants to speak to you. Hold on."

After some moments, during which James believed the line had gone dead, the President's secretary came on. His manner was typically precise, his information spare. "The President has returned within the hour. Wants you in his office pronto, Jimmy. Alone. I could send a car out for you if you need one."

"No. Thanks, Bill, a cab'll probably be faster."

James felt the eyes on his back as he returned to the table. He bent over May Fielding and said, "Something's come up. I have to leave. Don't leave the office today until you hear from me."

She blinked once and said, "This isn't your way of sticking me with the check, is it?"

He smiled and began reaching for his wallet. It was the first meal he had paid for in more than nine months.

As James stepped into the President's oval study precisely at 2:07 P.M., he discovered a man transformed waiting for him. The chalky grayness that had been FDR's post-Teheran complexion was gone, replaced by a soft glow of health. The dark arcs under his eyes were now merely accidents of age. Energy and strength were in the voice naturally, in the smile and gestures; they came now as a matter of course, not as an aging man's act of will. The President had become the antithesis of Washington's depressing wartime mood and lousy weather. He wore his old personality easily now and an old maroon button-down sweater of Jimmy's that had been passed on almost ten years earlier. It bulged here and there, but not too much.

The father quickly read the son's surprise and pleasure and said, touching the point of his chin with a middle finger as though his head were a work of art being shown to a prospective buyer, "Three days in Warm Springs will do it every time."

"But I didn't even know you'd been out of town, Pa."

"You weren't supposed to, Jimmy. That's how that damned Secret Service earns its money. How's your office shaping up?"

"Fine. We're just waiting for the correspondence to come rolling in like the tide." James sat down on the sofa. The prow of the *Half Moon* pointed so directly and close to his temple that he swung it back toward the fireplace.

FDR rolled himself in front of his son. "But it wasn't only Warm Springs. No, important things have been happening since we last spoke. The next two years, I believe, will be absolutely crucial to the fifty that follow. Fifty years! And we've got to be up to the challenge." He spoke confidently, as though he were an athlete who had found a second wind. Not merely breath, but second strength and second sight as well.

"I could kick myself, Jimmy. I should have started moving on this thing at least a year ago, if not sooner. Never should have let you go off in the first place. I needed you here. My God, it's so clear to me now . . ."

James wanted to reach out and rest a hand on his father's shoulder, a gesture, nothing more. *I'm really with you, Pa*, it said.

". . . seriously underestimated postwar problems. I was thinking in terms of petty differences, philosophical, territorial. And for that sort of thing, some judicial body—a League of Nations with some real oomph—probably would be enough. But that's not what's shaping up, Jimmy. I swear, if it weren't so deadly serious, it'd be a grand, celestial comedy. It seems to have a life, a momentum of its own. Right now everyone—and I mean *everyone*—is jockeying for position, to be in the right place with the right forces when the final bell rings. Getting ready to gobble up everything that isn't nailed down. And believe me, when I say *everyone*, I am talking about factions within fragments within splinter groups within . . ." FDR pulled at a piece of wool that had unraveled at his cuff. "I had a dream about it in Warm Springs. You play Joseph to my Pharaoh."

James smiled and nodded.

"I saw a gazelle brought down by a lion. There was the ripping of flesh and then the lining up of all the waiting scavengers. Hyenas, vultures, rats and ants; one by one they edged forward to get what they believed was theirs. And it seemed there was always something to be found somewhere and contended over. Until at long last there were only bones blanching on the plains. Well, Joseph, what do you make of the dream?"

"It's easy, Pa. It means you're working on a plan to turn the whole bunch into vegetarians."

The release in FDR took the form of a rich and sustained belly-laugh. Twice he tried to pick up the dropped thread of his briefing and twice dissolved into milder versions of that same laughter.

"Heck of a good way to begin a session, Jimmy, heck of a good way." And again he chuckled and wiped at a tear that wasn't there. "Still, my dream is nothing compared with the appetites of our friends. They're getting ready to devour one another, and will if they think they can get away with it. If we give 'em their heads, Churchill and Stalin would go at it before the last shot is fired. And not just them. It's everywhere. In Greece and Yugoslavia, you've got partisans killing partisans. There's still the struggle over Poland—Churchill hasn't given up on that one. De Gaulle and Giraud. Not to mention what is coming with Chiang in China. And India is—well, India." FDR's cuff was unraveling faster; he bit off the thread and picked up a folded paper from his desk. "And now there's this. It was here when I arrived." He handed his son a decoded communiqué and indicated the lines he had underscored in red.

. . . EARLIER SUSPICIONS. THERE HAS APPEARED IN THE AREAS OF VITEBSK, SMOLENSK, MOGILEV STRONG ELEMENTS OF NEW GERMAN DIVISIONS. ALREADY THEY HAVE BEEN PRESSED INTO COMBAT AND ARE FIGHTING STRONGLY ALTHOUGH THEY TOO WILL BE OVERCOME BY THE RESOLVE AND SKILL OF THE RUSSIAN PEOPLE. THESE DIVISIONS ARE THE FIFTH AND SEVENTH OF KESSELRING'S FOURTH AND VIETINGHOFF'S TENTH. AS RECENTLY AS NOVEMBER LAST THEY WERE KEPT OCCUPIED ON THE "WINTERSTELLUNG" IN ITALY. HOW AND WHY HAVE THEY BEEN RELEASED TO FIGHT AGAINST OUR FORCES? WHY IS YOUR PRESSURE AGAINST THE ENEMY SUCH THAT THESE FORCES MAY BE EASILY WITHDRAWN AND TRANSFERRED TO FIGHT RUSSIANS? THERE IS A STRONG SUSPICION NOT EASILY OVERCOME ANY LONGER BY GOOD INTENTIONS AND ELABORATE EXPLANATIONS.

V. MOLOTOV

"The tone, that's what's important here, Jimmy. It's Stalin talking; don't let Molotov's name fool you. In every pouch that comes in now, the suspicion and hostility rise just a little closer to the surface. Last week he accused the British of failing to support Tito's people; three hundred of them were captured and executed by the Germans. This note is the worst so far. I think it's fair to say that a peace based on mutual trust and admiration is not a very strong bet at this point."

"Soooo, to make a long, unhappy story short, we are going to move a little on FAMILY MATTER." James uttered the statement more as a hope than as a firm conclusion.

"Well, let's just say that we have to have our weapon

ready as soon as possible. The timing will be crucial; if we don't have a bomb that works, we'll have very few political options. But by the same token, we can't wait until we have an operational weapon to get things moving on the political front. I've been getting my information from Marshall and Stimson and Dr. Bush over at National Defense Research. There are reasons to believe problems are developing on the project, just a strong intuition at this point. I want you to check things out. I want a complete update, and whatever else you can dig up. You'll use your new position to cover yourself."

"What sorts of problems, Pa?"

"Talk to General Groves, he's directly responsible for the bomb project. Talk to the European scientists working on the project—Enrico Fermi, Leo Szilard, Hans Bethe. You'll learn the names soon enough. Talk to Oppenheimer; he runs the show at Los Alamos. Dr. Bush has put a listing of all Manhattan Project personnel together for me with a general description of duties and responsibilities. Hassett's got it and will give it to you before you leave. Commit it to memory, then destroy it completely before you leave your office. Stimson has had orders cut for you, and Marshall's counter-signed—Top Secret clearance. That phony Co-Ordinator mumbo jumbo and Hearst's attacks will make you appear irrelevant. I want two things, Jimmy." FDR leaned forward slightly and lowered his voice. First, an accurate target date for a practical weapon. Second, the best method of getting any plans, blueprints, designs, things of that nature, into my hands with the least disturbance."

"And the greatest secrecy."

"Precisely."

Then nothing more really had to be said. His father had given the orders; now it was a matter of getting the job done. Finally, something tangible. The directness was certainly encouraging. "When do you want me to get started, Pa?"

"Yesterday. But Hassett's put you on a five P.M. plane

tonight. Murderous trip out to New Mexico. Los Alamos, that's where the final assembly is to take place. I certainly don't envy you that trip. Shame, though."

"Why a shame? I can use the travel time to study some of the background and get a sense of how I want to attack this thing."

"No, no. I meant it's a shame because your mother's expected back later tonight. She'll have hated just missing you."

"Just as well," James said.

"Keep your eyes open. Turning Hearst on is one thing; turning him off is something else again. There's not a doubt in the world he's got someone tracing your every move. I wouldn't want him to get even a sniff of what we're up to with this. He's served his purpose, and that's quite enough."

"I'll be careful, Pa. But something you said the other day troubles me."

FDR's eyebrows went up.

"You said something about letting the Russians steal our secrets. You weren't really serious, were you?"

The President's eyes glinted. "Let me tell you something about our Allies. We all spy on each other all the time, every bit as much as we spy on the Germans and Japs. You see, there has to be some way to corroborate at lower, field levels what the big shots say is really going on. So, for example, if I tell Winston we have such-and-such a production capability at a California war plant, you can bet their intelligence will have someone pay a little visit. Probably one of those English movie stars who is working in California. Same with the Russians. Of course they don't have as many movie stars over here and have to use second-class spies. Now isn't that a convenient state of affairs for transferring information—*if*, of course, we ever had to use it." The President shrugged and touched a desk buzzer. Bill Hassett entered. "Bill, is the material for Jimmy ready yet?"

"Sure is, Mr. President." He left and came right back carrying a leather briefcase and placed it squarely on the small table that separated father and son. "The orders and the list of personnel are inside," Hassett said. Then, instead of leaving, he stepped back and smiled broadly. All eyes were on the briefcase.

Finally, James understood. "Dad. No. Why?"

"Why not, Jimmy? Served me well enough when I needed it. Thirty years at least. No reason why it shouldn't bring you some good luck." It was the briefcase FDR had used as assistant secretary of the Navy back in 1913, originally a gift from Eleanor.

"I know, Pa, but . . ."

FDR pulled the top button of his sweater and released it. "One good turn, son, that's all. Don't make so much of it."

James ran his fingers along the top of the upright case. He remembered first seeing it at eye level when he was six years old, remembered the musky odor of it on a humid day when he was hiding in a closet and discovered it on a shelf. "Thank you, Pa."

"One final thing, Jimmy. Check in regularly. Make sure it's safe. Call Hacky, leave your number and wait there. She'll get back to you with some information."

"If you really think it's necessary, Pa."

"It's necessary, I can assure you of that."

They clasped each other's hand. James looked down and saw his hand wrapped by a more worn version of itself.

Saying good-bye to May Fielding so soon after hello would be a very unpleasant experience in person. James's inclination as he left the oval study was to call her from the barracks or even the airfield with instructions for running the office. As he approached his office door, however, the sign painter was in the process of deleting and correcting his final "a." The old man stepped back to let the Major pass.

May Fielding was on the phone. She covered it with her hand and whispered, "It's Mr. Henderson at OPA. You haven't returned any of his calls, and he's livid."

"Tell Mr. Henderson to go to—Interior. Secretary Ickes will be taking all my calls for the next few days. And if he can't get through there, have him call my mother directly."

May Fielding frowned her face and said into the telephone, "But he has been unavailable, Mr. Henderson. He's been checking all our people in the field. I'm certain he will return your calls when he comes back to the office." When she finally hung up, she said, "Was that mistake on our door in any way your doing, Major?"

"I have made it a policy never to interfere with the work of artisans, Captain." He had a sudden urge to ask her along on his mission, but that was, he also realized, impossible.

"Then it's a good thing I do."

James blurted, "I'm going to really have to be away for a while, Captain. Very hush-hush. I'll be calling in from time to time. Matter of fact, why don't you use my office—it's warmer. Please set things up without me." There was more to say, much more, but James merely indicated what was unsaid with a shrug. He was lousy at good-byes, he knew it, and now May Fielding knew it too.

She jotted some instructions in her notebook, nodded and said, "I'm not at all surprised, Major. It *is* Washington and the year *is* 1944."

"That's not much of an explanation," he said.

"True. But it's all we've got these days, isn't it?" She stood up, folded down her cuffs and said, "I'm sure you'll need a lift somewhere."

He smiled and nodded.

The sign painter still had not quite finished when she closed and locked the door behind them.

Part Two

The World in a Grain of Sand

Chapter

8

Two THINGS had misled James in his choice of attire—the plane's southern routing and his destination, Santa Fe, New Mexico. He wore a lightweight tan civilian suit and had stuffed some changes of socks, underwear and an extra white shirt into his antique briefcase. As the cargo plane tipped a wing in the clear, early morning light, James Roosevelt, hugging that briefcase on his lap, looked out expecting to see desert. The abundant snow on the mountains to the north and west of Santa Fe surprised him.

On the ground it was sunny, dry and in the upper forties; certainly an improvement over the meanness of Washington. The old taxicab drove northwest over rolling arroyos and into higher terrain marked by stark buttes and mesas—the mountains James had seen from the air—and the temperature dropped quickly. "You ain't 'xactly dressed for this country, mister," the cabdriver, a tight-lipped Mescalero, said, his eyes framed in the rearview mirror. James shifted his weight and did not reply.

The briefing notes had told James how this site had been chosen for the bomb lab. It could not have been an East Coast city susceptible to a possible enemy air attack. Certainly the kind of absolute isolation and control that the security people demanded could not be found on even a small western Army base. And after considerable scrutiny a variety of possible Rocky Mountain sites had been eliminated.

It was J. Robert Oppenheimer, the brilliant young physicist who had been named director of the laboratory, who had first suggested Los Alamos as a possibility. Pure chance, really. As a boy he had ranged on horseback through the forbidding canyons and pine-scented woods of the Pajarito plateau. Memories of an isolated boarding school, the Los Alamos Ranch School for Boys, had flashed tentatively through his mind, and he, even more tentatively, for such was his nature, had suggested the site to the project's overseers and his military superior, General Leslie R. Groves. That was back in the fall of 1942. Barely a year and a half later six thousand people were working on or associated with the atom project at Los Alamos, although most of them didn't exactly know what they were all doing.

The driver directed the taxi up the long curved incline that began at the Indian ruins. Then slowly past a sign that read: LOS ALAMOS 5 MI.

The information James carried in his briefcase was not extremely detailed. The biographies were sketches, really, compiled from personnel files and secret progress reports that Hassett had requisitioned through channels, Department of the Army clearance checks, for the most part. There was, however, some important information on Oppenheimer, a copy of a memo from the War Department's Office of Engineers alluding to some vague political activity that should have kept Oppenheimer from receiving the clearance he had needed to organize the laboratory at Los Alamos. And there was also a copy of General Groves's reply. James read it as the taxi bumped forward: ". . . clearance for Julius Robert Oppenheimer irrespective of the information which you have concerning his past associations and activities. Mr. Oppenheimer is *absolutely essential* to the project's ultimate success." With a copy to Groves's immediate superiors, General George C. Marshall and Secretary of War Stimson.

Oppenheimer could not know of the existence of such reports. And similar correspondence existed on Hans Bethe, director of the Theoretical Physics section; Otto Frisch; Edward Teller; and half a dozen other outstanding physicists, all European émigrés who had been recruited by Oppenheimer as soon as he was finally allowed to take charge of the Los Alamos project. James reread Groves's memo and admired its clear, no-nonsense stand.

James had begun to develop a feeling for the texture of professional life at this isolated place. Certainly there was not enough information for him to be sure exactly how to proceed, but the reports began to provide a sense of possible weak spots, of allies and antagonists. Groves, he felt instinctively, even with his support of Oppenheimer, would not be the sort of man with whom he could share any confidences. In a nutshell, Army careerist. From a sketchy, one-page biography James constructed a picture of a taut, energetic, self-important professional Army man whose talent was organizational and who probably lacked very much of an imagination.

"I can see why even the Indians cleared out of this place," he said, peering through the dirty window as the cab drove past a deserted village of asymmetrical clay huts. He immediately regretted the word "even." He had actually wanted to say something about the strange beauty of the place but hadn't.

From the top of the mesa he could see in all directions for many miles. Tumbleweed rolled everywhere if one looked hard enough. The land held such a spare beauty, its colors were so rare to an easterner's eye, that Indian magic was not an impossible quality to attribute to it. The mystery of a bomb that could reproduce the sun's force was as appropriate here as were the holy altars of the Taos Indians. James simply assumed he could share this observation with Oppenheimer when they met. Never with Groves.

The road was full of ruts that trucks had dug up when it had begun to thaw; now it was freezing again. And then suddenly, just ahead, a military roadblock. A striped barrier tipped across the road, large drainage ditches to each side that would have made a detour impossible, and two MPs standing alongside a jeep. James fumbled for his orders.

The driver pursed only a lower lip and said, "Looks like the end of the road, mister."

One MP snapped to attention as the cab approached; the other stepped into the jeep and started up the motor. Even before the driver had the window halfway down, the MP leaned in and said, "Welcome to Los Alamos, Major Roosevelt." There was a leer on his face at the mention of the name. "General Groves has been expecting you. Transfer to the jeep, please." And at precisely that moment the wind howled viciously.

His picture was snapped by a soldier at the gate before the jeep was cleared for entry. Then they proceeded slowly to a small whitewashed building. Awaiting Major Roosevelt on the porch was General Groves himself and a small, expressionless Colonel whom James took to be Groves's adjutant.

In no way did the General's appearance coincide with James's projection. He was a fleshy man tending toward plumpness all over but most noticeably just above his belt buckle. The mustache and the gray-streaked hair were dapper touches Roosevelt would never have imagined.

Groves and the Colonel stepped off the porch as the jeep stopped, and the visitor got out. Even though James was not in uniform, he initiated a crisp salute, and as they were shaking hands, Groves said, "Welcome to Los Alamos, garden spot of the West, Major. Been reading about you quite a bit in the newspapers."

James recognized the not-so-oblique reference to Hearst. He had control of his facial muscles, however, and was looking directly at the General's braided visor as he said evenly, "It's a pleasure to be here, General Groves."

"Might be a pleasure, Major, but you sure didn't dress for the place. Maybe we can do something to rectify the oversight." James decided not to say anything. "This is Colonel Ishmael," Groves went on. "He's, well, he's the house detective." James and the dark, expressionless Colonel shook hands.

They walked into the building and along a narrow hallway toward the General's office, a warm, cheerful oasis decorated with military photographs featuring the General and commemorative plaques that marked successes in his career. "I'll bet," said Groves, "you were a little surprised that I anticipated your arrival, Major." The sentence was uttered very quickly; and it wasn't easy for James to understand.

"Indeed, General."

"Like to know how I do it?"

"Of course I would, but I wouldn't want you to breach your own—"

"—Security system? Ha. That's a good one. I've got such a solid damned system here that I couldn't break it down myself even if I worked at it twenty-four hours a day, seven days a week, fifty-two weeks a year until the day of my retirement from this man's army, Major. You get my drift? Actually, it's nothing too tricky. That's the secret right there. Nothing tricky. Just your basic diligence and precision and hard work. We run checks on all arrivals, *all* arrivals; no one takes us by surprise, especially folks on military flights like yourself. Keep track of everything on the road for damn near a hundred fifty miles. Actually, I can't take all the credit. Part of it is Colonel Ishmael. He keeps his ear to the ground, nose to the grindstone, and his eyes everywhere else." Only then did James realize that the mysterious Colonel had disappeared. But at least Groves's staccato rhythm was becoming easier for him to follow.

"Quite impressive, General. Really." Roosevelt reached into his briefcase, brought out a copy of his orders, and handed them over the desk to Groves. As the General read through them slowly, the jaw muscles just below his ears started pulsing. "You realize"—he was speaking more slowly as his eyes traversed—"that it's unprecedented, a junior officer from the 'wrong' branch, heh heh, being authorized to—"

"I hope Secretary Stimson's endorsement gives you the authorization you need to allow me to carry out my mission, General." Said without emotion and with the barest hints of ingenuousness and threat.

General Groves's jaw pulsed a little more. He read in silence. Then he folded the orders neatly back in thirds and pushed them across his desk toward the President's son. "Well, Major, what can we do for you?"

"Nothing earth-shaking, General Groves, I can assure you. Just making an update report on the state of the project." He pulled a lined notebook from his briefcase. "Trying to get the big picture on this thing for the President. Determining how close to target. Just in case some senators or a congressional committee or two start giving him a hard time about next year's budget. We've heard so many different estimates over the years, and still there's . . ."

But Groves was not to be put off by Roosevelt's matter-of-factness *or* by the implied dissatisfaction *or* by the Hearst cover. He was a career soldier, and an administrator at that; the final rule was, Always protect yourself at all times. Anyone coming in from the outside asking questions was considered a snooper and a potential troublemaker. The higher he was connected, the greater the potential trouble. Groves had many protective colorations; he opted now for his "straight-from-the-shoulder-look-around-we've-got-nothing-to-hide-from-you" approach.

"By the way, General, what are we talking about now for a possible target date for the weapon? A functional weapon."

"Well, I could tell you a year, Major, that's our standard answer, but if I did that, I'd be telling you exactly what—I won't mention names here—what was told to me back in March forty-three, almost a year ago. Matter of fact, I've spent too long listening to what some of these crackpot scientists have told me, Major." Groves shaped his face into that of an innocent victim. "Just goes to show you what can happen if you get away from what you know, get too far away from trusting your own judgments. All my life I've had the ability to get things done. No matter what. You see, I'm a projects man. You need a project done, see Leslie Groves, he's your man. I'm the guy who got the Pentagon complex built for the War Department even when I didn't know the first damned thing about construction." James nodded even though the information was news of a sort. "I'll tell you something strange, though. Every day I see the tide turning for us in the war, I have really mixed feelings. Not that I don't want those bastards defeated, not that at all. It's just that I worry the war will be finished before our bomb is ready."

"And you believe that's a possibility?" asked James.

"Not if I have my way, Major. But I can't build the freaking thing myself. Wish I could; it'd be done by now. They tell me there's still some important theory work to be done. And we're in a bit of a 'doubting time' around here. I've seen it on just about every project. You just hit a time when people sort of tighten up, hit a flat spot. Here, we've got the situation where too many important people are beginning to doubt it can even be made. None of my project directors, though."

"Professor Oppenheimer?"

"Right. Not him. He's driving himself like mad. Some of

the others. Don't mind telling you we'd be much better off if we used only Americans on this thing. There's absolutely no way to get into the heads of some of these . . . I'll give you an example. Other day I'm sitting in a session with some of our theory people. Okay, you say I'm in over my head with them, but I think it's important to keep a high profile. So I'm just sitting there watching, being visible, scratching some things in my notebook. Teller is at a blackboard doing some calculations, and I see he multiplies 8 by 7 and comes up with 58. Now, these are supposed to be the best brains in the world, right? They win Nobel Prizes? So stand up and say, 'That's a mistake up there, Professor. Eight times 7 is 56, not 58.' And he looks quick and shrugs and says, 'It's not important.' And the others all laugh, not at him but at me. And there's never an 'I'm sorry' or a 'thank you.' So I stand up again and tell them that this is a billion-dollar project we're involved with and, more than that, we're trying to save the goddamned world and *every freaking thing is important*. 'My God,' I say, 'you guys can't even multiply 8 times 7, how the hell are we ever going to make the bomb?' And they all laugh again, even harder. Real crackpots. But as to a target date, I'm afraid I can't say until the theory stuff is done. After that, I can really swing into action."

"What I'd like to do here, General Groves, is just look around a bit, as inconspicuously as possible, talk to a few people, and be off. Just a couple of days, nothing very extensive."

"Glad to put you up in my quarters, Major, if you'd—"

"Actually, General, I'd prefer something near where the scientists are housed. Something informal. I don't want to call any undue attention to myself. That's why I'm wearing civilian clothes."

"I'm pretty sure something can be arranged, Major. How about if I take you on an official tour of the place first? Tomorrow you can be on your own. How's that strike you?"

"Fine. There is one thing, though. But you've been so direct, so straightforward with me that I feel I can confide in you. You see, General, I really don't know what the devil's supposed to be going on out here. It's slightly embarrassing." That much, at least, corresponded with Hearst's editorials. But there was both tactic and truth in James's admission. He didn't really know what the project at the laboratory was all about other than in vague, generalized, comparative terms, and he certainly couldn't ask the right technical questions without having a sense of what general processes were being attempted. The tactic was simple flattery. Groves's ego, as evidenced by his allusion to the Pentagon and his "8 times 7" story, was a setup for anyone who tapped his self-image as an expert. "I might not be able to understand even when you explain it, so bear with me. At Harvard I was abysmal in chemistry."

Groves closed his eyes and breathed deeply. "It's physics, Major, physics. And it's very simple, really, if you understand a few basic principles." Groves reached into a desk drawer and pulled out a tennis ball and a Ping-Pong ball. He had delivered this demonstrated talk to every VIP with clearance curious enough to ask the key question—"How will it work —if it works?"

The clearing of his throat marked Groves's change of roles from "projects man" to Professor of Physics. Groves began in a voice that made Roosevelt realize there was a very mediocre academic locked in the corpulent Army career man. "Now, of course, there's a lot of technical, newfangled language attached to all this stuff, and that's what throws you at first. But what's actually happening is simple if you don't let the nomenclature throw you and once you understand your premises. First principle: Every element in the world is composed of atoms, infinitesimal particles of matter. Second principle: An atom is built exactly like our solar system." He held up the tennis ball. "This is the core—like the sun, but they call it the nucleus. And around it circles smaller particles—like the planets." He moved the Ping-Pong ball around the fuzzy gray core. "Principle three: It is possible to knock one of these little planets out of line and get it to crash into other planets until you get what they call a chain reaction. That means they crash into each other until one picks up tremendous speed and crashes into a core, the nucleus. And when *that* flies apart, you get one hell of an explosion. *WHAM . . . !*" Groves smacked his desk so hard and suddenly that James felt his head jerk backward. He suspected that Groves had made the dramatic slam plenty of times before, and usually with impressive effect. ". . . just like breaking the balls on a pool table. We call that splitting the atom."

"Sounds simple enough, General." James's humor was wasted on Groves.

"Problem number one: Certain elements lend themselves better to atomic reactions than others—their planets are not so stable—and these elements have to be manufactured. We need an awful lot of this matter and we need it very pure. My plants are beginning to produce it at Hanford and Oak Ridge. Problem number two: We had to know if the theory actually would work. Experiments in a control reactor in Chicago have proved positive, so that's no problem any more. Problem number three: We've got to find a way to scale down the size, find a triggering mechanism that's reliable, and design the whole thing to fit a bomb that works the very first time and every time—engineering problems, in other words." James noted the "every time."

Groves picked up the balls, smashed the small one into the larger, and said, "Ka-boom." Then he cleared his throat and lowered his voice. "And that's what Los Alamos is all about in a nutshell, Major." It seemed the Professor had finished his lecture—but no, not quite. "Oh yes, I darned near forgot. Problem number four: The Germans knew everything I've told you back in 1938."

James had begun to like the blowhard General in spite of himself. "Well then," he said, "if we're going to beat the

Germans to it, I'd better get out of your way as fast as possible."

"Not a bad idea at all, Major. Let's give Mr. Bradley a call."

The name had not been on his briefing list, so James said, "Mr. Bradley?"

"I've assigned code names around here. Oppenheimer is 'Bradley.'"

Wearing one of General Groves's tweed overcoats that could not really have fitted much worse, James Roosevelt stepped down from a jeep before a large, unimpressive log cabin. "Hard to believe, isn't it, Major," said Groves, slightly breathless as they mounted the porch, "that the brains to win this war are behind that door?" With a sweeping gesture he announced, "Our Theoretical Division, and a bigger bunch of prima donnas you're not likely to find anywhere."

A thin, almost gaunt man all but devoured by two bulky sweaters and a floppy brimmed hat came out the door as Groves was straightening up. "Mr. Bradley," he said, "we were just coming over to see you. This is Major Roosevelt. He's doing some official snooping."

Oppenheimer's eyebrows rose as if "Roosevelt," too, must have been a code name. Then the distracted man shook hands timidly with James, never keeping eye contact, and said in a weak voice, "Problems over at Ordnance. There's a struggle to the death over comparative triggering systems. I'd like to be able to spend some time with you. But you're in very good hands with the General. Sorry, perhaps later." And he hurried down the steps and into a black Chevy without glancing back.

The interior of the cabin was brighter and more active than its woeful exterior could have suggested. Groves introduced Roosevelt to a small man with a heavy German accent. The General said, "Mr. Herman, Major Roosevelt." But the man glared at Groves and said, "I'm Hans Bethe, director of the Theoretical Division. Mr. Roosevelt, I must tell you how much I—we all—admire your father."

"Actually," James said, "I'm here partly to indicate his own support for your work on this project."

"Ach, but you also probably meant to say 'concern.' And he is correct to have concern. I have concern now too. That is the only thing we are producing enough of around here these days."

Groves chuckled as though Bethe had said something funny.

"Concern, may I ask, Professor, over feasibility of the project or over timing?"

"Have you ever heard, Mr. Roosevelt, the classic expression of the difference between the theoretical and the experimental physicist?" James smiled, puffed his cheeks and shook his head. "Well, the theoretical scientist knows what's wrong with the radio but does not know how to fix it; the experimenter has no idea of what has gone wrong, but he could repair it if you let him fiddle with it for a while. And that's where we are at the moment. There are those who have proven the theory. There are those who think they know how to make it work. So when are the two going to come together already? Isn't that when you'll finally have your bomb?" The question was aimed right at General Groves, who chuckled again, as was the suggestion that followed. "If Mr. Roosevelt is going to be with us for a while, then we should have some time to talk."

"Two or three days perhaps," said James.

"Then he will certainly stay with us." Hans Bethe tapped his chest.

Leslie Groves explained, as though to a child, that the Major preferred his own quarters.

"This is true?" Bethe questioned, and James nodded. "At least then, Mr. Roosevelt, you will do us the privilege of dining with us tonight. My wife is a marvelous cook. She and I will be pleased if you accept, *ja?* Insulted if you will refuse." He handed James a card. "Call this number when you are settled in, and we will make the arrangements." James couldn't be certain, but he sensed an urgency behind the hospitality. He smiled and nodded again.

In James's meetings with most of the staff members, the preponderant tone was cynicism, often in the form of irony and sarcasm. Groves had dropped the code names after Bethe.

Edward Teller, a theoretician who itched to cross over to experimental, told James, "This is what we are good at here, a chain reaction of rumors; that is what we can put together here." He wouldn't elaborate. "A joke, Major, just a joke."

Anton Feinmeister in Experimental volunteered, "If the right hand does not know what the left one is doing, or even if there *is* a left hand, you could not even open a bottle of wine." And Groves was always right there with an explanatory or, more often, a cajoling remark. He was the master of the belittling chuckle. James's favorite remark of Groves's was: "Little good old-fashioned Army discipline'd straighten all you crackpots out in a hurry, heh heh. My guess is haircuts would probably double productivity." To which Otto Frisch replied, "But there is nothing to put out, Herr General. You cannot make a bomb any faster out of haircuts than out of theories."

Except for the Ordnance people, who were mostly military personnel or young technicians with shaves and good manners and haircuts, the people James spoke with were either edgy, guarded, evasive, disgruntled, nasty or completely unwilling to speak personally about the project. Morale was clearly not good.

"You see. Prima donnas," General Leslie R. Groves explained by way of summarizing the day's tour, "and exactly the way prima donnas are supposed to act when they've been waiting this long for the curtain to go up and for each one of them to be the star."

"That could well explain it," James agreed. He made sure his face supported the statement.

"What appears to bother some of our people—and they may have a valid gripe from a scientific point of view—is the compartmentalization. One group doesn't know what the others are doing. Security matter. Truth is that here I'm the only one who knows how everything fits together, organizationally speaking." Now Groves was tapping his chest repeatedly. James stifled a shudder. "It might not be the most efficient method—duplication and whatever—but let me tell you, strictly between us, Major, security has discovered some pretty nasty things about some of these people. I figure it's better to go just a little slower in order to make sure there are no slipups. At any rate, things'll change pretty damn quick when we get close enough to move some of the Chicago team down here. That's when it'll all begin to come together. Until then . . ." Groves made a vague gesture with shoulders and arms.

"And when will they start to be moved down?"

Groves whispered, "Actually, we've already started. Not all the people up there. Just the ones we're sure of."

When James was driven to the guest cottage, he felt absolutely bone weary from sheer physical displacement again and the bombardment of new faces and the searching out of important words. After taking off his borrowed overcoat, suit jacket, tie, shirt and shoes, he lay on an Army cot, fingers folded under his head, his heels elevated on the bar at the foot. He noticed a telephone on a small table alongside. *No, he realized, this certainly wasn't the place to check in from. Nothing concrete to report anyway.* He reached over and picked it off the cradle. After a moment, the base operator's voice came on: "Number please."

"Operator, I'd like to call Washington, D.C."

"Your clearance number, please."

"I'm visiting the base. I arrived today. Major Roosevelt."

"I'll check that." The line seemed to go dead. Then the voice came back: "Yes, sir. What number do you wish in Washington?"

"That's the problem, operator, I don't have the number; but I'd like to place a person-to-person call to Miss May Fielding. The residence is probably listed under General Walter W. Fielding. Please check out both names for me."

"That's F-I-E-L-D-I-N-G, Fielding? May or Walter?"

"Correct."

"Hold on please."

"Operator. Sorry. I've changed my mind. Cancel the call." From the phone James heard the hissing sound of expended air.

Chapter

9

JAMES ROOSEVELT was greeted at the door by Hans Bethe's wife, Rose, a demure, handsome woman. One of his reports told him that she had been pressed into service operating the housing office at Los Alamos. The cramped, unimpressive front room of a small log cabin made it rather obvious that she had not used her position to give her own family preferential treatment. She announced with a soft Viennese lilt, as she shook his hand, "It is a very great honor to have a Roosevelt in our house." As she leaned forward to kiss his cheek, her smell, a combination of lavender and disinfectant, evoked a vague memory of the maids' quarters at Hyde Park.

In the front room four men stood up at the same moment, bumped one another, and filled the space completely, even though only one, Edward Teller, could have been considered a large man. James had to stoop as he entered; the ceiling gave him less than four inches of clearance. None of the words in the round of greetings formed a complete thought; fragments and phrases flew around: "My pleasure . . . best meal you are likely to . . . I don't think I've ever . . . of course . . . why not?"

James was slightly embarrassed because he had read secret information on all the men present, but he easily masked his feelings amid the awkwardness of the introductions. Oppenheimer, far more at ease and relaxed than he had appeared while on the move that morning, Bethe and Teller were all dressed casually in sweaters and slacks. The fourth man, Otto Frisch, was in an ill-fitting brown suit whose jacket and slacks missed each other by a shade, and a wide blue tie. He was in the Experimental Division and working on the specific problem of finding a technique for triggering an explosive reaction within the confines of a large-sized bomb shell. Bethe introduced him by saying simply, "This is Frisch." And then, "We all have him to blame for the twist our lives have taken in these last five years."

James looked confused, so Teller added, "He discovered how fission works." The word "fission" meant nothing to James. "In Germany, five years ago. Who could have guessed it would have brought us all to an asylum like this one?"

Otto Frisch smiled shyly and said softly, his words less clear in English than those of his colleagues, "I would have thought the mad paperhanger more responsible for our lives now than I have been."

"All is read-dy," tiny Rose Bethe sang from the kitchen, and again the men bumped into one another moving to the small round table. *Had they been atoms*, James thought, *we'd have had an atomic reaction.*

"You'll excuse me, gentlemen," Rose announced when the kitchen was filled with men. "Everything is ready, so seat yourselves. Hans, you closest to the stove. You will be serving."

There were five chairs around the table, and when the men finally allowed her to seat them, Teller said, "And for you, Rose?"

"No, no. I must go back to the office tonight. There is work to be done. I have already eaten. Hans will take care, but it is up to you all to be certain he does not forget anything or drop it in your laps when he is serving you. He has been known to."

"But we can make room, Rose," Teller pleaded, even though it was probably physically impossible. "Please."

"No, no, Edward. I really have work to do, and I have already eaten." She placed her hands squarely on her husband's shoulders and kissed his temple. "Please don't rise, Mr. Roosevelt. Gentlemen."

Teller and not Bethe served dinner—chicken with dark rice, a salad, chilled chablis. The informal conversation at table consisted of some polite comments about the food, the delicacy of the embroidery on the linen napkins, Rose's kindness, the dreadful weather. An artificial expectancy seemed heavy in the air. Until Oppenheimer cleared his throat and announced softly, eyes still on his plate, "I've been asked, Major Roosevelt, to convey some information to you. And hopefully through you to your father. In other words, I've been commissioned to relay some concerns, and they are not the sort we wish to be shared by anyone else." Oppenheimer, characteristically, had trouble facing such matters head-on. "In other words, we do not wish anyone else to be told of what is said here tonight, with the exception of the President, of course. We do this, mind you, not to deceive or confuse; rather, to try to constructively alter . . ." Here he stopped, thinking he had botched matters, but decided to continue: ". . . the course of events here and perhaps in the world. Even so, we are running something of a risk and would welcome your assurances that what we have to say will be for your—and his—ears alone."

It was James's turn to look thoughtful. He finally said,

"Gentlemen, that is precisely the reason my father sent me here." Of course, it wasn't, but it was the expression called for by the situation. "You have my personal assurances of absolute secrecy." There seemed to be a palpable release of tension in the room, and Bethe and Teller began to speak at the same moment. They stopped at the same moment also and smiled at each other.

So it was Oppenheimer who delivered the overture. "We do not want this to sound like a list of petulant grievances. And there is a wide range of differing opinions on many things here, but I believe you ought to hear some things from me first since I happen to have the organizational responsibility, scientifically speaking anyway." He glanced around the table, and each of the physicists nodded assent. "It has to be said, Major. Morale on this project has never been worse. It's as simple as that." Hearing his own direct judgment seemed to embolden Oppenheimer. "And not merely here. It seems to be a project-wide malaise. Professor Frisch here can tell of discontent at the metallurgy lab in Chicago as well. And in New York. And especially with the British at Harwell. Something is going to have to be done."

Silence. After the first rush of willingness to speak, there was now restraint, perhaps self-consciousness. James waited and said, "Morale problems of what sort? Specifically."

"We are dealing with a complex matter humanly and structurally," said Teller, pushing his chair back slightly from the table and smacking against the sink. "On one level there is the incompatibility of the personality of the physicist with the military mind. And although it bothers many of our colleagues, it is an irresolvable conflict, to my thinking. It is a way we must live, an accommodation most of us have learned to make. We may not be happy with it, but we appear to be powerless to change it. So our mail is read each day, and we are spied on from time to time as though *we* were the enemy. Still, these are the conditions that prevail, as they say, these days."

"At least," said Oppenheimer, "we won the battle of the uniforms."

"Uniforms?" said James.

"Oh, yes. G. G. got it in his head that since we are in effect military personnel, we ought to wear those silly Army uniforms just to prove it. Can you imagine Teller here in such a uniform? But it was not an easy struggle, I can assure you."

"G. G.?" Roosevelt asked.

"That's what almost everyone here calls Groves," Oppenheimer said. "His nickname at West Point, we have discovered, was 'Greasy.' So it's G. G. for 'Greasy' Groves." James sat back, uncontrollably smug with the secret information that "Greasy" Groves had gone to bat for this man's position and reputation.

"But the problem now is neither a matter of style," Teller interjected, "nor of personal restrictions. It is nothing less than the Army's interference in the project itself. In the work of the physicists themselves. It's their insane policy of compartmentalization that drives me to distraction. I don't want to debate the issue here. All I know is that it inhibits me in my own work." He smiled at James. "Technically speaking, Major Roosevelt, I am suspect in being at this table with Frisch here: he is Experimental; I am Theoretical. If we communicate on the project, we may learn too much about the weapon as a whole, Groves believes. But if we do not communicate, we won't even *have* a weapon! I just would like you to know that it is seriously hampering our effectiveness and hope you can convey that information to the President."

James nodded, but Teller had prepared a logical proof, so he continued: "Compartmentalization may have made some sense at one time, but when the various parts are ready, as they almost are, to begin to be brought together, then we . . ."

James interrupted. "What is your best estimate of a date for a workable weapon as of right now?"

"That is precisely the point. If they let us proceed as we

should, seven, eight months perhaps. But even that estimate is uncertain because I do not have all the information I would need. It could be sooner. They do not tell us, for example, if we will even have all the fissionable material we will need. Or how pure it will be. Such things are mysteries. No good, Mr. Roosevelt, no good at all. Ask Oppenheimer here. He is the project's director; perhaps he will know." Things were beginning to heat up a bit.

Attention turned to the spare man whose pale eyes fluttered. "Maybe I have more of the missing pieces than Teller here, or most of the others, but I simply do not have what I would really need to make a scientifically accurate estimate. And much of the information I do have was gotten—well, by slipping into compartments even I had been excluded from. This is simply not the way we ought to be operating at this stage of the game, Mr. Roosevelt."

"Groves," said Teller, "Groves and Colonel Ishmael— they're the only ones, of all people, who are in a position to know what is really going on. If you wish to alarm the President, relay that particular piece of information."

"It could, of course, be argued," said James, while cutting some lettuce, "that the closer you get to completion, the greater the need for control. Hence, the stepped-up security."

"Fine, fine, fine." It was the excitable Teller. "So long as the security—the control, if you will—doesn't keep us from solving the problems we need to solve to make all the parts fit together. And that is precisely what is happening now. And we run the risk of 'security-ing' ourselves right out of the bomb!" He raised his hand as if to strike the table but realized the inappropriateness of the gesture and dropped his hand slowly into his lap.

Hans Bethe was up now, trying to circle the table and take some of the dishes. There was no room to maneuver, and Teller said, "Bethe, for God's sake, sit down. We are men of science, are we not? We can surely devise a method of getting the dishes to the sink more efficiently. We must cooperate." Teller cocked a thick eyebrow in Roosevelt's direction so the analogy would not be lost. "Here. We pass the salad plates first. To the right."

Slowly the dishes came around, and Bethe flicked the uneaten food and bones into a can and rinsed off each plate before placing it on a pile in the sink for Rose. He began to speak in midsentence: ". . . quite a paradox. There are those, like Teller here, who are upset that the bomb will not be available quickly enough. Then there are others—more than you can imagine, Mr. Roosevelt—who are coming to believe that we do not even need such a bomb. Who are absolutely convinced that Hitler no longer has the capacity to produce a bomb." The expression on his face indicated that he was sympathetic to this view. "And if that is so, the world would certainly be a better place without such a thing."

Hans Bethe did not look toward the table as he went on; rather, he stared at the reflections of the others in the darkened window above the sink. "You see, they are having second and third thoughts about the need. They no longer trust the information that we are in a desperate race with the Germans. They reason that here in America with the very best scientists, with a triple-A priority, with unlimited funds, with no bombings, we still just have nothing more than a pile of hot graphite in Chicago. So how could the Nazis, now that things have turned so decisively . . . oh!"

Hans Bethe realized at this moment that the hot water had run out. He dried his hands on a dish towel, sat and continued at the table. "Now that things have turned so decisively and they are bombed and harassed day and night, it is not likely they will be able to do what we cannot. So I am glad you are here tonight, not so much to tell you the things about our work which upset me, but, more, to find out from you if our work is absolutely necessary . . . humanly speaking."

James sensed that the discussion was approaching a critical point. First Oppenheimer, then Teller, and now Bethe were, in varying depths and directions, voicing criticism of the program, and in so doing, had left themselves vulnerable. Now James was being asked to show he could be trusted by offering some critical information. He had no choice but to seize the moment; after all, his mission for his father was to devise some method of bringing him plans for a workable bomb, and these were the men who could deliver. James did not hold back. "Professor Bethe—"

"Call me Hans, please."

"Hans. There's a good deal of logic in what you say, but let me put it this way. With so much at stake, can we take even the slightest chance the Germans won't get the bomb somehow?"

"Is it pure chance then, Major? You will offer no concrete information to help someone like me who must make a life and death decision? Eh?"

James said softly, "The truth is I do have something helpful to offer." All but Frisch leaned forward. "Unfortunately, it doesn't entirely resolve the moral dilemma you've suggested. Still, I believe men such as you are entitled to know. Regardless of what rumors you may have heard, we have not yet completely destroyed the German capacity to produce an atomic bomb."

Bethe sank back. Teller, his eyes flashing, said, "All the more reason to pull these military counterweights from our backs and let us get on with what we can do."

Oppenheimer was seriously considering the implications of Roosevelt's words.

Now it was finally Frisch's turn. He was patting his pale, heavily lined brow when he said, "Forgive me, Mr. Roosevelt, but I am not at all surprised by your information. To me it is no information at all, and I treat it as such. You see, you could not really have said the German capacity has been completely destroyed, even if you knew that to be the case, for by doing so you would have been encouraging a revolt in our project. Although you are no doubt a very honest, up-standing and honorable young man, you are certainly not a fool. No, you could not possibly have been allowed to tell us that. However, you could have remained silent or enigmatic on the subject, but most of us would have taken your evasion as an unwillingness to confirm our fears and to allow us to assume the German project was smashed. So you see, you could really have only said what you have said, and that very fact removes a certain, shall we say, authority from it. For me, at least."

Edward Teller interjected: "If I am not mistaken, Major, I believe you have just been called a dissembler in the most circuitous manner you're ever likely to encounter. But that's old Frisch for you. We are used to him, you see." Everyone but Frisch and James laughed nervously.

"Coffee, gentlemen?" The host looked helplessly from face to face around the table and received nods from everyone except Frisch, so he bumped his chair back once more and began rattling among the pots and pans in the cabinet be-hind him. It became immediately evident that this was not going to be an easy task. After a few moments of clatter, Bethe found the various sections of the percolator, which he placed on the table for assembly while he began to look in other cupboards for the coffee, all the while muttering curses in English and German. Assembly of the parts on the table did not go smoothly. First Teller and then Oppen-heimer took turns trying to find the proper combination of stem, basket, lid and container. James had the knack and reassembled the parts into working order. By now Bethe's curses rolled out in a torrent; he turned and announced that there was no coffee to be found anywhere. James pointed to a red bag on the counter near the toaster. After they fig-ured out where the coffee and water should go and approxi-mately how much of each was needed, Bethe said, "See, it is exactly like Army compartmentalization. We need people who know how all the parts fit together." He was serious.

"I have some deeper fears than compartmentalization or even the Germans, if you care to hear them, Major," said Otto Frisch, picking up his dropped thread. "Maybe you will dismiss what I am about to say with, 'That Frisch, he is too full of conspiracies.' If so, there is no retort required. Nevertheless, since I have the ear of the ear of the President, so to speak, I must say into it what I believe to be so and run whatever risks." The silence as Frisch spoke now was somehow deeper than it had been earlier, heavier with drama.

"I ask myself questions. I say, 'Frisch, if we are really in a race against Hitler for the bomb and survival, then why do we have a system that is so very slow?' Could it mean that it is known Hitler cannot really produce a bomb? And could it be that there is some *political* reason for the compartmentalization? Could it not ensure that the men who will control it will *not* be the scientists? Will they not be militarists and bureaucrats? Will they not be the people who will finally determine when and where and on whom to use it? You see, I ask many questions." He was staring unflinchingly at James Roosevelt, who was staring directly back. "And I have concluded that the people who will control the bomb have already made decisions, gentlemen. Decisions that go even beyond the end of this war. Political decisions. I give an example. Huge plants have been and are still being built—don't ask me how I have found out; the information is there if you look for it—to produce fissionable material for the bomb. But how much? Enough for one bomb? Two? Half a dozen? Or for as many bombs as Ford has made automobiles? Let us assume one or two would end the war. Why then make such a tremendous investment in these plants? Has it been decided by someone already that we will be in the bomb business for a great many years to come? And who has made that decision? Can you answer some of my questions, Mr. Roosevelt?"

James shifted in his seat. "My problem in responding now would be the same as before, Professor. You see, if I said it was true, I might be prompting a revolt . . ." There was some laughter from Teller and Bethe and nods that acknowledged James's cleverness. But Frisch was narrowly serious.

"Major"—his voice had an emotional edge to it—"do not patronize me about this. I have seen too much in my life, too much go wrong, and it is too personal a matter. Yes, the swine must be defeated—absolutely obliterated if necessary —but it is becoming more complicated now that we get closer, and we must begin to look beyond. We who are the responsible ones must know everything we can about what it is we are doing. This weapon will be a political force when the war is won. *The* political force. Who will control it? For what purposes? Will America share its peaceful possibilities with the world? Or will she use it for a *Pax Americana?* Now, I say, is the time to raise these issues." He turned his steady gaze slightly away from James and addressed his colleagues. "Forgive my passion, but I believe these decisions have already been made and that it is now *our* business to discover what they are and, if necessary, redirect them. Or I worry for our souls."

For a moment there was not a sound. A floorboard somewhere cricked. James cleared his throat and said, "I'm sorry for my feeble attempt at humor, Professor Frisch. Of course you are correct; it is a deadly serious matter. I guess I fall into both of your dangerous categories—the military man *and* the bureaucrat. The simple truth of the matter, gentlemen, is that I don't know any more than you do about what plans there are for this weapon. Obviously this is one of my father's concerns at the present time or I would not be here now. I can only tell you that I will forward to him everything that I gather in my inspection of the project." A correct and fundamentally evasive response that everyone at the table recognized as such.

There was some fidgeting of hands on the table. Then

Teller burst out with: "Bethe, our coffee." All eyes turned to the stove, where the pot sat on an unlit burner.

The following night, while the ringing buzzed in his ear, James looked out through the window of the Santa Fe Pharmacy and Drugstore into the darkened street at the swirl of debris being tossed about by miniature twisters and at the car he had borrowed from Hans Bethe. Only a hand-written pass from General Groves and a telephone call to double-check got him off the installation. On the third ring, a response: "White House. Central."

"Hi, Hacky. Good to hear a friendly voice. Major Roosevelt checking in."

"Yes, sir."

"My number here is LI 9-3823."

"That's LI 9-3823?"

"Roger."

"He is free, I believe. Will call back shortly." James hung up, waited in the booth and watched the deserted street. At the far corner, there was a flash of headlights and then darkness. He saw a figure leave a car and walk in the shadows on the near side of the street. Then a jeep with two MPs turned the corner and stopped in front of the First Chance Saloon. The man in the shadows, seen only by James, approached Bethe's car and opened the trunk with a key. When he leaned in, even James couldn't see him very clearly, but it appeared as though he removed one small object and replaced it with another. James understood the situation immediately—recording machines!

Groves's security people probably knew what everyone at Los Alamos had been saying. In James's mind, there was a hurried rush to try to reconstruct everything he'd said since he had arrived. It was crazy. There was momentary panic. Then came the general feeling that since he'd been on his guard because of FAMILY MATTER, there couldn't have been anything particularly incriminating. After all, he was there to spy himself, and that meant holding back and picking up whatever was dropped. Still, a moment's letting down of the defenses, a careless word . . .

The ring he'd been expecting stunned him when it came. "Major Roosevelt?" Hacky's voice again.

"Right." James eyed the shadow as it retreated into the darkness.

"Just one moment." A series of buzzes and clicks. When FDR came on, each man was oblivious to the fact that the other's speech pattern was almost identical. Had there been an eavesdropper on this line too, he'd have had a hard time keeping track of the shifts in speakers.

"Some interesting developments here, Pa. Seems that morale isn't quite what it should be. Variety of reasons. Seems the man at the top here ought to be shaken up a bit." He hoped a recording of *that* got back to 'Greasy' Groves. "But we can talk more about it when I get back. There is, in fact, quite a bit to talk about."

"How worrisome do you make matters?" FDR asked.

"Well, that's not really too easy to say yet. I've seen situations where there's grumbling and discontent, and things still run along as smoothly as they're going to anyway. The other thing is that they might be getting close to something on this project, and a certain amount of anxiety might be feeding the situation. Really hard to tell at this point."

"In other words, Jimmy, you're definitely hedging."

James had been made wary of what was and was not safe to say on a public telephone in the Santa Fe Pharmacy and Drugstore. There was actually no telling if Groves was monitoring the trunk lines leading out of town, but it was necessary to assume that he was. James said very carefully, giving emphasis to certain words he hoped would allow his father to understand, "*Pa*, it's the sort of thing that is better discussed *in person*. Too complicated, too many conflicting things to *talk about now*. I just don't have enough information *yet*. I'd like to visit the other installations *first*."

"Which one?"

There was no way not to give a direct answer. "Chicago."

"To see whom?"

Fortunately, this question allowed some flexibility. "Everyone I can set up any time with."

"Well," FDR said, and then took a moment to think and swallow, "I suggest that you change your itinerary a bit, Jimmy. My information here is that we may have the beginning of a small house revolt on our hands. A number of the Chicago and New York scientists, and perhaps some of the others too, may be having second thoughts about this bomb of ours. It seems that they've sent a delegation to Professor Einstein at Princeton. He telephoned me earlier in the day. I'd like to be able to telephone tonight or tomorrow and say you'll be up there to talk to him. You've heard no rumblings about any trouble out where you are?"

"None at all, Pa," James lied, and envisioned Otto Frisch's narrowed eyes as he did so. "And, Pa, tell him I'll be up there day after tomorrow, okay?" James all at once realized that his briefcase with information on Enrico Fermi, Leo Szilard, Bethe, Teller, Frisch, Oppenheimer and even Albert Einstein was still on the front seat of Hans Bethe's car. He hadn't taken his eyes off the car since he noticed the shadowy agent; still, it was a dumb thing to have done. That briefcase would become a part of his body from the moment he touched it again. "Take care of yourself, Pa. I'll be in touch after I see what's up in Princeton."

"I may be down in Warm Springs, but Hacky will put you through, won't you, Hacky old girl? You realize, Jimmy, that she listens to everything that comes in and out of this office. Good luck." His laughter faded and was cut off when the line went dead.

Chapter
10

ONCE AGAIN Major Roosevelt found himself shuttled and buffeted across the continent; this time in trains and planes, in buses and taxicabs for crucial connections, on an irregular course that dropped him in the unlikely, random cities of Colorado Springs, Topeka, Memphis and Pittsburgh and Allentown, Pennsylvania. He found himself, finally, on a cold, slowly moving, often delayed mail-train on the last leg of a journey up from Philadelphia, rocking and dozing fitfully as he reclined on his briefcase and two sacks of mail. He needed a shave, and his tan suit was woefully crumpled and baggy. The coat he'd expropriated from General Groves had actually served as a cushioned sleeping bag on his journey. It was only slightly more than thirty-six hours since he'd left Santa Fe so abruptly. His physical wariness and discomfort were only slightly less than on a Raider operation; that much, at least, satisfied him.

The earlier train stops had been at grimy Pennsylvania and New Jersey factory towns, one indistinguishable from another. Then flat suburban villages of small, comfortable-looking homes. Only after the train had been switched and shunted off the main line did the landscape begin to become variable, interesting. The sun had come up suddenly and strongly just before the mail clerk shook him and said, "Princeton, next stop."

As he stood on the station platform, James Roosevelt was overcome by a palpable wistfulness; a rush of feeling tinged with melancholy entered his tired body. This was a town very much like the fondly remembered towns of his childhood—vacation towns, visits to friends' families, summer camps. Upstate and New England relatives had often come to meet him at stations like this one. He couldn't remember when he last stood quietly at such a charming railroad station. Much too long ago, he realized sadly.

The house at 112 Mercer Street was typical of the secure confidence of an old university town: it was, if anything, understated and unpretentious to the degree that the large trees behind it gave it the only distinction it held. That, and the prominent genius of its chief resident.

The taxi deposited him at the curb. And, after knocking twice, he was admitted by a small, gray housemaid more concerned with preparing breakfast than impressed by a Roosevelt. A vague odor of old, cooked cabbage permeated the entire house. She led him to the study, a book-lined room with three chairs and a large rectangular table placed in the geometric center. All the light came in from a French door that opened onto a slightly diseased lawn.

James stood in the hallway behind the tiny maid, who impatiently but silently waited to be noticed. In the room a small, dark woman was reading, actually dictating sets of numbers and phrases in German to a smaller figure hunched over the table. It went on for the better part of a minute until the woman noticed the maid and the tall man in the doorway and exclaimed, "*Ach*. Professor. Our guest. Hilda, shame on you. You should have said something." Hilda shrugged and left.

Then the man at the table looked up, blinked, rose and stepped gingerly forward. He looked so very much like the world-famous image of himself that James was surprised by the perfect duplication. The unkempt mane of white hair, the small, twinkling brown eyes over an absurd organ grinder's mustache, were comic replicas. Even his clothing was predictably famous: baggy pants, a too-large sweatshirt, one tip of the shirt collar out, the other tucked away. Albert Einstein.

"Forgive, forgive, forgive, Mr. Roosevelt," he said as he shuffled forward. "So, so, so." He examined each feature. "*Ja,* you do look a great deal like your father. No doubt you are told this all the time. Perhaps it disturbs you, the comparison."

"No, sir, not at all. But please forgive my appearance; I've been traveling the last two days."

"*Ach,* appearances. They are no concern here. Substance matters, eh?" Then Einstein explained, with a certain mock embarrassment in his tone, the scene James had walked in on. "I mean to say, that it is, of course, somewhat unusual to see a secretary dictating to her boss. Is it not?" His accent was extremely thick, the vowels slurred and the rhythms unconventional. "But for this even there is an explanation. Possible, of course, that Helen is the genuine physicist and I am merely her mask to the world."

At this point Helen Dukas, realizing that she was not going to be introduced to the President's son, introduced herself. Volunteering that she greatly admired James's father, she offered to bring the men some coffee. The idea of a steaming cup revived James's flagging spirits.

"But that is not the truth," explained Einstein. "Actually, we have been told that someone will pay much money at a war bond drive if we are to auction off the original calculations of my general theory. Who could have imagined that relativity would help to win the war? But, alas, I have kept none of the original work. You have caught us making up a forgery, Mr. Roosevelt. And, what is worse, I do not even remember exactly how it was organized. Helen must read it to me from a book. That is what you have seen. Please keep our secret."

The admission, although meant to amuse, caught James by surprise, and he did not know how to respond. He was perhaps supposed to laugh or to offer a denial that the great man could actually be so forgetful. Each response seemed wrong at the moment. So he smiled and said nothing whatever.

"It is good," said Einstein. "Your demeanor seems very correct for the seriousness of the matters to be discussed. Cigarette?" James rarely smoked. Never in the morning. Yet in this room with its smell of rich and tangy leather and old paper and cooked cabbage, it seemed appropriate. Professor Einstein brought a wooden box out from a drawer in the table, opened it clumsily, and James selected. "For me, my pipe." It lay on the table, a bastardized construction with a conventional briar bowl fitted to a straight chrome tube about a foot long. "We can sit by the sunlight if you wish." James lifted each chair to the glass doors, and the men sat quietly for a while, looking out. A small black ashtray rested on the old briefcase that rested on James's knees. Specks of dust floated in all directions through the stillness of sunlit air. Smoke began to rise and curl. The silence was a presence, not an absence of sound.

"I have seen that it has happened before—this appropriation from science by politics. I am not really a child about such things. Then, maybe I am. As a young man perhaps I paid too little attention to the politics, but in Europe it is not possible to remain always naive about things political. Did your father—the President, I mean to say—did he convey to you my concerns?"

"Only in the most general way, Professor. I was in the

West; we spoke rather quickly over the telephone. It would be well if you assumed I knew nothing and began from the beginning."

Einstein was squinting directly into the sunlight as he pulled with soft, regular lip-smacks on his elongated pipe to stimulate the burning deep in the distant bowl. "In physics it is always good to begin with speculations, but with politics conditions as they exist are often the more effective. Political speculation usually is not relevant, except perhaps for the radio or for books." The great man punctuated each sentence with a draw on his pipe that sounded like a leaky faucet—*plip*—but that had a slightly hypnotic effect on the tired major. "My worries are the worries of the men you have already spoken with—Bethe and Frisch, in particular —and of others you have yet to meet—Fermi, Szilard, Sachs and Bohr." *Plip.*

Jesus, thought James, *between Hearst and these atomic scientists, there are no secrets!* He said, "But the worries of Professors Bethe and Frisch seem quite different to me. Professor Bethe was concerned that our weapon would not be ready as quickly as it should be, and Professor Frisch thought it may not even be needed at all."

Plip. Plip. Plip. "Ah, what you say surprises me. It is not precisely what they tell me privately. When *we* speak of it, Bethe and Frisch are of one mind—that the weapon is no longer a necessity. This is also the position of Bohr and Sachs, Szilard and Fermi. And others—many others—I am not at liberty to name at the present moment. They—and I—sincerely wish work on the bomb project suspended." *Plip.* The small brown eyes were smilingly fixed on James's face.

James had hoped that Einstein would continue speaking. For Einstein to have ended with a specific request made his own evasion more difficult. He elected a stance of bewildered indignation. "Suspended. I—we—couldn't. It's just not feasible. We are in a life and death struggle, Professor. Why, if Hitler were to—"

"He has not the capacity, Mr. Roosevelt. You certainly must know this. If I had even the slightest doubt that we were dealing with a dangerous possibility, do you believe I would interfere?" *Plip.* "It is a practical impossibility that they would have sufficient fissionable material. No, no, they lack the capacity utterly, thank God. Certainly your military intelligence must have told you this fact. If they have not, perhaps there are even deeper problems involved. But I cannot believe this to be the case."

"And just what is the source of *your* intelligence, Professor?" James could not keep the edge out of his voice.

"Echoes, Mr. Roosevelt, especially clear echoes we scientists have received from the Continent and elsewhere."

"Germany?"

"*Ja,* Germany." *Plip.*

"Have you given this information to our intelligence people?"

"This is what I am doing now, am I not?"

"Professor Einstein, it is certainly not my place to question your judgment, but if we must make a determination on the basis of what you call your 'echoes,' well then, it is fairly obvious that we must of course continue. If, however, you have some firm information we could check into . . ." It was hard keeping a patronizing tone out of his voice, and James did not fully try.

Nor was Albert Einstein without pique when he responded. "Do you actually believe, young man, that I would be so frivolous as to ask such a thing if I were not certain? There are more relatives and friends than I can possibly count who are imprisoned, and God only knows what else, by Hitler presently. Do you think I—or Fermi or Bohr or Frisch or any of the others—would make such a formal request if we had even a trace of doubt? Perhaps I should not have said 'echoes'; this was a mistake. There is information from our fellow scientists in Europe that convinces us." His agitation was made evident by a muscle that started pulsing below his right eye. "It was I, after all, who wrote to your father in 1939, telling him that I thought a uranium bomb was feasible and should be attempted. That was also not an easy decision. Nor was it impulsive." *Plip. Plip. Plip.* "Hitler had the capacity then and none of the scruples. He still does not have the scruples, but now also not the capacity. So now I sit before you, the same man who urged your father on then, urging him to stop now."

Here was Albert Einstein making a—what?—"demand" was not the right word. Neither was it a "request," exactly. The secretary entered with a pitcher of coffee and large cups on a silver tray; she placed it on a corner of the table nearest the men, caught the troubled silence in the room, and left on tiptoe.

The weight of silence worked to James's advantage. As the representative of the government that held the power in the matter, he did not even have to respond. The burden was of course always on the petitioner to prompt a response. This fact of political life was understood by both men.

"There are times when there seems no doubt that God *is* malicious," Einstein said wryly. "And He often does His painful jokes through cruel timing of events. Not many months ago these same men could have brought the project to an absolute halt merely by withholding their efforts. And I would not have had to beseech you in the name of conscience and simple humanity. We would have met on the terms a high government representative could understand. We might then have had the power to . . ." He allowed the voice, which broke slightly on the word "power," to trail away, and James leaned forward to try to catch the final phrase, but he could not. "General Groves and Dr. Bush, Mr. Stimson and your general staff—"

"We call them the 'Joint Chiefs,'" James heard himself

correct the professor impulsively, as though he found the European terminology in some way personally insulting.

". . . it is a well-known fact that things have gone far beyond the theoretical. It has become a task for technicians and engineers, trial and error."

There it was, dropped so matter-of-factly into a prefatory statement, the most definitive piece of information James had collected on the true state of the project. It explained the growing desperation of the theoreticians who wanted the project stopped.

"Nevertheless," Einstein continued, "I must make the naive appeal for which I, as the person most responsible for events, have been selected. Please convey to the President our request for an immediate suspension, if only a temporary one, in order to examine the implications of the various possibilities. A letter is being drafted now and will be circulated among the scientists. This will take some time, but we wish to tell the President of our concern immediately."

"I understand, Professor Einstein. Of course I'll do exactly that. But I'm curious. When you say, 'Examine the implications,' what sorts of things do you mean?"

A long, thin cloud that neither man had noticed before had been moving on a direct path toward the sun. Now the leading edge touched and then covered it, plunging the Princeton study into late morning gloom. Einstein had not drawn on his pipe for many minutes, so he *plipped* repeatedly now, trying to bring a fire back into the bowl. Doing this, he suddenly seemed so helpless, so small, insignificant and frail to James. "It is partially a question of responsibility, Mr. Roosevelt. If there is a superbomb and it is used inhumanely, we who urged its development will always carry the weight of guilt. Well, if we are to bear that guilt, we should be given some responsibility in determining its use. You see, there is a sense in which I"—he touched himself over the heart with the tips of all his fingers—"in which I will have pulled the trigger. We are men, Mr. Roosevelt, who represent many different nations of Europe. We can even see this power used as a weapon for peace. We have talked about international control of it. There is much, very much, that can be done, but we must not rush headlong into . . ." Einstein had no exact words for "what we must not rush headlong into."

James recalled his father's phrase "a headlong race toward destruction." He also knew that things had begun falling intriguingly into place in the darkened silence of the study at 112 Mercer Street.

There was no need to say anything more. Not really. This didn't mean, of course, that nothing would be said. In fact, James still tried to punch some holes in the "echoes" theory. He surprised himself with an impromptu argument he'd never really considered before: "If Hitler used poison gas or some other form of outlawed mass destruction, wouldn't we need a retaliatory weapon then?" He was becoming a very clever apologist for the bomb.

Einstein did not respond.

James introduced a second justification: "And we haven't even mentioned the Japanese. Our intelligence says that they, too, might be in the process of developing an atomic weapon of some sort. Surely, we can't sit idly by."

Albert Einstein looked deeply into James Roosevelt's eyes and smiled very sadly. "Suddenly, young man, I feel very weary and old. On most days I rest after breakfast. If you wish some more coffee . . ."

In the sky a dozen long clouds had now formed and were on a direct sun path, even as the first one had not fully passed away. A front from the west had begun moving in. As James sat alone in the darkened room waiting for word that his taxicab had arrived, he worked at repressing his satisfaction. He imagined the phone call he'd make within the hour. *Pa. I can talk now. I think I've brought home the bacon: we've got both the things we've wanted. First,* MANHAT-TAN's *just about ready to pay off. Seven or eight months at the most. Second, I think we have a foolproof way of getting all the information we'll ever need—plans, designs, formulas, you name it. The source? I'd rather not say over the phone, but you're not going to believe it when I tell you.*

James was roused from his imaginings by a coldly efficient Helen Dukas. "Mr. Roosevelt, your cab is here."

As he sat in the cab, he rehearsed the telephone call over and over, each time changing the dialogue slightly or delivering a phrase with a slightly different emphasis. It required, in each version, a mighty effort to edit out a phrase that, like the thin, broad smile he could not repress, kept insinuating itself against his will. "Actually, Pa, it was just like taking candy from a baby."

Outside, a misting, late-night January snowfall went almost unnoticed. Upstairs at 112 Mercer Street, in Helen Dukas' room, a phonograph was playing Beethoven's *Emperor* Concerto. The exultant piano in the final movement was merely quietly joyous after it filtered through the carpets, floorboards and walls before arriving at the study below and far to the rear. It wasn't at all usual for him to be in the study this late; had Helen suspected he was working, she would never have risked the possible annoyance. But Professor Einstein was not annoyed, nor was he working, in the usual sense of the word.

The evening had been orderly and predictable: he had dictated two letters to Helen and played with some formulas on random motion, a final pipe, a bowl of soup, a warm bath, bed at nine—a pattern seldom varied these days. But the sleep that always punctuated the pattern did not come tonight. He knew why, of course. It was only partially the visit of the Roosevelt son. But far more, it was Bohr. It was impossible to think of random motion of particles and not think of Niels Bohr and the early days.

Bohr was in America now, having been smuggled out of Denmark by the British. When he had finally met with Bohr in New York last week, Einstein had left deeply disturbed. His anger and confusion had not been fully dissipated by the return to the isolated life and work at Mercer Street and at the institute. Now, tonight he had heard the bells of Nassau Hall chime ten and he had slipped out of bed, into an old brown robe and fleece-lined slippers, and padded down the hallways and staircase to his study.

Einstein had heard the *Emperor* for the first time in Munich at the old municipal auditorium. He even remembered the date—March 14, 1891—his twelfth birthday. Now the rondo theme had begun again in earnest, the bursts of piano alternating with the insistent orchestra. Bruno Walter was conducting. *My God, where is he now? Los Angeles. So out of touch we all are here.*

Einstein sat at his worktable in the half-light, tapping his foot and distractedly pulling bread crumbs into a tidy pile with the edge of his hand. Then, just before the orchestra's final seven notes, which were as clear and definite as steps to a familiar destination, he noticed the tin of pipe tobacco that sat atop his papers and was struck, after all these exiled years, by the name of his favorite American brand—"Revelation." He left his crumbs and began to tap the can, hearing the rondo clearly in his memory, unaware that it had ended upstairs. *And Artur Schnabel,* he thought, *where is he? No one now can play Beethoven like that man.* He laughed. *In this strange country* Revelation *is a tobacco.*

The revelation he knew he would have to deal with, however, was Bohr's. Einstein believed the level of secrecy surrounding Bohr's presence in New York—the code name "BAKER," the constant surveillance and protection—to be one of the usual excesses of government, any government. Now he understood, finally, what was really at stake.

He remembered the despair on Bohr's face as the Dane recounted his recent escape from Norway and then the meeting with Churchill. "He was vicious with me, I tell you, Einstein. He said I was a dangerous person, almost a Nazi collaborator. I will tell you what I think. He said the bomb was necessary to win the war; this he said over and over. Yet I know the Germans can never make such a weapon. Of this I am absolutely certain. I have told Churchill this. He went into a rage. The Frenchman, Joliot-Curie, he has, I believe, also conveyed to you the German incapacity." Einstein had nodded; he nodded again now in his darkened study. "We must try to stop the bomb production, Einstein. If it comes about, it will be too late. Joliot says he will give what he knows to the Russians someday if he must. But the Russians having a bomb to create a certain equality of destruction is not so satisfying a solution as to stop completely the making of this terrible thing."

Einstein had not remembered filling and lighting his pipe. Pale smoke haloed his head and moved on a draft of air toward the rear door. Outside, the snow swirled, the wind blew. The old house groaned continually.

All of my life I have most wanted isolation. Just to be allowed to work, my work. Other things, ja, *but the quiet to work most important of all. I have this now if I want it. But the world does not allow; it simply does not allow. My life is always this struggle against the world, and the world will have its way.*

He saw his options clearly. Stop the bomb. Or. Share the secret with other countries. Or, perhaps, withdraw completely into his own work. *This last I cannot do. I have written to Roosevelt and urged him, first, to build a bomb. Now I have telephoned and asked him to stop. He must think me mad. But I am already involved. Deeply involved.* He realized then that the Roosevelt son did not seem at all enthusiastic. Perhaps he had better call the President again tomorrow. *But they will not stop. The British and Americans will not stop. They have come too far. Szilard and Frisch have said it often enough. Bohr confirms it. I did not want to think the situation hopeless, but it already may be so.*

The logic was clear and painfully direct: If the project

could not be stopped, and if he could no longer isolate himself from the problem, then the secret must be shared, exposed. *But I am an American citizen now. I have pledged my loyalty. It is American loyalty.*

It annoyed him that he could not think of the name of "the Roosevelt son." *Helen will know it. I must write to him and determine if there is any chance. Persistence here is a virtue. As long as there may be a chance . . .* He began to draft a letter in his tiny, illegible hand. After "Dear" he drew a long dash to be filled in later by Helen. He recalled what his Uncle Jacob once said about the unknown when he was a child: "Albert, you call the unknown 'X,' and you chase after it as you would an animal you wanted to trap." It never occurred to Albert Einstein, as he penciled an "X" over the dash, that he himself was in the process of being trapped by that nameless "X."

Resolution of the old man's dilemma, however, did not seem a possibility as he composed gentle, but, for him, firm sentences asking for a formal written response to his earlier request. The very act of writing to "the Roosevelt son" was to reject his comfort and isolation.

In his last sentence he crossed out the word "request" and wrote "urge"; then he made an overall revision that firmed his tone even more. He reread the letter and felt a bit more satisfied. Although they were merely words on a page, they represented a position, a moral position and, as such, a form of power. He nodded in agreement with himself as he read. Scratches on a page. His life's work consisted of that in the end. Einstein placed the draft of his letter on Helen's desk as he passed to the kitchen to heat up some milk.

But in the country where Revelation was a pipe tobacco, "the Roosevelt son" was about to deliver the real thing.

Chapter

11

THE SNOW of Princeton, New Jersey, was a persistent rain in
Washington, D.C., important to James only because it was
impossible for him to get a cab during the great evening
exodus. The weariness he felt, the cumulative effect of days
of uncertainty, anxiety, subtle pressures and sheer physical
discomfort added up now to a mild state of fatigue as he
walked toward the row of phone booths in Union Station.
He brought the back of his hand across three day's stubble
and fished in the pocket of Groves's overcoat for a piece of
Spearmint to freshen the stale taste in his mouth. The packet
was empty.

Although there was fatigue, there was little disappointment. After all, he'd accomplished his mission faster and
more efficiently than his father could possibly have expected. Still, he couldn't shake that adolescent sense of
wanting to make Pa proud of him. He really needed a
shower, shave and a good night's rest, but he was driven

even more to make his report and win FDR's approval. As he pulled the nickel out of the depths of that pocket, he wasn't sure whom he'd call. After the number was dialed, he realized it was probably too late to expect an answer.

"Co-Ordinator of Military Manpower and Materiel."

She was still there. James thought fleetingly of hanging up and then of asking for himself in a gruff voice. She repeated, more firmly, "Military Manpower and Materiel. Whom do you wish to speak to, please?"

"Nice to know you're so dedicated to your work, Captain. By my calculations, you should have closed the office an hour ago." He could hear the telephone being transferred from one ear to the other.

"That we can talk about when you get here, Major. At least it's reassuring to know that you're alive," she said, an undercurrent of pleasure beneath the surface sarcasm. "You *are* alive, aren't you?"

"Alive, at Union Station, and utterly unable to get a taxi."

"I'll be down in a few minutes. Exactly where are you?" Although the offer was sincere, there was a distinct note of annoyance in her voice. James attributed his perception to his weariness.

"At the present moment I happen to be in a phone booth, but I'll be waiting at the West entrance. I'll be the one who looks like he's hit the skids."

There were at least thirty people huddled under the filagreed canopy, and May Fielding, who drove up in an immaculate black thirty-nine Plymouth coupe, picked him out of the crowd immediately. James tossed his briefcase onto the back seat and then slid next to May Fielding. He had an urge to kiss her cheek. "I think," he said, "I ought to be offended that you spotted me so fast."

"It's just my OSS training." The windshield wiper on his side didn't work. As they rolled into the traffic on Constitution Avenue, it made him nervous that he couldn't see. "It just needs a little tightening," she explained. "You're just going to have to trust me, aren't you?" There was still that edge to her voice, clearer than ever now. They drove in silence until the first red light at Eleventh Street. "After I heard from you I got a call from Hassett, couldn't have been more than thirty seconds. He wanted to know your whereabouts. You sounded so tired on the phone, I almost lied and said I didn't know. Bad luck, if he had called first . . . Anyway, seems the President wants to see you *toute suite*."

"Just where I was headed anyway, but I could have used a shave and a shower."

"I guessed that and asked him if we could have half an hour or so. He said, 'Immediately if not sooner,' in that imperious way he has. You know? Sounds more like the President than the President?"

James had plucked the *we* from her words and was smiling weakly. "No matter. Half an hour couldn't get me over to Alexandria and back."

"You could have freshened up at my place."

"Your place?"

"You're not the only one who's involved in secret stuff. I've taken an apartment on M Street." The light changed and she shifted smoothly forward.

"Speaking of the office"—which, of course, they hadn't been—"how are things going?"

"W-e-e-e-l. If you insist. It's a disaster. There's a WAC corporal and two WAVES doing the filing, or rather trying to do the filing. I'm there till eight or nine every night typing form responses. But there are more papers coming in each day than it's humanly possible to handle or find space for. In addition, there is a constant stream of phone calls from the War Production Board, the War Labor Board, the War Manpower Commission, the War Shipping Administration, the Office of War Mobilization, Office of Defense Transportation, not to mention Henderson at OPA, the DPC, BEW, OWI . . . should I go on?" Her voice rose a note with each rendition, and still she had sung only a partial scale of the wartime bureaucracy. "And they all want to speak with you. All of them want to know exactly how our office changes their jurisdictions and functions, and I don't honestly know what to tell them. It looks to me as though we really *are* just duplicating a little piece of all of them."

"We're not really in full operation yet," James said flatly.

He could make out the White House ahead on the left. The two sat in silence again. She swung across Pennsylvania Avenue and through the east gate, where a guard looked in, smiled and waved her straight toward the South Portico. James said, looking back over his shoulder, "Funny. I never get that sort of treatment around here."

"You're a VIP. I'm just one of the help." Her annoyance had become stronger still and rose to just below the surface. They arrived at the entrance, and May said, "See you tomorrow morning, Major."

As James picked up his briefcase and ducked out of the car, he realized that it was the first time since he'd met May Fielding that he'd felt even slightly uncomfortable with her. He said, "Something bothering you, Captain?"

She nodded and replied, "It'll keep till morning, Major."

James said, "In the morning then," and pushed the door closed behind him rather strongly.

One of a battery of Presidential aides, Bill Hassett was the one FDR called "my all-around man." That meant he had to be everything the President needed or wanted on demand, from chief clerk and record keeper to trouble shooter and *ad hoc* ambassador to the Hill. Tonight he would be in his office until well after 1 A.M. readying outlines of the President's new legislative package, trial balloons that Hassett would float over to the offices of Speaker of the House Sam Rayburn and Senate Majority Leader Alben Barkley the next morning. They'd know precisely how to handle things over there. "No, you never get into a bad-smell contest with Congress if you can help it, and Hassett and my congressional people know how to keep the air fresh," FDR had once told Jimmy.

James watched from the uncomfortable straight-backed chair alongside the President's closed door as Hassett carefully collated eight neat piles on his desk. The work was not exactly automatic, and the weary James, watching with a curious detachment, realized there were probably slight differences in the various copies going out. Hassett penciled light marks in the corners of certain sheets. Here, James thought, was exactly the man to record and maintain the documents of the Roosevelt years. In fact, he realized, the small office had taken on the aspect and atmosphere of a museum—the dim light of a Regency lamp, the perfect variety and blend of early American furniture, unbroken walls of alphabetized books and filing cabinets.

"You're sure the President wanted me immediately, Bill?" It had been twenty-five minutes. Hassett didn't make mistakes.

He said, "He's got someone in there. Pertains to you."

Then James lapsed into a bit of a funk. Satisfying images of his father's approval clashed with imagined scenes of a bitter misunderstanding with May Fielding. Then Bill Hassett was leaning over him saying, "Jimmy, he wants you in there now."

James had not fully collected his thoughts when he entered the oval room, but he stepped in quickly and gave the natural impression that he had come a very long distance at great personal effort. He expected his father to comment immediately on his ragged, impressive appearance, but he did not.

FDR was in his wheelchair drawn a few feet back from his desk, the position he usually assumed when he'd been listening, and James understood from his general demeanor that he had just received some important information. His body was tipped to one side, and he propped up his jutting jaw with a hand rolled into a loose fist. He wore the tattered maroon sweater. The room smelled strongly of cigarette smoke and perspiration. "Seems," the President said without moving, "as though you've been cavorting with traitors, Major Roosevelt."

Indeed FDR had been gathering information, and James realized that the source of it was in some important way related to FAMILY MATTER. Ordinarily, he would have to sit back and wait to be told, in FDR's own good time, whatever morsels of information the President offered. FDR had developed the galling technique of holding back information in precisely the way other men in power use threats.

Since his father had coyly "Majored" him, James responded grumpily from a less-respectful distance. "Pa, I'm dog-tired and could use a good hot bath and eight hours' sleep, so I'm not really in the mood to be toyed with. If you'd like my report, I'd be more than glad . . ." The fact that his father was beaming unrelievedly made it impossible for James to continue. Both men knew that when FDR was inclined to tease his son, irritability only prolonged the operation. James took the only course open to him—capitulation. This man had the power to exasperate him as no one else in the world could. James dropped his briefcase, pulled off his coat, and dropped silently into the chair in which the President's recent informant had been sitting.

"That's the ticket, Jimmy. When in doubt, sit it out—an old Roosevelt family strategy in certain circumstances. Now tell me, who is this Ishmael fellow who seems to have emerged as our number one annoyance?"

Whatever information had preceded his son's entrance, the pleasure it gave FDR revealed itself in the tone of his question. But James felt his face elongate; he feared that his dumbest expression was beginning to impose itself. And he blanked. *Ishmael*—damn it, he knew that name. *Ishmael*. But his weariness saved him some embarrassment, for he was simply too tired to try to bluff or stall, tactics he might have tried had he been fresher. "You know, Pa, when the time comes, I'm sure you'll manage to beat the Devil."

FDR said, "And the best thing is that it's all done behind this benevolent, patriarchal face the world—well, a healthy majority of Americans, at least—could never imagine masked such cunning." FDR's smile deepened. "Don't," he advised his son, "don't underestimate the things that can be done behind two rows of regular white teeth and a strong chin. This Ishmael matter, for example—"

A loud, persistent buzzer began in double bursts and irregular intervals. Then muffled sirens wailed outside, and through the window the two men in the office could begin to see the lights of Washington going out in patterned sections. On the mantel the small clock in the hull of the S.S. *Farragut* began to chime the hour. The lights in the room dimmed to a glow. "The shades, Jimmy," FDR directed. The Oval Office was secured for the air raid drill.

"Let's see. We were discussing Ishmael, *Colonel* Ishmael, to be more precise . . ."

Ah, the title—the military rank that his father had withheld—that made it clear now. "General Groves's security man," James blurted like a student still trying to get credit for a correct answer. Almost immediately he detested his lack of control. *Always*, he thought, *always boxes within boxes within . . .*

"None other."

"*He's* been here to see you?"

"No, no, of course not. But Groves has been. At this Colonel's insistence, it seems, to deliver a rather fretful plea of some sort. Claims there's a precipitous threat to the MANHATTAN PROJECT. What seems most significant about his sudden request for a meeting with me is its timing. Appears as though he's afraid you've come up with something he could be ashamed of and didn't want to get caught hiding."

James said nothing, but he was feeling both less fatigued and a more necessary part of what was unfolding.

FDR winced, lifted one hip, and placed it carefully down in a different spot. His days were spent in such minute physical adjustments. He rolled his large head in a great, slow circle and said, "Would you mind, Jimmy?" The special shrug he gave meant that as weary as James might be, his father was probably in greater need of relief.

James rose in the half-light and stepped behind FDR's wheelchair. He rested the palms of his hands heavily on the old man's neck muscles; the tips of his massaging fingers reached down to the collarbone. The long fingers moved, stiffly at first, up and down as the cupped palms worked laterally. FDR uttered a soft sound of deep, controlled need and satisfaction. After a moment he said, amid pauses during the moments when the son's hands squeezed him to silence, "And have you come up with anything Groves could be ashamed of? If you've accomplished nothing else, I think you've at least made him wash his hands."

Now it was the son who shifted his weight from one leg to the other as he said, "Tell me what Groves said to you, and then I'll tell you the truth of the matter."

"Well, for openers, he told me that this Ishmael fellow has —oh, there, that's where it's knotted—has uncovered a spy ring. Claims to have had them under surveillance for almost six months. Russian. Guess he was worried we had the same information and naturally assumed that was why you suddenly showed up. Didn't want us to think he wasn't doing his job. He wanted me to be sure to know they had matters very much under control. What do you think?"

"Spy ring." Doubt struck the dominant tone in James's response. Frisch was certainly cynical and despondent, and Oppenheimer, Fermi, Szilard and Einstein were full of very deep reservations about proceeding, but *spy ring!* Would they have been so candid about their dissatisfaction had they been already undermining the project for six months?

Preposterous! "Pa, I've talked to the top men out there. They've got lots of doubts and gripes about the project, the way it's being run, even the need for it at this point, but I'd bet my bottom dollar they're not Russian spies."

"When I asked Groves for names, he tried to bluff me. Imagine, bluff me. I'm afraid I had to get a little rough with him. There was barely a dry spot on his uniform when I was finished. Names are on my desk. They're not the top people. I've already checked."

James took a step backward and glanced at three names printed on a small unlined piece of paper: "FUCHS, SOBELL, ROSENBERG." James was puzzled—none of the names was at all prominent.

"Know them?"

"No, Pa."

"Didn't think so. One is a very junior physicist, an Englishman transferred over from Harwell. The other is a low-level engineer. And the third isn't even assigned to the project—I'm still having Hassett check the name out. What do you make of it, Jimmy?"

"Nothing very much, Pa. Probably a fishing expedition: these security people have to justify themselves somehow, and one way is to discover spies every once in a while. I came up with something very different, something very helpful."

FDR emitted a sound that indicated, *Let's hear but continue with the massage*. He opened the top buttons of his shirt and pulled at his sweater so James's fingers could press the uneasy flesh directly.

"Well, Groves was not at all what you'd call cooperative. On the basis of what you've told me just now, I can see why. But he might have a bigger problem on his hands than a Russian spy ring. He might not even have a bomb in the first place. There really is a house revolt in the making among the very top people—Frisch, Fermi, Szilard, even Einstein. Did he mention anything about that?"

"Not word one."

"It seems that the closer they get—and they're pretty darned close now—the less certain these people are about the need or the wisdom of continuing. That's one thing." He expected a response; there was none. "The other side of the coin, the important side for FAMILY MATTER, is that their reluctance means we're really coming very close to a bomb."

"Jimmy, I've heard too much of that sort of talk before. 'Anytime now.' 'Brink of a breakthrough.' And we still don't have anything but rumors."

"Pa, I'm certain. Fermi's controlled pile worked in Chicago, and that proved it was feasible. Einstein let it all slip out. He told me the bomb was now a task for engineers and technicians, said it could be made if all the physicists packed up and left tomorrow. It's true. Trust my judgment, Pa."

"How long?"

"I'd estimate six, eight months at the outside. Possibly sooner."

The sound of his own excitement embarrassed him, especially since he didn't feel his father's body respond with an energetic pulse of belief. In fact, the lack of a reaction caused the tired James to become slightly more combative. "There's more. I believe I've discovered the best possible way to get our hands on any of the atomic information you might want. Secretly. Safely. And it's neither a rumor nor an abstraction." James felt his father's shoulder quiver. "If he can be convinced it is being done in the name of maintaining world peace after the war is over, I believe Professor Einstein himself could be made to act as a clearinghouse for us, to turn over whatever technical information we might need. He could easily be convinced that it is too late to stop the bomb but that the next best thing would be to share the secrets with certain of our Allies." The phrase *like taking candy from a baby* leapt into his mind, but James was ashamed to utter it.

FDR rubbed the last joint of a forefinger slowly back and

forth across his upper lip. He was so deep in thought, he hadn't been aware that James had lifted his hands off the loosened neck muscles and returned to his seat. Even though he had always realized that luck was often the residue of careful planning, it was not easy for Franklin Roosevelt to accept the fact that so much sheer good fortune seemed to have attached itself so quickly to FAMILY MATTER. But such appeared to be the case.

"So you say you're relatively certain we can have safe access through Einstein to any technical information we may need?"

"Right. But I've held off until I cleared things with you."

"Then let's say, just pure supposition, of course, that I wanted to use a tidbit of this information to strike some sort of bargain with Uncle Joe—how precisely would I go about it?"

James raised his eyebrows and shrugged. "Usual method, I should think. Acquire the papers from Professor Einstein and simply arrange a delivery at some prearranged place with couriers."

FDR thought for a moment. "Do you have anyone in mind for the job?" James smiled broadly. "But let's continue this little hypothetical tale. Let us assume that the Tartar receives the, oh, let's say a set of blueprints, what is the first thing he does then?"

An involuntary stammer laid James open. "Wh-why, I assume he begins with the terms of whatever agreement you've made with him."

"Wrong. Oh, no, not that, not by a long shot. The first thing any of us do is to check the accuracy of the information. We may be Allies, but we're not fools and we're very cautious bedfellows. We first check the information with our espionage people. Remember when I said we'd have to let the Tartar steal the secrets? Well, Colonel Ishmael's little spy ring conveniently offers us a double protection. First, it lets Uncle Joe check whatever information we may give him.

Second, if anyone were actually to stumble on our activities, we would have a disreputable band of Red agents to offer up. So, you see, it's in our interests that they be allowed to continue operating."

James frowned at the naked cynicism of his father's final statement. "Jimmy," FDR snapped, "for heaven's sake, try to realize what's at stake here. We haven't the luxury of the fine ethical distinctions they make in philosophy classes. This is as real a part of the war as those shells you were so fond of dodging in the Pacific. We are talking about trying to control a weapon that may eventually destroy the human race. So let's get down to basics: what do you want to do with this Colonel? Groves has been scared witless with the dressing down I've given him, so we won't have to be worrying too much about him. Do you think his security man can be controlled, or should we simply replace him?"

"I can't really answer that, Pa. I haven't been able to size him up. He's practically an unknown quantity as far as I'm concerned." Then James remembered the shadowy figure he had seen removing the recording machine from Hans Bethe's automobile. Whoever this Colonel Ishmael was, he knew a great deal indeed. Replacement would certainly be the cleaner, easier solution, but James said, "If we move out the man who discovered a spy ring, it might look a little queer should word leak out." Something within him seemed to be accepting the unstated challenge of that strange, dark Colonel.

"Suit yourself, Jimmy. He's in Washington. Came East with Groves. Staying at the Mayflower. Why don't you pay him a little visit and see how well he fits into our plans."

"Okay, Pa."

The silent moment that followed was terminated by the all-clear sirens calling the lights on in sections eastward into Virginia. The White House buzzers sounded, and the lights in the office flickered and came all the way up. James stood and took a step toward the shades. "Better just leave them,

Jimmy. But while you're up, open the closet next to the bookcase." James walked over and opened the narrow closet door. It was empty except for a large safe on the floor. "Took five men to get it in this morning. It's foolproof, and only I have the combination. And now you have the combination." He offered his son a small piece of paper. "You see, I fully expected you to bring home the bacon, Jimmy. In truth, I didn't expect you to bring it home quite so fast or looking the way you do, but give me some credit—I *do* know how to pick my people."

James looked down at the paper in his hand. He was moved by his father's words and demonstration of confidence.

"Destroy it after it's been memorized. This is still very much a family matter. But I need some time to think about our next move; things have been happening too fast since you left. Tell Hassett to put you down for ten A.M. tomorrow. And, Jimmy, if you really need the words, you've done a first-rate job."

Still the boxes within boxes, James thought.

Then there was nothing to say.

In the taxi that drove him over to his barracks in Virginia, James resolved to make his visit to the mysterious Colonel Ishmael a grand, early-morning surprise. Utterly forgotten was his promise to talk things over with May Fielding.

Chapter

12

For many hours after the taxi had deposited Major Roosevelt at the officers' barracks at the base, all the lights in room 912 of the Mayflower Hotel burned brightly. A tiny beetle-browed man, whose height was actually three-quarters of an inch below the Army's wartime minimum, paced the red carpet in polished leather slippers. He muttered to himself as he moved crisply back and forth before a small table that held a portable typewriter. Then he turned abruptly, sat down, and began furiously striking at the keys. Sitting in pressed flannel pajamas before his typewriter, he was a man transformed.

If it hadn't been for some letters an aunt had passed on to a maid and the zealousness of that good woman in finding their rightful owner, Colonel Gregory Ishmael might never have been able to document his family's heroism, especially his father's daring raid on Rostov. The attack had been the most remarkable maneuver that the White Army would manage during the entire war against the Bolsheviks; nothing General Kornilov or Admiral Kolchak, the most famous of the anti-Red leaders, ever attempted could match General Vassily Ishmaelevskiy's courage and tactical brilliance.

The Ishmaelevskiy name had been notable for centuries in Russia; in America it was trifled with and dissected to "Ishmael" and still thought rather odd. But Colonel Gregory Ishmael's book, fifteen years in the making, would change that accident of history. After all, there was a good deal of misinformation about the civil war in Russia that needed rectification, especially now that the propaganda agencies were making the Bolsheviks seem so benevolent and brave. But, ah, there was at least that glorious attack on Rostov.

His memories were not exclusively of the war, of raids and skirmishes and slaughters. There were recollections of earlier days with the family. Gentle, pleasanter days. In the sitting room with his older sisters and their gentlemen; of interminable hours of religious training with Father Markov; of formal dinners with dozens of well-dressed aristocrats seated around the polished table and always his father at the head, tall and elegant, always with a smile in the eyes when they caught Grigor examining him. Memories of the great sprawling house on the Dnieper near Smolensk. He could, even in the steam-heated stuffiness of the Mayflower's room 912, reproduce the odor of the peasants' barley fields when the wind came off the river, and of his pony's stall. Colonel Gregory Ishmael now reached up and patted the air reflexively as though to pat his horse's neck. Memory had given way to reverie, and each image he retrieved pulled with it half a dozen others.

Writing and continually rewriting his father's history anchored his mind. The act of recreating that glorious evening of the raid and the week-long forced march that led up to it provided him with a continuity of purpose. The tiny man in the pressed pajamas sat back from the typewriter with eyes closed tight, feet out, arms on the carved chair rest, head thrown back. He saw his father on his horse stepping into the murky waters of the Don, the first of nine hundred men —some swimming, some horsemen, some on rafts they had made—to cross north of Rostov so as to approach the city from the unprotected west. Ishmael roused himself and typed furiously again for about half an hour. It was almost 2 A.M. when he rested.

He had composed the scene dozens of times before. Each time he recalled something new. This time it was how, from his position in the rear, he saw the silent advance of his father's soldiers in the moonlight across the newly cut wheat fields. The sudden, swift success of the raid, a total surprise, he had recorded before, but the slovenly cowardice of the Red defenders he hoped to capture even more perfectly this time. The world should know this. Must know this.

Now, his eyes closed, he saw his father at sunrise, standing tall at the central square of Rostov before the mounted statue of Alexander II. General Ishmaelevskiy was ordering the execution of ten Bolsheviks, criminals all, murderers of defenseless families. The men were crying and retching.

The counterattack came later that day; the entire Red garrison had been sent up from Novocherkassk. Outnumbered 5 to 1, General Ishmaelevskiy rallied his men brilliantly. Not until two other Red regiments with much artillery arrived was it certain that the city would be recaptured.

On the night before the final, hopeless battle, the General ordered Major Zdovskev away with Grigor. Gregory Ishmael, slumping back in his seat again, warm tears on his cheek, thought he felt the final embrace, the stab of his father's collar medallion against his hairless cheek. The last time he ever saw his father. Nor did he ever again see his mother, sisters, aunts, uncles—anyone who carried the name Ishmaelevskiy. Dead. Lost. Finished, along with Russia. To retrieve them—that was the purpose of his book.

But, of course, the struggle was deeper. In Ishmael's mind the two roles—historian of the White cause and Colonel in charge of MANHATTAN PROJECT security—were not unrelated. The second had become for him a clear continuation of the first. He was sure that his vigilance would make a significant difference.

He pulled the typed page out of the machine and placed it neatly in a manila folder thick with similar pages. Then he loaded another sheet and began a brief, factual biography: "Gregory V. Ishmael, Colonel, Army Security Agency. Attached office Brig. Gen. Leslie R. Groves, command unit, special venue, Santa Fe, N. Mex. Born: Smolensk, Russia, 16 July 1903. U.S. Citizen: Providence, R.I. 3 October 1922 . . ." Again he stopped. Again his eyes clouded over. Even such a cold compilation as this brief professional biography triggered memories of all the things that had been lost. He decided to finish it in the morning.

"Get 'em where they live. Go get 'em alone. And get there early." The dictum had come from his father and was of the same vintage as his briefcase. It came, in fact, when FDR, as undersecretary of the Navy, had broken a lockout at the East Coast shipyards. His father didn't tell the story much any more, but there had been a time when it was a tactic he always used successfully whenever he was having problems with a troublesome and powerful individual. The trick was to show up unannounced at the troublemaker's home, never the office or a restaurant, very early in the morning, usually before breakfast and before the opponent had set himself for the day's business. "Gives you a heck of an edge, Jimmy. Throws the other fellow right off balance, and it's just a matter of timing. You set the rules and the tone," was how his father had explained the technique. It seemed to James the perfect follow-up for Colonel Ishmael. He'd be telephoning Ishmael in his room at the Mayflower at around seven forty-five tomorrow morning—from the reception desk downstairs! James's lips moved as he practiced, "I'll be up directly, Colonel." He smiled tightly as he closed his eyes.

At 7:24 A.M. the lobby of the venerable old Mayflower Hotel was listless even though a brave veneer of mauve-colored paint was supposed to convey the impression of renewed charm and youthfulness. Perhaps later in full daylight the illusion might work better, but the dank heaviness of the winter morning seemed to have rolled through the revolving doors and colored the lobby gray even before Major Roosevelt, looking very determined, arrived.

The newspaper clerk was slowly arranging the morning's papers. A bellboy stepped off the elevator with a suitcase and moved at half-speed toward the desk, where a tall young man leaned over the counter with a pen placed over his lips. A plate fell somewhere but did not smash; it rang itself to eventual silence. James had the bracing feeling of launching a sneak attack on an unsuspecting enemy, once again a Raider, but this time holding all the advantages.

He hadn't slept very well or very long, but that didn't matter. He was braced by a night of planning, improvising. He carried no sense that confronting Colonel Ishmael directly and alone might be a mistake. The seriousness with which he approached the desk caused the clerk to draw back, as though avoiding a taxi in the street. "You have a Colonel Ishmael, I-S-H-M-A-E-L" was all James said; it wasn't a question. He tapped the breast pocket of his uniform just below his campaign ribbons; it was an unplanned gesture but suddenly seemed right to him, the way an inspired piece of stage business comes to an actor.

"Yes . . . sir." The implication of the pause was "anything you'd like, Major." And he was off to a file alongside the mail slots. "That'll be 912, sir."

"I'd like to see his registration." This, too, was no question.
"Certainly, sir."

The card read: "Col. Ishmael, Gregory V., Santa Fe, N.

Mex." Roosevelt's eyes ran back over the spare information. "Santa Fe" told him a little; the "V" piqued his interest. "I'd like to phone the Colonel's room," he announced.

The clerk pulled out a large black telephone from under the counter. "Just dial 0-1 and then the room number." He glanced at the card—"9-1-2, sir." The static on the line gave way to an echoing ring.

The voice was distant but composed. "Ishmael here."

"Colonel. Major Roosevelt. I'm downstairs. It may be a bit early for you but—"

"Nonsense, Major." The voice became suddenly cheerful. "Nonsense. It was inevitable we get together sooner or later. I was hoping for sooner. I've already ordered some coffee. Come on up."

"I'll be up directly, Colonel," James said with unnecessary authority: it was done more for the benefit of the clerk, who had been shuffling cards and listening.

The slow response and ascent of the elevator enabled James to evaluate and adjust. Ishmael's obvious confidence and ability to shift gears so smoothly bothered him. There was even the vague thought that his visit might have been expected. But smooth and clever as the response was, it was a forced response. And James had forced it.

At precisely the moment he brought his knuckles up to tap just below the brass numerals, the door opened. Colonel Ishmael, immaculate in pressed gabardine shirt and pants, tie folded perfectly away between second and third buttons, belt buckle and shoes agleam, stood compact and erect before James Roosevelt. There was a brief, frozen moment of eye contact. And James was struck again by how short his adversary was and by a thick brow that thinned only slightly across the bridge of the nose. Not at all an imposing physical presence. James straightened and squared himself.

"Ah, Major. Come in, come in. I like your timing. I'm a morning person. Always have been. The morning's really the right time for dealing with . . . complexities." Colonel

Ishmael paused, creating a silence that his guest might want to fill with an explanation of how he came to be standing in the doorway at—the mantle clock read seven thirty-four. James let the void remain.

Finally, Ishmael backed into the room and with a sweep of his arm made an invitation to enter. "I've packed already," he announced, pointing with his chin toward a briefcase and a small leather satchel resting at the foot of the bed. His typewriter was still on the desk. "Anxious to get back to work." The strangely accented words, the sibilant hissing of breath between sentences, created a vaguely enigmatic mood.

James still said nothing. His presence was his advantage.

"But you are here, are you not, for some clarification?" Colonel Ishmael pivoted and wavered slightly as he spoke; he seemed just the slightest bit vulnerable, and one of his hands pointed in the direction of a striped chair that was angled before the desk, and James almost said, "No, thank you, Colonel." He avoided the error by reminding himself that one didn't take the trouble to surprise an adversary early in the morning and then thank him for the offer of a chair. Nor did you, in any way, acknowledge his superiority of rank. *You are the President's son. Use it.* He left the Colonel's offer unacknowledged.

A soft tap on the door came from a waiter, a light-skinned Negro with white hair. He carried a tray of coffee and buns and slid silently between the two men. James noticed the *two* cups. The waiter placed the tray on the bed table while Ishmael fumbled for change in his pocket as James stood stock-still. The Colonel was deciding whether to give the man two nickels or three when he said, "Have you ever seen the motion picture *La Grande Illusion*, Major Roosevelt?" As the waiter heard the Major's name and caught the facial resemblance, his eyes widened. He'd sure have something to tell them at home tonight. He closed the hand around two nickels, bowed slightly, and backed out the door. His eyes never left Roosevelt.

"I haven't come here to talk about motion pictures. Last night General Groves indicated to the President that you assured him a plot was brewing around our A-bomb project. That's a pretty damned important piece of information. So serious, in fact, that I'd like to know exactly what you have. I'd also like to know why I wasn't informed of it when I was out there last week?"

"Precisely why I mentioned *La Grande Illusion,* Major. There is a scene in it that reminds me very much of this meeting. The one in which a German officer tries to convince a captured French officer that as officers and cultivated gentlemen they have much in common despite the mere happenstance of the war that temporarily separates them. An antidemocratic, somewhat patrician notion, no doubt, but I am, for some reason or other, reminded of that scene now."

"I thought our uniforms made it very clear that we were on the same side in this war, Colonel Ishmael." He wished he hadn't mentioned Ishmael's rank.

"Of course, of course they do, *Major.*" Ishmael emphasized the final word.

The little man's smile offended Roosevelt. He would have liked to thrust a fist into those curling lips, a quick, stabbing blow that drew blood. But Ishmael, he knew, would never relinquish that smile. "I'm here to clarify some statements you made last night." Still Ishmael smiled. "I will tell you honestly and directly that the answers you give me now will determine whether or not you retain your position on this project. Perhaps even your career is at stake."

The smile bowed into a slightly defensive smirk. His dark eyes began to burn like an admonished child's. He nodded.

"Now tell me all about this plot to give away our atomic secrets."

"I have documented—exchanges." That was all Ishmael intended to say for the moment. James reminded himself how much was at stake and stared directly into the bright, dark eyes. He resisted even the urge to shift his weight. He felt his nostrils flare. It was Ishmael who broke the gaze.

The silence, which had begun as an absence, was now a presence in the room. Ishmael moved first, flicking a limp hand at the air in front of him. He cleared his throat. His face displayed his deepest resentment. It was clear that control of his investigation was about to be taken away from him. Clear that this liberal upstart who controlled his future and was making no bones about it wouldn't be put off or outflanked this morning. But that wasn't the only source of resentment; there was also the accident of birth that gave this Major authority over a colonelcy achieved through merit. His resentment burned and announced to James, wordlessly, that sometime in the future, somewhere, in some way or other, there would be a retribution. So he was forced to elaborate on his last word—"exchanges."

"My surveillance has produced evidence of exchanges— written and spoken communications that indicate there are individuals in the program who plan to give our secrets to the Russians."

"Names. I want their names."

"Fuchs, an Englishman in Theoretical. He has made contact with certain known Russian agents in New York, Chicago and other places. Also one Morton Sobell, an engineer, and his contacts in New York, a husband and wife named Rosenberg. At this point only verbal information has been passed. I have been waiting for an appropriate time to move. No damage has been done thus far."

"Whose idea was it to finally inform the President?"

"Why, General Groves's, of course."

"And that is *all* the information you have on espionage activity?"

"Personally, I believe the security problem with the British project at Harwell and with the Canadians to be even greater, but this is what I am responsible for specifically at Los Alamos. Of course, after the first bomb is tested, the list of potential traitors will quadruple and will probably reach into the upper echelons of the project."

"I don't have time to indulge in speculations with you this morning. The people you have named have been known to us for over a year and have been under the strictest surveillance by us." Ishmael could not control the mixture of surprise and disappointment that leapt to his face. A security man's greatest fear—that another agency, the FBI for example, had been in on an operation—was always present and very easy to take advantage of. Since an Ishmael saw plots everywhere, James simply handed him this new world of possibilities. "Under no circumstances are you to go meddling into this thing on your own." The word "meddling" came down on Ishmael like the Red counterattack that had broken his father's army.

James said, "Should you continue in your position, Colonel, you will be required to send all security reports to the President through my office on a regular basis. Your surveillance can continue, but it will only be in the nature of a backup or corroboration. Do you understand?"

The trace of a smirk had already returned to Ishmael's lips. He swallowed, closed his eyes and nodded.

"My own investigation into the entire program is far from complete. I do not want it jeopardized by your gumshoeing. And, needless to say, Colonel, I do not wish to be followed, recorded, or in any way impeded by you or your people. Is that also clearly understood?"

The gall of listening to this tone coming from a junior officer was almost too much to bear. Ishmael smiled and said, "Major, I would not presume to take such liberties . . ." What he obviously left unstated was ". . . *with the son of the President of the United States.*"

"But that is what you have done already, Colonel. And I

want to tell you I didn't enjoy having my conversations re-corded, not one little bit. There'll be no more of that busi-ness either." James's final trump.

Colonel Ishmael was forced into a nod; his eyes were more hurt and vengeful than ever.

"Fine. Then I see no reason why we cannot work together in containing any threat to security that may arise." James did not quite keep the sarcasm out of his voice.

The slightest of twitches—a sustained quiver across the cheekbone—was on the Colonel's face.

James, his expression impassive, had begun to enjoy the heady feeling of attack, especially when a cunning adversary had been forced to give ground so completely. "I've a very busy day ahead of me, so I'll pass on the coffee this morning."

Ishmael turned and stepped swiftly over to the type-writer, from which he pulled a sheet of paper. "Major Roose-velt, anticipating all eventualities, I took the liberty earlier this morning of preparing a condensed biography, a *curriculum vitae*, so to speak. Such things are helpful in transfer decisions."

James took the sheet, folded it neatly into quarters, and placed it in the breast pocket of his uniform. "That's about all I have, Colonel. If there's anything you would like to ask me . . ." Roosevelt left the request open-ended so it would not sound like a legitimate offer.

"Nothing to ask, Major. You have made things quite clear."

The elderly white-haired waiter was in the elevator when Major Roosevelt stepped on. He gaped openly. James was unaware of the inspection this time. His thoughts were ex-clusively of Ishmael, of how he had prepared that thumbnail biography in anticipation of James's visit, as though he had expected the possibility of a transfer. James didn't under-stand why this made him feel so uncertain. Maybe his father was right; maybe it would be a good idea to have the subtle little man replaced. The FAMILY MATTER mission was, after all, completely in James's hands now—at least the legwork and its implementation. He saw in his mind the dark, enigmatic face, the lips in that almost perpetual half-smirk. But he chased the image and the unwarranted uncertainty away as the elevator arrived at the lobby with a little bounce.

Chapter

13

LISTENING TO the typing and humming in the outer office, to the telephone ringing and to the sliding of file drawers, James felt as comfortable as he had ever since leaving Makin. Even the weather had turned encouraging, clear and crisp. If his next meeting with his father went as he expected, he would probably be taking the next, most concrete, step in FAMILY MATTER very shortly. That safe in his father's office had made the whole enterprise very tangible, very real. He smiled at the thought, shaking his head in disbelief: *It's really just a simple matter of filling it up with illicitly obtained top-secret documents!*

To make the morning even more enjoyable, he actually had a legitimate piece of work to do. It was a letter to Henry J. Kaiser, the shipbuilder, requesting a temporary transfer to the Navy of a dozen of his company's barges in the Baltimore yard to be used for the summer landings in France; because it was an urgent need for OVERLORD and because it was so straightforward a request, it was a pleasure.

"Captain Fielding," he called, having eliminated the

buzzer when he wanted to see her, "may I see you for a moment?" He sealed the handwritten note and stamped it "Top Secret."

She was in the doorway, smiling coldly; her eyes were frozen on him. James remembered then the unstated and unresolved problem she had raised in the car from the railroad station.

James said, "If you have some free time, Captain, I thought we might get whatever's been ailing you out in the open." He was glad he had remembered.

May Fielding scowled, "I'm not sure I like the way you put that, Major. Your 'ailing you' seems to strike the wrong note. Maybe we'd better wait."

James, using the cajoling tone his father had long ago mastered but not quite hitting the mark with it, said, "Why don't you just let that chip fall off your shoulder and sit down. After all, you *are* among friends."

May closed the door firmly behind her and brought a chair alongside his desk. "I'd like to believe that, Major. In fact, I accepted the position here with that as an unstated premise. But the evidence seems very much to refute it now."

"Specifically?"

"Specifically, the fact that there's something funny going on in this office, and I feel like a complete fool being left in the dark about it. Oh, I know all about the stiff-upper-lip business and giving your unquestioned loyalty to the home team, but this is absolutely ridiculous."

"Specifically," James said again, drumming his fingers silently on the edge of his desk.

"Well, for openers, this office has no legitimate function. It's a cover setup if I've ever seen one, and so patently so I could scream. Now, if I thought"—her voice became a whisper—"if I thought for a single moment the cover-up was for the reasons Hearst's been spewing, my request for transfer would have been on your desk days ago." Her cheeks glowed with excited challenge.

"But what makes you think that's not the reason?"

"It's not. I know you well enough to be able to tell something like that."

"Your woman's intuition?"

"My intelligence. That's not the point. I don't like the idea of being used, especially when I've the highest military security clearance—"

James interrupted again: "not to mention your OSS training."

May Fielding's eyes narrowed. "Precisely. *Not* to mention my OSS training."

James saw his options. He could deny everything straight out, attribute it to an overactive imagination on her part, and be sweetly forgiving. That way, he'd lose her. He could, of course, invent another espionage scheme and by degrees bring her into its machinations; that way, at least, he would hold on to her. Could even call it OPERATION SCHEHERAZADE. But he'd have to stall until he had more time to think of a secretive but believable justification for the existence of the office as a cover. The one thing he could not do and still keep the "family" in FAMILY MATTER was to tell her the truth.

"May," he announced sincerely, this time hitting the mark exactly, "you're quite right, of course. I can't honestly deny anything you've said. This is, indeed, an office that duplicates the work of dozens of other offices. In your words, a cover. And, no, it was not set up to keep me out of harm's way in the Pacific. I never doubted that you were bright, but your having seen through it so quickly is rather embarrassing. You should also know that I've hated keeping anything from you, but my own orders required it. And, I'm afraid, will require it until I can get you cleared to participate. I'll see what can be done about that immediately." The lie was so gentle and full of good intentions that it didn't even seem like a lie to him.

Captain Fielding wore the haughty expression of a skeptic who had just been proved correct. But his response didn't

170

completely satisfy her. "In that case," she said, "I've got a—I don't quite know what to call it—it's not exactly a proposal and even less a threat. At any rate, until you decide to let me know what's really going on here, I'm going to try my darnedest to find out for myself." She drew back slightly, waiting for a reaction.

"Fair enough. Just let's call that a sporting proposition." He thrust out his right hand.

She took it and said, "It's a deal, then. And I'd say that strange-looking little Colonel who dropped off that envelope a few minutes ago is a part of whatever is really going on around here."

James said only, "Colonel?" But he knew.

"I'll bring it in. It's marked 'Personal.' He just placed it on my desk and left. Didn't wait for a response. Didn't leave his name. Just handed it over and left like the Lone Ranger. Strange."

May retrieved the envelope from her desk and handed it to James. It was an odd size, small and square. When he opened it, the embossed card said.

THE FRENCH COMMITTEE OF NATIONAL LIBERATION

PRESENTS

AN EVENING OF CINEMA

La Grande Illusion

AND

DANCING WITH

Le Jazz Très Hot

AT THE FREE FRENCH MISSION—1250 INDIANA AVENUE

8 P.M.—DONATIONS TO THE COMMITTEE—8 P.M.

James handed the invitation to May. "There, does that look like a smoldering plot to you?" She shrugged. He smiled and said, "Now that I think about it, maybe we'd better show up at the place. I'm sure you'll want to look for spies in all the closets and under the rugs."

She handed the card back between second and third fingers as though she had just touched something unclean.

"Let's say seven-thirty. I'll pick you up. And I don't think dress uniform would be especially appropriate." May Fielding was composed and smiling broadly. Just then the intercom buzzed. A secretary's voice said, "Mrs. Roosevelt for you, sir."

James picked up the phone, expecting to hear Malvina Thompson, his mother's secretary, and was mildly surprised by Eleanor's voice. "Mr. A. Philip Randolph has just stood me up, and I feel terribly rejected. Why don't you come on over here and hold my hand, Jimmy."

He'd actually been intending to see her to find out something about her activities and travels. "Certainly, Mother. Where are you?"

"Where would I be? *Toujours* my office."

"Yes, of course. But which one? I just happened to have guessed right last time. The odds are against my being lucky twice in a row."

"Jimmy, don't tease. Second-floor sitting room."

There was an ease in his step as he walked up the old staircases and through the halls that stretched almost two hundred yards from one wing of the mansion to the other. As he walked, he realized that he looked forward to tonight, seeing the invitation from Ishmael as something a little more than merely an evening's entertainment, but, nevertheless, nothing to be upset about. And May Fielding, of course, was an unexpected bonus. So James felt comfortable with himself as he approached the door to his mother's office. At the door, however, the connection between his mother and Romelle reasserted itself, and he felt his body stiffen—a conditioned reflex.

This time all activity stopped when he entered; he had been expected. "Tommy" Thompson came toward him to take him to the inner door, and heads swiveled with his advance. A light tap on the closed door and the cheerful words, almost sung, from within, "That you, Jimmy?"

He answered her question with his tall presence in front of her desk; the faint smell of lilac again touched his nostrils. Her biography, he realized, ought to be called "Lilacs and Steel." She looked up from her letter writing, took off her glasses, which were attached to a colorfully beaded string around her neck, and let them fall into her lap. "My God, look at you. Did I tell you how good, how remarkably impressive you look in your uniform?"

"I don't remember offhand, Ma, but my guess is that you probably have."

"Well, you do, you really do. Tommy, some tea, in here, please," Eleanor said as her secretary left.

"Did you know, Ma, that according to an unimpeachable source, you have become the most traveled woman in the world?"

"And who, may I ask, held the previous record, and who is your unimpeachable source?"

"Record holder—Queen Mary. Unimpeachable source— Walter Winchell, on his Sunday radio program."

"Oh, Jimmy, hardly unimpeachable. In fact, he's eminently peachable." A blushing shyness that revealed itself only for the briefest of moments charmed the son. He recalled such rare moments from the past; it brought them immediately closer. And it was a very relaxed conversation they had, each updating the other on recent events and activities, the doings and whereabouts of the other children, future projects. James, of course, deceived her whenever necessary. But when he said, "You know, I'd like some of that tea after all," it indicated more than a simple request for tea.

No sooner had the tea been brought in when Eleanor changed the pleasant mood abruptly with a sigh. "There *is* a matter, Jimmy, with which I'd like your help."

She had promised not to interfere with Romelle, but she was a woman of deeply felt allegiances. James braced himself for a gratuitous lecture on his marriage and his irresponsible behavior. He knew his mother to be the kind of person who did not consider a rational attempt to persuade an act of interference. He flushed with sudden but mild anger: "Mother, as far as Romelle is concerned . . ."

Eleanor Roosevelt looked hurt; her face bore the expression of a sudden betrayal. "I had no such intention," she explained. "We have already spoken of that once. I've made my feelings very clear, I think, and it's over." She stopped and placed four spread fingers on her bosom, the thumb reached to her shoulder. The posture was one of wronged innocence.

"Sorry, Ma. Guess I'm feeling guilty about it." He didn't believe he was feeling guilty. Looking for something to do, he stirred his tea excessively.

"It's your father's health that worries me."

"But he looks better these days."

"He's the sort of man who can mask his true condition, but I know he's very, very run down. That's the reason these colds recur and linger on and on. And he hasn't been sleeping particularly well either. He's simply driving himself too hard, harder than ever before. And now he's circulating talk of a fourth term." She shook her head in mild bewilderment.

James said, "There are times when I see him and he looks fine, showing a bit of age and wear and tear naturally, but generally fine. He really does."

"And other times," countered Eleanor, "when he looks dreadful, like a man ten years older. He needs complete rest. He needs a physical examination. Everything, from A to Z. Complete. I'm starting a campaign for it and would like your support. Can I count on you, Jimmy?"

The son pulled up a trouser leg at the crease, crossed one leg over the other, and poised his teacup on his knee. He felt foolish having jumped the gun about Romelle and wondered how his mother would report the incident to her. "Of course I'll help, Ma. I think it's a darned good idea." He continued to stir silently.

His mother was placing her cup back in its saucer and looking intently at the liquid. She added softly, "And now, Jimmy, what's all this bother about Professor Einstein? Apparently, you've gotten him terribly upset."

James's first concern was for his teacup. His second was for masking his reaction. The expression of confusion that covered his face had a genuine source, but he edged it toward ignorance with little effort.

"You see, he's written me the strangest sort of letter. Its tone is quite unlike him—upset, anguished, even a little belligerent . . ." As she spoke, James's face took on a believable bewilderment. ". . . and he mentioned you in connection with problems on a large military project. Obviously something is going on I should know about. So what's it all about, Jimmy?"

The personal implications of her question fell on him heavily. FAMILY MATTER wasn't really much of a family matter at all, merely two Roosevelts and a distant German "cousin." He understood the poignant irony of Einstein's writing to Eleanor for help on ethical grounds. But James's qualms did not make him doubt in the least his role in the operation or his ability to navigate these murky family waters. The most effective deception, it seemed to him then, should have at least some basis in truth. "There's a Top Secret project about which the Professor is concerned, and legitimately so. It comes partially under the control of my office. I visited Professor Einstein, who had, you should know, originally argued in favor of the project but has since become dissastisfied. I took his recent recommendations under advisement. What, by the way, is the date of his letter to you?"

She didn't have the letter before her. But she put on her glasses anyway, squinted and looked over her shoulder toward the window. "The twelfth or thirteenth, I expect. I have it in my bedroom. Tommy could fetch it."

The falsehood seemed to form itself without great effort: "I've already gone to see Professor Einstein after that letter, and we've arrived at an acceptable compromise."

"You mean I needn't worry?"

He laughed his confident laugh and said, "I mean you needn't worry."

Her turn to be taken somewhat by surprise revealed itself by a catch in the voice and a confusion of the hands. "When I respond, will it impede your work in any way if I tell him that we've spoken and that you've told me his concerns have been dealt with? Or some such thing?"

"Seems like the best and most direct way, Ma."

Malvina Thompson knocked, stuck her head in and announced, "Mr. Randolph has just arrived, Mrs. Roosevelt."

Eleanor rose first and sighed, "Ah, will there ever be time, Jimmy? Will there ever?"

He almost said, *There never has been*. But he kissed her softly on the cheek and said, "It doesn't seem so, does it? By the way, when have you last had a physical examination yourself?"

She patted the back of his hand sweetly, almost condescendingly, he thought. "Good, good. It's nice to know you haven't forgotten my main concern—for your father."

Walking back toward the East Wing, he realized once again that his mother was a marvel. " 'Lilacs and Steel,' " he muttered, "Steel and Lilacs. I don't want to forget that title." But the main effect of the meeting was a slightly upsetting realization. Eleanor's connection with Einstein and May Fielding's conclusion that there was something covert she would try to discover—both formed a very discomforting coincidence. But there wasn't much he could do about them but bide his time and keep a low silhouette. Ishmael was another matter entirely: nothing random there; he was the kind that set booby traps. Still, the best defense would be the same: stay down and stay put.

He didn't notice the cozy charm of her new apartment because May Fielding had somehow found the time to get her hair cut. Her brand new page-boy threw James very much off balance; that might have been its purpose.

"Like it?" She fluffed the perfect, turned-under roll of rich red hair at her neck.

He didn't but only said, "It's going to take some getting used to."

As he and May walked toward it in the crisp night air, James recognized the "Free" French Mission as the old Buchanan Library. At the door two French ladies in identical tricolor feathered hats would accept nothing less as a donation than ten dollars each as an admission fee. May's scowl tightened. James paid with a twenty-dollar bill, smiling broadly. "A Roosevelt," he whispered to her, "has to look very magnanimous in public, but that certainly was steep."

"I know," she said, the faintest suggestion of a smile playing over her lips as they joined arms and the crowd following the red arrows to the auditorium. Even though most were speaking and stepping softly, the marbled floors and echoing acoustics produced a bubbling torrent of sound.

May looked up the Doric columns to the domed ceiling, a fresco of rosy-cheeked angels in a twined circle overlooked everything and everyone. The moviegoers were funneled through large oak doors and into the auditorium, a great salon with huge paintings of American Revolutionary War scenes in the style of Delacroix, with Washington's Army merely blue-coated versions of the immaculate red British. James observed some military uniforms in the noisy crowd, and those he noticed were, without exception, very high-ranking officers. Most of the other men wore blue serge suits, neatly striped, and their women's bare shoulders were draped in fur stoles. Hundreds of wooden folding chairs had been set up and a screen hung between two immense paintings of Washington in action: at the left, mapping strategy in his tent by candlelight; at the right, praying to God Almighty for victory at Saratoga.

Given the babble in the room, James decided to sit close to the sound speaker in the rear of the hall in case an echo made understanding too difficult. It was also a place where they weren't likely to be too easily noticed. The language heard around them was mostly French, and the people employing it all seemed very stylish. During the period when nothing was happening, May and James inspected the room. Finally he turned to her and said, "*Comment allez-vous, mademoiselle?*"

With perfect ease and inflection May responded: *Monsieur, j'ai mal de tête. Je voudrais aller chez moi.*" Her response caught Jimmy so off guard that he drew back in noncomprehension. "I said, 'I've got a headache and would really like to go home.' "

Before he could answer, one of the tricolor-hatted ladies was standing before the screen with her arms held high above her. Very slowly the roar in the great room died. When she spoke, her words rolled over one another; James could not even be absolutely sure which language she was speaking. May came to his aid. "French," she whispered, and translated. "She said they have collected more that five thousand dollars. And it will be sent directly to General de Gaulle in London. Then she said something I couldn't quite get and after that that ultimate victory is assured." That explained the shouts of "*Vive la France!*" and the applause that stayed in the room until long after the hands had stopped. "After the film there will be dancing right here and wine that has been donated for the occasion by M. Something-or-other. The director of the film, M. Renoir, is now living in America. He is here and will say a few words."

There was applause, this time more restrained, and a

tall, plump man replaced the mistress of ceremonies. Monsieur Renoir. He spoke in English and too softly to be heard very well in the rear, only a few phrases here or there: "Light the lamp of freedom . . . defeat this inhuman menace . . . perhaps the last war young men shall be asked to . . ." May was smiling tenderly, sadly, her lips tightly closed, her brow furrowed; it was an emotion she rarely allowed to show. James looked at her as the lights dimmed; he wished the protective feelings her face held were for him, but he felt pleasure in witnessing them nonetheless. He continued to look at her after the title and credits came on the screen; his gaze was only broken by the collective and disappointed "ahhh" in the room; the film had slipped off its track, but the problem was quickly corrected.

From the opening moments, when the two French officers, who had just been shot down by a WWI German ace, are captured and led to the officers' mess, the film took complete possession of James's attention. Given the impossible acoustics, the subtitles were the only way he could understand. Ironically, in the scenes where two aristocratic officers, Erich von Stroheim as the German and Pierre Fresnay as the Frenchman, spoke English, he heard very little, although the gestures told him all he needed.

For May, the film was all Jean Gabin. When his name first appeared, she leaned over and whispered, "Jean Gabin. I just love him. I think my headache's disappeared."

The film, which built subtly and steadily in mood from lighthearted prison camp banter to the most serious of philosophical matters, almost caused James to forget its chief significance to him: What was the message in the film that Ishmael wanted to relate? Within the first half-hour that question was replaced by one that ran broader and deeper: What really was the Grand Illusion of the title? The film itself never answered that question for him.

The lights came up too quickly. James closed his eyes and massaged them lightly with thumb and forefinger, his father's gesture. He needed a last moment to think. There was no ambiguity in what he perceived to be Ishmael's message: James may not have been a career officer but he was an American aristocrat. Just as Von Stroheim directed Fresnay as a fellow officer and a gentleman not to aid a prison camp escape, Ishmael asked for James's loyalty in controlling whatever problems developed at Los Alamos.

He blew some air lightly through rounded lips to relieve some of the tensions the film had created and whispered, "Quite a film, *ne c'est pas?*"

She was completely drained and answered weakly, "Quite."

The immediate transition from film to music was not an easy one for them to make, but not many others seemed to have a similar problem. There was already laughter in the room and the same low roar as earlier. White-jacketed Negro boys and elderly men were taking the folding chairs away; others were draping a huge tricolor over the movie screen; and still others were wheeling out a piano and setting drums for the band. Captain and Major finally had to relinquish their chairs to the expanding dance floor.

James considered leaving when May said, "You know dancing doesn't seem very appropriate after that. I could brew us up a very tasty pot of coffee." But just as they turned to leave, Colonel Gregory V. Ishmael stood directly in their path.

"I'm very glad you could make the showing this evening," the Colonel said softly, bringing his heels together silently. "I do hope you found it worth your while."

"Entertaining as well as informative, Colonel."

Ishmael seemed to peek around James's shoulder, prompting him to step aside and offer a grudging introduction: "Colonel Ishmael, this is Captain Fielding, my secr . . ."

"Your secretary, of course, and even more accurately, your trusted assistant, daughter and only child of General Fielding. I am, you see, cursed with this mind full of data regarding the military. If I may take the liberty of the place we are in, perhaps you will not greatly mind. *Enchanté, madamoiselle,*" he said, bending from the waist, placing the back of May's hand to his lips and looking up into her eyes through half-closed lids.

Her smile was sickly. The band started to play a jazz version of "The White Cliffs of Dover."

Colonel Ishmael's attention did not stay on her long. With a conspiratorial grin that could only be termed sly, he said, "Of course, it would be pleasant to discuss the film at some length, and perhaps we shall someday. But there is some information of which you may wish to be made aware. Major, your wife is in attendance this evening. I saw her a short while ago with the Loring woman." Only the confused look in his eyes was necessary to prompt an Ishmael explanation: "The one who writes the society column for the Hearst newspapers. They were, let me see—" he spun around slowly to examine the corners of the hall—"by the rear door when last I saw them. They are not there at the moment, however. Now I'm sure you'll both forgive me if I make my apologies. I shall be leaving for the West again tomorrow morning, Major, so I had better take my rest tonight." The two men exchanged a private glance. "Captain Fielding, it has been a genuine pleasure finally to have met you."

As he walked away, May drew closer to James, so close that her shoulder touched his, and she said softly, "He gives me the creeps. Reminds me of that horrible German in the movie."

"He gives everybody the creeps, May." James was slightly upset, feeling that Ishmael had taken the initiative away from him this evening. He just might have to get rid of the man after all.

"Who is he, anyway?"

"Just one of our charming security people. Come on. I'll take you home in a cab, if you don't mind."

"Mind? I'd love it. And there really is that hot coffee I told you about. And, Jim . . ."

"Yes?"

"Don't wait too long to decide to tell me what's really been going on around here, okay?"

He didn't answer. He took her arm, and they walked quickly in step toward the large oak doors. They swung sharply to the right in the marbled hallway and almost bumped into a babbling group of people clustered near the cloakroom. A willowy dark-haired woman in a green chiffon evening dress and pearls turned abruptly around. The woman and James froze, looked directly at each other. She seemed momentarily stunned; he nodded slightly. Colonel Gregory Ishmael stood with his coat on against the wall of the lobby and, without moving, caught James's attention. He smiled and brought his hand to his brow in mock salute.

On the chilly street outside the Mission, May Fielding said, "Your wife?"

"My wife," he confirmed.

The trappings of serenity did not come until, sitting on the green velvet sofa in her apartment, he put the steaming, cream-rich coffee to his lips. "Hmm, that's good," he said, and he meant it.

"I grind my own beans." She sounded naughty. "I get them from Mr. Black, I'm ashamed to say."

"Do you have any idea how this compromises me? What if Hearst found out that Jimmy Roosevelt's secretary bought coffee on the black market? Don't you care at all about my reputation?"

Her response was a soft kiss on the cheek. A mocking attempt to passify his mock anger. James placed his hand on the turned-under roll of hair at her neck and drew her closer. She understood and brushed his cheek. When they drew back, there was no banter, no jokes nor remarks. Only silence and modest smiles.

Chapter

14

FDR WAS already behind his desk, scanning pages quickly and then signing his name in a broad, confident hand. "Come in, come in, Jimmy," he said without looking up. "I can take care of these while we talk." His voice was thick this morning, and twice he blew his nose into a crumpled handkerchief that had been on his desk. Sunlight streamed into the gracefully sculpted room; here the ease and certainty with which his father held power seemed as natural as a monarch's—more natural, in fact. The polished woods and rich leathers were the democratic equivalents of plush and gilt, and Franklin Delano Roosevelt wore them like elegant but comfortable clothing. Even with a head cold.

"Are you all right, Pa?"

FDR took off his glasses. "Sinuses. Just sinuses. It's the change of climate that does it to me. Sit down." The scratching of the President's pen was the only sound for some seconds. He picked up a pile of signed papers and placed them in the wire basket on his desk and put the pen upright in the holder shaped like the Democrat donkey.

When FDR looked up, James saw that his father's eyes were watery and red-rimmed.

"You could use some warm sunshine, Pa." It was said by way of introducing the subject of his father's health.

The old man didn't respond to his son's concern. Instead, he came, directly and uncharacteristically, to the point. "We're ready for the next stage with our FAMILY MATTER. I'd like you to gather any valuable information about the project, anything another government might think worth a considerable risk to obtain. That's the stuff I want. Accumulate as much as possible, and be sure you have some sense where it fits in the overall plan for the weapon. In case—let me stress this, Jim—in case I might have to use it, I want it right here where I can lay my hands on it." This last statement struck James as though it were a slight backing off, but the fact that he was now cleared for the next step was sufficiently satisfying. "In a sense, Jimmy," the President said before blowing his nose again, "in a sense you'll be on your own in this. A good deal of my time is going to have to go to OVERLORD, and probably even more to the election coming up." He grimaced at the latter thought.

"It's beginning to sound more and more like a contingency plan, Pa."

"Always was. But if it's needed, I want everything right there at the ready." FDR placed his elbows on his desk and folded his hands. "Hassett has orders to admit you to the office anytime you want to make a deposit in the vault, but he knows nothing else about it." His eyes shot to the closet and back again. "What have you finally decided to do about Groves's troublesome Colonel?"

James smiled. "We'll go with him, Pa. I paid Colonel Ishmael one of your famous dawn visits the other day and can say that he's pretty well defused now, although 'redirected' is probably a better word, since I'm sure he'll do a heck of a job capturing the 'bad guys' for us." Conveniently, James neglected mentioning the evening at the French Mission.

"Be careful of the fellow, nonetheless, Jimmy. Here." From under the desk blotter the President pulled a plain sealed envelope. "This is for Einstein. It tells him that you are acting for me in this matter, that for all intents and purposes you *are* me." With lowered voice he added, "Be absolutely certain this document is destroyed after he has read it." The letter went into James's briefcase.

"You don't mind if I get started on this right away, do you, Pa?"

FDR allowed his face to register annoyance. He didn't answer. "Don't see him in that uniform. It might scare him off. Wear something diplomatic."

"Diplomatic?"

"Conservative stripes and a homburg—or two."

He had decided that he wanted to take May Fielding up to Princeton with him even before he returned to the office, which was buzzing with meaningless activity. May eyed him as he entered. As he edged his way through, he said back over his shoulder, "Captain, I'd like to see you for a moment, please." May Fielding closed the inner door behind her without being asked. "Something's come up," he said enticingly, and turned to look out the window. "I'm going to have to leave for an overnight trip. Be back tomorrow morning." A pause for drama. "I'm going to want you along this time, Captain."

"Certainly, Major."

He pulled up his sleeve to check his watch. "It's ten-fifty. I'll be back as close to eleven forty-five as I can make it. Will you need much time to prepare—?"

"No, sir. I was an Army brat and learned to travel very well on a moment's notice. Do you want me in uniform for this, Major?"

"No, no uniform. And I'll see you back here in an hour. Let's meet at the South Portico."

"Fine, sir."

The timing was fortunate for James. In another few minutes midday traffic would have clogged the streets and especially the narrow Theodore Roosevelt Bridge into Arlington, but he easily drove around the ellipse, on to Constitution Avenue and across the Potomac. U.S. Highway 1 took him past Arlington Cemetery and the world's largest office building, the Pentagon. 'Greasy' Groves, he now knew, had organized its construction, and he recalled the General's words: "I'm a projects man. You need a project done, see Leslie Groves, he's your man." James considered the building's immensity as he drove by. Every bit as stunning to him was the logic that equated the construction of buildings with the construction of an atomic bomb. "My God," he said aloud, and almost missed the Twentieth Street turnoff.

He owned nothing truly diplomatic, neither the striped suit nor the homburg, but he had a pressed gray flannel with a vest and a camel hair overcoat. It was as diplomatic as he could get at the time. The truth was that he regarded the visit as a formality: Einstein seemed to have no other choice but to cooperate.

As he drove back over the bridge, traffic had begun building up, but most of it was leaving the capital. She was standing at the entranceway to the South Portico, dressed elegantly in a tailored blue suit with a tan coat over her arm and wearing a floppy felt hat, the kind May Craig, the reporter, always wore, but on May Fielding the effect was stylishly cool. "I suggest we take my car. If we are traveling 'civilian,' a staff car might not be appropriate, and we won't have to fill out motor pool forms," she alertly suggested.

"Good idea." *She is sharp*, he thought.

May drove. Jim gave some general directions out of the center of town, and not a word was uttered until New Jersey Avenue became Rhode Island Avenue and then crossed the

Maryland state line. Both noticed the open ashtray at the same moment, and May said, "There's a fresh pack of Lucky Strikes in the glove compartment."

"I'd thought they'd gone to war."

"No, no, not the cigarettes, just the color of the pack. They're not in green any more."

"One thing," he said as he opened the cigarettes, "we have to eliminate is any Major-Captain business away from the office."

"I'm game, Jim, but does the mission call for it, or do you just prefer it that way?" She said it with so straight a face and serious a tone that he completely missed her irony. Then slowly they began to continue the conversation they had begun weeks earlier at the Statler, each talking easily about simple things—growing up, going to school, family histories. "By the way," May asked a half hour north of Washington, "should I have some idea about our destination?"

"Princeton, New Jersey, May." Now that he could use her first name, he found himself using it even when it was quite unnecessary. He pulled his sun visor down, put his elbow on the ledge of the window and turned more comfortably in his seat.

When they passed just north of Baltimore, the trip became a lovely bucolic journey: trees, rolling hills, horses, cows, sheep. It remained that way well into Pennsylvania. They spoke little and enjoyed the silence, the time passing and the pleasant countryside. James felt very smart in having invited May along, having conveniently forgotten that deception was a significant part of his motivation.

May finally said, "Will Professor Einstein be expecting you, and will I get to meet him?" Its intention was to startle, and because James was so comfortable and unprepared for it, her question did. She looked over at him before he could mask his surprise. He said nothing. "Well, Jim, is he?"

"What in the world makes you think I'm meeting with Professor Einstein?"

"Well, four things, actually. First of all, he's Princeton's leading citizen. Second, he sent you a letter a while back. Third, it's a top-secret meeting, by your own admission. You see, it's elementary, my dear Major."

"Jim," he corrected. "But you said there were *four* things."

"Oh yes. There's also my OSS training that you are so fond of throwing up to me."

Then more silence, broken finally by, "I hope I'm right. I'd love to get to meet him. He's my dream man."

Jim said, "How fickle you are. I thought it was Jean Gabin. If you're getting tired, I wouldn't mind driving for a while."

"Do you have a driver's license?" He hadn't thought about it before, but his license had actually expired while he was in the Pacific. "I'd hate," she announced, biting her words off sarcastically, "to see you have to bribe a New Jersey policeman."

"Yes," he capitulated, "it *is* Einstein and it *is* very secretive and you *will* get to meet him. Friends?"

"Friends," she agreed. "Enjoy the sunset. You're safe with me. And, Jim, thanks for trusting me and letting me participate."

The lights of Mercer Street had begun to take effect in the early winter twilight. May Fielding parked in front of the house, stretched like a sleek cat, and asked, "How do I look? I want him to like me."

"How could he possibly resist. Of course everything is relative." She winced at his lousy joke.

It was good to stand up and good to walk toward the house and good also to feel the smack of cold air on their faces. Helen Dukas answered the door and didn't recognize James at first, perhaps because he appeared so much more presentable than on his previous visit. She said, "James Roosevelt?" It came out a question. "I realize it may be a bit late, but I would like to have a word with Professor Einstein if it's at all possible."

"*Ach*, of course, Mr. Roosevelt. It is you. Come in, come." She didn't take her eyes off May Fielding the entire time.

"This is Miss Fielding, my secretary. We were on our way to New York on some government business, and I realized that there is something I would like to discuss with the Professor."

Helen put out her hand to May. "I'm Helen Dukas, Professor Einstein's secretary." Her voice in the hallway softened noticeably. "The Professor is having his soup. Also, he has a touch of the grippe, so I am keeping an eye on. But I will tell him you are here. Come, you will sit in the study."

Einstein scraped and shuffled into the room on slippered feet. He was bundled in a plaid robe and seemed much smaller and more frail than James remembered him. The lids of his eyes were reddened, and the eyes themselves were very dull.

When James introduced May Fielding, she smiled so broadly that her admiration almost became an aura around her. She gave the Professor immediate pleasure, and he said to Helen, who stood in the doorway, "Some tea for our young guests, *ja*." His head was completely congested, his discomfort great. Sensing James's need to get immediately down to business, May said, "You gentlemen must have some things to discuss, and if there is any soup left over, I'm absolutely famished." She threw James a wink no one else saw. Einstein seemed genuinely disappointed and complained, "But, no, certainly there is time for some moments of simple—"

Helen, whose allegiance could never be mistaken, stepped in and settled everything. She undraped a green afghan, which she threw over the Professor's knees; she also took May by the hand and began leading her to the kitchen for soup. Before leaving, she announced firmly that there would be no smoking in her absence. As the door closed, Einstein said, "So." He added, "That is how it is with me, these days." It was an unconvincing complaint. He eyed his nearby pipe.

James made an indistinct and slightly affirmative gesture while reaching into his briefcase for his father's letter. Without a word he handed it over and watched Einstein open the envelope with some difficulty and read the single page very slowly. Luck was with James because when the old man had finished, he couldn't quite reach the table to put the letter down, so James took it from him and placed it on his own lap.

"My father asked me to tell you, Professor, that for a great variety of reasons we needn't go into unless you absolutely wish to, it is not possible to stop production. His letter makes that point most strongly, I believe. He also told me to say he would have stopped the thing if he could have. But we have simply passed the point of no return. Too much is already known about it; it has simply gone too far. There are reactionary elements who are participating in the project or are very close to it. It would be very unwise strategically and politically for my father, especially before a very important election, to stop the program now. In that sense, he is a victim of this project in somewhat the same sense you are. What he would like to do, however, is neutralize those elements. This, he believes, is possible."

Einstein looked very depressed.

"But," added James, "he believes that you and some of your colleagues are absolutely correct in your concern and is prepared to do something concrete about the situation." His tone mellowed. "In other words, Professor Einstein, I'm here to make a counterproposal he believes will satisfy most of your objections." He saw Einstein take heart, and a part of James wished this assignment were slightly more of a challenge. "He believes the best possible existing solution to be the sharing of the atomic secret with our Allies and eventually with the entire world. If you'd like, Professor, I could enumerate the advantages of this approach as we see them."

Einstein had had enough time in the days since hearing Fermi, Szilard, Frisch, and especially Bohr in New York, to develop a sense of hopelessness about the matter. He had come to realize on his own that his attempts to stop the project were really the desperate acts of a guilt-ridden man, with little genuine hope in them, no practical chance for success. He had discovered and weighed all the practical alternatives. That President Roosevelt had responded in the form of an emissary was an unexpected sign; that there was an alternative proposal about to be presented seemed to him a miracle of sorts. Einstein nodded and with raised eyebrows said, "You have the specifics?"

"The President must act privately and secretly in this matter for the moment. After the war, the situation will change. When a functioning world peace organization is established, it will become the international agency used to control this weapon. But before that, for the present time, the President wishes to use the information in ways that will best promote the peace."

"So," Einstein said expectantly, a slight impatience present this time.

"He would like you to direct, through me, whatever information—formulas, designs, reports, anything pertinent, in other words—he could use in bargaining for the peace we all desire."

"But he is the President. He is in charge of the very project he wishes information about. So why does he not simply order what he requires from the people in control?"

Helen tapped on the door and entered with a tray. "Tea with lemon," she announced, "it is good for loosening the chest." The flowered cups were gigantic. "There is honey, also good for keeping pure the lungs." And she glided out.

Responding to the Professor's last question, James said, "There are, as I have mentioned, reactionary elements"— that phrase seemed to have magical properties as its effect registered on the old man's face. "It is necessary, at this stage at least, to work without their knowledge."

"Take your tea, Mr. Roosevelt, before it cools." James nodded and sipped. "You must know, if it were anyone but your father making such requests, I would not be inclined. However, I respect and I trust him a great deal."

Roosevelt dabbed his lips with a napkin. "We must," he stated a bit too dramatically, "sometimes take greater risks for peace than we take in wars."

Einstein's face disappeared into his teacup, and his voice came indistinctly. "So what do you wish from me specifically, young man?"

Now James was a salesman clinching a big and certain deal: "First, that you agree to act as a conduit for atomic information with the dissident scientists, only those you absolutely trust. And, second, that you channel that information to the President through me."

"Just so simple as that, eh?" It was meant ironically.

"Indeed there are precautions that must be taken. It must be a very well-guarded secret. You must never tell your sources the purpose to which the material is being put. And you should know that for our part, we will guard all identities. However, we can guarantee you and your colleagues no protection should problems arise."

"As you say, Mr. Roosevelt, sometimes we must take certain risks for peace, must we not?" He shook his head and patted the white hair billowing from his temples. "Do you know what Frisch would say if I were to tell him of this meeting? He would say this is merely another trick of the government to make us finish the project quickly." James looked hurt. "But that is Frisch. A cynic. I am certain he will supply information when I request it."

"There is another thing. You can remind your colleagues of something they already know, Professor."

"And this is . . . ?"

"That they are all being closely watched and must be exceedingly careful. I cannot stress that enough."

"Again, we must take risks—that has become the *leitmotif* of this memorable visit. Does that then complete our business? I would like to spend some moments meeting your charming wife." James did not correct the misunderstanding.

"Well, sir, there is one other matter." Einstein's eyes widened. "My mother. Please do not correspond further with her about the project." The wide eyes bulged, but Einstein said nothing. "As a starting point, the President has chosen the pile in Chicago. Please try to accumulate as much information on it as possible. And, you should know, time *is* something of a factor."

"Ah, that is Fermi. It shouldn't present too great a problem. I know much of it already. How do I transmit the information?"

"It is best if you never contact me, sir. I will be in touch with you from time to time."

There was something about that last statement, as well as the news that Eleanor Roosevelt was not a participant, that appeared to make Einstein a little squeamish. It smacked too overtly of espionage, and the difference between theory and unpleasant practice was never an easy one for the physicist to bridge. Bohr, Einstein realized, had confronted just such difficult situations. So had some of the others. Now it had finally touched him.

Einstein sat silently for a long moment, his small eyes watery with discomfort; he sniffled and dabbed at his nose with a balled handkerchief. His energies—intellectual as well as physical—had been sapped. Now James felt the intruder.

"Naturally, I have reservations, but you may tell your father that I will do what he asks."

It was a capitulation; James had been hoping for more willing compliance. The difference was not one of substance but of style; nevertheless, it took some satisfaction out of the success.

In the act of rising, James quickly, and unseen by his host, slipped his father's letter into the briefcase. "I shouldn't keep you any later, sir. Your secretary won't forgive me if you don't get your proper rest."

"*Ach*, Helen protects me too well, don't you think? But the world will win out. Complications will always pierce the best defenses. It is so with the grippe. It is so with this business tonight also."

"And both problems will be overcome, Professor."

Einstein groaned with effort as he rose. "*Ja*, temporarily, perhaps."

In the hallway the four came together, and Helen allowed her charge to give May Fielding a kiss on each cheek. He did and said, "The pleasure is mine, I can assure you, Mrs. Roosevelt." At which, May darted a quick glance at James, suspecting he had purposely misinformed the old man in the study. Then there was a final round of handshakes accompanied by vague apologies and hospitable phrases premised on the idea they would all meet again under more favorable circumstances.

In the car there was no talk, only the *whirr* of the heater bringing the temperature up slowly. The night was as clear as the day had been; the moon was almost full. James looked heavenward as the car sped south on a road that produced regular bumps over tar seams. The movement and sound had a hypnotic effect. It suited him, for there was little satisfaction in his having "closed the deal." He ended his dissatisfaction with a justification, which he repeated each time the wheels thumped a ridge of tar on the road. It was *duty*. *Duty . . . duty . . . duty . . . duty. . . .*

He hadn't remembered looking at the stars since Makin. The secrets he and his father were after were of the same order as those hidden in the stars—Groves's exploding Ping-

Pong balls. The realization frightened him. Was there any-one alive who could really understand the forces involved? The power of the sun in a grain of sand. The future of life on the planet transformed. *My God*, he realized, really for the first time, *we're talking about the entire planet!*

The stakes were suddenly so high that James Roosevelt felt the physical sensations of fear—a tingling at the base of his spine, irregular breathing, and a metallic taste in his mouth. He, too, had begun to sense the void between plan and action, between theory and practice. And, as suddenly, he had a new and overwhelming sense of awe and respect for his father.

"What?" James asked even though she hadn't said any-thing.

Part Three

Boxes Within Boxes . . .

Chapter
15

HE COULD tell from the way they looked at him that the worst was probably over, that he'd begun to regain at least some of his glow of strength and energy. But Franklin Delano Roosevelt knew without reading the faces of the people around him how much the ordeal had taken out of him and how narrowly he'd pulled through. His performance on this, the afternoon of his fourth inauguration, was a triumph and a cumulation of sorts: the single-minded physical effort of the past year had brought him to the South Portico ceremony on this cold January 20. He had played out his personal resources extremely carefully throughout the campaign of 1944, finessing them like a master card-player, and he began the new year again with very little margin for error.

Convenient research had provided the information that during the early Presidencies short and simple inaugurations had been the rule, so FDR arranged one of the shortest and simplest of them all, and he justified it with the irrefutable explanation that the money saved could buy bullets for the boys at the Bulge. There would be neither a parade nor an inaugural ball; he knew he'd have to put forth one more extreme effort for the swearing in and a brief but inspiring speech.

Fewer than three thousand people stood on the gray, frozen snow of the south lawn, stamping and clapping hands to stay warm. The worldly ones carried flasks. When the red-uniformed band began "Hail to the Chief" almost on time, the President came through the doors in a manner that first stunned and then moved the viewers—walking erect, without the aid of crutch or cane. His knees were locked in place, and he slid each leg forward until, through a series of twists and pivots, he advanced forward to a chair at the balustrade. He was without coat or cape but wore a "diplomatic" blue suit, and even though his face maintained the most confident of Roosevelt smiles, his exertion was enormous. There were cheers as he reached his seat, where he shook hands warmly with Harry Truman, his new Vice President. When it was time for him to take the oath, he wrapped his arm around Jimmy's neck and was lifted to the speaker's platform. Jimmy hadn't remembered his being quite so light before. As Chief Justice Harlan Stone administered the oath of office, FDR looked out over the crowd and into the winter haze that shrouded the Jefferson Memorial and all but obliterated the Potomac.

He had long known that for most Americans he was only a smile and a voice, and the sense of trust that voice could engender had given him his mandates. The speech was short and businesslike, adhering to the no-nonsense, we've-got-a-job-to-finish character of the whole ceremony. But the rich voice rang clear, like that of an elegant but feisty patriarch who really did know what was best for his privileged children. He accepted the challenge head on: "Make no mistake about it, we Americans of today, together with our Allies, are passing through a period of supreme test. It is a test of our courage—of our resolve—of our wisdom—of our essential democracy." Yes, FDR was personally convinced, and now he persuaded any reasonable doubters that we would pass our test with flying colors.

"Not too bad for an old man, eh, Jimmy?" he said as James helped him down from the podium, into his wheelchair, and through the crowd of well-wishers on the crowded balcony. Flashbulbs popped, hands were shaken, flying compliments thrown and caught. The navigation of this past year had been a deep personal triumph. But he hadn't achieved it alone. That young Navy officer, the cardiologist at the Bethesda hospital, Lieutenant Commander Bruenn, had first spotted the heart problem during his physical examination in the spring. The regimen FDR went on wasn't easy—a low-fat diet, reduction of cigarettes to no more than five a day, ten hours' sleep, no swimming and, worst of all, only one martini—but by August he had shown improvement. The gray pallor and particularly the blueness in his lips which had prompted Frances Perkins, the labor secretary, to pay him a worried visit in April began to change for the better. Her face at cabinet meetings had become for him the litmus test of his health. It hadn't registered any real concern for months.

He did not know at first that the green pills Dr. Bruenn had prescribed were digitalis. Only after they had success-fully controlled the enlargement of his heart and improved its capacity to circulate the blood—in other words, only after the danger had passed—was he told how seriously ill he had been. Among close friends he was jovial and breezy about his "close shave," as he called it. Personally, he was very concerned; he knew that 1945 would be the most im-portant year of his life, perhaps an epochal one in the life of the world.

Indeed, FDR had learned the essential flexibility of poli-tics early on, and he never had any trouble accepting it as "the art of the possible." In fact, for him compromise, horse trading, as it were, was at the very core of change, and for him finessing his way to a winning position was the sweetest of satisfactions. It didn't surprise him, then, that there was a price to be paid for the benefits of his digitalis medication: his appetite fell off sharply and he lost fifteen pounds almost immediately—his clothes looked almost ludicrous on him— and he often suffered with stomach cramps.

As they were going upstairs in the elevator after the swearing-in ceremony, he told James, in a perfect *non sequitur*, "The trading off of effects is all that can ever be accomplished in this world, Jimmy. And all you can ever bargain for is a little time, but one hopes during that time . . ." And he made small circles with limp hands. It was a very different statement and tone of voice—even out of context— from those he had employed just a few moments earlier out on the White House veranda. When his father said, "I'll be having a light dinner in bed. Stay around here this evening, I'm sure I'll want to talk to you," James had the sense that a crucial card was about to be played.

As he had most evenings, Arthur Prettyman, the President's valet, helped Franklin Roosevelt into his pajamas. He, more than anyone else, had seen the changes in the body; his large brown hands had removed the clothing, the braces, efficiently and tenderly for more than a decade. Those hands had eased the muscles with thoughtful massage. Tan flannel pajamas with chocolate piping felt warm and comfortable against FDR's skin, as did the steaming towel Prettyman applied slowly to his face. The weariness and weight of the day began to lift. "Arthur, I'd like to have my martini now," FDR said as he pulled toward him the papers Hassett had arranged on his bed table.

"But, Mr. President, you had one just before the ceremony. For dinner there is poached egg, juice, whole wheat toast."

"I'm not a child, Arthur. I'd like my martini first."

Prettyman was upset, but there was no recourse except to make sure Mrs. Roosevelt got a report on the transgression.

"Gin, you mean," the valet muttered. "That ain't no martini cocktail any more. Hasn't been for two, three years now."

"That'll be quite enough, thank you, Arthur." Their relationship had always been an informal one, with respectful teasing permitted on each side, but ever since the warnings of FDR's heart condition, Prettyman's protection had become slightly overbearing. Before the valet left the room, the President's voice softened. "Arthur. I can assure you that a nightcap is really perfectly acceptable." And Prettyman left, still mightily upset.

Events on the western front, while troubling, were not really serious. General Bradley had already succeeded in containing the German counterattack, so it was restricted to a small bubble that would soon be pinched off and stuck with a pin. In the East the Russians had taken Warsaw, run through East Prussia, besieged Budapest. The destruction of the German air force was practically complete, German cities were bombed daily, there were slow but steady advances in Italy and almost everywhere else. Yes, the German collapse was inevitable. But the alliance might have begun to fall apart.

Churchill had visited him in Hyde Park in November shortly after FDR's reelection and, although there was much other important business to be discussed, he seemed obsessed with what he still called the TUBE ALLOYS Project. One image and sentence stayed with Roosevelt and returned again now as he sat up in bed bolstered by two pale blue pillows: Churchill had a forkful of rare roast beef before him, his ruddy cheeks squeezing his eyes closed, and he was saying, "Victory, it's wonderful. Peace, ah yes, it's marvelous. But the balance of power, 'tis that makes all the other things possible." Then he hoisted the meat into his mouth and said, while chewing, " 'Tis Tube Alloys, atom bombs, whatever we call 'em, they're going to shape our peace, by God." And FDR could see that it was a wrathful God to which the Prime Minister referred.

Churchill had also complained bitterly that the British were being frozen out of the MANHATTAN PROJECT. After all, hadn't they agreed at their Quebec Conference to exchange all information freely. Did the President know that His Majesty's Government had already arrested one of the scientists at Harwell for attempting to pass plans to the Russians? And there were plenty of other scientists who bore careful scrutiny. "The Ruskies know about it and want it very badly, *very* badly," he had warned.

The days at Hyde Park had been intended as a preparation for the Yalta Conference, but Churchill kept hammering away at the bomb and the "postwar balance of power." From Churchill's lips that phrase only meant tipping the balance in his favor. FDR's atomic plan would be an attempt at a truer balance, a condition where East and West had the same potential for destruction and, hence, no inclination to really carry it through. If and when that finally happened, then, and only then, did a need for a referee—FDR's world organization—have any real significance.

So strongly had the President come to believe in this postwar blueprint that he had risked everything on a fourth-term campaign. He simply had to see his plan through to its conclusion. He had to be there to steer between and around the power politics of Churchill, the potentially dangerous insecurities of Stalin, and the naive errors of Woodrow Wilson. It explained sacrificing Henry Wallace as Vice President: if the party bosses wanted Truman and that choice helped him win, it simply had to be made. Unpleasant, of course, but he'd made hundreds of unpleasant choices in twelve years as President; he was used to it. At least he'd managed to keep Wallace on as commerce secretary, and Harry S Truman seemed an innocuous enough little man.

Of course, FDR had given Churchill the assurances he wanted. But assurances were one thing; atomic information was something else again. The struggles, the deception, the compromises and sacrifices were finally behind him. Matters had now come down to a single event, to a . . .

Arthur Prettyman knocked once and entered with the President's martini on a silver tray. "You'd like a light massage, sir?" It was offered by way of accommodation and apology.

"I would indeed, Arthur. Perhaps later. I've got some work to do first. Would you find Jimmy and fetch him up here? He may be in that office of his or with Early."

"More'n likely he's wherever that pretty WAC captain is." FDR raised his eyebrows and smiled. Prettyman smiled and left again.

Franklin Roosevelt would have to prepare himself for one final effort; he would have to be physically and mentally ready to take on Churchill and Stalin once more, and on Stalin's home turf. Everything had to be made as ready as possible for Yalta. Yes, another prodigious effort on his part. He worried that he might already have cut things too fine; he might not have left himself enough time to prepare himself properly. The conference was scheduled to begin in two weeks. There was a limit even to the restorative powers of Warm Springs.

James sat alone at his desk. The outer office was dark, and the green-shaded desk lamp threw an ominous circle of light into the gloom. He was drafting a typical busywork letter to Admiral Leahy, Chief of Naval Operations. In this sense his cover job as Co-Ordinator of Military Manpower and Materiel hadn't changed very much throughout the year.

But some events of the year back in Washington had given him a solid feeling of accomplishment and made him realize that he had been something of a dabbler most of his life. He had even come to understand, from his regular discussions with Einstein and some study on his own, the principle and practical value of releasing atomic energy. It was no longer a pure abstraction. The knowledge satisfied him and made him feel that he was something more than a government snooper. He believed in FAMILY MATTER now.

And there had been, above all, May Fielding. At the thought of her now, he put down his pen and rubbed his cheek approvingly. She had begun to make an honest man of him: he'd formally separated from Romelle, who was in the process of suing for divorce. And he'd taken an apartment on M Street diagonally across from May's. He smiled, relishing the satisfaction he felt about the turn his professional and personal life had taken in Washington during the last year. But the pleasurable moment was shattered by the abrupt ringing of the telephone. "Major Roosevelt here."

It was Prettyman. "Your father would like to see you now, Mr. Jimmy. He's in his bedroom."

"Thank you, Arthur."

"And, Mr. Jimmy?"

"Yes."

"See what you can do to get him to listen to the doctors. He's had two martinis today. And one's his limit."

"Will do, Arthur."

James had been pointing toward this meeting for more than two months, ever since the election. He knew that political conditions had deteriorated to the point where FAMILY MATTERS had become almost a necessity, and he had guessed that Yalta would be the place for the first step to be taken. From his rear pants pocket he took out a tiny alligator-skin wallet; from a pouch inside he extracted a key and opened a flat drawer at the bottom of his desk from which he plucked a folder. *Boxes within boxes within boxes,* he thought.

He walked across to the White House and took the red-carpeted steps two at a time up to the third floor. Naturally, he was pleased that the efforts of more than a year were going to be employed, but there was the faint taste of fear too. The immensity of the destructive power he had begun to understand and of the risk his father was taking now intruded itself against his wishes.

After knocking twice and being unsure if he had gotten a response, James opened the door and saw his father propped up in bed so deep in thought that James realized he hadn't been heard. "Pa," he said quietly and then "P-a-a," almost twice as loud. A single table lamp cut only a limited circle out of the darkness.

"Jimmy, yes, come in, come in." FDR tipped an already empty glass into an upturned mouth; he was hoping for a final drop but nothing fell. He put the glass on the table and said, "Pull up a chair, Jimmy. We've got some serious business tonight."

James placed the folder under his arm and lifted a Chippendale chair close to the bed.

"I need you tonight, Jimmy, not so much for discussion as for specific information."

This is it, thought James.

While he spoke, the President twirled the monogrammed ring on the small finger of his left hand with his thumb. James remembered when the flesh used to swell around that old ring. His father still hadn't made direct eye contact with him. "Sometimes there comes a situation where the last resort is the next resort. It just sort of happens that way if you live long enough. And that time has come. I fully expect to have to put FAMILY MATTER into effect at Yalta." Now they looked into each other's eyes. A long look, something deeply shared. The President said, finally, "The reasons for it are indisputable. The top two dispatches are from Churchill; they're Yalta pep talks. Read them."

"You don't have to justify anything to me, Pa. I trust your judgment."

"No more than I do, I can assure you, but take a look anyway."

The top sheet, a cable on pink paper, was devoted exclusively to Tube Alloys; its tone was a dire warning. The sentences that caught James's eye began with:

> IT WOULD NOT SURPRISE ME AT ALL IF YOU HAVE FOUND THIS
> BOHR'S ARGUMENTS PERSUASIVE. BUT UNDERSTAND ALSO THAT HE
> IS NOT TO BE TRUSTED. HE HAS SMUGGLED INFORMATION TO THE
> RUSSIANS WHILE IN YOUR COUNTRY. . . .

The second cable was buff-colored:

> IMAGINE POOR UNCLE JOE UNWITTINGLY SITTING DOWN IN
> CONFERENCE WITH MEN WHO HAVE THE POWER TO BLOW HIM
> INTO THE ATMOSPHERE AND WHO CAN TELL HIM FINALLY
> WHERE TO GET ON AND ESPECIALLY WHERE TO GET OFF.

"And it has been like that since we met at Hyde Park. Picking away constantly, as though he suspects something. And Stalin is every bit as surly. By the way, is there any truth to the Bohr thing?"

"I've got no firsthand knowledge, Pa. But do you think it's possible with that psychotic Colonel Ishmael on the job? I do know they've had a blanket over Bohr ever since he arrived last year. But I'll check into it and give you our best information before we leave. The important thing, I believe, is keeping Ishmael away from those technicians who are doing that low-level spying. But speaking of leaving, just when will we be going? I've got some preparations to make."

FDR was no longer twirling his ring but sliding it up and down. He said succinctly, a note of weary certainty in his voice, "I don't want you with me for this. I'll handle Yalta alone. You'll stay here until I send for you." Then he brightened. "It's been a year of successful prophecies for me. My record was excellent, the result—well, that's another matter. I warned you Yale would beat Harvard, and they mopped us up. And even after we drafted the best players off every other team and put them in the Army, the Washington Senators still couldn't beat anyone; I told you they wouldn't, but remember how hopeful you were? I even predicted that Dewey would find a way to lose the election to a tired old war horse. So, without rubbing it in too much or trying to be an 'I told you so' on that bomb of ours, I will ask you what seems to be your latest, best idea of when we'll have the infernal machine." While James was wincing, and before he could respond, his father added gratuitously, "The entire year of 1944 has come and gone without so much as an atomic belch."

James extracted a letter from his folder. "It's from Groves to Marshall," he said.

FDR scanned and then read aloud: " 'The first gun type bomb, which will produce at least a ten thousand ton TNT yield, should be ready by or before 1 June 1945. A second one should be ready by August and others at shorter intervals thereafter.' "

"Has Groves," the President asked, "ever committed a specific date to writing before?"

"No, Pa. First time. And it's to Marshall."

FDR slapped his quilt with both hands. "When a born hedger like Greasy Groves puts himself on the record in writing, then we've got something we can really believe in. Important bit of information. Thank you, Jimmy. If I'm going to the mat with Uncle Joe on this, there are some things I'll have to know." James was nodding. "First, I'll need some idea of what information he might already have."

"Okay, here's what we know. The Russians do have a program. Not a heck of a lot is known about it, but it's pretty rudimentary stuff at best. Their people probably understand atomic theory and may—I stress *may*—even understand the bomb itself in principle. It depends on what, if anything, they've gotten from their agents in Los Alamos."

"I'd be better off assuming that they understand and have nothing, and when we start trading, it will be up to Uncle

Joe to make demands. Certainly then we'll be able to tell what they do and do not have."

"Precisely, Pa. What they asked for would tell us exactly where they were in the process. My guess is, not too far along."

"But I have to know the entire process, each of the various stages for producing a bomb, if I'm going to do some horse trading. I want a *quid pro quo* situation with the Tartar so I can get the concessions I want by degrees."

James smiled, leaned forward and said softly, "Pa, you've come to the right place. I've been anticipating this, and am in the process of writing something up for you. I'll make sure you have it before you leave."

"I'd like some idea right now," FDR said flatly. "I don't like the feeling of having something this big that's Greek to me. I remember the Ping-Pong ball demonstration you gave, but I'll be darned if I'd try that on Stalin. I would really like to understand the whole process—and exactly what's been holding it up."

"Okay. Fermi built something in Chicago called an atomic pile, and in it he controlled the release of energy from certain kinds of metals. What's important about that is that it proved lots of energy could be released in an atomic explosion, that in fact the theory was right."

"Step one, the atomic pile."

"Correct. Step two, the atomic metals that have to be used in the bomb are uranium and plutonium. The scientists call them U 235 and Pu 239. And they have to be manufactured. And that has taken a lot of time, first, because they couldn't find the right technique and, second, because the process that works is very, very slow—that's partly what has been causing the delay."

"Uranium 235, plutonium 239. Manufacturing them is step two."

"Check. Step three, this is where we are now. It is theoretically the simplest part, but it happens to be causing the greatest problems."

FDR's lips twisted and he said, "Not to mention the problem with the scruples of some of the scientists now that the Germans are practically whipped."

"Step three is bringing two masses of these atomic metals together very hard and very fast. The problem is this: You only get an explosion if the metals are of a certain, specific weight, and we haven't produced enough of the material yet to discover through trial and error the exact amounts that are needed. They call the correct amounts 'critical mass.'"

"Determining critical mass—step three."

"Step four, we already have. The bomb design and the triggering. They will simply shoot a wedge of one atomic metal of the right weight into another. That's the 'gun type' that Groves wrote to Marshall about."

"Sounds wonderfully primitive for all the fancy scientific terms," said FDR. "You have all the specific data we'll need in the safe?"

"All except the solution to the critical mass problem. We're waiting on that one. It's Otto Frisch's baby. When Einstein has it, we'll have it."

Then there was a silence that seemed timeless as well as deep. Each man was imagining in his own way the destruction such a weapon could cause, the fearfulness of which seemed to precipitate increasingly depressing thoughts. James understood that when the power to destroy became this enormous, you didn't merely have an old problem enlarged—you had a new and perhaps insoluble dilemma. FDR had been having the same general thoughts but accepted with a mental shrug the ultimate existence of such a weapon and the realistic need to try to do something to neutralize it.

"In spy movies," Jimmy said at last, "you'd probably be

expected to memorize and repeat those steps to me before I left. Can you, Pa?"

FDR snickered and placed his hand on his son's while saying, "Jimmy, you've done a very fine job. And I'm grateful. I hope someday the entire world will be grateful. Why not take yourself a little vacation while I'm away; you've certainly earned it. Arthur tells me you're particularly close to your charming WAC assistant; why not chase the sun with her for a few weeks?"

James's mouth fell open by small increments. His eyebrows went up and his eyes rounded. FDR enjoyed the stupefaction his comment had caused. "Seriously, Jimmy, I'd like to put some distance between us now, especially if that mad Colonel is still as dogged as you've made him out to be. Let him see you as the playboy the world believes you to be. I'll be sailing off in a week or so, and I'd like this to be our last meeting until I return. Unless, of course, I need you quickly. If things at that conference table work out as I suspect they might, our next meeting will be to arrange an exchange of some sort. Get ready for that possibility while I'm gone and keep up with any and all developments on the bomb."

"But take a vacation too," James added sarcastically. Then seriously: "I'm in touch with Professor Einstein twice a month."

"Good. You know, Jimmy, in those same spy movies," FDR continued melodramatically, "the chief spy would say something like this: 'Remember, you'll be completely on your own from here on in. I won't be able to protect you.' Wouldn't he?"

"Something like that. Yes."

"Well, he just did." And FDR offered his hand. Jimmy took it, not to shake but to hold. Firmly. Again he felt the limits of his father's strength.

At the door, he heard the President say, "Find Arthur and send him in to me. I could use one of his neck rubs."

"Certainly, Pa."

As he closed the door behind him, James Roosevelt experienced a sudden pang of loneliness that quickly depressed him. His father had lived with that same feeling for so long that it had become, more or less, a permanent condition.

"It is not my intention, young man, to lecture you, but it seems to me you run the dangerous risk of an excess of rectitude." Professor Otto Frisch uttered the words kindly, wisps of smoke rising from his lips. He looked not at his young guest but at the cigarette he held pinched, European style, between middle and ring finger.

The young man, his brown hair lank across his wide forehead, his horn-rimmed glasses a perfect adjunct to an impassive face, smiled only with his lips. With a voice extraordinarily reasonable Klaus Fuchs, the youthful British physicist, said, "That seems to be my legacy and my curse—to be irremediably moral. My father is a minister, a high church moralist of the highest order."

Then for some moments neither man spoke, for Fuchs had earlier presented Frisch with a stunning proposal as they sat amid the clutter that was Frisch's cramped study in his small Los Alamos cabin.

For the past week Frisch had succeeded in dodging the eager Fuchs, intuiting something troublesome, maybe even dangerous, about his request for a private meeting. Indeed, the older man had been impressed by the younger's abilities as a physicist, by his solid mathematical grounding combined with an adventurous theoretical imagination; nevertheless, he did not like or trust Klaus Fuchs. And unlike some of the other older men, Otto Frisch was not the sort to jealously guard his own reputation by holding back a new generation of physicists. He liked young Panetta and Feynberg, for example, but there was just something about Fuchs that put him off.

Finally, he had consented to the meeting, but only in his rooms and only after he had made still another thorough check for one of Colonel Ishmael's ubiquitous listening devices. And as expected—or perhaps feared—Fuchs had indeed made a disconcerting request.

Now Frisch broke the silence: "You realize, of course, what you are asking me to do. You are asking me to become a traitor to this country. To be willing to pass on plans and formulas to which only the senior members of Experimental and Theoretical may have access, and, as a consequence, perhaps spend my last days in an American prison. Yes, with a straight face you sit in my study and ask me to do this. Do you not think that somewhat presumptuous and insulting, young man?" Frisch realized, when he had said 'straight face,' that he had never seen Fuchs laugh or, for that matter, display any human emotion. Perhaps that was why he didn't trust him.

"You know as well as I do, Professor Frisch, why the work on this bomb is continuing. It would be a charade for either one of us to proceed on the assumption that it is still needed to win *this* war. Perhaps the next one—"

"But why, of all the possibilities, have you come to me?" He neatly tapped his cigarette ashes into a coffee cup.

Was it the flicker of a smile, somewhat smug, Frisch had seen cross Fuchs's lips? "Isn't it a logical fallacy, Professor, for you to assume that because I've come to you, I've come *only* to you? And I might also point out that it would be equally erroneous for you to assume that no others have seen my request as a reasonable one."

"And agreed to participate?"

Fuchs tipped his large head, and his lenses caught the light in such a way as to turn them into a pair of blank discs. "There is not another person on this project to whom I would admit that the answer is yes."

That singular admission had made the men unequal: Fuchs was now extremely vulnerable; he had, in fact, offered him-

214

self up to the older man. The discomfort, however, was all Frisch's; the knowledge made him feel like a conspirator. He said quickly, "If there are others, then why do you need me?"

Fuchs seemed pleased by the question. Frisch had in fact asked, *Why me?* No need to delve into the political situation of the world, no interminable theoretical or philosophical discussion required. Just a frank and pragmatic *Why me?* "Because I have reason to believe that you accept our premises about the continued building of a bomb now. And if that is true, it is reasonable to believe that you would, like us, be willing to risk what has to be risked. It is as simple as that, Professor."

"But you have merely told me why you believe I might join you. You have not yet told me why you have sought me out."

"Ah, yes. That, too, is not very complicated. There are a great many of us at work on the project who believe it will utterly disrupt the political stability of the world for generations to come. Some—a few—have already stopped working on the project. Although that may be salve for an individual's conscience, it does nothing to prevent the bomb at this point. Then there are those souls who are, in quiet ways, trying to convince the American and British governments to stop the project while they continue to work on it. Finally, there are those who believe nothing can stop it and are willing to take whatever risks are necessary to insure that if there must be a weapon, it will not be the exclusive property of one nation."

"Still, you have not answered—"

"I was just about to, sir. What is required, we believe, is a united front—sheer numbers, in other words. A mere handful of us can never be respectable; we can only subvert and eventually we will undoubtedly be caught and offered up as traitors and spies. If we have to take that route, we shall. With greater numbers, however, and with men of stature in those numbers, we become respectable. Every man like yourself who joins with us adds to our credibility and our capacity to stop the project in one way or another. That is essentially *why you,* Professor."

"It seems to me, young man, that you are willing to take some rather severe personal risks in this matter."

"How could it be otherwise, considering what is at stake?"

Otto Frisch knew, had known, in fact, long before Fuchs even proposed anything, that he would not, could not consent. Now he resented the challenge the young man had presented; he resented, as well, his unshakable commitment to action; and he resented even more the personal courage of these people who were willing to risk everything. He knew even as he began to frame his rejection that he resented most of all what Fuchs made him feel about himself—burnt out, lacking the ultimate will to resist directly. Envy was, of course, the undercurrent for all the resentment. That Fuchs was smug and righteous made it somewhat easier to dismiss him, if not the issues he raised.

Frisch tamped out his cigarette and then combed his fingers through his gray hair as he said, "I cannot agree to participate with you in any capacity. And since you have been so direct with me, I shall give you my assurance that everything that has transpired here today shall be kept in the utmost confidence."

"And your reasons?"

"A single reason. A question of trust. President Roosevelt. If he is not to be trusted to control the weapon, why have we even bothered to come this far? What indications have there ever been that he is to be considered power hungry or inhumane?"

Fuchs's glasses flashed, and his eyes again disappeared behind white discs. He said, "Roosevelt is also an old man. What if he becomes suddenly ill, unable to function, to control the project? As a matter of fact, how can you be certain he actually knows what is really going on here? That Groves and Ishmael and the whole swarm of warmongers even allow him to know the truth? And, in the end, is it worth the risk?"

"If he has not a direct interest or concern, why would he send his own son on an inspection here twice within the last year? And as far as his age goes, that is a less crucial matter for other old men than it might be for you, Fuchs. Since it is, finally, a matter of trust, I shall continue to place mine in the President until I have reason to doubt him."

Klaus Fuchs rose and said without expression, "For those of us who believe there is simply too much at stake, your good, old-fashioned trust is just not adequate protection. Thank you for receiving me, Professor Frisch."

That evening, as Otto Frisch pulled still another cigarette from his pack, he realized that information about the bomb was probably being passed along on two levels. Fuchs and his friends were scraping together whatever they could. On the other hand, he and Fermi and Szilard and Bohr had all agreed to send some elemental but crucial formulas and designs to Einstein. They had Einstein's assurances that since it was too late to stop the project, sending him the classified information would be the next best thing. Einstein's word was sufficient.

In fact, Frisch intended to duplicate his latest and most successful critical mass calculations after dinner and encode them in a friendly letter to Princeton. He smiled wearily at the bitter irony of Fuchs's request: For Frisch it was, after all, as Fuchs himself had mentioned, nothing more than a matter of respectability.

Chapter

16

FROM THE moment his plane, the *Sacred Cow*, touched down at the ice-coated airstrip at Saki until he had been taken by the heated, oversized black Packard to Yalta, seventy-five miles away, Franklin Roosevelt was repeatedly surprised. The Crimea amazed him. The airport had been surrounded by Russian soldiers with submachine guns poised. Molotov had greeted him warmly but with disappointing word that Marshal Stalin had been delayed and had not yet arrived from Moscow. The President's limousine then made its way for about twenty miles over what would have been familiar American terrain—gentle hills, rolling farms, small clumps of trees—except for the signs of tremendous devastation. Everywhere bomb craters and burned-out buildings, demolished tanks, trucks and railroad cars. Everywhere. FDR had heard that the fighting in the Crimea had been fierce, but he expected nothing quite like this. Along the entire route soldiers with rifles snapped to attention and saluted as the Packard rolled by. At first FDR didn't notice how many of them were women.

The road and the terrain after Simferopol, the Crimean capital, changed abruptly. It became suddenly mountainous, circuitous, and the entourage progressed very slowly, but after the mountain pass had been breached, there was an unexpected and majestic view of the Black Sea. Miraculously, the sun chose that very moment to break through. Mike Reilly, FDR's chief bodyguard, sitting in the front seat next to the Russian driver, whistled and said, "Reminds me of California, down around Santa Barbara."

The road descended sharply and followed the undulating coast past once-grand, aristocratic country estates, now the broken relics of revolution and war. Two miles to the south of Yalta the President ended his four-hour automobile trip alongside a huge building built in the Italian Renaissance style and seated in a mountainside overlooking the dark waters. It was the building in which, for better or worse, a good deal of the world's future would be forged by three men. The Livadia Palace.

The palace seemed fated for such a momentous task. Its history, its very character and design, symbolized all the violent turnings that had characterized the century. Built in 1911, it was the Czar Nicholas' "little summer home," testimony to the casual and confident power of Russian royalty. After all, it had only fifty rooms.

For two decades after the Revolution it was a sanitorium for tubercular workers. At capacity, almost five hundred patients filled it without very much crowding or discomfort.

The German high command occupied it in late 1941 and all but destroyed it when the Russian counteroffensive forced them out in forty-three. They left little more than a shell, devoid of windows, doors, paint, plaster, plumbing, lights; they had left plenty of rats. Two frantic weeks of repairs were almost completed when the two hundred Americans in the Presidential entourage had begun to arrive.

Windows and doors had been replaced, most of the rooms were plastered and painted, the heating and electrical systems worked some of the time, and the vermin had been pretty much eliminated. But there was only one private bathroom—the President's.

In the few minutes he had alone in his suite, the Czar's former billiards room, Franklin Roosevelt felt tired but fairly strong, given the ordeal of the ocean voyage, the flight from Malta and the long drive. The Black Sea, almost directly below him, he could see and hear and smell through the row of windows in the south wall; perhaps this was the source of his unexpected strength. There would be very few minutes alone before General Marshall would brief him one final time on the Allied military position. He had heard that problems had developed between the British and American combined chiefs yesterday during discussions at Malta. On military matters, he trusted Marshall and would support his position. There would not be many such quiet moments alone as this one during the fateful days ahead. But sitting as he did in shirt sleeves, the collar open, cuffs turned up, in a green velvet armchair with his legs propped on a boldly designed oriental ottoman, he concentrated on clearing his mind and reaching into the physical consolations of a lifetime, the sun and the sea.

Through the window he saw a U.S. cutter under full flag cruising toward the port of Yalta; he wished he had a pair of binoculars but didn't call for them for fear of breaking the isolation of the moment.

The complexities of the conference would not affect him, would not draw him away from his very specific and limited objectives—he wanted his kind of world organization, and he wanted Russia actively involved in the attack on the Japanese mainland. Simple as that. Churchill and Stalin had different priorities. Churchill's concern was the Russian control of Eastern Europe and trying to reestablish noncommunist governments there; he would undoubtedly be continually hammering away at Poland. For Stalin it would be maintaining political control of the areas his armies occupied and the task of dismantling Germany completely when the war finally ended. FDR smiled crookedly to himself. "So I'm Wilson at the conference table whether I like it or not," he said to the ship steaming toward Yalta. "But with a slight difference: I've got a hell of a lot more than good will and moral indignation in my pocket."

A knock at the door brought Marshall, and FDR used the intrusion to send for binoculars. "Well, George, you look well. Sit down and give me nothing but good news about your talks with our British allies."

"You want the play-by-play, Mr. President, or just the final score?"

"The final score first and then some of the highlights."

"Eisenhower remains supreme commander. Montgomery's thrust across the Rhine in the north gets top priority, Bradley's secondary."

"Whoa, back up a minute, I must have missed something, George. Was that the score or the highlights?"

"The score, sir. How we came to those conclusions wasn't an easy matter. The British tried to force Eisenhower out as supreme commander and replace him with their own man, most likely Montgomery. They tried to have Bradley replaced too, tried to control Patton, tried to get all military commitments in writing. Let me tell you, sir, meetings between allies are usually a lot rougher than with the enemy."

"Know the phenomenon well, George, know it well."

"And I'm still not absolutely convinced it will hold together. Montgomery is a particularly hard man for some of us to stomach. War has become almost totally mechanized; yet their top military people act as though it's still Balaklava with the charge of the light brigade."

"That's precisely the mentality that caused their defeat at Gallipoli in the last war, George. They are, for the most part, pampered, nineteenth-century aristocrats. With all the excesses of the breed, most of the good as well as the bad. And Churchill's as bad as any of them. Maybe we can help bring them into the twentieth century at this conference. Let me just say that I'll be leaving all military matters here in your and Admiral Leahy's hands. You've got my complete trust and support. My energies must be with the larger political questions. I simply ask that you keep me well informed."

George Marshall did not know what specific decision-making powers those instructions left him with, but he did not ask for clarification because he wanted to give the President as much time to rest as possible before the conference began in the morning. "I really have nothing else to report, Mr. President."

"And the Bulge?"

The General flushed because he was of the opinion that the temporary success of the German counterattack had been the result of faulty tactics and communication. It should never have been allowed to happen. Its mention now embarrassed him. "The containment is assured, sir. The initiative regained." Marshall clasped his hands in such a way as to indicate an impatience to leave.

"Fine. I won't be dining with our delegation tonight, George. I've still some important homework to do before we get started. Please explain my absence. And, before you leave, would you mind handing me those binoculars so I can watch the sun set on the U.S. Navy." Marshall handed over the glasses and was on his way out of the room when the President said, "The attack on Japan, what's our target date?"

"One October, sir."

"And what are the casualty estimates for our troops?"

"Five hundred thousand at a minimum. Of course we could always get lucky."

"Thank you, George." The General turned and left.

The President brought the double fuzzy image together

and then into focus. There was something very familiar about the ship. The name—U.S.S. *Jamestown*—was of no help. He scanned the bridge area and the entire superstructure. Then he brought his glasses down. Something about the hull intrigued him, something about the unique rhombic shape. Of course! It was the old *Paterson*. He'd christened it when he was Navy undersecretary in 1921. That was the hull that was supposed to revolutionize naval design. Ha! It had been a light cruiser back then; now it was nothing more than an escort craft. They had rebuilt the entire superstructure. "But it's still serviceable," he muttered, and chose to take this for a good omen.

Like a wily old boxer who had just enough left to go the route if he didn't make any miscalculations, Franklin Roosevelt, after four full days at the conference, was still very much in control of himself. It helped significantly that the plenary sessions were held at the Livadia Palace. He slept much later than usual, took breakfast on the sun porch, and was conserving himself wisely. As at Teheran, the informal sessions—the late dinners, drinking and exchange of ideas— were the most difficult and demanding. He took some solace from the fact that he saw Stalin adding water to his wine.

The exchanges between Churchill and Stalin had become sharper with each passing day. He was the peacemaker, saying nothing for the most part, nodding no matter who spoke, agreeing with parts of each point of view, explaining his position in general terms and only if it was insisted upon. But there were moments when his attention wandered, when he looked about the huge round table and fastened on a detail, a gesture. Today, for example, he had noticed that Stalin wasn't smoking dark Russian cigarettes but Western ones, although still holding them strangely between thumb and forefinger. FDR realized that the Russian hadn't taken his pipe out since they had arrived. Yesterday Churchill wore a colonel's uniform and the day before that a naval outfit of indeterminable rank. On the second day it had gotten suddenly cold in the conference hall and a fire was ordered lit in the fireplace; it compelled Roosevelt's attention much of the time. These diversions did not trouble him; on the contrary, they indicated his resolve to wait for the proper moment to act. Stettinius, the new secretary of state, was beside him, constantly attentive; Hopkins was sitting directly behind him, ailing but observant and as helpful as ever.

In addition, the division between Churchill and Stalin over the questions already discussed—the dismantling of Germany and which government would represent the Poles in lieu of elections—was so intense that the questions were certainly going to be thrown back to the foreign ministers for more haggling.

"It is getting rather late, gentlemen," FDR heard himself inject during a pause in the Polish debate, "and I would suggest that we prepare to move on to the question of establishing a world organization. Tomorrow is open. It strikes me that a great many of the problems we leave unresolved here might be properly the province of such an organization in the long run." The same expressionless man wearing the same gray suit as at Teheran the year before whispered his translation into Stalin's ear. FDR saw Stalin stiffen and Churchill's glasses slide down his nose while trying to hold back a smile. But there was no disagreement over tomorrow's suggested agenda, and Roosevelt adjourned the meeting. As usual, the Russian delegation was the first to stand.

Stalin whispered something to Maisky, his ambassador to Britain, who seemed to style his beard after Prince Albert's, and Maisky then announced, "Marshal Stalin wishes to invite his dear friends to dinner. You have not yet visited the Palace of Prince Yusopov, who was the man who killed the monk Rasputin. It is said the crazed monk placed a curse on the palace before he died, but the Marshal urges you to overcome your fears and be in attendance."

A problem for Roosevelt. Tomorrow would be a tiring and critical session; he didn't want to dissipate his energies tonight. The most diplomatic possible ways of withdrawing began to run through his mind. Then he realized that Churchill was already responding: ". . . the Marshal that as much as I would like to be in attendance, this evening is simply not possible for our delegation. Internal domestic problems have developed that need our immediate attention. We are at this moment trying to ring up London and will be making such attempts throughout the night. Although it may be a somewhat indiscreet request, and without seeming ungrateful, I wonder if we may not dine with the Marshal tomorrow evening instead." Then he added hurriedly, "If it does not create too great an inconvenience." He looked over his glasses at Roosevelt.

Ah, that changed matters for FDR. It might provide him with the time he needed alone with Stalin. But he had neither energy nor appetite for a full dinner, so he said, "You see, Marshal Stalin, Rasputin's curse is already at work." Maisky laughed and so did Stalin a translation later. "I'm curious to see the palace, but I, too, have some pressing work to do this evening. If the Marshal will not object to giving me a late tour of the place, perhaps a simple nightcap will suffice . . ." He left the counteroffer open-ended. Stalin was clearly still upset, and Churchill took FDR's offer as a gesture to placate the Russian.

Maisky whispered with the angry Stalin and said finally, "If ten o'clock is agreeable, the Marshal will send an automobile and looks forward to seeing the President for drinks." The Russians formed a phalanx with Stalin at the point and swept out of the room.

Before they were quite through the door, Anthony Eden, the dapper British Foreign Secretary, approached and handed Roosevelt a penciled note:

Franklin—

Must plug away even harder on free elections for East.
Europe. Will support your world organ. all out tomorrow.

Winston

FDR looked across to the standing Churchill and nodded.
Churchill smiled. Eden took the note back, crumpled it, and
placed it in his vest pocket.

As Reilly was wheeling the President out of the great hall,
FDR said to Stettinius and Hopkins, who were walking
slowly at each side, "I'll see Uncle Joe alone tonight. Won't
talk politics, just try to soften him up for tomorrow. Chip,"
he called, and Charles Bohlen, his interpreter, came forward. "Maisky will be there tonight, and I won't be speaking
about anything of consequence, so you can take the night
off."

"It's no problem, Mr. President, I actually enjoy . . ."

"A night off," the President repeated, smiling. "I'll just
take Reilly here in case a fistfight breaks out."

His chamber was warmer than the conference room, and
the fire in the fireplace was augmented by another in the
wood-burning stove. Reilly wheeled him in front of the fireplace and waited. "Mike, would you go get Dr. Bruenn, and
do it quickly, please."

Time became a flame leaping from one log to another, and
Reilly was tapping him on the shoulder saying, "Commander
Bruenn is here, Mr. President." Then FDR saw the doctor
over by the bed taking his serpentine stethoscope out of his
black bag. "Problem, Mr. President?" Bruenn asked consid-
erately.

"A cough at night. Could be the dryness here."

"Anything else?"

"I get tired too quickly; yet I don't sleep as I should. I
thought perhaps a pill of some sort . . ."

The doctor clipped on his stethoscope and said, "I don't
like your color, sir. Help me lift him over to the bed." And

Mike Reilly cradled the President in the air and placed him down softly. "Take off his jacket and open the shirt."

Dr. Bruenn probed the chest, abdomen and back. Slowly, carefully, saying only, "In—out." Then he thumped with knuckles and listened. He said, "Hmm."

The President trusted Bruenn: he was competent and straightforward. Some of his physicians in the past had not been. "Is that a good 'hmm' or a bad 'hmm," Doctor?"

"All 'hmms' are by their nature ambiguous, Mr. President, but your heart sounds fine, the murmur has been controlled. Your lungs are clear."

"So it's a good 'hmm.' "

Bruenn strapped the cuff of the blood pressure device around the President's arm, pumped, held and released. He uttered an obviously unhappy 'hmm.' "It's 186 over 108. Don't like that a bit. Clearly a hypertensive situation. You need complete rest, Mr. President. Relaxation and no people."

"Well, I've certainly come to the right place for that, haven't I? What can you give me that'll help me function? And not a word of this examination to anyone, by the way." He looked first at Reilly and then back at Bruenn. "Churchill and Uncle Joe probably know already that you've been called in."

"I'd like to put you back on digitalis, the same dosage." He took a small bottle of green pills from his bag. "And one of these pink pills each morning, noon and night. In fact, I'd like you to take one right now."

Reilly poured a glass of water from a pitcher, but Dr. Bruenn took it and spilled it in the basin. "Just to be safe, take it with this," and he took a small bottle of water out of his case. "They are supposed to be using the bottled water we've shipped in, but I only trust it when I see it in the bottles," Bruenn explained while the President took his pills. "I'll check in with you again tonight, sir."

"Make it around nine."

Lieutenant Commander Bruenn nodded and saluted informally.

FDR smiled wanly. "Thank you," he said. "Reilly, help me over to that armchair by the fire." As the doctor left, Mike Reilly eased the President into the dark green velvet chair and propped his legs on the ottoman. FDR buttoned his shirt, and Reilly helped him into a sweater. "That blanket, Mike, and I'll be fine." The President pointed with his chin, and the security guard draped it over him and tucked it snugly up to his chest. "I'm going to try a nap. I'd like you to accompany me tonight when Stalin sends the car. Wake me at"—he checked his watch—"a quarter after eight."

"Right, sir."

He wished the moment had not seemed quite so fateful. Even the full moon, a pale red disc over the dark southern waters, appeared to be a sign. He had, he recalled as the black car sped along the beach road, considered this action for well over a year. He reviewed: *If the bomb is ready, we give the Japs a demonstration, perhaps even use it on an isolated, military target. If not, we attack. The Russians from the northwest, we from the southeast. But 500,000 casualties!* Now it had become a matter of making all the contingency arrangements—so why did the moment seem so fateful? *October, I just have to hold on until October to be certain Stalin will comply.*

Nothing was said in the car. The Russian driver and the Russian major sitting alongside him had same-shaped heads, haircuts and necks. FDR elbowed Mike Reilly and indicated the curious fact with a raised eyebrow and an upward pull of his chin. They shared a smile.

The mantle of the huge fireplace in the main hall of Yusopov Palace was a foot above Joseph Stalin's head. He was not only in his stiff mustard-colored jacket with red pants, he was also wearing his scowling, proud-leader-of-all-the-Russians demeanor, obviously still upset at having his dinner invitations spurned. Seeing him posturing so blatantly, a small, pompous figure overwhelmed by the cavernous room, FDR realized for the first time in many years that even the name "Stalin"—Man of Steel—was not his birthname but the result of a willful choice. He had renamed and remade himself.

Franklin Delano Roosevelt wore his black fur-collared cape and had an expression on his face that was nothing short of regal. In it was the confidence and ease that could come only from a sense of supreme power. The calming effect of the medication added to the aura. And none of it was lost on the Marshal.

Reilly tried not to look anywhere but forward as he wheeled the President in. Nevertheless, something in the moment—something greater than the setting, the lighting, the costumes, the postures and expressions—something made him, a man who prided himself on his coolness, swallow hard and breathe deeply.

Ambassador Maisky was the only other person present, so obviously Stalin, too, had private, personal discussion in mind this evening. Roosevelt did not want Maisky there when serious discussion began, since he, like Bohlen, was a high-echelon diplomat. Men like that would be writing memoirs in twenty years, and the President wanted his secret much better kept than that. There would be no way to ease Maisky out of the room; it would have to be done directly. "I stand because all day I sit," Stalin said in barely discernible English, the consonants forming liquid blends. He looked at Maisky proudly as a successful student does to his hopeful tutor.

"I sit all day, Marshal. And I sit all night also," Roosevelt said in an attempt at humor that, from Stalin's reaction, did not translate as humor.

Then Stalin suggested cognac, and FDR accepted. It was a simple offer that, like a huge raise in a poker game, eliminated Mike Reilly. "If you won't be needing me, Mr. President, I'll . . ." Maisky filled two glasses with a light-bodied Napoleon as Reilly closed the large doors softly behind himself.

The talk, through Maisky, was of the weather, the accommodations, the food, the transportation, the possible length of the conference. Innocuous but preliminary matters that were necessary approaches to the stunning specifics that lay ahead. It was Stalin more than FDR who seemed somewhat impatient to have the introductory dance over. Stalin, still framed in the fireplace with the soft glow of an old fire behind him, suddenly raised his glass and said, "*Za pabiedu.*"

"To victory," Maisky explained.

"To peace," FDR responded. The cognac warmed him as it went down.

"Does the President not find the Prime Minister somewhat changed these days?" Maisky translated. "More argumentative, more easily annoyed and carrying many chips on the shoulders. Perhaps he is afraid that after we barbarians finish with the Germans, we will not stop and come right across the channel after him?" Stalin's grin lifted his mustache at the ends.

The President said, "His people have suffered a great deal —not as much as have yours, to be sure—but he must act in their interests as he sees them. We all must do that. I realize for the first time the changes that come from approaching a long-desired and awaited goal. We all are somewhat changed by our successes, are we not?"

"When I look around the conference table," Stalin said, "I realize that in ten years we all will—may—be dead. Old men are sitting at the table. Ten years is not a long time in the world. In twenty years a new generation may not understand what the war has been about. In thirty, they may have made Hitler a hero again. Our grandchildren may be the enemies of each other if we do not make the proper settlements here."

For FDR it was the moment to get rid of Maisky. "I have come to discuss a matter of great delicacy. Since Mr. Maisky holds a formal position in your government, I cannot be certain in advance whether you do or do not desire him to hear my words. I wish to speak, as we say, off the record. Perhaps a translator who holds no formal position . . ." If the message was conveyed properly, Stalin could not possibly miss FDR's intent.

After relaying the words, Maisky asked the President if he wished his glass refilled. Roosevelt merely covered the top with two fingers. Stalin said something crisply in Russian to Maisky, who, in turn, said to Roosevelt, "If you will excuse me, Mr. President." Walking over the marble floor on tiptoes, the ambassador silently left the room. Now, thought FDR, there are two career diplomats, one on each side, who've been offended and will lose more than a little sleep during their lifetimes trying to figure out what really occurred during this night.

The awkwardness of the moment caused each man to smile at the frustration of being unable to communicate. Stalin spoke. FDR took it for English. "Yalta you like?"

"*Da*, Marshal Stalin." He nodded emphatically.

Then the uneasiness of silence returned until a gentle knock at the door brought the pale, expressionless young man who was Stalin's interpreter at the conference. He received instructions from Stalin and took a position three paces away from the Marshal, just outside the frame of the fireplace. He looked frightened.

Roosevelt began tentatively, looking and speaking to the translator. "Tell Marshal Stalin that I have come here tonight on a matter of great importance. A matter of the greatest secrecy." He spoke slowly, enunciating each word carefully and choosing a simple vocabulary. "I would like him to honor my request for secrecy." As the translator passed along the message, Stalin looked confused. He asked a question, the answer to which took away his confusion.

The translator, like Maisky, spoke with a clipped English accent: "If you will forgive my suggestion, Mr. President, I can work more effectively if you would speak naturally and to the Marshal. Thank you. The Marshal offers his word that all will be held in confidence of the strictest order."

FDR looked directly at Stalin, took a deep breath and began in earnest. "I have a specific proposal to make, one which will be, in a sense, between my government and yours, or more accurately, strictly between you and me. There is, before I begin, however, a crucial preliminary question I am confident you will respond to candidly." The interpreter's continual whispering did not bother FDR as much as he thought it would.

Joseph Stalin nodded.

"Are you aware of our project to make a superbomb?"

A crucial question indeed. If Stalin acknowledged the existence of the program, then he had been snooping; if he did not, the American President might perceive him to be a liar. It was indeed important to set the proper tone for this meeting. Stalin looked into Roosevelt's eyes for a long while. Slowly he said, in English, the single word "MANHATTAN." He knew, and now Roosevelt knew that he knew. Things could proceed. FDR said, "There exists a form of negotiations in America known as an escalating agreement. Are you familiar with the way it works?"

Stalin shook his head uncertainly.

"The first party, in this case it is I, will offer you something of value on the basis of your promise to reciprocate in the future. When you do reciprocate, I shall offer you something more valuable, and the process is repeated until each of us has attained his goal."

"What," the interpreter relayed flatly, "is to be exchanged?"

"I would like your agreement to establish and support a world organization under the blueprint I have submitted in my report to the conference."

"That is all?"

"In addition, after Germany has been defeated, you will be a full participant in the attack on the Japanese mainland should such an attack prove necessary."

Stalin's eyes glinted. "To the first, I say I do not like the arrangement of power within such a body as you have proposed. To the second, Russia has paid by far a greater price in lives than anyone else in this war. An attack on the Japanese, if they decide to fight to the death, is something I cannot ask the Russian people to do."

FDR knew that the major tactical error would be to try to persuade or to bargain. Nothing could proceed until Stalin responded by asking what Roosevelt was willing to offer, and that bait had already been set. Roosevelt stared into his folded hands and waited.

"No, no," Stalin grumbled, "these are things too costly to consider. If a world organization is not fair for the Russian people, we would be fools to join. And the attack on Japan this year, or even next year, no, no, no."

FDR waited.

"And what would the Russian people be offered in return for such sacrifices?"

"You would be given the plans for the MANHATTAN PROJECT weapon."

Stalin did not skip a beat. He had a stream of petty objections to what was being asked of him. FDR listened and then interrupted: "That is why I have designed an escalating agreement. Here is specifically what I propose. If you agree to the general plan, I will arrange to have you given the first part of the information for producing the weapon. When you formally agree to participate in the proposed world organization, you shall have the second part. After the Japanese attack, part three. The agreement may be terminated by either side at any stage. I would be the one taking the greatest risks. Let us assume you decide to join and then withdraw from the world organization, you would already possess a significant amount of information on the super-bomb."

"It is not," Stalin replied in a huff, "my nature to break agreements if I have given my word on behalf of the Russian people."

"I merely was attempting to show that a control mechanism exists if either side finds itself unhappy with the terms of the agreement later on."

Stalin was nodding and thinking. He said, "I believe this to be an informal understanding. Not a matter for governments. A matter, rather, between ourselves. It would not be put on paper."

"That is correct. It would be a verbal commitment between us. The world needn't know. If either of us felt it was not being honored, it would be terminated."

"And Churchill? Where is he in this?"

"His scientists will give him a weapon before too long, but neither he nor anyone else knows of my offer to you tonight." FDR could sense that the bomb was a very enticing prospect for Stalin; it would mean absolute parity.

The impassive interpreter relayed a question to Roosevelt: "For when is the attack on Japan scheduled?"

"Tentatively, early this autumn. But it can be adjusted to meet your military requirements."

Stalin nodded and said, "In these United Nations, as you call them in your report, Russia would have to keep the power to veto, and she must have many votes to counteract the ganging up of other, smaller countries against her."

"No, you may not have both. The veto power is sufficient protection. I wish it for my country as well, but not it *and* a weighted voting system. But, Marshal, I assure you, these are details. I understand that you may publicly have to say many different things. It matters not to me how it looks to the world. I may even have to do the same from time to time, but for the continuation of this agreement between us, we must act as we have pledged. Only then will the other have to reciprocate."

"You call this by some fancy name—escalating. For us it is nothing more than an old-fashioned carrot and a stick."

FDR smiled and nodded. "With a slight difference. We each carry both the carrot and the stick for the other."

Stalin tossed down the cognac he had forgotten he was holding and, probably because he was a bit tense, began to cough. His face reddened. The young translator froze with fear and indecision. "Slap him on the back, " Roosevelt ordered. After four slaps, the first two deferential, Stalin regained some control.

"And so," the interpreter said for him, picking up the Marshal's words once again, "when do you wish a response to your proposal?"

"Since you have to invest nothing tangible until you receive my first offering, I thought I could have your agreement in principle tonight. Now." FDR grinned.

Stalin laughed and sputtered a series of laughing coughs. "Remarkable. You are indeed everything I have heard about. I had never quite believed the words. But if I say I agree—"

"—in principle."

"Very well, in principle, you will give me stage one of the MANHATTAN bomb . . .?"

Roosevelt interrupted again. "We will have to make arrangements, but you will have the information shortly."

"How long?"

"No more than one month."

"Well," announced Joseph Stalin, looking like a man who had just been handed a great deal of money, "I would be a fool not to say I agree—in principle. I get something valuable just to say I agree. And because I trust you, I agree." Stalin stepped forward and strongly took Roosevelt's hand; he was startled by how firm the President's was. Then he said, "We drink to escalating agreement also called getting your way with carrots and sticks."

FDR put his glass forward to be filled and said again, "To peace."

The military photographers were preparing for their final shots of the conference room; chairs, ashtrays, writing pads and the day's agenda had just been arranged on and around the table. Roosevelt had slept until noon and awoke, strangely enough, with a ravenous hunger for bacon and eggs, surprising because the digitalis had usually killed his appetite. Dr. Bruenn had reported his blood pressure down considerably that morning, so it was a rested and confident United States President who took his seat before the small American flag on the stand in the center of the table.

He felt a tap on the shoulder and expected to see Hopkins or Stettinius, but it was Churchill, who looked a bit disheveled and very secretive. His face was very red, his hair like molting feathers. FDR could see the handle of the revolver protruding slightly above his belt. "Morning, Winston," Roosevelt said. "Everything straightened out back in London?"

"London be damned. I've got better news than that." He pulled an empty chair very close to Roosevelt's and whispered, "I visited Uncle Joe this morning. He'll take a United Nations; the great national council and a general assembly. It was quite a selling job I did, let me tell you. Took three solid hours, but he bought the idea finally." A flashbulb went off as though for emphasis.

"Why the sudden change?" Roosevelt whispered, wide-eyed, tongue moving in his cheek.

"I just kept punching away at him all morning. You've absolutely got to stand right up to the man all the time. Only thing these Ruskies respect. If we stick together, maybe now we can get him to back off on Poland."

"Perhaps, Winston. At least we have to give it another try."

More bulbs popped; the Russian delegation had entered.

236

Churchill rose to return to his place at the table. He put a hand on Roosevelt's shoulder. "The way Montgomery is driving, we'll have a good part of Germany to bargain with too. And don't forget our TUBE ALLOYS, old man." His ruddy cheeks rose until one eye closed. A wink.

Across the table Stalin sat down. He put on his picture-taking face: stern, one eyebrow arched, nostrils flaring. Churchill patted at his unkempt hair. Roosevelt smiled patiently with hands clasped while waiting for the photographers to finish. He cleared his throat and said, "If we may please . . ." Something slightly different was translated into Russian by Maisky, and all those who were not attached to delegations moved toward the doors of the great hall.

Stalin removed a package of cigarettes from his breast pocket, American cigarettes. They were Camels.

Chapter

17

SS OBERGRUPPENFÜHRER Karl Wolff, Himmler's former adjutant, was not a worrier by nature. Certainly not when it came to carrying out his specific SS duties in Italy—observing and policing the civilian population under German military control. He did his job very efficiently and with great ease of conscience. He took personal pride in the fact that camps in Italy were among the best-run in Europe. Wolff had even developed a deep affection for the Italian people. However, only a fool could not fail to be concerned over the military reversals of the past year. Even the brilliant General Kesselring was continually yielding ground, albeit grudgingly: Florence was lost in January and Bologna was now under heavy siege. Karl Wolff didn't really give a damn about the south of Italy; the Americans could keep it forever for all it really mattered. But Florence was a blow. No longer to walk to his office in the Pitti Palace, to stroll alone through the Uffizi galleries, or to dine on trout along the Arno—these were losses of a personal nature and as such were of genuine concern to him.

So SS Obergruppenführer Wolff wrote a letter to Reichführer Himmler. Its tone was not that of a lieutenant general to his immediate superior; rather, it was cordial and intimate, a personal request for important, perhaps privileged, information from one old friend to another. Buried in the second paragraph was the core of his concern: "Heinrich, it would be a wonderful thing indeed to know that the Führer's superweapon, the one he speaks of often and which can change the present direction of this war in an instant, is in readiness." But concern became doubt by clear degrees in subsequent paragraphs: "Now is the time to use such a weapon. . . . If, however, it will not be prepared in time, should we explore the possibilities for making the best terms for peace?" Karl Wolff had thought and committed to paper the unthinkable.

For three days after the letter was sent off, he had some vague doubts about its propriety. Fortunately, it was for Himmler's eyes alone, and their friendship ran very deep; he would not be betrayed. *After all, it was not so terrible to want your doubts removed,* he rationalized as he returned in his staff car from a pleasant visit with Schuster, the aristocratic Cardinal of Milan. *We must be realistic about these matters, mustn't we? Still, I should not have suggested suing for peace quite yet. I was very foolish putting such thoughts in writing.*

When he returned to his headquarters in Magenta, there was a telegram from Himmler. The envelope was stamped "URGENT—SECRET," carried cities and times of transmission —Berlin, Munich, Innsbruck, Balzano, Milano—and had been relayed within the hour. Obergruppenführer Wolff tore it open.

LT. GEN. WOLFF, SS.
 YOUR MEETING WITH FÜHRER APPROVED STOP   BERCHTESGADEN
MORNING 11 FEB STOP   PRESENT YOUR PLAN THEN STOP   END
                         REICHSFÜHRER HIMMLER

PLAN! What *plan?* There was no *plan.* What did it mean? Wolff reread the cryptic message. He would meet with the Führer in two days, Berchtesgaden, yes, that much was certainly clear. Did *plan* refer to his suggestion about making the best possible peace? It must, it could mean nothing else. He had no plan, no clear proposal. Certainly, however, it would be wisest not to ask for a clarification if the Führer was involved. He would use the time in transit to improvise something or other.

His itinerary to Berchtesgaden would be, as far north as Munich at least, the reverse of the telegram's routing. From Munich he would have to backtrack southeast to the Austrian border and Berchtesgaden. The bombings of the rail lines had been so severe that his adjutant had to make plans for automobile alternatives. The continued bad weather—daily rain or snow—that had slowed General Clark's advance up from the south became an even greater blessing when one was traveling long distances. One could only hope the bad weather would continue.

Wolff ordered a tray of food brought to his dressing room as he changed into his black SS uniform. "Contacts would probably have to be made through Switzerland. I know many people here who have reliable Swiss connections. Certainly Cardinal Schuster would be able and willing to help, and he is a confidant of the Pope himself." Karl Wolff realized that he was talking to himself in the mirror while buttoning his collar, but the realization didn't deter him. "Yes, I must develop a plan."

General Wolff had been waiting for almost two hours in the sitting room—it was a hallway, actually—of the Führer's mountain stronghold. He had been told when he arrived, by Erich Kempka, Hitler's aide, that Foreign Minister Ribbentrop was in the map room with the Führer, had been there all morning, and would most likely be out before noon. That was forty-five minutes ago. Wolff checked his watch nervously at shorter and shorter intervals.

The Obergruppenführer sat rigidly in a straight-backed chair with his black briefcase pinched between high black boots. There were, of course, some papers in it, and a few could even relate to a possible peace plan, but essentially it was a prop. One simply could not go in to see the Führer empty-handed. Elsewhere in the fortress he could hear doors closing and heels walking over stone floors. Through the tall, narrow window high on the ghostly white wall opposite, he saw fleecy clouds moving westward against an azure background: a beautiful day, the overcast lifted. The bombers would be up again.

Ribbentrop came through a low door and up three steps toward him. It was not as though he accidentally discovered Wolff waiting; rather, that he knew Wolff would be there. The two had undoubtedly discussed him while in the map room. Wolff had last met Ribbentrop at the Reich Chancellery more than a year earlier when he needed some clarification on the handling of Italian Jews. The situation had become an embarrassment to the Pope; something had to be done. Ribbentrop dropped the problem back in Wolff's lap.

The Foreign Minister, looking dapper in a dark blue suit and a wide blue tie, carried a briefcase identical to Wolff's. He approached in a relaxed manner, smiling, and offered his hand; Wolff stood, brought his heels together softly, and accepted. "Wolff, old man, it is so good to see you again after so long. Things are well in the south?"

"As well as can be expected, Herr Minister."

"*Ja.* Of course. I know what you mean. But perhaps we can do something to change that. He asked me to send you in right away. I look forward to seeing you again soon, General."

"It was my pleasure, Herr Minister."

Karl Wolff was suddenly as frightened at the prospect of

this meeting with the Führer as at the initiation into Hitler's elite guard ten years earlier. *Ten years,* he realized as he was about to knock on the door, *ten years already. Bad and good. But mostly they were good years, and they shall be again.*

Adolph Hitler stood and almost obliterated the southern portion of Germany on a map of Europe that hung behind him. He wore a light brown uniform with not a single insignia or decoration other than silvered buttons and a small swastika in the lapel, an even lighter shirt and dark brown tie. Wolff was struck by how peaceful, almost beatific, the usually active face was, so unexpected an expression that Wolff found himself even more confused. Part of that face seemed to have retreated—the forehead, the jaw—since Wolff had seen it last. The general's voice betrayed him and cracked during his salute: "Heil, Hit-ler."

Both of the Führer's hands remained in the large side pockets of his jacket, the left one seeming to hang limply as though in a sling. The fierce brown eyes were watery and somehow much paler than Wolff remembered them; even his hair seemed lighter. "Heil," Adolph said with a nod of recognition. "You wish to sit? I have spoken to the Foreign Minister about your suggestion of using a peace initiative in order to divide the enemy alliance." He spoke slowly and with a peculiar lack of emphasis that gave the voice a distant, detached quality. "I am glad Himmler shared with me your ideas, General."

Wolff, now seated but still disoriented, wondered what in the world Himmler had done to his simple request for information, but at least he now had a context in which to think. He said, "And I am glad to be of service to my country and my Führer." He realized that his voice now had something of the same flattened timbre and cadence of his leader.

"It is true, as you have conjectured, General, that matters are serious, but they are not desperate. Know this well. If they were desperate, panic and not a reasoned, thoughtful approach to the problem would be the expected reaction.

Let me ask you, Karl, do you see a man in panic standing before you?"

Wolff was expected to answer the question. He said, smiling broadly, "Not at all, mein Führer."

"Remember this, it is always possible to pull victory from the jaws of defeat. Frederick the Great did it often. Never through panic. That is the enemy—defeatism. Unacceptable. There are always tactics." Hitler pulled his right hand, the one that was said to be injured in Stauffenberg's bomb attempt on his life, from his pocket and pointed a finger at Wolff. "You will play a major role in one of our tactics." The gesture and the calmness of the voice did not seem to correspond. Wolff's mind whirled.

Hitler's tone moved from controlled to even more controlled when he said, "Often in strength there is weakness if one can only find it. Our enemies are strong now because they manage to work together. Ah, but as you well know, all coalitions are basically unstable and never more than when they are about to divide the spoils of their supposed victory. Only three men keep it together. If Roosevelt were to disappear from the scene . . ." And his eyes became even more dreamy. Wolff had thoughts of an assassination squad making a daring raid on Yalta. "But this is wishful thinking, and that can be as dangerous as panic, can it not?"

"Indeed, my Führer. If you could just give me a date for the wonder weapons we are preparing . . ." Wolff stopped abruptly because the tightness developing around Hitler's eyes warned him to do so.

"Our superweapon is a final resort. I have already told you, Wolff, there are many tactics available as long as one does not panic." The tightness about the eyes began to ease slowly. Hitler licked his lips and flicked at his trim mustache. "Himmler tells me you are very respected in certain high Italian circles. Would it be possible for you to make contact with the Americans, the British, and offer terms for peace?"

Obergruppenführer Wolff nodded.

"You are to begin with tokens, perhaps the release of political prisoners, the immediate surrender of some of Kesselring's troops, gestures of that nature. I leave the details up to you. But you must make them realize that what is really involved is the complete surrender of Germany under certain conditions into the hands of the Americans and the British. The Bolsheviks we will fight to the death. This they must understand. They well might find it appealing at this point, so unnatural is their alliance at this stage. What do you think, Wolff?"

"A separate peace is a capital idea, my Führer. It is something I have thought about and am well qualified to undertake. Through the Papacy, contacts can be readily made. Through well-connected Italian aristocrats, industrialists, in the name of peace and stability after the war. There is in Milano a colonel of British intelligence whom I have cultivated. I keep him around, we dine, we play chess, discuss politics. All of these people are anti-Bolshevik. Believe me, my Führer, arrangements can be readily made. You speak the truth: that alliance, that unnatural alliance, has never really been tested. Now is the time."

"Precisely, Wolff. So it is important that a condition for negotiation be complete secrecy from the Russians. It is a schism we wish to create with this maneuver. And you are undoubtedly the man for the task. You are widely respected." The last statement was made without particular conviction, but the stated thought was sufficient to thrill the SS general. "The specific procedure I desire is for you to contact a certain American in Berne. He uses the designation 'Special Assistant to the United States Minister.' Ribbentrop tells me that is a preposterous label, meaning nothing whatsoever. He is actually one of their finest and highest-placed intelligence agents. The man we have chosen to approach on this matter. His name is Dulles."

"Mr. Allen Dulles. I have heard of him through my friends."

"He is extremely clever, but he is also believed to have attitudes . . ." Hitler searched for the right phrase.

". . . inimical to Bolshevism," Wolff essayed.

"Precisely. But I do not have to tell you how to proceed on this mission. Channel all communications directly to me through Netteburg in Zurich. He is in direct radio contact. Speed is of the greatest importance." It was the end of the interview although General Wolff hadn't realized it.

Even when Hitler smiled its termination, Wolff missed the point. He said, "My Führer, it is a worthwhile tactic even if it accomplishes nothing more than give us the days we need for the completion of the wonder weapon."

"Yes, of course, the wonder weapon. That would end all our problems at once, wouldn't it? But you must be on your way with your great responsibility. Much lies on our shoulders." He stepped around the great desk and offered his hand to the startled general—it was known to be a very uncommon gesture for Hitler to shake hands. His clasp had great vigor. "Send Kempka to me when you leave, General."

During the week before the two representatives were scheduled to meet in Zurich, much groundwork had been done in a short time by a variety of contacts. On Wolff's behalf there was Elgin, the British intelligence officer; Rhighetti, the white-haired priest, emissary of the Cardinal; and Count Luigi Pallazzo. Dulles responded through a Swiss banker and the consul general of Genoa. Naturally, there was a great deal of overlapping and repetition of information on both sides, but a pattern of general interest emerged. For Dulles matters were simple; he would discuss only an unconditional surrender. Wolff requested only the containment of a preliminary session to himself and Dulles. A meeting was arranged at a Zurich restaurant—La Gardiole—for the following Friday evening. It would be no easy journey for SS Obergruppenführer Wolff, who was known and despised by more than a few in Switzerland.

Supplied with a false Swiss passport bearing his photo and the name Otto Forsch, occupation, jewel merchant, home office, Basel, General Karl Wolff, dressed like a middle-aged and prosperous businessman, entrained from Lake Como on an often-halted six-hour ride to Zurich. His black briefcase now bore the initials "O.F." embossed in gold. In it were papers with the Forsch letterhead, Otto Forsch's checkbook, and letters from his wife and daughter. His camel's hair coat carried the same personal label. He had also the time and address for the rendezvous and a small photo of Allen Dulles, code name, "Mr. Givans." His intelligence had informed Wolff that the man he was looking for was large with a full mustache, a pipe smoker who usually wore tweeds and a gray fedora.

Wolff arrived at the restaurant early and took a small table with a commanding view of the entrance, from which he never removed his eyes. He sipped a Dubonnet and felt just a little of the headiness of being in a place where the war was only a backdrop, where the sirens meant a traffic accident and never canceled dessert. Women entered on the arms of men. They laughed and patted their hair. Would life ever be like this again for him in Germany, he wondered.

Then he jumped reflexly as an unexpected hand touched his shoulder, and he looked up into the fleshy face and full mustache of the man he had been waiting for. The American said, "Herr Forsch, I presume?"

"*Ja*. Mr. Givans?"

"*Professor* Givans," the American corrected him. "May I join you, Herr Forsch?"

Wolff half stood. "Of course, of course. Do sit down. I am surprised only because I was looking out for you, observing the entrance, and *poof*, you are mysteriously materialized from elsewhere."

"There are always a variety of entrances and exits, Herr Forsch. You are enjoying your visit to Zurich?" Allen Dulles was seated now directly across from him.

"I have just arrived, but I expect to enjoy it a great deal." A waiter stood beside them with two menus. Dulles didn't accept his, saying, "I've eaten already, thank you. Just some Amaretto and black coffee."

Wolff was extremely hungry, having imagined the wonderful possibilities of this dinner all day, but it struck him as inappropriate to eat in front of the man with whom one was trying to negotiate. His stomach growled as he returned his menu. "Later," he said. "I'll have another Dubonnet." He tapped his empty glass with a polished fingernail, and the waiter removed it swiftly.

Dulles leaned over and said confidentially, "I know it appears boorish, but I've never adjusted to these late European dinners. Are my ground rules acceptable?" The strange, offhanded manner of this man unbalanced Wolff a trifle. His quizzical expression prompted Dulles to explain: "I am here to discuss only the subject of the unconditional surrender of all German forces." As he spoke, he absently patted his breast pocket and removed a meerschaum and a wrinkled leather tobacco pouch. He acted as casually eccentric as an Oxford don. And undoubtedly was, Wolff assumed, every bit as clever.

"Yes, those are acceptable terms. But you must know that I do not speak officially for the German Government. What I am doing might be considered treasonous in some high governmental circles. I, therefore, wish for your assurances of complete secrecy."

Dulles nodded.

"I am negotiating on behalf of Generals Kesselring and Hausser. And, of course, for myself and the SS in Italy. I cannot speak for anyone else in an official capacity. It is our hope, however, and our considered opinion, Professor, that many other generals are waiting for this initiative and will follow suit. So, although surrender will be immediate and unconditional, you must know that only a segment of our armed forces are represented by my presence. I do not wish to misrepresent."

Dulles looked beyond Wolff and with tilted head pulled regularly on the meerschaum. "Why?" was all he said.

"Excuse me?"

"Why? Why do you want to do this?"

"Ah, there is the essential question. You are indeed a man who gets down to business. But the answer is so deeply felt and complicated that words cannot explain it exactly." The romantic in Wolff liked what he heard himself say.

"But I find that I must have the words, Herr Forsch. I must judge them and pass them along."

Wolff shrugged. "The war is finished. Hopeless for us. Why should there be more unnecessary killing? Hitler is committed to the bitter end. We—Kesselring, Hausser, myself—we are not. I wish to dine in a restaurant like this in Munich someday to—to . . . The war has been fought. We were winning; it was good. Now it has been lost; so enough, we say."

Still the regular puffing of the pipe. Dulles took the cordial glass and tipped the Amaretto into his coffee. "Then it's patriotism?" he said.

"Well, yes, there is patriotism, if wishing to save one's countrymen needless destruction is called patriotism. I believe, however, it is something much simpler than that."

"And that is . . . ?"

"Simple physical and mental and emotional fatigue."

Dulles nodded thoughtfully with a compassionate expression in his eyes that indicated he had been convinced. "No, that doesn't fully satisfy me. You do not look at all fatigued to me, Herr Forsch, neither physically, mentally nor emotionally. What you have said is part of it, no doubt, but it is not at the core of your motives. What I am after is something that smells like a human truth. Once, a few years ago when I was practicing law, a client told me he wished to sue his own father for everything he owned in a breach of contract suit. I asked him why, and he gave me a dozen good reasons, but it wasn't until he glared at me and said, 'When we were children, he always gave my brother things he never gave me.' And I knew I had the truth. There was a certain"—he sipped his coffee—"texture to it."

Wolff pursed his lips. He was indeed in a struggle with this man. It did not seem like it, but such was certainly the case. "I have developed an attachment, a fondness even, for many Italians—in the north." No, it didn't sound quite right, even to him. "Well, more than a fondness. There are investments we have made in Genoa, Milano, Turino. Professor, every day the battles rage, certain elements—the bands of Communists—grow stronger. The war brings chaos, discontent—this is what they feed on, these parasites. Already they have become very strong in Bologna, in the mountains. In France they will be a force to contend with shortly, I can assure you. If there were to be an immediate turning over of power from our military control to yours, their power would be minimized. Certainly, you would not wish them any more success than we do." Karl Wolff felt that was better, closer to Dulles' texture of truth.

"You want them to become our problem then?"

Wolff smiled and nodded.

"And your investments to be protected by us?"

He continued to nod. "Does that smell better to you, Professor?"

"A good deal better, Herr Forsch." He placed his coffee cup back in the saucer and puffed for a few moments. "You must realize that this is merely the first stage in our negotiations. My task tonight is elemental: it is for me to report to the higher-up whether or not it is worth our while to pursue these matters."

Wolff didn't believe Dulles. He said, "And what will be your recommendations?"

"It is still too early to tell."

Wolff cleared his throat and said, "Each day is crucial. There are more bombings, more devastation, the Communists grow stronger and bolder." For a while it seemed as though there were nothing more to say. Wolff was slightly upset but seemed calm enough. He snapped off the end of a bread stick.

"Before I report to my superiors," Dulles said, seeming more serious than at any other time, "I need some gesture from you. Some act on your part that shows good faith and the ability to do what you say you can do. Something that would indicate we were not wasting our time with you."

Wolff was disappointed. He had hoped for further discussions at least within the week. But such was the price one paid for losing a war; the American could afford to wait, he could not. "What sort of gesture do you wish me to make?"

Dulles acted as though he were thinking. "The release of some prisoners is traditional," he said flatly. "Jewish prisoners in this case."

Wolff laughed ironically. "Jews. Always Jews. You want Jews, those I have. Of course I can oblige. How many? Fifty? One hundred? Two hundred? It shall be my pleasure to send them to you with my compliments." He realized that his response was probably inappropriate for this exchange, had perhaps too much of the smell of truth to it. Although Dulles was smiling broadly.

Dulles removed a folded sheet of paper with five names on it. Wolff knew four of them. All were accomplished or influential Italian Jews. "Just these people and their families would be sufficient as a gesture of good faith. The day they are delivered to the Swedish consulate in Geneva, I will contact you. At that time the British will be brought into our negotiations. I recommend the *veau à la Matignon*." He stood, placed his fedora at a jaunty angle, and sauntered toward the rear of the restaurant.

Too many spy movies, Wolff thought as he finished the

bread stick. But he took encouragement from the fact that the Jews could be quickly delivered and that there would be a new, widening round of discussions soon. Yes, there was a distinct interest on the part of the Americans; there was something positive to report to the Führer. The waiter approached again with the menu, but Karl Wolff said, "No, that is not necessary. I shall have the *veau à la Matignon*."

"A very wise choice, sir."

Joseph Stalin was livid, barely able to control his rage. His voice was slightly shy of shouting, and he brought his hand down forcefully on the writing desk in Roosevelt's suite at the Livadia Palace. FDR sat back in the green armchair, perceiving Stalin's actions as a critic would a great dramatic actor. Detached and judgmental. The phrase *tour de force* ran through his mind.

The gray little interpreter could not quite keep up with the stream of invective spewing from Stalin, and he finally editorialized: "The Marshal is indeed extremely upset—annoyed—disgusted—dismayed." He sounded like a dictionary of synonyms. FDR was certain Stalin was cursing viciously as his spittle flew across the room. Some of Roosevelt's detached amusement revealed itself against his will in and around his eyes, even though he realized it could antagonize this "Man of Steel" even more. After all, he had burst in just minutes earlier and struck a series of outraged poses; now he was almost shouting, and FDR had, as yet, no concrete idea of what in the world had prompted his posturing. He waited.

Certain translated phrases had been grasped. "This last day of the conference . . . Russia betrayed . . . complete lack of trust . . . outraged . . . no joint communiqué will be signed . . . betrayed . . . betrayed." No choice, Roosevelt realized, but to let his anger run its course and then try to get to the bottom of things. The President tried to maintain eye contact, but through the window behind Stalin he again saw the cutter *Jamestown,* this time steaming out of the harbor. He longed for the week of sea air and buoyant movement that would be part of his return to Washington. But he quickly brought his eyes back to Stalin's and waited patiently for the anger to subside, which it did in the manner of a volcano, with slowly diminishing shock waves. The interpreter became more helpful then: "This is no way at all for a so-called ally to behave behind the back. Do you think I am a fool to be so easily betrayed? You wave your carrot and I jump? No, no, we will sign no joint communiqué today. No, no, impossible. This conference will not have our official blessing. We are not fools!"

Stalin's invective seemed finished. Each man then simply looked into the other's unflinching eyes. But the tirade was not quite over: "I was warned. Oh, yes. I cannot say that I was not warned. But of you, I did not expect *this.*" There was the barest trace of embarrassment on the face of the interpreter, and FDR took it for an improvement in relations —at least momentary and between them.

"It is," Roosevelt said patiently in his most aristocratic tone, "it is indeed a weak alliance that brings accusation and bitter invective before anything else. Now tell me precisely, what is the cause of your anger?"

"You pretend not to know."

It was Roosevelt's turn to explode. "Damn it, man, I don't know! Do you understand—I do not know what you are accusing me of." And then, more calmly, "Unless you tell me."

Stalin glowered as though to suggest that having even to state the cause would be a further humiliation. He looked at his interpreter as at an impartial witness and, with a contorted expression, conveyed exasperation at Roosevelt's unmitigated gall.

The President's voice became remarkably reasonable: "Please, my dear Marshal, if I do not know of what I am accused, I cannot possibly defend myself. You would certainly not wish to convict an innocent man. And there is always the possibility—however remote, I grant—that I am innocent of this betrayal, as you call it."

Stalin's foot tapped and his cheeks puffed. He made it clear that his explanation was a mere formality; there would certainly still be no joint communiqué. "There have been surrender neogotiations in Switzerland—of how long the duration we do not know exactly—between the Germans, the Americans and the British. This is no mere rumor. This is fact. The German is Wolff, an SS general, a pig of a man; Dulles, your own representative in Switzerland, has met with him. As have American and British officials. Wolff has even delivered a bus load of concentration camp Jews to the American consulate in Geneva as an act of good faith. But why do I waste my time? You know of these things already. Perhaps you knew them when you came to visit my palace the other night."

Roosevelt had some difficult determinations to make hurriedly, since word of these surrender meetings had never reached him. First, he had to make a judgment on the accuracy of Stalin's intelligence. He believed it immediately because unless it was true, Stalin would not jeopardize the deal for the atomic weapon. Second was the embarrassing matter of letting Stalin know that such things could be going on without the President's knowledge. This idea he rejected too, almost out of hand. Not only was it a matter of personal pride, but Stalin would probably not believe that FDR could be kept ignorant of such a major policy decision. *Why indeed?* FDR thought, and seethed at the idea that the OSS and the Army had kept the lid on something so potentially dangerous. But no one, not even James, would have been able to read the anger in the tired old man who smiled and then laughed as though at a trivial and comic misunderstanding.

"My God," Roosevelt said, "how in the world did you find out about it so soon?"

Stalin's eyes narrowed.

"You really did believe I was interested in a separate peace with Herr Hitler, didn't you? Actually thought I was going to sign a piece of paper with that maniac and not tell you about it? What kind of monster do you take me for?" FDR's indignation was utterly real.

"There has been a pattern of deceit. I have never been satisfied that you are fighting as you should on the Italian front. I have sent you cables about this. Why, then, have the Germans been able to send whole divisions from Italy to Poland to fight against us?"

"That's nonsense, utter nonsense. Let me tell you directly —those negotiations are phony, fake. The whole purpose is to squeeze General Wolff and get information out of him. Among the Jews he has released is a man very important to our atomic project. I don't know how to convince you that nothing very significant is going on in Switzerland." Here he took a crucial, but calculated, gamble. For the first time FDR said, "Joe." Then again, "Joe, there is no chance for a peaceful world without some trust between the two of us. If I am culpable at all, it is only of not thinking to inform you ahead of time of this Swiss . . . diversion. I've had a great deal on my mind these last few weeks. I apologize abjectly and can absolutely assure you that neither you nor Russia will ever be betrayed by me. But, you see, even this comes down to a matter of trust, does it not?"

Stalin's immediate response was the thought, *Damn this Roosevelt, he always is so convincing, so sincere.* The Marshal's mustache fluttered irregularly as he pursed his lips. He said, "Do you have an American cigarette?" The very question meant that the difficulty would be overcome.

Roosevelt took the Camels from his sweater pocket, and each man lighted up. There was silence.

One of Franklin Roosevelt's greatest tactical strengths was improvisation. Upon this marvelous impromptu performance he added a virtuoso touch. "There is a saying in English: Every cloud has a silver lining."

"It is the same in Russian," Stalin and his interpreter said almost simultaneously.

"These meetings in Switzerland, they afford us the possibility to effect the first transfer of atomic information. If you will agree to send an observer to these talks, someone you trust completely, I shall send someone also—my own son James—with the information. This certainly is not the action of someone who wishes to deceive the Russian people, is it?"

The Marshal's eyes narrowed in a smile. He drew on his cigarette, tilted his head, and blew the smoke upward carefully. "You see, it is as I said before. You have this carrot and merely have to dangle it in front of my eyes; I have no choice other than to acquiesce."

Roosevelt, who had begun to feel comfortable again, said, "You poor fellow. I hope there are compensations." Then it was time for silence, and the two men watched the U.S. Navy cutter diminish in size as it headed toward the Bosporus and access to the Mediterranean. "Is it still very dangerous getting your ships out through the Straits?" Roosevelt asked, a personal interest in the ending of the Yalta conference slipping into his voice.

"Always dangerous," Stalin replied. "We have better control of the situation, but there are still U-boats there. Access to the Mediterranean, however, this is a matter for another postwar conference to settle. Control of the Bosporus, the Dardanelles, has always been a way for Western nations, especially the British, to control the Russian fleet. It should be freely navigable water under international control."

FDR was smiling broadly and nodding his agreement. "Precisely why you have decided to throw your unequivocal support behind a United Nations organization, is it not? And why also you intend to announce your wholehearted pleasure at signing the joint communiqué this evening. Thrilled by its spirit of cooperation and hope for the future."

The ashes of his cigarette broke off neatly as Marshal Stalin tapped it on the tray. "I have rarely met a man as persuasive as you are, Mr. President. Is it an acquired trait, or were you born with it along with the silver spoon in your mouth?" He was smiling slyly.

"Born with the propensity and the prosperity," Roosevelt said, realizing that the word play would not be understood, but unable to pass it up. "But the skill was forged in the world of American politics and in my pleasurable dealings with men such as yourself."

The comment elicited a brief eruption of laughter from Stalin coincidental with the tamping out of his cigarette. But his face turned suddenly very serious and he asked, "What specific arrangements must be made for the first transfer of information?"

"Let me see. Today is the tenth of February. Precisely one week from today, the seventeenth, my son will await a message in Mr. Dulles' office at the American consulate in Zurich. The message should refer to a 'FAMILY MATTER'—you understand, a 'FAMILY MATTER'? Jimmy will then make contact and we'll have our first exchange. Send someone very reliable."

Stalin frowned and said, "In one week."

Roosevelt nodded.

" 'FAMILY MATTER.' Why such a name as this?"

"No reason, really. It just popped into my head."

"I doubt, Franklin, if anything just 'pops' into your head. So now I have become a member of your family. This is why, perhaps, behind my back you have referred to me as 'Uncle' for so long?"

FDR raised his eyebrows and said only, "Perhaps." Their morning's business had been completed. "Now you must excuse me, Marshal Stalin; I must practice my signature for tonight's signing. I trust you intended to do the same."

"*Da*. Of course."

When FDR heard the cars start up and begin to roll out of the driveway, he reached into his small reserve of energy and bellowed, "Hopkins. Stettinius." But it was Mike Reilly who trotted through the doors first. "Get them in here. I want all of them, every last one of them in here and make it on the double."

"Who do you want exactly, Mr. President?"

"All of them. The whole delegation. All of them, damn it, all of them." And Reilly double-timed out into the palace.

FDR had a moment to think, to plan. It was sufficient. Certainly things were going on at lower levels that he knew nothing about—the Dulles news proved that. But it didn't upset him unduly. Nor would he become paranoid at the idea of adventurism in the OSS—that was, after all, their stock in trade. But keeping the President in the dark, for whatever reason, over something that had these kinds of potential repercussions, well, that was just plain unacceptable. Of all the things that burned him, looking like a sucker was the worst. So this seemed like a perfect time to shake all the boys up a little. After all, they needed it.

The men drifted in alone and in pairs. Marshall and Leahy. Hopkins. Harriman and Stettinius. Bohlen. Jimmy Byrnes. The President's obvious and extreme anger caused them to form a cluster. "Not only," he began, "have I just been subjected to personal humiliation, but the entire conference has all but come apart at the seams and collapsed around me. It seems that our Uncle Joe somehow got word of surrender talks going on in Switzerland that I didn't even know about. OSS, Dulles and some German general. Mr. Stalin felt that we were being somewhat secretive in selecting this method of stabbing him in the back. Now just what the hell has been going on out there, and why didn't I know about it?" The assembled statesmen and warriors all looked as innocent as choirboys, and as naive; they looked at one another and shrugged.

Edward Stettinius, the new secretary of state, squared his shoulders and leaned forward. "Apparently, Mr. President, we all are in the dark about this matter. I shall be glad to take it upon myself to get to the bottom of it and have a report in your hands, sir, as soon as possible."

There was really no reason to belabor the point. These men, he realized, would now be worried enough to see what was going on below ground in their own departments. FDR made a note to clean house in the same manner in the domestic agencies when he got back to Washington. "We were lucky this time. I was able to bluff Stalin. The Russians are going to send a representative to those talks just to be sure we weren't trying to pull something behind their backs. That'll put an end to the idea of a separate peace all right." Then he reconsidered: "*Their* backs, hell—someone's trying to pull something behind *my* back!"

Expensively shod feet scraped the palace tiles nervously. "What's my itinerary back home?"

Again the shuffling of shoes and the clearing of throats. "Well, sir," Stettinius explained, "there are courtesy calls in Alexandria, Athens, I believe Algiers . . ."

FDR's tone was laden with mock impatience: "Perhaps we're all a bit weary and not reading one another. These have been difficult weeks for all of us. Nevertheless, I don't believe we ought to break down quite yet, gentlemen. So how about specifying that itinerary."

While the others waited in strained silence, Chip Bohlen ran out of the room and returned with a copy of the itinerary on a crumpled piece of onion skin. The President read silently. "Kings," he said, "a parade of kings. Farouk in Egypt. Ibn-Saud, Arabia. Selassie, Ethiopia. Why didn't I know about this. I don't want to see kings."

"But I've been sending you memos right along, Mr. President," a worried Bohlen explained.

FDR had succeeded in getting their attention, so he backed off slightly. "It looks like a page out of *The Arabian Nights*. Kings! But where's Malta?"

"We had to cancel Malta, Mr. President. And move you on to Algiers to meet with De Gaulle. I left a memo on that for you almost a week ago," Bohlen said weakly.

"Water under the bridge, Chip. Rearrange Malta and push De Gaulle back." Then he smiled his widest smile and said, "I wanted to thank you all personally for your help these weeks. I really don't believe I could have made it successfully without your support." The words were uttered absently and almost without conviction, but the listeners were pleased; at least the smile and the words "thank you" were there. "Why don't we all gather here for drinks after the closing photographs this afternoon?" Nods and smiles. "Chip, stay around for a minute and we'll revise that return schedule."

Alone with Bohlen, FDR said, "Something's come up that needs my attention. I'd like Malta for the fifteenth. Maybe you can squeeze a couple of kings together and push the Frenchman back a day or two. In fact, give me a two-day stop over in Malta to rest up, the fifteenth and sixteenth."

"Certainly, Mr. President. I'll arrange whatever you wish."

"Fine, Chip, fine. And be of good cheer: from Yalta to Malta and let us not falta, right? I'm sorry for the confusion and the inconvenience *and* the short temper."

"Oh, that's quite all right, sir."

As Charles Bohlen exited, FDR picked up the pencil that lay on the desk and began printing a note in clear, block letters. Then he edited and cut it until it read:

TO MAJ. JAMES ROOSEVELT, DIR. OMMM, WHITE HOUSE, WASH D.C.

MEET USS QUINCY, MALTA MORNING 16 FEB.   THIS IS FAMILY

"Reil-ly," he called melodically. And Mike Reilly, who
must have been awaiting a call at the door, was at his side in
a flash. "Two things, Reilly. Which one do you want to
tackle first?" FDR smiled. It was their joke.

"Give me the tough one, Mr. President." Standard answer.

"Okay, prop up those pillows and carry me over to the
bed." Mike Reilly lifted under the arms and legs, and Franklin Roosevelt rose easily off the chair. His burly attendant
floated the President tenderly to the bed and set him down
softly. "Thanks, Mike. Here's the easy one. Take this message down to radio. Get it coded Top Secret and sent out
Priority/Extreme Urgent. Stay with it until you see it get off.
Then destroy the original."

"Will do, Mr. President."

"And, Mike. Hand me those binoculars. I want to follow
my past as it steams away." It was not meant as a cynical or
depressing comment; rather, as a weary epilogue to a successful Russian adventure.

Part Four

End
of the
Matter

Chapter

18

"SORRY TO have to be calling so early on a Sunday morning, Major Roosevelt, but . . ."

James looked over at the clock. Six-forty A.M. Still, he threw a cheerful note into the phone. "Oh, no problem, I've been awake for hours." And then the unnecessarily ironic words, "I'm a very early riser, you know."

The unidentified female voice explained, ". . . but there's an urgent cable from the President for you, Major. I didn't want to have to bother you so early, naturally, but it *is* an urgent—"

He smiled and said playfully, "This isn't the late Louise Hackmeister, by any chance?"

She gasped a laugh. "At any rate, Major, a message is here for you. Top Secret. Requiring your immediate attention."

"You couldn't possibly read it over the phone just this once, Hacky?" he chided.

"Major" was all she said.

"I'll be right over."

James Roosevelt, eldest son of the President of the United States, sat silently on the edge of his bed in his khaki military underwear rubbing his face with his large hands. Since he had lived only a few days in his new apartment, the surprise of the phone call added to the strangeness of his environment gave him a sense of bewilderment. James shook his head and said aloud, "Top Secret. Message untouched by human hands." He picked the phone up and dialed the number slowly and carefully.

Naturally she thought the periodic and distant buzzing was coming to her in a dream. Only very slowly did it draw her out and become the telephone ringing alongside her bed. May Fielding sighed, picked it off the cradle, and tried to sound as though she had been awake for a while. "Hel-lo."

"Hi. Since I'm up, I thought I'd call and see how you were doing."

May Fielding cocked an eye at the clock and said, "It's not funny, Jim."

"Actually, I'm calling to ask a favor. I've got to get over to the White House. I'd like to borrow your car."

She winced and smiled at the same time. "So, satisfied with destroying the happy tranquillity of my Sunday morning, you think you're going to drive up to the White House in my car at seven o'clock on a Sunday morning without a moment's thought. Do you have any idea how something like that would compromise my reputation in this town?"

He said, smiling winningly with his voice, "Are the keys in the same place?"

"Glove compartment," she shot back. "Will you ever run out of ways of complicating my life, James Roosevelt?"

"I'll try not to." He threw a mock salute into the mirror.

As he backed into a parking space reserved for Steve Early under the South Portico, he imagined Louise Hackmeister

264

peering from behind the blinds in her West Wing office. In fact, as he left the car, he waved up to her window just in case the thought had stumbled on reality.

The cable, Louise explained after excessive apologies, was actually up in Mr. Hassett's office. James took the stairs two at a time as he neared the third floor, anticipation building to expectation. Early Sunday morning and Bill Hassett was already, as James had last seen him, collating copies of newly mimeographed pages. The visitor looked on in silence for a moment and knew he was seeing government working, the nuts and bolts construction that maintained the continuity. Here was the loyalist worker who left the President free to follow his creative political instincts. James realized again at this moment that one of FDR's greatest talents was to surround himself with a good many such people.

Then Hassett looked up. "Ah, Jimmy. Sorry to inconvenience you." His hands continued their business without pausing. When he finished the pile that occupied his attention, he took a key from his pocket, unlocked a lower drawer, pulled out and handed James a buff-colored envelope.

With another key Hassett opened the door to the President's office, and James entered alone. He threw his tan coat over the arm of the dark sofa and opened the envelope while walking to his father's desk. The cable's meaning was immediately clear because the words FAMILY MATTER first jumped out at him. Without realizing it, he was sitting at the President's desk, smoothing the cable in front of him, rereading it aloud softly so as not to confuse even the simplest instructions. Two things: take the information for the first stage of the bomb and bring it to Malta by the sixteenth. Simple, really. He looked at the desk calendar and realized that he had to make arrangements to leave immediately.

The safe didn't open at the first try and prompted a nervous cough. When it did open, he realized that he had some not so simple decisions to make: where exactly did step one of FAMILY MATTER leave off and step two begin? Did his father want the option of using some transitional material? They didn't have to use it, but shouldn't it be there? How many copies of each should he take? He had prepared for many eventualities, so he extracted a folder of photographic copies of all the material and laid it before him on FDR's desk.

The material on top of the folder marked "A" was certainly what he wanted—diagrams of Fermi's pile, a copy of his final report, pages of mathematical formulas, two pages of notes describing early errors in theory and later ones in computation. All had come via the Einstein network. It was probably better, James was convinced as he placed the excess material back in the safe, to take at least all this information on the pile and also the pages giving the desirable properties of the applicable uranium and plutonium isotopes also. The ultimate content was, after all, his father's to choose, and he should have all the options. As the safe clicked behind him, James Roosevelt realized that the process begun back in December forty-three with his recall from the Pacific had entered a decisive and probably final stage. Impulsively, he reached for the phone to call May, just to say the single word, "Malta." But the ghost of the ever present Louise Hackmeister killed the impulse.

Instead, he called out to the adjacent office—"Bill." After a moment the door opened and Hassett's head poked in. "I'm going to need a little help on this one, Bill." Hassett walked in; Jim stood and picked up his coat.

"What sort of help?"

"That cable ordered me to Malta immediately, and I'd like you to arrange the most direct transportation possible."

"Malta," Hassett said slowly as though he were weighing a great ethical dilemma. "That might take a while, Jimmy."

"It's a Top Secret clearance, Bill. Presidential priority. How long?" James was slipping an arm into his coat for emphasis.

"Give me an hour just to see what can be done. Where can I get in touch with you?"

"I'll be at my apartment." Immediately he wished he had said, '*the* apartment.' James placed the cable in his folder and tucked both in his briefcase.

Hassett said, "Malta," again with even greater wonder.

"That's right, Bill. You got it. *Malta*, M-A-L-T-A. I'm meeting the President there. Please get on it right away." He stopped at the door and looked back slowly around the room. "My assistant, Captain Fielding, will be joining me."

As the Fairchild 91, the seaplane they called the "Baby Clipper," made its sweeping turn, a flaming reflection of golden light leaped off the center of the island and momentarily blinded Major Roosevelt, who was peering intently down from a round window. The flight had proceeded from Annapolis, Maryland, to the Azores through continually shifting fogs and mists. On the second leg—the Azores to Malta —the weather had improved suddenly and markedly. James could not know that the burst of reflected sunlight he had just seen had come from the Golden Dome of Malta, a magnificent cathedral landmark located at the island's geographical center.

Now Malta stood out in such clear relief below them that it appeared to hover well above the green water. Walled cities, terraced farms and vineyards, the ruins of ancient temples and modern churches, paths and roads, were easily discernible on the island.

The harbor of Valetta awaited them: the U.S.S. *Quincy* was angled into the quay with a semicircle of smaller Navy ships protectively surrounding her. James tapped May Fielding, who was seated directly in front of him, and pointed below to their destination. She shuddered at the prospect: the idea of being in an airplane that landed on water was sufficiently uncertain to give her cause for concern. James tapped again, and when she finally acknowledged him, he formed a confident circle with thumb and forefinger and winked in a slightly offensive manner. May stared daggers back over her shoulder.

The skipping run into the long, narrow harbor was so noisy that May Fielding cupped her hands over her ears, but the roar continued while the plane turned and came back alongside the *Quincy.*

A launch pulled up to the plane, and after a round of salutes and handshakes, the transfer of the smiling Major and his chalk-white companion was smoothly effected. Neither was dressed for the hot, humid Maltese climate. James in his woolen, short-jacketed uniform, May in a tailored burnt orange suit. Dozens of pairs of military eyes were riveted on her as the open launch slid effortlessly around the smaller ships and then cut directly toward the *Quincy.*

The golden sun and serenity of sea were lost on James as he shielded his eyes from the light and scanned the *Quincy* for some sign of his father, who he certainly expected to be taking the air. And then he saw him—there—under a colorful canopy on the afterdeck, in shirt sleeves, waving easily from a lounging chair. The son returned his father's waving arm signal but much more vigorously.

By the time she had climbed the wavering ladder and the deck staircases that brought her to the President, May discovered that she had become a little more composed. James had her elbow firmly in his hand as he escorted her to his father, who smiled contentedly up from the book in his lap. FDR, on his third day of complete rest after Yalta, was taking the sea's therapy and looking like a man recovering well from an operation. There was still a careful, fragile quality to all his movements, but some of the concern and anxiety had already begun to fall away. The glow of returning health in the form of a light tan on his skin was, if not already noticeable, at least strongly suggested. He tipped his head forward in greeting.

"Mr. President," James announced proudly, a bit too much

like a child with a trophy, "this is my aide, Captain Fielding. If you recall, you advised us to follow the sun, and we've taken you up on that suggestion." James was already covered with perspiration.

FDR was not at all thrown off balance by the unexpected complication. "Ah, Captain Fielding. Of course. I've known your father for quite a while, a little better a few years back than recently, unfortunately. But you're certainly a good deal prettier."

As May stepped forward to take the President's hand, a barge putted by below the group on its way farther out in the harbor to refuel the seaplane. May said something that the President didn't quite hear, but he smiled broadly and indicated a chair near the foot of his, which she took.

"You two look uncomfortable. Why don't you slip off those jackets and pour us each a glass of that martini elixir, Jimmy." FDR pointed to a shaded table with a cocktail shaker and an ice bucket. James unbuttoned his jacket, removed it, loosened his tie and rolled up his sleeves. He never relinquished his briefcase. May slid demurely out of her woolen suit jacket. The President appreciated the modest grace of her movements and her need to let some air circulate under her blouse by pulling at the bodice periodically. "D'you have enough ice over there, Jimmy?" he asked, and was answered by the clink of cubes falling into glasses.

FDR addressed May Fielding directly. "I can't tell you how pleased I am finally to meet you, my dear. And how wise it was for Jimmy to have brought you along. Good for an old man's morale, especially after weeks of seeing nothing but Russian women."

"I-I'm not sure I've just been complimented, Mr. President." And the faint blush that swept her face made her look even lovelier. FDR laughed.

James brought the glasses over, saying, "Pa, how did things come out at Yalta?"

"Unfortunately, you won't be here long enough to get a

detailed report. But, in a word, 'complicated.' " His glass was raised in a welcome toast. Jim and May raised theirs. "To youth and beauty," the President said only to May.

"And intelligence," James added, to her further embarrassment. "What in the world do you mean, Pa, that we're not going to be here long enough?" he asked after his first stinging sip.

"It may look like a vacation to you, Jimmy—the Mediterranean, the sun, the breeze, drinks with a rich old man on a glamorous cruise ship—but, in fact, you are on an important assignment. You'll be leaving very shortly." FDR looked out into the harbor where the barge had hooked a refueling line to the fuselage of the plane. "It's something rather important. Came to my attention toward the end at Yalta. Darned near threw a monkey wrench into the whole works."

"Mr. President," May said prudently, "if you'd rather discuss this alone with the Major, I can assure you . . ." Her hands were on the arms of her chair; she seemed about to rise.

"Nonsense, nonsense, my dear. You're Jimmy's aide de camp. If *you* can't be trusted, who can?" May's eyes flashed. "In fact, the more I think of it, the more I realize it's the sort of assignment for which two people will be needed. I assume you have top clearance, Captain." He scanned her face. She pursed her lips, smiled and nodded. James had promised she'd eventually be included in his activities, and she was thrilled that it was finally happening.

"*And* OSS training," James added facetiously.

"Oh. I wish you hadn't mentioned that organization, Jimmy. 'Office of Strategic Services' leaves a very bad taste in my mouth these days. They're the reason I've brought you out here." And FDR went on to recount and explain events from the moment of Stalin's blowup at the Livadia Palace over the OSS peace initiative with the Germans to the present. "It came within a hair's breadth, you see, of destroying everything that had been set up at the conference."

"And our mission?"

"Let me fill you in a bit more first. I think I've gotten to the heart of the matter. Just spoken on the phone to both General Donovan of the OSS and Dulles. They swear up and down that the whole thing was a fishing expedition and in too early a stage to have bothered to report it to me. You both should know that I don't buy that baloney. Why, for example, were the British brought in before even I got wind of what was going on? No, their story doesn't wash, but I'm letting it all go for the time being. I'll take care of them when I get back to Washington." He sipped his drink and began to speak before he had swallowed completely. " 'vertheless, I've had to placate Stalin. Humiliating, let me tell you, to have to sit in front of him and pretend I already knew what he was talking about . . ."

"Nevertheless?" James cued.

"Nevertheless, I've worked out a plan. I've directed Dulles to have the meetings continued—no other choice really. To string the Germans along until the Russians can send an observer to verify that they haven't been sold out. You, of course, will be my representative to the talks."

"Then," James added knowingly, "after the Russians get there, we break off the negotiations cleanly and the Russians are satisfied."

"Precisely. End of problem. And end"—he glanced again at May—"of exotic European vacation." She smiled.

"Where are these meetings taking place? Here on Malta?"

"No. Zurich. Dulles has been instructed to meet you at the American consulate there tomorrow morning."

James said, "Well, at least we'll have time to finish our drinks." And May added, "At least we'll be better dressed for it."

FDR smiled. "I'm not so certain about that. I'm told it's well below freezing there right now. Cheers." The conspirators emptied their glasses at the same time; May Fielding placed her drink on a nearby table.

"Now, Miss Fielding, I must rudely beg your indulgence. There *is* a matter for which no degree of clearance, other than having the last name 'Roosevelt,' is sufficient. There are some rather delicate family matters I must discuss with Jimmy." He appeared genuinely embarrassed, and May was immediately on her feet. "If you wish to freshen up, my cabin is at your disposal." He called softly, and a tanned young officer in starched whites appeared and escorted May Fielding below.

FDR's face was suddenly as serious as his son had ever seen it. James brought his chair alongside his father's. "Jimmy, I've set up the first exchange." James was nodding, no surprise on his face. "You will be contacted at the consulate in Zurich sometime tomorrow. The code words will be—"

"FAMILY MATTER."

The old man's eyes smiled sharply into his son's. He said, "Naturally. Set up a meeting with the caller. You select the time and place. And hand over the first batch of papers."

"There's some question about that, Pa. Exactly what do you want transferred?"

FDR looked disappointed. "You're my expert on that. I left it up to you to decide. What have you brought?"

"All the Fermi material and some introductory stuff about U 235 and PU 239, just in case you wanted to whet their appetites a little more."

The President thought for a moment and said, "No. The atomic pile is quite sufficient for now. Quite sufficient. The first material is really a test of good will, and they're going to want to check it out against what they're getting from their lower-level spies."

Then there was nothing to say. The two men watched the barge moving away from the plane.

"That's a lovely-looking young woman you've got there."

Jimmy hadn't expected those words. He said, "She's very bright."

"Not *too* bright, I hope, or too curious." FDR's glance at his old briefcase completed his thought.

"There's nothing to worry about on that account. It's still exclusively a family matter," the son said. "How're you feeling?"

"Truthfully, Jimmy, I'm bushed. Need at least three weeks in Warm Springs to bounce back after I make my report to the Congress. No, make it a month."

The launch that had carried the pair to the *Quincy* from the Baby Clipper had again started its motor. And a young officer, in almost all respects the duplicate of the one who was May's escort, appeared and announced its scheduled departure.

James was surprised and said, "A bit of a fast shuffle after coming halfway around the world, isn't it, Pa?"

His father laughed. "Admiral Roosevelt runs a very tight ship on a very tight schedule. Where is that lovely young thing again?" And May Fielding appeared, as though on cue, from around the corner; a freshening breeze had come up, and with it some of May's ease and composure. Wisps of dark red hair now blew around her relaxed smiling face. The Navy officers formed an appreciative matched set standing at the ship's railing.

James said loudly to his father, for May to hear, "I don't want to be the one to have to tell her. Since it's all your idea, you will have to deliver the bad news, Pa."

FDR beckoned her forward with all the fingers of his right hand. He said, "I look forward to seeing more of you back in Washington, young lady. And remember, if Jimmy gives you any trouble, report directly to me—I'm his commanding officer." He put his face up to kiss her and be kissed. Her lips sought his cheek, but his lips touched hers lightly and lingered a moment. She saw him smile.

"I hope," the President added, "you can both drop in again sometime when you're in the neighborhood."

The suddenness of events had her bewildered again; the

thought of reentering that plane depressed her, but she was smiling gamely as she picked up her jacket and traveling bag.

James leaned over his father and said, "See you back in the States, Pa." He had taken his father's soft hand.

The launch finally emerged from the prow of the cruiser, and FDR waved to the two standing figures below. May's arm made slow, sweeping arcs. Jimmy saluted once and patted the briefcase rhythmically.

Chapter

19

THE WINDOWS of the oak-paneled room in the Gothic building that was the United States Consulate in Zurich looked out over the gardens of the Sechselauten Platz. From where he sat at the conference table James could see two stooped gardeners scratching at the ground and throwing shovelsful of dark soil on the bases of shrubs. The city was cold and gray, but it hadn't snowed in more than a week.

Allen Dulles, sitting at the head of the table, revealed nothing of the disappointment he had felt since the President had telephoned him. The smoothly shaved, ruddy face had its usual luster; the tweed jacket and sweater were, as always, standard dress; he still pulled on his pipe with the same imperturbability. Only the tongue's occasional flicking at some random hairs from his mustache was a minor sign of discontent. Earlier that morning Major Roosevelt had confirmed what General "Wild Bill" Donovan had prepared him for earlier: the discussions with Wolff were to be terminated shortly after the Russian observer arrived.

The man seated across the table from James made almost

no effort to conceal his discontent. He bit at his lips, snorted and glared at James from under his bushy white eyebrows. Brigadier General Alec MacIver, highest-ranking officer in British intelligence, didn't like being told what to do by a junior officer, a mere boy, actually, and an American to boot.

No one spoke, but it was obvious from his agitation that MacIver would speak first. "You realize, of course, that His Majesty's Government, should it so desire, is perfectly free and justified in continuing these discussions unilaterally. It has made no agreement either to abide by any decisions made here or to discontinue any contact with the enemy at your recommendation." The words themselves were actually far more moderate than the hostile manner in which they were being delivered.

Dulles knew what James did not, that General MacIver was nightly on the telephone to number 10 Downing Street and had been taking his instructions directly from Churchill. If, therefore, President Roosevelt wanted the talks broken off, and broken off dramatically in front of Uncle Joe's emissary, Churchill would be risking a very great deal on this single act of defiance. There would go any chance of Poland, the countries of the East, perhaps even the Tube Alloys. So, it would not happen. In fact, MacIver's angry threat was a clear indication that Churchill had acquiesced to the political reality of Roosevelt's calling the tune once again. Dulles realized that the scene had, nevertheless, to be played out.

"I remind you, General," he began, his tone a little too avuncular for the older man's liking, "that we were the ones who brought you into the picture in the first place. It's our baby, after all. Seems reasonable to assume that if *we* see no future in the operation"—here the General glanced over at James—"it ought to be terminated once and for all."

"But what if *we* still consider it useful? What is to prevent us from keeping this flame alive if we so choose? Certainly there are intelligence advantages in it for us. Wolff is so desperate he will do almost anything we ask."

"International considerations prevent it, General Mac-Iver," James interjected, his eyes still on the gardeners below. "Agreements were made at Yalta, and Teheran before that. They must not be altered. We are none of us free agents in any of these matters any more—certainly you must realize that." The very flatness of his tone was an insult to MacIver.

"It seems rather clear to me that you gentlemen are acting somewhat freely in declaring what will and will not happen here," added the General.

As though his tone and refusal to look directly at MacIver were not sufficient, James suddenly felt like insulting the Englishman directly. But there really wasn't a good enough reason to yield to the impulse, and he checked it. After all, MacIver's presence was actually immaterial to his actual mission. Perhaps it was that mission that had made him so edgy. James seemed to feel the pressure all the while he was in the conference room. He knew he would be better when contact was made with the Russians.

Allen Dulles, having just thrown a smoking wooden matchstick into a pewter ashtray, spoke now with the omniscient voice of a great peacemaker: "It is always unpleasant to have to terminate, for some greater good, a project that has begun with such promise. But that, after all, is the essential nature of this intelligence business, gentlemen. I recall earlier in the war, while I was—" A knock at the door caused his abrupt halt. "Ye-es."

A stout woman, her gray hair in a severe bun, stepped partially into the room and announced, "Mr. Forsch has arrived, sir." There was more than a trace of a German accent in the thick roll of her pronunciation of General Wolff's alias.

"Have him wait a moment, Mrs. von Strauch. We'll be ready presently," Dulles said. He placed his pipe alongside the ashtray, moving it slightly with his thumb as he spoke, looking apparently for a satisfying symmetry. "I'd like to remind you gentlemen"—he was looking only at James Roosevelt—"that even though these talks are to be terminated shortly, there is still some important information that may be drawn from our guest. Namely in the areas of Kesselring's real strength in Italy and the names of other generals who are wavering toward surrender. Wolff's been holding back a little there."

James was absently nodding in agreement when General MacIver, who, after an introductory snort, asked, "And precisely when will our Russian comrades arrive? How long shall we have to continue this peace charade? I've got other matters that require my attention."

It was a question for which James had no definite answer. "I can assure you, you'll know just as soon as I know, General."

MacIver glowered.

"Well," Dulles announced cheerfully while walking to the door, "why don't we have him in then."

SS General Karl Wolff, wearing a pale brown suit—one of the six he'd had tailored for himself since he had arrived in Zurich—stopped in the doorway and, smiling, surveyed the room. Even while shaking hands with the British officer, his eyes rested on James. From his expression it seemed clear that he'd been forewarned of Roosevelt's presence.

The surprise was all James's. Here was the first Nazi officer he had ever faced—an SS man for good measure—and Karl Wolff was in all respects the amiable, successful Swiss merchant of Hollywood casting. Tall, good-looking in an open, unthreatening way, Wolff had the smile and manner of a man who had little trouble making people like him. Roosevelt was not prepared for this and had to manufacture his dislike.

Karl Wolff made his way around the table directly to James, who had remained seated. The smell of an antiseptic cologne approached with him. When Wolff stuck out his hand, James had no alternative but to accept it, reluctantly, but to take it nonetheless. Wolff sandwiched James's hand with his second one, pumping slowly as he spoke in precise, clipped English. "We will see some tangible results, I hope, now that so eminent a guest has joined our discussion." This was said loudly, for the entire group. More softly and with genuine sincerity he added, "For what it is worth to you, Major Roosevelt, you must be told that there are a great many others like me in Germany who have a wonderful respect—a *wonderful* respect, let me assure you—for the way your father has led his nation. We believe he has made some errors; naturally, this cannot be helped always, we are human. Some mistaken choices of allies, but this is merely politics. But of the ability to mobilize and achieve objectives swiftly, these have won from me a great deal of personal respect."

He had used precisely the tone of the fan of one athletic team who displays a grudging admiration for the manager of an arch rival. And done it as well as possible under the most awkward of circumstances. That MacIver and even Dulles were beaming bothered Jim more than Wolff's virtuoso performance. His face remained expressionless, and he still had not said a word, but Karl Wolff forced that issue as well by pulling out the chair next to him and asking, "May I sit alongside you, Major?" Wolff stood poised, waiting for a verbal response.

"Certainly, General. Here, let me take that briefcase out of your way."

As Wolff settled in, Dulles, with pipe raised, was organizing the meeting: "Unfortunately, today's session will be somewhat abbreviated owing to Major Roosevelt's arrival just this morning. It is going to take a while to brief him, fill him in on recent developments. As a matter of fact, it might prove beneficial even for the old-timers, so to speak, to use today as a rehash."

The request drew from MacIver a sniggering laugh.

Wolff asked, " 'Rehash'? This means a going over again, no?"

Allen Dulles nodded and said, "Precisely."

"A rehash, then, is a good thing. It is a postmortem that I would not like to participate in today. That would mean our conference was finished," Wolff explained. "But, of course, a slight delay is a small price to pay to have the presence of a man who puts our discussion on a . . ." He struggled for some words and raised a finger in the air when he had found them. ". . . a plane not so theoretical. So let us, by all means, commence our rehash."

The knock on the door this time was insistent, and a uniformed May Fielding did not, under explicit orders from Major Roosevelt, wait before entering to announce the phone call he had been hoping for. "Telephone for you, sir. Appears to be rather important."

James was on his feet, his briefcase slapping against his side, taking great strides. A muffled "Excuse me, gentlemen" was his only, halfhearted attempt at explanation or apology. He had already begun to dismantle the negotiations.

The tall Swiss telephone, an imposing piece of black machinery, sat on the cluttered desk of a clerk who had been removed by May when the call came in. There was nothing tentative about his "Hello."

The line was crackling, and the voice on the other end sounded very distant. It said "He-el-lo" in three distinct syllables. "I am to speaking with Major Roosevelt, please." All the accents were wrong, but the pronunciation was fairly close to English.

"This is Major Roosevelt speaking."

A pause, a rustling of paper. "There is, Major, a matter of our families I have to discuss." There was a slight note of rising expectancy in the voice.

If "matter of our families" was supposed to be FAMILY

MATTER, something was indeed being lost in the translation. "When did you arrive?" James asked.

"This very morning amid confusion. But I am now accommodated and prepared for meeting the family matter."

"Are you free to meet with me this afternoon?"

"Of course. Yes."

"It is now, let's see, eleven-fifty. Would it be possible to meet at two o'clock?" And then James realized he had no meeting place planned in a city with which he was completely unfamiliar.

"Certainly possible. I shall be at a destination of your choosing."

A printed card, stuck in the corner of the desk blotter on which James's elbow rested, caught his eye. It read: DAS MUSEUM DER NATURGESCHICHTE—ZURICH: 10–12/1:30–5. Nummer 15 GABLERSTRASSE. "There is a Natural History Museum, number 15 Gablerstrasse. Can you find it?"

"Museum. Fifteen Gablerstrasse. I shall be in this place precisely at two o'clock."

"How shall I recognize you?" James asked innocently.

"I shall be the one among the large stuffed animals. The one who will be wearing a red flower." James thought he heard a smile carried on the voice.

"Two o'clock," he said.

"Yes."

James Roosevelt returned to the conference room, where, in his absence, Wolff had begun telling some jokes about Hitler. The present one was about his absentmindedness.

Now that he had made contact with the Russian and would soon make the first exchange, James began to enjoy his secondary mission, the undermining of this German attempt at a separate peace. So satisfying was the anticipation of seeing General Wolff's expression when a uniformed Russian entered that paneled room tomorrow morning that his manner was noticeably softened when he sat back down alongside Wolff. "Gentlemen, excuse me. Only a message of the greatest importance could have taken me away. My assistant had orders to interrupt. Now, where were we?"

As Dulles delivered a slow, painstaking history of the events that had led to this meeting, James, his body turned slightly toward Wolff now, nodded attentively. General Mac-Iver occasionally added a detail or offered a slight correction. Roosevelt actually listened to none of it. He was anticipating the meeting at the museum, the culmination of more than a year of planning. One by one the faces, fragments of scenes, were dredged up by memory. Marshall and Einstein; Ishmael and Hassett; Frisch and Groves; Oppenheimer and the Bethes—each appeared momentarily, played a silent scene, and was chased by the next one off the screen of recollection. All the while, there was the trace of a smile on James's lips—an encouraging sign for Wolff—a narrowing of the eyes, and the illusion of paying attention to the speaker.

At a quarter to one, James raised his hand slightly, and Dulles slowed in midsentence; he stopped when his thought had been completed. "Gentlemen, this strikes me," James announced politely, "as a very good time for a luncheon break."

Only the flicker of anger across his face and a reddening of his neck at the collar revealed Dulles' rage. It was his job to make these decisions. He tapped his pipe twice to regain absolute control and said, "Owing to the importance of these talks, Major, it seems reasonable to simply have some food sent in."

"Had I not"—James reached down for his briefcase, which had fallen over, and began to stand up—"had I not made other plans, I certainly would have been willing to go straight through." MacIver made an audible, exasperated "hmmph." "There's no reason, however, why we can't continue at three o'clock when I plan to return." James looked down at his wristwatch. "I should certainly be free by then. How long do you estimate this briefing will have to last? Can we finish up tonight and get to the new business tomorrow?" The Major seemed so perfect a fool that Generals Wolff and MacIver stared at each other and raised their eyebrows in identical expressions of helplessness.

"Three o'clock then." Allen Dulles bit off his words.

James knew as the taxi turned into Gablerstrasse that Zurich's Natural History Museum would be more mausoleum than museum. And not a very elegant mausoleum at that. The limestone facade and columns were soot-blackened; the brass railings blue-green from disuse. James smiled as he walked slowly up the uneven marble steps. *My God, it's right out of a Hollywood spy movie,* he thought. *Ridiculous.*

In the dank gloom of the lobby the idea was reinforced, but he was no longer smiling. A white-haired woman, extremely old and frail, sat behind a desk at the glass-partitioned entrance. Floorboards creaked beneath his feet as he walked toward her. No one else was present.

Her bony finger pointed to a handmade sign: EINTSITTSKARTE—1 Franc. Roosevelt placed a Swiss franc in her dish and waited as her palsied hands slowly tore off a gray ticket from a roll. On closer inspection, James discovered the old woman's pale skin to be almost transparent, a white veil covering but not hiding bone and vein. Her eyes were yellowed and watery.

In a glass case immediately beyond the partition two large vampire bats hung upside down. The barest quivering of a wing and a trace of respiration were the only indications of life. A fetid pool immediately ahead held two small living crocodiles. The room James stood in opened on to dark hallways, spokes leading out from the center. A sign over one read: DAS REPTIL; another said: DAS SÄUGETIER. Because he

283

heard footsteps coming only from this direction, he chose the way of the mammals.

The exhibits of stuffed animals in the rooms along the hallway were logically ordered according to mammals of increasing size. Display cases of insects gave way to rodents and then primates, marsupials and, finally, large carnivores. James noticed that there were people in some of the rooms, usually old scholars hunched over books at poorly lighted carrels. In fact, the lights in the museum seemed to have no other purpose than to cast shadows. The rooms seemed darker for their presence.

He made quick tours of the cavernous side rooms and, finding no flowered lapels, moved on. By the time he reached the canines, the specimens were no longer encased. His watch read two-ten as he stepped quickly into the room he had been searching for. Standing directly beneath a huge brown bear in a fierce fighting posture—arms and claws ready to lash out, black lips curled back revealing sharp yellow teeth—standing under this rigid protector was a small, blond young man with a deep pink carnation in the buttonhole of an ill-fitting blue suit. The humor of the setting came to James only after a moment's thought.

The man was handsome in the regular-featured, open manner of an American motion picture cowboy, except for the hair parted neatly down the middle and plastered to his head. He was smiling broadly in appreciation of the visual joke he had created. "Major Roosevelt, your face is known in my country," he said as he offered his hand. "You must to forgive my English. I practice it not often enough."

"I can assure you, it is far, far better than my Russian, which I am ashamed to admit, does not exist. Perhaps someday . . ." James let his thought dissolve.

Never for a moment had he taken the time to think that the person with whom he would be making contact would be another human being. This man's youth, his obvious sense of humor, threw him. James was unready for a human exchange, which was why he hadn't even thought to ask the Russian his name. "May I ask you to repeat the phrase you used over the telephone?"

The Russian's brow knitted but smoothed as he said, "I have a matter of the family to discuss with you, Major Roosevelt." He smiled like a child who had surely given his teacher the correct answer.

Visitors to the museum passed the two men during their brief exchange. Not many, but there were more than James had noticed a few minutes earlier. An oriental couple, a tall man in an English greatcoat, three tiny men speaking Greek. A camera clicked somewhere in the rear of the room.

James placed his briefcase on his thigh, unhitched the clasp, and drew out the manila envelope he had prepared. The Russian's blue eyes were smiling as he accepted it and somehow made it disappear under the breast of his suit jacket. James expected it to fall out, but it did not.

Still put off slightly by the man's youth, James assumed him to be merely a trustworthy messenger for some important diplomat. He said warily, "Your people will send an observer to the discussions tomorrow?"

"Of course. That is, after all, the reason I am in Zurich, is it not?" He tucked his chin down sharply, executed a military turn, and stepped off into the main hallway.

Roosevelt decided to wait a while before leaving and took a turn around the room. The bear specimens were caught forever in lifeless reality. The room groaned now under the feet of new visitors. James realized also that it smelled acrid.

Then he was walking down the hall back toward the crocodile pool when from behind he heard running footsteps and a call—"Major. Oh, Major Roosevelt." He walked on. Then a man was at his side. Breathless, short, face upturned. In dress uniform, the golden eagles on his epaulets catching and focusing what little light there was in the hall. Colonel Ishmael!

"What an incredible coincidence, Major. You here. I had

no idea you were an appreciator of the taxidermist's art. But you've certainly come to the right place. The specimens here are the finest in the world, but of course you know that. And I've got them all." He tapped the small camera that hung around his neck.

James was caught off guard and he showed it—worried, confused, ashamed. He said nothing; he merely glared down. But after the initial shock that came with being caught in the act, his indignation at being spied on took over. He was obviously supposed to concoct an excuse for being in Zurich and at the museum. It was a game he refused to play. His heavy breathing conveyed his anger.

"It's an amazing device, really," Ishmael explained ingenuously about his camera. "Needs almost no light. Sharp as a tack, as they say. Hate to admit it though—it's German."

James saw no reason to participate in a duel with Ishmael. "I have a very important appointment. I'm late already." He began to walk toward the exit.

The Colonel trotted along for a few steps. "Where are you staying, Major? Perhaps we could get together for dinner tonight?" James continued alone toward the crocodiles.

The taxi ride back to the consulate on Sechselauten Platz was an emotional roller-coaster for James. After the first ten minutes he came to understand that, personal insult aside, Ishmael didn't really have anything tangible. Photos perhaps of James and an unknown Russian courier. But the President had authorized this mission to Zurich to bring the Russians in on the Wolff talks. A number of important people knew about it, so just what could be more natural than a meeting with the Russians on the day before they were scheduled to step in? No, Ishmael had nothing substantial. James, after about ten more minutes of great agitation, found himself much more relieved.

Of course Ishmael's very presence in Zurich and the coming forward to confront James meant that he knew more about James's real mission than anyone could have imagined. But how? An informant? A wiretap? Was Jimmy being followed constantly? Had Ishmael simply thought the matter through? His father had been right; he should have gotten rid of the man. It still wasn't too late.

And then, as the taxi sped along the Limmat River quay, he began to be worried that Ishmael might even have some way of getting the material from the courier. The next possibility struck like the bomb itself: *My God, that 'Russian' might have been one of Ishmael's own men!* The difficult thing was that there would be no way of knowing if the worst had happened until he had some moments alone with the Russian delegate tomorrow morning. He was an extremely worried man when the taxi deposited him at the Gothic building across from the gardens.

James had arrived early for the morning meeting and taken his place at the table. He had a fresh legal pad and two sharpened pencils already on the table when Dulles and MacIver entered together talking uneasily. James's presence froze their conversation, and MacIver, barely civil, acknowledged him with a cold nod. It was understood that today would mark the arrival of the Russian and the beginning of the end of their enterprise.

Wolff arrived jovial, confident, in a dark brown version of the previous day's suit. No sooner had he greeted everyone cheerfully and taken his place next to Roosevelt than a knock at the door preceded the entrance of their newest member.

The first thing James saw was the uniform: the color of hot mustard, a breast full of medals, with red collar and cuffs and a row of golden chevrons on the shoulders. The face of the young man who had stood under the bear told James everything he could have hoped for. He had not passed the atom secrets to one of Ishmael's agents after all. James's relief was almost inexpressible. The smile on his face as he stood was in marked contrast to the Russian's most serious demeanor.

MacIver, seated with his back to the door, swung this way and that trying to get a clear look at the visitor. He wasn't particularly fond of Russians to begin with, but his anger deepened at the recognition of rank. It was a comic offense to him that this young officer should be permitted to wear the uniform of a major general.

SS Obergruppenführer Karl Wolff was completely unprepared for what was occurring before his eyes. A subtle and sophisticated man, usually ready for all political eventualities, he was aware now only of something quite unexpected. Because he had been rather encouraged by young Roosevelt's presence the previous day, he could not instantly imagine that the mere introduction of an exotic military uniform could doom his mission.

Then, like a film being brought slowly into focus, Wolff realized that the uniform was Russian. The expression froze on his face, his jaw slack, the upper lip curled over perfect incisors. One eyelid flickered; red blotches slowly came to his cheeks.

Dulles was the only one present who recognized and knew the Russian by name. He stood and said, "Our efforts here must be deemed important indeed for the Marshal to have sent his son to our talks. Welcome General. Gentlemen, let me introduce Major General Vasily Stalin, Soviet Air Force."

All the men were now on their feet being personally introduced by Dulles.

Names didn't matter a whit to MacIver. A Russian pipsqueak had just arrived, and his aloof expression reflected MacIver's attitude.

If the Russian uniform had been the first nail in the coffin for Wolff's plan, the name "Stalin" was all the rest of them. The handwriting was now clearly on the wall. Wolff and the Third Reich had been trifled with, humiliated. The plan to split the Allies with a separate peace was utterly doomed.

The betrayal Wolff felt was directed at Roosevelt through narrowed eyes.

Seeing them, James realized that to the wit of the pink carnation and the snarling Russian bear had been added the immense irony of an exchange between the sons of Roosevelt and Stalin—very much a Family Matter after all. As they all began to sit down again, James said to Stalin, "All is well, I trust, with your . . . family."

"Of course," Stalin said smilingly, "what could be a problem?"

The dirty work fell to Dulles. He lighted his pipe and began, "Gentlemen, our preliminary meetings have gone so well that I thought it was time to broaden the base of our discussions, so to speak . . ."

Karl Wolff rose. He picked up his thin attaché case. His voice was weary. "No. Mr. Dulles, please do not bother on my account. I have too much respect for you and General MacIver. Please." That was all he had intended to say, but he added, "Spring is on its way. In Italy the winds have already become warm. To miss even one more day needlessly would be unforgivable." He shook Dulles's hand and MacIver's. And left.

The relief James felt had outward expression only when he burst into the office in which May was typing a letter to her mother. He threw his briefcase across the room and announced, "We're going to take a real vacation now. We've earned it."

He kissed her neck.

"Not here, Jimmy," she said, squirming. "And we can't take a vacation. We've just had one on Malta."

"True, true, but that one left something to be desired. Now we're going to chase the snow. Two weeks of skiing in the Alps."

"But who's going to watch the office? What if Hearst gets wind of . . ." He stopped her in midsentence with a kiss that, after a moment, communicated his joy.

Chapter
20

WHEN THEY finally returned to Washington in mid-March, May Fielding and Jim Roosevelt were berry brown. Certainly more deeply tanned from their quest for Alpine snow than from that for Mediterranean sun, and bound together closer than ever. Even in the office his hand often rested on May's shoulder as he leaned over her desk; her smile matched his for a few extra seconds; their communication deepened through gesture and facial expression. Now that their love had gotten beyond misunderstanding, the Office of Military Manpower and Materiel had become a happy place. The secretaries did their busywork with a smug contentment.

Washington acknowledged spring with sunny days in the 60s and bursts of cherry blossoms. James, basking in the success of his triumph in Zurich, eased slowly back into the monotony of his manufactured work. Something still had to be done about Ishmael, who had clearly overstepped his bounds, but James wanted to give his father some time to recover from the monumental effort at Yalta and the equally exhausting report of what had happened there that he had recently delivered to Congress and the country. Jim had seen his father only once since his own return and recognized the President's need for a Warm Springs recuperation. "Got to snap back" was the phrase FDR had used repeatedly. Since his mother had just left on a tour of Latin America, James was looking after the White House.

Spring, love, the smell of blossoms and success, just plain inertia—whatever the excuses he allowed to explain it, two weeks slipped by without his dealing in any way with the Ishmael matter. Regret arrived in a manila envelope tucked under May's arm on the unseasonably warm and sunny morning of April 11, 1945.

As she stepped toward his desk, she was thumbing through the letters in her hand. She said slowly, "The usual, Jim. Nothing appears to be exciting." May placed the pile before him on the desk. "That's the way it is around here, either exotic Malta and Zurich and Princeton, New Jersey, on a minute's notice or boring business as usual. No middle ground. Curious. This doesn't have a return address on it." She had extracted the large envelope and handed it to Jim. The postmark—"SANTA FE, N. MEX."—was sufficient warning. James broke open the seal and pulled out a note clipped over a large photograph of some sort. He seemed anxious. He read the neatly printed hand:

Dear Major:

Since you were on the run when I last saw you, I was unable to show you the marvelous results my camera got even in that extremely difficult light. All of my negatives were perfect. Clear enlargements are possible. If you see any shots you like especially, drop me a note and I will send them on.

James knew immediately, but he didn't want to examine the photographs in front of May, so he flipped the note to the corner of his desk and started opening the rest of his mail. After a moment she walked to the outer office. James got up and closed the door soundlessly.

Under the note was a photographic contact sheet with three strips of interior scenes of the Zurich Museum of Natural History. Three of the photos were circled in red crayon: in one James and Vasily Stalin are shaking hands; in another Roosevelt is handing Stalin a large envelope; in the third Stalin is placing the envelope under his jacket. James took a magnifying glass from his desk drawer, leaned down and squinted over that envelope, trying to determine if any writing on it was legible. Some was, but James could not make it out.

He swallowed hard. This evidence didn't actually make things any worse; it merely documented a meeting between him and Stalin. But Dulles and MacIver could certainly do the same thing. The worst that could ever come out was that Roosevelt had undermined a German plan to split the Allies. Still, the photographs made James feel very uneasy.

He picked up the telephone and dialed "39." In the middle of the first ring there was a one-word response: "Hassett."

"Morning, Bill, this is Major Roosevelt. Do you know how much longer the President plans to stay at Warm Springs?"

"The original plan allowed for another week, but you know him, Jimmy, he might stay two weeks or be on his way up here now. Wait a minute. Steve Early blew in last night and probably has the latest word on his plans. Why do you ask?"

"Well, something important has come up. I'd like to see him about it."

"Tell you what. I'll give Early a buzz and come back to you with what he knows in a few minutes."

"Thanks a lot, Bill."

While he waited, he scanned the other pictures with the magnifying glass. The clarity of detail, given the darkness of those rooms, really was amazing. The phone rang and James answered: "Yes, Bill."

"This is Steve Early, Major. Hassett just called. Listen, I'm on my way back down to Warm Springs this evening. The President'll be there. Why don't you come on along with me?"

"Great idea, Steve. Thanks."

The windows were wide open. A warm Georgia breeze wafted through the study, billowing out the dotted-swiss curtains but not upsetting any of the papers the President was signing on his desk. The odor of wild flowers mingled with the smell of barbecued beef and chicken. FDR stopped reading in midsentence, sniffed and swallowed.

"Madame Shoumatoff," he said politely to the artist making pencil sketches across the room, "we've got just ten minutes more, I'm afraid." He disliked posing for his portrait.

She was a bit annoyed that he had not held his position, so she moved a little to the left herself in order to find her original perspective. By then, however, he had slipped a cigarette into his holder and tilted his head back. No, she thought, not a very satisfying day's work. Perhaps tomorrow.

Franklin Delano Roosevelt was intent on the distant sound of barking dogs coming from the direction of the Pine Mountain Road. Why didn't Fala join in? That wasn't like him. FDR listened for a pattern of canine communication, the number of barks and changes of pitch. So deep was his concentration that he didn't feel the pressure beginning to build in his left temple. The pain, when it came, was sudden and withering. It forced him out of himself. He was not even aware that he had raised his left hand to his forehead in obedience to its command.

Certainly, he would not have believed that the hand he felt squeezing the back of his neck was his own. And the words he heard coming to him as though through a thick door surely could not have been his own. "I-have-a-terrific-headache."

Extreme pressure in his head. That rushing noise he heard

now, that at least was clear. The roar was like the torrent pouring out of the water pipe when they filled up the swimming pool. It even throbbed in the same regular way.

But those muffled noises, the distant shouts for help, a woman's scream—they certainly could have nothing to do with him. Too distant. Must be those dogs. Pine Mountain Road. Paralysis.

The pool must be almost full by now. That rush of water, diminishing. The pool filled up. He had the sudden urge to *run* to the pool. Crazy. Why not? Out through the porch, down along the rows of magnolias and over the rise to the gazebo, then along the narrow back path to the pool. Running, of course, why not running?

He'd never felt lighter on his feet. Still, it *was* a few hundred yards. He thought he heard his footfalls reverberating on the soft earth. Once or twice, as he cut to change direction, he imagined his bare feet slipping, but he never really came close to falling.

Now his breath began to bite in his lungs, but he'd be damned if he'd slow up even a little. His knees still seemed to be driving beautifully, the stride too long, but he enjoyed pushing himself just this one last time.

Then the rhythm came. Breathe, stride, stride, stride, stride, exhale. He imagined he was on the path now. The dark, cool blur of woods on either side he thought of as a threat. In fantasy he raced on.

Before him, finally, the pool. Still and clear blue in the sunlight. He ran directly toward it. Burst from the bushes and small trees toward the clearing. Without missing a step, the ball of his right foot planted itself on the pool's edge, and he launched his body in memory flight.

So perfect was the long, low dive that he knifed into the cool water without a sound.

The body of the slumped old man was raised from the floor and carried to the bathroom. Dr. Bruenn cut away his shirt and undershirt expertly and injected adrenalin directly into the heart muscle. Franklin Delano Roosevelt, thirty-second President of the United States, was dead at 3:55 P.M. James's train had just passed through Columbia, South Carolina.

Chapter

21

EVEN AT night the planes were coming in so low over the Wilhelmplatz that the vibrations could be felt in the Führer-bunker below the Chancellery building, which had already been reduced almost to rubble. The continuous *thud* of Russian artillery, however, hadn't gotten any louder since Tuesday. In the war room of the bunker, where a haggard, uniformed Adolph Hitler was sitting alone and motionless at his desk in a flickering brown light, the telephone rang. Before he picked it up, the sound died away, and a slight electronic hum came from it. His eyes were bloodshot and glazed over, the face unshaven. He stared hypnotically at the dead telephone. His fingertips were quivering until he shaped his hand into a tight fist; he smiled at his small triumph of will.

The phone had done this—rung and stopped—earlier in the week, and each time it had been Goebbels, who had the only direct outside line to the bunker. He raised the telephone to his ear and waited for Julius Schaub, his adjutant now, to respond to the light blinking at his desk in the outer office.

"My Führer."

"Schaub, did you just call me?"

"No, my Führer."

Hitler hung up and waited for the call to come through. If indeed it had been Goebbels, it might be good news—a break in the Russian front, a split finally between the Allies. His hand rested in the air above the telephone; he would not let the news slip away the next time.

When it rang, his anticipation actually worked against him: he was momentarily frozen because the expected had occurred. But he clutched it before it could fail again. "*Ja.*"

"Füh-rer." Goebbels' voice and so full of good news it could barely control itself.

Warily, Adolf Hitler said, "Well."

It was not easy for the deformed little man calling from his shelter in the Propaganda Ministry to control his enthusiasm, but he made the effort. The tension produced a prophetic smugness of tone: "It is happening as was predicted, my Führer. The second half of this month will produce a startling reversal of our fortunes. We have the first tangible sign." He stopped abruptly for dramatic effect.

The word "tangible" was the basis for a slight shudder deep in Hitler's bowels.

Then the news burst from Goebbels. "My Führer. I congratulate you. Roosevelt is dead." Said as though the Führer himself had murdered the American President. "This is Friday the thirteenth. It is an important symbolic event. Other misfortunes will surely follow for them." The universe had stepped in, the Propaganda Minister was saying. Even at the eleventh hour, there could still be a final justice.

"*Ja, ja,* certainly, Goebbels. You bring very good news indeed." The weariness remained in the Führer's voice, much to Goebbels' chagrin. Didn't he see? Couldn't he read the unmistakable signs?

Hitler placed the phone on the cradle very gently. Of course the dramatic last-minute salvation was a genuine possibility now—he believed that. But the immediate news was much more satisfying. Roosevelt dead.

The smile came slowly to his face. They had come to power in their respective countries at exactly the same time; the world measured them against one another. Now, whatever else was to happen, the other was dead, and he was alive. "Even," he said aloud as he rose, "if I were to kill myself tomorrow, this no one can take from me—I exist and he does not!"

His next thought was more pleasurable: "He knew it. I am certain he knew he was dying while I still lived. It must have been an anguish for him. He must surely have known this, the uncertainty of the outcome. Had I surrendered, the satisfaction would have been his. This proves absolutely that decisions have been made correctly."

He walked over to the map pulleys and selected GERMANY.

On the desk of Winston Churchill's study at 10 Downing Street lay the papers of three reports, mixed and scattered randomly, the top sheets stained by the brown ring of a brandy glass. The luxury of nights without flying bombs had already been taken for granted, except when an ordinary fire brigade siren awakened latent fears. Such was the case now, and the Prime Minister reflexively leaned forward, about to leave for his air raid shelter. He grunted at his stupidity, pulled the belt of his plaid robe a little tighter about his waist, and reached into the drawer for his private stock of cigars. He took a single Habana Perfecto from the humidor —a gift from FDR at Yalta—clipped it and lit up. Extraordinary. As he stretched his legs forward, his slippers tumbled off his feet.

The tap on the door was a bit strong and caught him in the midst of a particularly pleasurable exhalation. "M'yes."

"Sorry to disturb you at this late hour, sir, but you ought

to have this bit of news. Just arrived. Hasn't gone out yet." Stepping toward the desk, envelope in hand, was Gerard Gresham, the young assistant to the minister of information. Nothing else was said as he handed the message over and left.

In the envelope was a tear sheet that had come off the Reuters Teletype machine at the Whitehall office:

12:03 AM 13 APRIL 45
PRESIDENT ROOSEVELT DIED 3:55 PM 12 APRIL, WARM SPRINGS, GA. MORE INFORMATION TO FOLLOW.

Churchill's first reaction was disbelief, not because the information was completely unexpected; as a matter of fact, it was more likely than not, given the way Roosevelt had looked at the end of Yalta. No, the disbelief was there only because the sheet of paper he held in his hand contained nothing official. No department had authorized it, no one had signed it, no one had double-checked. Just young Gresham, a piece of torn paper, and "MORE INFORMATION TO FOLLOW."

But of course he's dead. No mistake. This is precisely how it would come. Torn sheet of paper. The world will dress it up, make it formal afterward.

His sorrow was compressed into a sigh, as much for himself as for Franklin. "Sloppy calling card," he said as he looked again at the spare message. "Damned sloppy."

The mouthful of brandy burned his palate just a bit, and he was glad it did. He pulled smoke deeply into his lungs and held it there. They had been rivals almost as much as allies. And there was never complete trust. It didn't matter— they defined each other.

For a moment Winston Churchill could not remember the year of his own birth. He sighed again without meaning to, and then again. *Things to be done,* he told himself. He reached for his fountain pen and an unlined sheet of paper and began to write:

Dear Mrs. Roosevelt:
I can understand how deep your feeling of sorrow must run at this hour. I had a true affection for Frank . . .

He stopped, crumpled the sheet suddenly and dropped it in the basket. The second attempt began: "Accept my most profound sympathy in your grievous loss . . ." He felt a little better about the tone.

Then the machinery that had been a lifetime in the making kicked into gear. He flipped the button on his squawk box and said, his voice as businesslike as at midmorning, "Raise up Eden and Macmillan and get them over here 'mediately. Emergency, understood?"

"Yes, sir, understood."

Again he picked up his pen and poised it over the words "grievous loss." But he wrote nothing. Instead he plucked another piece of unlined paper and began a new note:

13 April 1945

Dear President Truman:
Pray accept from me the expression of my personal sympathy in the loss which you and the American nation have sustained with the death of our illustrious friend. I hope that I may be privileged to renew with you the intimate comradery . . .

He wrote easily on because the unexpected, last-minute possibility of a new, unified and much tougher Anglo-American position against Russian expansionism now lay on his desk in the form of words on a torn sheet of paper. The moment had to be grasped. He would fly to America for the funeral. Afterward, talks with Truman. *Perhaps he will listen to my warnings, will do something about the Russian spies in the*

300

atomic program. Maybe some of the traitors will be caught and made an example of. Roosevelt, for some strange reason, had been far too lenient. When he finished his note to Truman, the new American President, he was satisfied, hopeful. Then he went back and added to the first sentence of his condolence to Mrs. Roosevelt.

By the time Harriman had left the Kremlin, it was after 3:15 A.M. The information he had given the uniformed Stalin had been spare: time and place but no cause of death. And the Marshal had asked about the cause of death a number of times.

"At this very hour," Harriman had said, checking his watch, "America most likely has a new President. I shall be pleased to forward any message you wish."

Stalin was confused. How could it all happen so quickly? "But you, Harriman, are always preaching about free elections," he had said, and Harriman explained the succession procedure again to him, but it still made no sense to the Russian.

No, the whole affair was much too suspicious. For power to be turned over so quickly, without a struggle. Very suspicious. Certainly the one who has the power now must be implicated in the mysterious circumstances of getting it. To Joseph Stalin the matter smacked of intrigue and always would.

"Shall I forward a message to the new President?" Harriman repeated.

"Of course. Tell him that I wish him well. I welcome his help in our effort to destroy the Fascists. I hope we will meet soon in a conquered Germany." It was obvious that Stalin was preoccupied as he spoke.

After Harriman left, the small man stood by the window that overlooked Red Square, floodlit once again as a symbol of Moscow's prevailing safety. Four dogs ran across the square from Oktyabrya Street. He still didn't like the feel of the news, but he came by degrees to understand its significance to him. To Russia. Churchill would hold sway now, that's what things had come to. Fleetingly, he thought that since Churchill had gained most appreciably from the shift in power, he must have been instrumental in causing the shift. A plot.

Still, there are advantages to this situation. At least it is cleaner this way, not so muddled by personal trust. Now we bargain purely from strength. . . . The realization that without Roosevelt there was no superbomb caught him by surprise. *If the new one gives the bomb to Churchill—Roosevelt's death has changed everything!*

Stalin's resolve was instantly set. In the morning he would have the scientists brought in. Russia must have the weapon as soon as possible. It was now an absolute necessity.

From his breast pocket he pulled out a flattened pack of Camels, the last of the cartons Roosevelt had sent him after Yalta. The struck match, as it reflected off the window glass, made it seem as though Red Square was aflame.

Chapter

22

JAMES FELT like a thief. Utterly without reason, for technically speaking he was merely completing a mission ordered by the President of the United States, operating perfectly legally in his capacity as Director of the Office of Military Manpower and Materiel. But justifications didn't matter: his father was no longer the President; he was in another man's office.

Nothing in the room had been touched. Too soon. The desk and chair seemed to be awaiting FDR's return; books, ship models, cocktail glasses and shaker, photographs and prints, the leather furniture, fireplace, bronze implements, even the "Dirty Word" cartoon—all as familiar as yesterday. And suddenly as irrelevant. The Presidential office was still in early morning gloom.

In a week everything would be changed to reflect the new President's tastes and habits. Probably Hassett would be gone. Certainly the safe and its contents would be discovered and removed. There would be questions. As difficult as it had been to leave Warm Springs, James really had no other choice: removing the atom secrets from the safe took precedence even over the personal grieving. Still, he felt like a trespasser.

For the first time, the combination came correctly to his memory and the door swung open at his first attempt. Eleven manila envelopes—ten compact and one overstuffed, bursting its seams—sat diagonally on the shelf like the spines of a skeletal fish. They barely fit into his briefcase. A sudden decision: To leave the door to the safe open or closed? No matter really, its function was over now; useless either way, but it seemed neater closed. *Close the door on it,* he thought. It made a certain poetic sense of the moment.

He elected to leave by the door to the main hallway, rather than through Hassett's office, as he had entered. With his hand on the knob, he stopped and looked back over his shoulder, remembering the first sun-drenched afternoon he had ever seen his father sitting behind the desk here. FDR had his hands clasped at the nape of his neck, head tilted upward and slightly cocked, wearing his widest Cheshire grin. President of the United States and enjoying the role. He didn't say a word, didn't have to. A dozen years had spilled away since that moment.

James looked around with sorrow; nostalgia momentarily welled up in him. But deeper feeling—the emotions that must certainly be stirred by a sense of irreplacable loss— these were not yet present.

In the same dulled state, he left the White House in a taxi for his apartment. He walked through the rooms in a mild dream state. But he wasn't there for either consolation or emotional release: he was simply completing his mission.

From the kitchen he brought an old newspaper and began to tear it in long strips, which he laid over the grate of the fireplace hearth, barely noticing the photo of his father addressing Congress on the front page. He tugged on the chain that opened the flue. His kindling consisted mostly of torn strips of a broken fruit crate. Only three pieces of a split log were left from the winter's burning, but they'd be sufficient. He needed a match.

He found a packet in the desk drawer and lit the edges of the paper. The fire burned blue for a few minutes until it met itself in the center and the kindling took hold; then it was a hot orange and the wood began to crackle. He placed the manila envelopes from his briefcase on top one at a time. They burned very slowly, and the thick one didn't catch at all.

Closing the mesh screen, James pulled up a chair and propped his heels on the edge of the hearth. The shaded room became warm, then hot as the fire grew in intensity. The morning of April fourteenth was a warm one, but from his chimney on M Street came a steady cloud of dark smoke.

His cheeks became hotter as the fire radiated its increasing heat into the room. James didn't realize that tears had been running freely down his face and neck, collecting at his military shirt collar.

Emotion was building with the flames. The mission—their FAMILY MATTER—was ending and with it the realization that his father was really dead. Cut off from the next stage. Forever.

James silently cried himself to sleep.

The fire burned for three hours and was smoldering when the ringing telephone stirred him. He knew it would be May. Of all people, she was the only one he was willing to share his sorrow with. Still, he could not respond, could not move a sleeping arm from here to there. After the fifth ring it stopped.

Scattered embers glowed in the ashes below the grate. *This at least finishes Ishmael for me once and for all.* He smiled at the bitter irony. *I just pity those poor bastards he's had the goods on all this time. There'll be no stopping him and Groves now.* Then the silent weeping began; then the sleep of emotional fatigue returned.

The second time the phone rang, James knew that he needed her voice, needed her presence.

"Jimmy, are you all right?"

"Yes. Just got some sleep. Feel a lot better. You?"

There was a pause on May's end, an awkwardness that James could visualize and that translated itself into care and concern. "Okay. There's nothing . . . I want you to know . . . I guess I'm trying to say that I'm glad I had the chance to meet your father even that once."

The realization that there were things to be done, functions he had to perform, came with his next question. "Has the train arrived yet?" James knew the plan: a train was carrying the body up from Warm Springs to Union Station. Then a funeral cortege to the White House and a service in the East Room, and then the next morning the train would continue to Hyde Park and burial.

"That's why I've been trying to contact you. The train is expected very soon. Your sister and brothers are meeting it for the family."

"Oh. Where's my mother?"

"At the White House. She arrived late last night."

He knew immediately what he must do. "Where are you now?"

"Across the street. The only thing at the White House today is the service and beginning to move the Truman family in discreetly."

"May. I'd like you to be with me this afternoon. I'd like you to be with me when I meet Mother."

The young, almost hairless Marine in dress uniform who operated the elevator looked frightened as it labored to the third floor. May was trim in her black coat, shoes and veiled pillbox. Jim's uniform was slightly wilted, the pants creased dully, and the back of his jacket held the folds of his earlier exhaustion. His eyes were red-rimmed and he was tired, emotionally and physically drained, but the lock of her arm around his was a constant assurance.

No one was in the upstairs hallway or in his mother's outer office. James called, "Ma?" And when a voice piped back, "That you, Jimmy?" he unhooked his arm from May's and placed his hand in the small of her back.

Eleanor Roosevelt had been looking out over the rolling lawn. She wore a black crepe dress that seemed to hang unevenly on her; the padded shoulders accentuated the poor fit. May immediately wanted to help redo the careless bun that had been woven of her hair. Her face was tired but serene. She had not been crying.

James came forward. Mother and son touched cheeks while he clutched her shoulders and held on. Flesh of her flesh. She closed her eyes and waited.

May, feeling terribly out of place and awkward, gazed down at her shoe tops. She was surprised to hear Mrs. Roosevelt saying, "You must be General Fielding's daughter. Franklin recently told me about you."

"Please forgive me, Mrs. Roosevelt. I feel very strange being here now, intruding, but . . ."

"Shush. Don't apologize, child. You don't have to explain Jimmy to me. He is just displaying an old Roosevelt trait. When things become very, very difficult, we only want people with us whom we absolutely trust. Welcome." Eleanor offered her hand.

"Well," she added, turning back to her eldest son, a note of resignation in her voice, "we've got some rather difficult hours ahead of us, Jimmy. People have begun arriving downstairs already. He'll be in the East Room then. See to the arrangements. Have you seen your sister and brothers yet?"

"Not yet, Ma."

"I'll expect you to say a few words at the service."

"Of course."

May understood the subdued, disjointed quality of their words and thoughts as an unwillingness to give way to emotion. Perhaps her presence reinforced this desire. Until, until she realized that Mrs. Roosevelt was repeating, "Of course there is no such thing as an appropriate time, but he was so close to seeing it through. So close . . . So close . . ." She had begun weeping.

James's breathing had become labored and slightly irregular as he fought back tears. He was certain at that moment he would someday tell his mother about FAMILY MATTER.

Downstairs, from the east end of the White House, came the muffled sounds of choral singing. The particular hymn was unrecognizable.

"They're practicing. It's almost time. Why don't you children go down. I need just a few more seconds to think."

"Mrs. Roosevelt, I'd be more than happy to . . ."

The widow, her face gone blank, her eyebrows raised in bewilderment, shook her head firmly. "No," she said. "I fear that the immediate future for the Roosevelt family may prove less difficult than the long-term future for all of us. If you're still offering to assist in helping us all get through a difficult postwar period a year or two from now, I'm certain I'll willingly accept it. Probably, I'll be soliciting it by then."

"*Lilacs and Steel*," James thought.

"My offer has no time limit."

James kissed his mother's cheek again and, placing his arm around May's waist, said, "We'll see you downstairs, Ma."

She said nothing but smiled and turned to the window, where she continued to watch the reflection of the sun on the surface of the distant pool.

Chapter
23

THE LIGHTS in the windows of the house on Mercer Street appeared to go on and off randomly. It was the second night after the revelation had first come over the radio, and Albert Einstein still could not sleep.

As they had sat at the kitchen table listening to the limited information first come in, Helen Dukas and the Professor reacted in very different ways. Madame Dukas was anguish itself: wailing, sobbing, sighing, a wellspring of tears. Einstein's sorrow was slower in coming because his main initial reaction had been disappointment, a response of which he felt ashamed.

So at 3 A.M. he sat in his study, having shuffled from bedroom to bathroom to kitchen to parlor to study, clicking lights on and off as he progressed. Helen lay upstairs in total darkness awake in her bed; she was listening, knowing he needed this time alone but also very concerned and ready to step in if he required attention.

He would have to write a letter to Mrs. Roosevelt, but he

didn't want to think about that right now, so he began scribbling a note in German to Niels Bohr. Many years before at the institute at Potsdam they had debated on the subject of God and the ultimate cosmic basis for physics. Bohr had contended that everything was totally random, always subject to unexpected and unknowable change. Einstein had said that God may be perverse sometimes but that He certainly did not gamble with the Universe. He began this note to Bohr: *"Du hast recht gehabt."* ("You were right.") And then he placed his pen down on the cluttered table.

Albert Einstein saw the immediate future very clearly. The bomb would surely be used on the Japanese—no way to stop that now. It would be a warning to the world, especially to the Russians. The only hope had been Roosevelt; hence, the abject disappointment. Einstein felt that he, the pacifist, had, by increments and in a manner totally random and unknowable, become the potential destroyer of life; hence, the guilt. Oh, it was all very reasonable to explain if you traced the process by logical stages—leaving Germany, coming to and staying in America, proposing the bomb to counter Hitler, then trying to stop its production, and finally agreeing to Roosevelt's secret plan for maintaining control. All so perfectly reasonable.

Had he not been trained as a scientist, he might have still clung to the theory and refused to accept the factual result. The decade ahead would be shaped by generals, militarists, and he had helped place the ultimate power in their hands. This he saw clearly and took responsibility. He filled the long-stemmed pipe with, first, a pinch of moist tobacco from the bottom of the Revelation canister and then some dry pieces off the top. As he sat in his study in the early hours of April 15, he knew his heart was going to break.

Of course, if there is no telling the future, if it is indeed all a random matter, there can be no certainty of disaster. The new President may be a man who . . . But he stopped when he realized it was his sense of personal guilt that required this pleasant reinterpretation of the future of the race. As he drew fire into the bowl of his pipe, he visualized again the meeting with Bohr at Potsdam. They had been seated at opposite ends of a leather couch. He recalled now that there had been others in the large room—students, colleagues, distinguished guests, all utterly silent. Bohr had been very deferential, but very firm, in asserting that there was no paternal force sitting on a throne out in the ether or beyond, playing dice, cards, roulette, and certainly not meting out universal justice either. "There is," he had said sorrowfully, "nothing out there whatsoever."

In Berlin later that week Einstein had dined at the Grand Hotel with his old friend Fritz Kreisler, the violinist. They had been taking after-dinner drinks alone in Kreisler's rooms when Einstein recounted his discussion with Bohr. Kreisler listened carefully, then walked over to his violin case and took out his instrument, a two-hundred-year-old Stradivarius. Without any preliminary movement, he drew his bow back slowly over the E string and commenced to play the Adagio from Beethoven's Concerto in A-Minor. Kreisler played it without flourish and without excessive sweetness; the effect was a tone so pure that it wavered perfectly on the edge between the pure physics of sound waves and the magic of dreams. Einstein didn't remember its ending. But he remembered Kreisler's putting the instrument away and sitting down opposite him again.

"Could such a thing exist in Bohr's universe," Fritz had said softly, and placed his cognac to his lips. Both men felt that Bohr's challenge had been met and disposed of.

Albert Einstein, thinking back to that evening for the first time in many years, now realized that even while Kreisler had been making the music of the spheres, outside, on the streets of Berlin, madness was in the air. He laid his pipe on its side, stood up and padded over to the book shelves, to his own violin, encased and at rest on a pile of philosophical tracts for over a year.

Upstairs, Helen Dukas heard a chair being moved, a snapping noise she did not recognize, and, after a pause, three notes played on a violin. As she swung her feet out of bed into her slippers on the floor, the notes were replayed and others were added. At the top of the stairs, she heard the music clearly: Professor Einstein was playing Beethoven's A-Minor concerto. His instrument was badly out of tune. But she did recognize the melody.

Epilogue

MAY FIELDING anticipated the decision before James realized he had decided that he would not be staying on as the director of the Office of Military Manpower and Materiel. She had perceived this without ever learning that his position had actually been a cover for a secret mission that had suddenly aborted. Of course, the new administration would be happy to have a Roosevelt on display—a sign of continuity in the face of drastic change. Word of a promotion in rank for him was being tossed around freely. But May Fielding knew instinctively that he would surely be leaving, drawn more to duty and adventure in the Pacific than the predictable safety of Washington, D.C. Even though she and the certainty of her affection were here. A general's daughter understood those things.

She would not, however, be the one to raise the subject, nor did she intend to be a "swell sport" when his frustration soon built to the point where he was forced to confront a dilemma she had already resolved. She had no intention of making it easy for him, inevitable as it was.

None of this awareness was on her face as she brought Major Roosevelt the mail on his first day back in the office after the burial ceremony at Hyde Park. Quite a backlog had developed, but because she had remembered his interest in that large brown envelope with the Santa Fe postmark and no return address, she placed the new one prominently on his desk.

His eyes picked it out immediately, and he showed more interest in the other mail until May left. James got up and closed the door, his anger mounting at the shameless gall of Ishmael. By the time he tore the packet open, he was muttering, "How dare that little bastard . . ."

On the white cover sheet was neatly printed:

MAJOR,

YOU WILL HAVE BETTER USE FOR THESE. OUR COMPETITION IS FINISHED. I FOCUS MY ENERGIES ELSEWHERE.

Clipped beneath were three photographic negatives. Held up to the light, they each showed James, Stalin's son, a great stuffed bear and a large envelope being transferred.

James was stunned. Then he wanted to tell somebody. But there was no one. He said, "I'll be damned." Dozens of times over the next few days he shook his head and said, "I'll be damned."

From the concealed vantage point of the rear of an Army truck at the top of the hill, Colonel Gregory Ishmael kept Klaus Fuchs continually on the cross hairs of his telescopic sight as the physicist moved from the Los Alamos laboratory toward Oppenheimer's office. With his right hand Ishmael kept the slowly striding figure in focus. With the first finger of his left hand he clicked a trigger mechanism that photographed exactly what he saw. He had helped design the device.

He clicked repeatedly during the very few seconds that Oppenheimer, who had opened the door, and Fuchs were in his lens together. When the door closed behind the two men, Ishmael rose and walked over to the sergeant who sat before a battery of radio receivers, amplifiers and tuners. Ishmael picked up a set of headphones, and both men in the truck listened intently, the sergeant adjusting the dials delicately. "Best I can do, Colonel," he said.

"What's the problem?" Ishmael asked.

"Direction. They must not be anywhere near the microphones in the office."

"Do you have recording quality?"

"Negative, Colonel. I'll record it, but I'm practically certain the background noise will kill it. If I bring it up any more, distortion will do it in."

"I'll make some notes then, just to be on the safe side."

Anything in the office would have been heard clear as a bell. Only the sheer chance that Oppenheimer was making coffee for his guest and that they settled conveniently at the table in the kitchen kept their voices from being recorded. Ishmael wouldn't come away with any hard evidence today, but he knew there would be other times. Roosevelt was dead; the son was just another lower-ranked officer now. He'd be permanently out of Ishmael's hair very shortly. Yes, there would be time to do the job properly now.

Even though a recording of the voices wasn't possible today, Ishmael could hear enough of the conversation to be certain he had his men.

He listened so intently, he hardly breathed. Amid the crackling static he heard Oppenheimer say, "Whatever my reservations may have been in the past, things are quite different now. Yes, quite different. I don't know exactly what I can do, but surely we must act to try to forestall the inevitable."

Fuchs said something unclear about Professor Frisch.

"I'll talk to him tomorrow. He's tractable," Oppenheimer said. And then the static obliterated everything.

Soon, Ishmael thought, *it will be time to move on these traitors. Of course, in the long run, it all depends on this Truman. Let's hope he's a little less squeamish than Roosevelt was.*